Last Call

W9-CCD-293

ALLYSON K. ABBOTT

KENSINGTON BOOKS
KENSINGTON PUBLISHING CORP.
http://www.kensingtonbooks.com

KENSINGTON BOOKS are published by

Kensington Publishing Corp.
119 West 40th Street
New York, NY 10018

All Kensington titles, imprints, and distributed lines are available at special quantity discounts for bulk purchases for sales promotion, premiums, fund-raising, educational, or institutional use.

Special book excerpts or customized printings can also be created to fit specific needs. For details, write or phone the office of the Kensington Sales Manager: Attn.: Sales Department. Kensington Publishing Corp., 119 West 40th Street, New York, NY 10018. Phone: 1-800-221-2647.

Kensington and the K logo Reg. U.S. Pat. & TM Off.

First Printing: August 2018
ISBN-13: 978-1-4967-0174-9
ISBN-10: 1-4967-0174-7

eISBN-13: 978-1-4967-0175-6
eISBN-10: 1-4967-0175-5

10 9 8 7 6 5 4 3 2 1

Printed in the United States of America

For Kate T

Acknowledgments

I can never say enough about the key people involved with creating these books: my new editor, Tara Gavin, for making the transition so easy; my agent, Adam Chromy, for his tireless efforts on my behalf and his unfailing belief in me and my work; and all those behind the scenes at Kensington Books, who help to make my books a success. It is a pleasure and an honor to work with all of you. Thank you.

A special thanks to the "Porch Wednesday" group for helping with my "research." You guys keep me laughing and inspired. And thanks to Kate Templeton for the great ideas.

With that said, the biggest thanks of all go to my readers, because without all of you none of this would be possible. You have brought joy into my life, and I hope that in some small way I can return the favor by bringing a small measure of joy into yours. Cheers!

Chapter 1

It is the beginning of a new year and, for many, it feels like a fresh start, an artificial marker that gives the day some imagined significance over its predecessor. For some, it signifies hope for the future; for others, it may mean establishing new motivations for personal growth. Sometimes it simply offers a fresh outlook on life.

For me, it means better-than-average business, and in the case of this particular coming year, a fresh—or at least different—outlook on death.

My name is Mackenzie Dalton, though everyone calls me Mack, and I own a bar located in downtown Milwaukee. The post-holiday season is a busy one for the bar. Some people come in hoping to extend their holiday spirit by lifting a few holiday spirits with their friends, family, or coworkers. Others come in to celebrate the end of the hectic, mad rush that always seems to be a hallmark of the holiday season. Still others come in simply because it's part of their regular routine to visit the neighborhood bar, exercise their elbows, and share their holiday tales with other regulars they see throughout the year. And more than a few come in simply to escape the bone-chilling cold that is part and parcel of a Milwaukee winter. Cozying up to a drink with some friends is a great way to warm both the body and the soul.

My bar has a lot of regulars, the most notable of whom is an assemblage of barstool detectives who call themselves the Capone Club. This group is an eclectic collection of folks from many walks of life who share a common interest in crime solving. The Club got its start through some tragic events that happened over the past year, not the least of which was the murder of my father, Mack, exactly a year ago today. My father opened Mack's Bar thirty-five years ago, naming it after himself and then giving me a name that would allow me to eponymously inherit. It was a huge assumption on his part that I would want to do that, but he guessed right. For me, the decision was a no-brainer. My mother died shortly after giving birth to me, so it was always just me and Dad, running the bar day in and day out. We lived in a three-bedroom apartment above it, and that made for a strange and memorable childhood. I knew how to mix a host of cocktails before I knew my ABCs, my extended family consisted of some of the bar's regular customers, and I was the envy of many of my high school friends who coveted my constant exposure to free alcohol. Despite my unusual childhood, I'd have to say it was a happy and simple one. My life up until a year ago was uncomplicated and enjoyable for the most part.

Of course, there were a few rough spots. One in particular that marked me as different from the other kids and nearly got me declared insane is a neurological disorder I have called synesthesia. It's an odd cross-wiring of the senses that results in its victims experiencing the world around them in ways others don't. According to the doctors who evaluated me over the years, my synesthesia is a particularly severe case. The most commonly ascribed-to theory about how I acquired this disorder is that it resulted from the unusual circumstances surrounding my birth. My mother ended up in a coma due to injuries from a car accident that happened while she was pregnant with me. She sustained severe brain damage that left her essentially dead, but her heart—and mine—kept going. So she was hooked up to machines and her body was kept alive until it was safe for me to be born. Then the machines were removed, and she was allowed to die. Whenever I asked about my mother's death, my father always told me it was peaceful—he believed my mother's soul had slipped away the night of the accident—but there was a haunted look in his eyes whenever he spoke of it that let me know he had his doubts.

The doctors speculated that the conditions surrounding my gestation and birth contributed to an abnormal development of my neurological system. The result was that I experience each of my senses—sight, sound, smell, taste, and touch—in at least two ways. For instance, I taste certain sounds; this typically is the case with men's voices. Other sounds, such as music, are accompanied by visual manifestations, like floating geometric shapes or colorful designs. Most of my tastes are accompanied by sounds. For instance, the taste of champagne makes me hear violin music, whereas beer makes me hear the deep bass notes of a cello. But there are some tastes that trigger a physical or emotional sensation instead. For instance, I confess to being something of a coffee snob, and when I drink coffee that's brewed just right, it makes me feel happy inside, almost giddy. Bad coffee makes me feel irritable and angry. I'm a coffee addict, and going without it for a length of time makes me feel almost homicidal, though I suspect that is more of a caffeine addiction issue as opposed to a manifestation of my synesthesia.

In addition to the five basic senses, I also have synesthetic reactions to my emotions, either a visual manifestation or a physical sensation. My emotions were put through the wringer at times when I was growing up. I would say things like, "This song is too red and wavy," or, "This sandwich tastes like a tuba." It didn't help me fit in with the other kids, and my teachers grew concerned when they realized I was seeing things that weren't there . . . or at least things that weren't there for most people. The visual manifestations I had were very real to me, and they still are. But the lack of understanding regarding my condition left many people fearful and confused. I quickly learned to keep most of my experiences to myself rather than share them. After spending time observing other people's reactions to things, and hearing their comments and descriptions regarding their own sensual experiences, I gradually learned which of my responses were considered "normal" and which were my own peculiarity.

When the hormonal surge of adolescence hit me, my synesthesia became even more pronounced. Had it not been for one particularly patient and insightful doctor, I would've ended up committed to a psychiatric institution. Instead, my father and I learned how to control my disorder and hide it from the outside world. However, in private, he and I played with my abilities from time to time. My synesthesia is not only more severe than most, my senses are greatly heightened. I can smell, see, and feel things that others can't. I can often tell when something has been recently moved because I can feel changes in the air pressure, or see a difference in the air surrounding the spot where the item used to be.

The aspect of my synesthesia that has turned out to be the most significant of late is that I'm something of a human lie detector. In the vast majority of people, the voice changes ever so slightly when they're lying—a subconscious thing. This results in a variation in whatever manifestation I experience when listening to their voice. Once I've learned what someone's voice normally tastes or looks like, I can tell when they're lying because that taste or visual manifestation will suddenly change.

Because of my experiences as a child, I spent most of my life trying to hide my synesthesia from the world. It was an embarrassment to me, a handicap, a disability, something to be scorned and laughed at, something that made me stand out from the rest of the world . . . and not in a good way. That all changed this past year, however. It began with the murder of my father in the alley behind our bar, though I had no way of knowing at the time how that one event would drastically alter the route my life was taking. Eight months later, Ginny Rifkin, the woman who was my father's girlfriend when he died, was also murdered, her body left in the same alley. Her death led to Duncan Albright entering my life, and my life becoming focused on death.

Duncan was a relatively new detective with the police force in our district, and he was the detective in charge of investigating Ginny's murder. When he determined that the culprit was likely someone near and dear to me, he decided to do some undercover work at my bar, pretending he was a new hire so he could gain the confidence of my staff and customers, and dig for information and clues. In the process, he discovered how my synesthesia helped when it came to interpreting crime scenes, analyzing clues, or talking to witnesses and suspects. With the help of some of my customers, who formed the basis for what would become the Capone Club, we solved the murders of both Ginny and my father.

Intrigued by my ability, Duncan invited me along to some other crime scenes, where I was able to pick up on subtle clues that led to solving the cases. Duncan started calling me his secret weapon, and I relished the fact that my synesthesia was finally making itself useful. Instead of feeling like it was a shameful secret I needed to hide, I began to think of it as my superpower. We made a great team. I enjoyed helping Duncan, and he reaped the benefits of my abilities. Unfortunately, not everyone saw it the way we did, and things got messy fast.

The press caught on to me, and sensationalistic news stories started cropping up about the police using magic, witchcraft, and voodoo to solve their crimes. Then I got a little careless on one case and ended up nearly getting shot. Endangering a layperson in this manner didn't sit well with Duncan's bosses, and, as a result, he was suspended for a few weeks and ordered not to associate with me.

This might not have been a huge issue but for two things. One, I had invited Duncan into my bed as well as into my life by then, and we were in the process of exploring the potential behind our relationship. Letting go of that wasn't easy. And two, I'd discovered I liked this crime-solving stuff, and putting my synesthesia to good use. The intrinsic high it gave me was strangely intoxicating and I didn't want to let it go. My synesthesia had been an albatross around my neck most of my life; almost literally so because whenever I grew nervous about exposing it, or revealing it to someone for the first time, it triggered an uncomfortable strangling sensation around my throat.

As if Duncan's suspension and the edict to avoid me weren't big enough nails in the coffin of our relationship, things got even more complicated when I attracted the attention of a deadly stalker, someone who wrote letters that demanded I solve a series of complicated puzzles by a prescribed deadline, and do so using only my "special talent" without the assistance of Duncan or the police. The consequence of failing to do so was the death of someone close to me. The letter writer proved this wasn't an idle threat by killing one of my customers—someone who was also part of the Capone Club—and using the first letter I received to tell me where the body was. Then, a week or so later, my bouncer, Gary Gunderson, was murdered in cold blood when I failed to correctly interpret clues in one of the letters by the set deadline.

After several harrowing and frightening weeks of skulking around so I could still see Duncan with no one being the wiser, the stalker was finally exposed and caught. Sadly, it turned out my stalker wasn't a lone wolf. One of the trusted members of the Capone Club was working with the culprit, and the whole thing left everyone involved reeling and feeling unsettled. We were all struggling at that point to regain some semblance of normalcy.

For me, the definition of normalcy remained unclear. In our hunt for the stalker, I was approached at one point by Mark Holland, the chief of police, and Tony Dixon, the current DA, both of whom had decided that a philosophy of *if you can't beat them, join them* was their best recourse. In a period of a few days, I went from being persona non grata with the police department to being invited to work with them on a consulting basis. While I suspect the motives of the chief and the DA were primarily political in nature, given an upcoming election, their offer benefited me in enough ways that I decided to accept their invitation. It not only allowed me to use my synesthesia in a way that was intrinsically rewarding, it provided me with a new stream of income, and freed me to openly pursue my relationship with Duncan.

So, after a year of incredible loss, emotional pain, tumult, and confusion, I found myself starting the new year with a renewed sense of hope for the future. Ironically, it resulted in me standing in a home and staring at a dead man on the anniversary of my father's murder. I couldn't decide if this was a good omen or not.

Chapter 2

I'd been brought to the murder scene by Duncan, who was with me in my apartment when he got the call. Knowing it was the anniversary of my father's death, he had made it a point to be with me. And because of the day it was, he had offered me an out when he got the call, even though my presence in my new role as a consultant had been requested. It took me less than ten seconds to decide what I wanted to do. I welcomed the distraction.

We drove to the site together in Duncan's car. I was encumbered by a cast on my left leg, the result of a car accident that had delayed me from making it to one of my stalker's locations. It was a delay that Gary Gunderson had paid for with his life. The cast was a nuisance in many ways. Not only did it make negotiating the icy winter streets a dicey prospect, my leg itched like mad underneath it, an annoying sensation that left me with a near-constant taste in my mouth of what I can only describe as salty dirt. It also smelled odd, which triggered a crunching sound that provided background noise all day to everything else. Fortunately, I was hoping to get the thing off soon. It had been just over five weeks with it so far, and I had an appointment with the doctor in the morning to see how well the bones had healed. For now, I was stuck with the thing and the crutches that went with it.

The home Duncan drove us to was in an upper-middle-class neighborhood that consisted of houses built during the first half of the twentieth century that had belonged to well-to-do German American families in their heyday. During the 1980s, the neighborhood had become a hotbed of crime, and many of the homes fell into disrepair. At the turn of this century, much of the crime was pushed out, the streets were cleaned up, and many of the homes were bought by people who intended to fix them up and restore them to their original glory. Now, fully gentrified, the neighborhood had become a popular one for young families, and it served as home to a mix of ethnic and economic groups.

The particular house Duncan steered me toward was a midcentury ranch-style built of brick. A large picture window in the front had blinds drawn across it, and the front door was a solid slab of wood. Though it was bitterly cold outside, the sun was shining, and when Duncan opened the door and steered me inside, I was temporarily blinded. It was dark, with only a lamp on in the living room and an overhead light in the dining area off to the right. As my eyes adjusted to the darker interior, I realized we were standing in a large, open great room: a combined living, dining, and kitchen area separated by a pony wall and counter between the living room and kitchen. The furnishings were Danish modern style, and the color scheme was blandly neutral in varying shades of beige.

While the visual impact of entering the house was a mild one, I was immediately assaulted by the sound of shrill, high-pitched notes that sounded like they came from a trumpet. I recognized the sound right away as my synesthetic reaction to the smell of blood, and I knew then that the crime scene would be a messy one.

There was a bag by the door that contained paper booties and two boxes of gloves, one large and one medium. Duncan helped me put a bootie on my casted foot—which only had a heavy sock covering it because I didn't have a shoe that would fit over it—as well as my other foot, and then he handed me a pair of latex gloves.

"Do I have to bootie my crutches?" I asked him. I was making a joke, but Duncan seemed to consider the question seriously.

After a moment, he shook his head. "I think it will be fine," he said.

There were five people—all of them men—standing in the dining room area next to a table, and Duncan steered me toward them. One by one they all turned and stared at me: two uniformed officers, two guys in casual street clothes, and one man in dress slacks, a dress shirt, and a tie. Their expressions as they watched us approach ranged from curious to suspicious. All but one of the men were still wearing their outdoor coats, and they looked uncomfortably warm. I had a feeling I'd be joining them soon. Dressing for the single-digit temperature outside left one seriously overdressed for the toasty warmth inside. But I supposed it was a discomfort one would have to bear because removing our coats would have risked contaminating the scene.

Duncan made the introductions. "Gentlemen, this is Mack Dalton. I suspect most if not all of you have heard about her in some form or another. She is here today because the Milwaukee PD has hired her on as a consultant to help us in assessing and analyzing both our crime scenes and any persons of interest related to those crimes. Mack has some unique abilities in this regard, and I promise you, she will enhance our efforts. Today is her first official day on the job as a consultant for us, so please be kind."

Duncan then pointed to the two uniformed officers, a Hispanic fellow who looked like he was barely out of high school and a big African American guy who looked like a linebacker. "This is Miguel Ortega, and this is Hank Johnson," Duncan said, gesturing toward each of the men in turn.

"Pleasure to meet you," Hank said with a nod, his voice as deep and rumbly as an earthquake. It tasted like potatoes. "I heard about you from Nick Kavinsky," he went on. Then he smiled. "He says you da cat's meow."

Nick was one of the uniformed cops who participated in the Capone Club on a regular basis. I'd been told by others in the group that Nick had something of a crush on me, and I wasn't sure what to make of Hank's repeated remark. So I smiled back at him and said, "Thank you, I think."

"That guy over there is Wesley Donovan, one of our evidence technicians," Duncan went on, pointing to the only person not dressed for the frozen tundra, a thirtysomething, short fellow holding a computer tablet of some sort. Duncan then pointed toward a tall, balding, older man in street clothes, who had his parka unzipped but still on. "And that's Charlie Hammerman, another one of our evidence techs."

Finally, Duncan gestured toward the guy in a suit and tie, a somewhat portly fellow in his late forties or early fifties with a heavily lined and wrinkled face that I suspected had seen lots of life, sun, and cigarettes. "And the overdressed fellow over there is Mike Linz, a detective from this district. This is his case."

No one said anything once Duncan was done, so I smiled at all of them and said, "I'm mostly here just to observe. If I do anything that interferes with your jobs in any way, or if you have any questions for me, please don't hesitate to speak up. I'm here to help, not hinder you."

Linz shifted his narrow-eyed gaze from me to Duncan and said, "Just what, exactly, is she supposed to do?"

His voice was hoarse and gravelly and tasted like raisins. I didn't miss the fact that he asked his question of Duncan, effectively dismissing and ignoring me. Before Duncan could provide an answer, I jumped in.

"I have a neurological disorder called synesthesia," I explained. "It's a complex and complicated disorder, but I can sum it up best by telling you that I have extremely heightened senses and can see, smell, hear, and feel things that other people can't."

Linz's eyes narrowed even more, but he said nothing.

Duncan jumped in and said, "It will make more sense if you just let her show you."

With that, the men shifted, turned, and separated, milling out around the table and allowing me my first glimpse of the victim.

The dead man was lying face down near the wooden dining table. The top of the table was covered with a spray of blood, and there were spatters of it on the back wall of the room and the drapes hanging in a window there. There was an expensive-looking wool rug beneath the table, a concession to the large expanse of hardwood floors. The original colors in the rug were black and white, a speckled pattern that reminded me of the static one used to see on a TV screen in the precable days once a station signed off. This pattern was now marred by a large splotch of dark red blood emanating from around the victim's head, with smaller specks of the same red spattered outside its circumference.

These observations were my first impressions, each one accompanied by a secondary sensory experience. I had known as soon as we entered the house that there would be a lot of blood because I could smell it, and I also knew that a gun had been fired because I could smell gunpowder, too. Each of these smells came with an accompanying sound: those shrill, high-pitched notes of a trumpet in the case of the blood, and something akin to a plucked string on a ukulele in the case of the gunpowder. These smells and sounds were in addition to numerous other smells I picked up on, including the various aftershaves used by the men in the room, the scent of their laundry detergents, the smells of the house itself, and the odors from the various soaps and shampoos used by those in the room. And this covered just one of my senses.

My first task was to sort through all my reactions to determine which ones were real and which were synesthetic, and to determine what exactly I was reacting to. This parsing of my sensual data is something I've learned to do over the years. When I was younger, it didn't take much in the way of jeering remarks and scathing looks from other kids before I learned to keep my reactions to myself until I could determine which ones were what the other kids considered normal. Over the years I have become accustomed to my synesthetic reactions enough to know what each one is related to most of the time. However, my work with Duncan has exposed me to a lot of new experiences and situations, and as a result I have a whole host of new reactions to deal with and interpret.

One of my regular customers at the bar, as well as a

founding member of the Capone Club, is helping me with this. Cora Kingsley, a single, fortysomething, man-crazy tech wizard is my right-hand man, or in this case woman. Cora owns her own company, one that deals with computer hardware and software, providing con-sulting services to individuals and other companies. Like me, Cora is a redhead, though her color comes from a box whereas mine is natural. Cora has taken it upon herself to create a database of my synesthetic reactions to everything in the world around me. It's been an eye-opening experience for both of us, and although it's an overwhelming task at times, it has proven useful.

In addition to helping me better understand and track my synesthesia, Cora is also the closest thing I have to a sister. I have no family of my own anymore; my father's death essentially left me alone. But I have an adopted family of sorts that includes Cora, as well as two elderly brothers, Joe and Frank Signoriello. The brothers have been coming to the bar every day since my father opened the place. Both made their living as insurance salesmen, but now that they were in their seventies, they were retired. They, like Cora, are my most trusted confidantes, and now that my father is gone, they do their best to fill his role, like two doting, elderly, dear uncles. I've grown close to other customers who are regulars in my bar, but none are as close to me as Cora, Joe, and Frank.

Then there's Duncan. Our relationship has been a confusing one, complicated by several things, includ-ing the edict issued by my letter-writing stalker to stay away from him at all costs. To appear to comply with this demand but still ensure my safety, Duncan had arranged for a friend of his, Malachi O'Reilly, to step in and serve as my pretend new boyfriend. Since Malachi—or Mal, as most of us called him—was also a cop currently working an undercover assignment, this little subterfuge came in handy. What didn't come in handy were the very real feelings that had developed between Mal and me. He laid his cards out on the table, letting me know how he felt, and giving me time to weigh my own feelings. I liked Mal a lot; I would even say I cared for him a great deal. But there was something between me and Duncan—a spark, a thrill of excitement, a depth of feeling—I didn't have with Mal. To his credit, Mal took the rejection well, and I knew I could count him among those I called close friends or even family.

The men in the room watched me, standing around and waiting for me to do or say something. I had no idea what they might be expecting but figured I should probably get with the program sooner rather than later. So I started talking, explaining aloud about the various synesthetic reactions I was having to the scene before me.

"In addition to having highly acute senses, I also experience every sense with at least one other one. For instance, I hear a lot of shrill, high-pitched trumpet notes right now, and I know that sound goes with the smell of blood. I also hear a note that sounds like it's being plucked on the strings of a ukulele over and over again. That sound I recognize as going with the smell of gunpowder. So I can tell a gun was fired in here recently."

Linz smirked and nodded toward the floor beside the dead man. "I don't need any special senses to tell me that," he said. "There's a gun on the floor here, and a bullet hole in the back of this man's head. It doesn't take any kind of genius or special talent to figure that out."

The older of the two evidence techs snorted back a laugh, and Duncan shot him a dirty look.

"I knew there would be blood and a recently fired gun the minute I walked into the house and before I saw any of this," I said, gesturing toward the dining room table and the dead man on the floor.

"So you say," Linz said dismissively.

"Come on, Linz," Duncan said irritably. "I've seen what Mack here can do. She's the real thing. Give her a chance."

"It's okay," I said, putting a hand on Duncan's arm. "I'm used to the cynicism, and I understand it. We'll get there eventually. Did I mention that the blood in here is from more than one person?"

This question was met with silence and a few exchanged looks of skepticism. After an uncomfortable period of quiet, Duncan finally spoke. "What makes you say that, Mack?"

"Those high-pitched trumpet notes I mentioned? I hear two slightly different and distinct notes, one when I look at the pool of blood around the victim and another when I look at these spots over here." I pointed to some drops of blood a small distance away from the dining room table heading into the kitchen.

Charlie Hammerman walked over to the more distant blood drops and knelt down to study them. "She may be on to something," he said. "The shape of these drops indicates they fell from above, as opposed to being spatter from our victim here."

Linz frowned, and after a moment he shook his head. "So you noticed the differing shape of the blood drops," he said, looking at me. "Again, it's not a huge leap of logic if you know anything at all about the physics of blood drops. Plus, it's pretty unlikely our victim here could've gotten up and walked into the kitchen after being shot in the head the way he was. So while I'll admit you're a keen observer, one who has apparently picked up some knowledge from hanging around Duncan here, you haven't uncovered anything we wouldn't have figured out eventually on our own."

"I haven't studied or been taught anything about the physics of blood spatter," I told him. "I just know that those blood drops over there smell different from the ones closer to the body. The logical conclusion is that there were at least two people bleeding in this house."

"If you say so," Linz said with a roll of his eyes.

Duncan let forth a perturbed sigh and started to say something, but I beat him to it.

"Detective Linz, have you examined that gun yet?" I said.

He shook his head, looking bored but exasperated.

"I'm pretty certain you'll find several fingerprints on it," I told him.

"Another brilliant deduction," he said in a tone dripping with sarcasm.

I bent down closer to the gun and stared at it. "More than one set of fingerprints, in fact. I detect several flaws or disturbances on the surface of the thing, and they appear to smell slightly different, suggesting they are not identical."

The two evidence techs exchanged looks; Linz just stared at me in silence for several seconds. "Wesley," he said finally, not taking his eyes off me, "see what you can get from that gun."

Wesley nodded and handed the tablet he was holding to Charlie. Wesley then retrieved a camera from a tackle box on the kitchen floor and snapped several pictures of the gun where it was. When he was done, he picked up the gun with his gloved hands, taking care not to touch the surface any more than he had to. He released the cartridge and looked at it. "There are three bullets gone," he announced. He then slid back a cover on the barrel and added, "And there's one in the chamber." He tipped the gun, dropped the chambered bullet into his other hand, and handed it to Charlie, who put it into a small paper evidence envelope.

"So there were two shots fired?" Linz said, but before anyone could answer, he went on, his eyes scanning our surroundings, focused mainly on the floor. "The victim was only shot once, and I only see one casing here. Its position is consistent with the head wound on our victim and the theory that someone shot him from behind. So perhaps that other bullet was fired sometime in the past."

"I don't think so," I said. My senses were picking up on some sort of odd dust in the kitchen area. The kitchen was separated from the living area by a breakfast bar, and the cabinets and appliances ran along the back wall of the house and around to the left of the breakfast bar if you were looking in to the kitchen from the living room. The bar seating was actually in the living room section, and on the kitchen side of the bar countertop was a built-in stovetop with an exhaust hood that hung down from overhead. Across from this, against the back wall of the house and bordering on the edge of the dining area, was most of the cabinetry and other appliances. On the end near the dining room, the counter had been converted into a small desk area with some overhead cabinets on the wall above it. Right next to this was the refrigerator, which had smaller, overhead cabinets above it. It was this area where I sensed the odd dust was present. "I think you should look at those cabinets around the desk and refrigerator," I told Linz.

"For what?" he sneered, clearly irritated.

"I'm not sure, but something is irregular over there."

Ortega walked over and shone a flashlight around and under the cabinets. He didn't have to look long. "She's right. There's a hole in the wall right here at the bottom of this cabinet." He pointed to the overhead cabinet above the fridge that was closest to the desk area. "It looks like a bullet hole."

Linz walked over to check it out, and the two men moved the refrigerator out from the wall, making the hole easier to see. Linz eyed the hole and then turned and looked at the rest of the house. "It looks like this bullet must have been fired from the living room," he said. "It went over the bar and zinged right in here between the fridge and the bigger cabinets." He frowned and scratched his head. "What the hell? This scene doesn't make a lot of sense to me."

"You're assuming that bullet is from the same gun that killed our victim," Duncan said. "Until you get it out and verify that, you have to consider there might have been another gun that fired that second bullet."

"It still doesn't make sense," Linz said. "Somebody fired a bullet into the kitchen and our victim, here, felt comfortable turning his back to this person? Or did they fire into the kitchen after they shot our victim? Why would anyone do that?" He looked over at Wesley and Charlie. "I want prints off that gun yesterday," he grumbled.

Charlie was the person actually holding the gun, and Wesley was typing a serial number into the tablet. "Got it," Wesley said when he was done, and then Charlie carried the gun into a corner so he could dust it for prints.

Duncan moved in closer to the dead man and studied the scene. "It looks like our victim was shot in the back of the head," he said. "Maybe there was a struggle before that and the gun fired during the struggle. That might explain your kitchen bullet. The killer won that struggle and shot our victim in the back of the head as he was trying to get away." He paused and bent down to look at the victim's head wound more closely. "It looks like the fatal shot was fired up close because I can see stippling in the victim's scalp." He stood and looked over at the back wall of the dining area. "Is that a hole in those drapes over there?" he asked, pointing toward the window.

Linz walked over and spread the drape fabric out, revealing a hole in it. Then he pushed the fabric aside to reveal another hole in the wall behind the drape.

I carefully stepped closer for a better look, saw something shiny in the hole, and realized the bullet was almost flush with the wall's surface.

Wesley set his tablet down on top of a duffel bag on the floor and removed a camera from the bag. He then approached the window and shot pictures of the drape fabric, which Linz once again spread out for him, and the bullet in the wall behind it. When that was done, he returned the camera to the bag and took out a small implement that looked like an ice pick or a screwdriver—I couldn't see it that well from where I was standing—and some needle-nosed pliers, and proceeded to work at removing the bullet. It came out easily, but the one in the kitchen wall proved to be a bit more labor-intensive. It was fascinating to watch all this, but I felt a little useless just standing around watching, offering up an occasional insight.

Officer Miguel Ortega, who had ventured into the living room after the discovery of the kitchen bullet hole, said, "Here's our second casing." He pulled it out from behind a cushion on the couch positioned on the front wall of the house. "Looks like your theory about a struggle starting here in the living room might be right."

"So we can't assume the victim was shot by someone he knew, someone he invited into the house," said Duncan. "The front door is too close to the living room. Someone could have knocked on the door and then forced their way in when the victim answered."

Linz nodded and sighed. "Let's hope it was someone he knew. Random crime involving random victims is too hard to solve."

"Do we know who our victim is?" Duncan asked.

Hank answered. "Assuming the wallet we found in his back pants pocket is his, the victim is the owner of the house, Sheldon Janssen."

I saw Duncan's face draw down into a frown. "Are you sure?" he asked.

"Well," Hank equivocated, "it's not a definitive identification. Obviously, we haven't seen his face, and even if we had, I'm not sure it would be helpful given the damage the bullet might've caused. As soon as the medical examiner gets here we can get a better look. But his lack of hair, his size, and his build, match what was on the driver's license in his wallet."

"If someone killed him, why leave the gun here at the scene?" I asked Duncan. "Isn't that risky?"

"Not in this case," said Wesley, who was once again looking at his tablet. "The serial number came back to our victim here." He paused and looked at the rest of us with a puzzled expression. "He was killed with his own gun."

"Well, that shoots some holes in our theory," Linz

said. "Pun intended, of course," he added with a roll of his eyes. "Did our victim answer the door with his gun at the ready? And if he did, why? Or did things escalate with someone who was already inside, forcing our victim to go for his gun?"

Duncan's frown deepened. "Wesley, don't you have a way to scan fingerprints in on that tablet you have there?"

"Sure do. I've already scanned in several prints that Charlie lifted from the gun, and I'm running them through AFIS as we speak." Wesley shifted his gaze to me. "AFIS is an acronym for automated fingerprint identification system," he explained.

"She knows that," Duncan said irritably.

I gave Duncan an annoyed look and then said to Wesley, "I've had AFIS explained to me before, but it's helpful to hear it again. Thank you. I'm still pretty new to this, so don't hesitate to explain things to me."

"Yes, ma'am," Wesley said. "And if you have any questions, please feel free to ask."

"Thank you," I said with a smile.

Duncan, apparently impatient with our proprieties, cleared his throat loudly. "The reason I asked about your tablet, Wesley, is that I'm wondering if you can run the dead man's prints for a definitive ID."

"I could," Wesley said. "But it's better to wait for the medical examiner to get here."

"Well, where the hell is he?" Duncan grumbled.

"I'm right here," said a voice behind us.

I turned and saw a short, portly fellow of about fifty approaching, carrying something that looked like a large tackle box, huffing and puffing with each step. His cheeks were slap red, his nose somewhat bulbous and heavily veined—a physical characteristic I knew was often associated with someone who has had a close relationship with alcohol—and from beneath the Packers knit cap he had pulled down on his head I saw tufts of gray, curly hair protruding. His crystal blue eyes were rimmed with crow's feet. They looked alert and lively, and I got an immediate sense that they, and their owner, didn't miss much.

"Dr. Al Spencer at your service," he said, looking at me. Presumably he knew the others in the room.

"Hi," I said with a nod and a smile. "I'm Mack Dalton."

"She's a consultant working with the police department," Duncan added.

Dr. Spencer had no reaction to this. He set down his tackle box, removed his winter gloves, and then slid off his cap, revealing a wild tangle of that curly gray hair. His eyes were focused on the dead man. He stood there for a good minute or more, just staring. Then he stuffed his gloves inside his hat, crammed the whole thing into a side pocket of the down-filled parka he was wearing, and proceeded to bend down and open up his tackle box. He removed a pair of latex gloves and pulled them on. Next, he removed a camera from the box and began snapping pictures of the body, slowly moving around it and getting as many angles as he could.

While he was doing that, Duncan was having a whispered chat with Wesley in the corner. Despite his attempts to be quiet, I was able to hear every word. At times my hypersensitivity could be a nuisance, but in moments like this one, it came in handy.

"I need to verify the victim's identity as soon as possible," I heard Duncan say.

"Why the urgency?" Wesley asked, giving Duncan a curious look.

Duncan opened his mouth to answer, but before he

could say anything, Wesley's tablet emitted a chime. Wesley swept his finger across the surface.

"I have an ID on one of the fingerprints from the gun," he said. He gave Duncan a surprised look. "It belongs to someone named Malachi O'Reilly," Wesley added. "And according to this, he's a cop."

Chapter 3

I stared at Duncan in disbelief. "Mal's fingerprint is on that gun?" I said.

Duncan gave me a sobering look. "This is worse than I thought," he said. "Is that the only print you've identified from the gun so far?" he asked Wesley.

Wesley nodded. "The others had less detail, so they may take longer to run and might not be identifiable. But given that the gun belongs to the victim, I'm guessing some of the prints must be his."

"Where are you going with this, Albright?" Linz asked.

"If this victim is Sheldon Janssen," Duncan said, "then Mal may be in trouble. He's been undercover for a couple of months investigating a construction company and its owner, Wade Klein. Klein is suspected of cutting corners, violating building codes, paying bribes, money laundering, and maybe drug dealing. Sheldon Janssen is the name of his number one, his right-hand man, so to speak. He has a reputation for being something of a goon who roughs people up whenever the owner asks him to. Maybe more than that," he added in an ominous tone. "Though from what Mal has told me, they haven't been able to pin anything on him yet."

The medical examiner squatted down beside the body—the cracks from his knees sounding loud as gunshots to my ears—and placed his hands on either side of the victim's head. Then he gently lifted it. Duncan bent down to get a good look, and instructed Wesley to snap a picture. Wesley fetched his camera and did so. When he was done, the medical examiner gently lowered the head back into the position it had been in originally.

I backed away from the scene, disturbed by this revelation. "When's the last time you saw or talked to Mal?" I asked Duncan.

"Two days ago," he answered. "You?"

"Yesterday," I said. "He's been sleeping in my basement for the past week or so, but I didn't see him this morning before we left . . . or last night, now that I think about it. He was there working with his family on the elevator installation early yesterday morning, but then he left because he had to go to work at his job site. I don't know if any of them heard from him again after that."

Duncan nodded, looking troubled. "I'll give them a call to see if they've heard from him today at all." He walked off into the living room area and took out his phone. I listened as he called the bar and asked someone—presumably Pete, my day bartender—to get one of Mal's family members for him to talk to. After a minute or so of waiting, I heard him greet Mal's father, Connor, and ask the last time any of them had seen or heard from Mal. He listened for a moment and then said, "I don't know. But I need to find him. If you hear anything from him, please have him get in touch with me." He then gave him his cell number and disconnected the call.

I distanced myself from the bloody scene even more, in part to be closer to Duncan and listen in on his phone conversation, and in part to dull some of the sensory input I was getting. There was a hallway running off the kitchen and living room area that presumably led to the bedrooms, and I felt oddly drawn to it. I looked down it and saw there were four doors, two on the right, one on the left, and one at the far end. The one at the end was a master bedroom. There was a large, king-size bed in view, the sheets and bedspread still rumpled. But halfway down the hallway I saw a bunch of balloons floating in the air, wavering slowly back and forth. I realized the balloons were a synesthetic reaction, because it was one I'd had before. It typically manifested whenever I heard the sound of someone breathing heavily, or when there was a strong breeze nearby. The presence of the balloons in the empty hallway was perplexing.

I backed up a few steps, keeping an eye on the balloons. They were ephemeral in nature—many of my synesthetic reactions were, and it helped me distinguish them from reality—and they became fainter, more ghostly. I reversed direction and moved back toward the hallway, and the balloons grew more solid. Puzzled, I looked along the walls and then studied the ceiling, searching for an air vent connected to the HVAC system. There was one located almost dead center between the doors on the right and directly above the door on the left. Satisfied that this was the cause of the balloon image, I started to turn away and go back to Duncan. But then I heard and felt a rumble, accompanied by the sound of air movement. The balloons began to dance.

I realized then that the HVAC system had just kicked on. The air from the vent set the balloons to dancing, but what had created them in the first place? It was mid-January, so it was unlikely that there were any windows open to allow a breeze into the house.

My confusion must have attracted Duncan's attention because suddenly he was standing beside me. "What is it, Mack?" he asked. "You have that look on your face, the one you get when you're experiencing a significant synesthetic reaction."

I looked over at the others to see if they were listening in, but they were paying us no attention. In a low voice, I explained to Duncan about the balloons and what happened when the HVAC system kicked on. "I'm a bit stymied as to why those balloons were there in the first place," I told him. "I saw something similar when Dr. Spencer first arrived. He was breathing very heavily, and I think that's why. Once his breathing was more regulated, the balloons disappeared. And these balloons do the same when I back away from the hallway."

"So . . . what are you saying, Mack?" Duncan asked.

"I assume the first guys here on the scene searched the entire apartment?"

"That's our normal protocol," Duncan said. "So I imagine they did." He turned and, in a louder voice, addressed one of the uniformed cops. "Ortega, did you guys search this place when you first got here?"

"Of course," Ortega answered. "Why?"

"What brought you guys here in the first place?" Duncan asked, ignoring Ortega's question.

"There was a 9-1-1 call from the house phone, but the operator said all she could hear on the other end was some heavy breathing, and then the line went dead. So basically, it was a welfare check initially. When no one answered at the door, we tried the knob and found it unlocked. We opened it and smelled the blood right away, so we went in."

"So who made the call?" Duncan asked.

Ortega shrugged. "No way to know for sure. It could've been the victim before he was shot, but how could he have done it if he was struggling with someone and the gun?"

"What time did the call come in?" Dr. Spencer asked.

Ortega consulted a notebook he pulled from his pocket. "Nine twenty-eight," he said.

Spencer looked at his watch. "It's ten-thirty now. I just checked a liver temp on our victim, and based on it, the temperature in the house, and the lividity in the body, I'd say he's been dead for close to three hours."

"So he couldn't have made the call," Duncan said. "That means that whoever shot him made the call, or someone else found our victim after the fact and called."

"Either way, make sure you dust that phone for prints," Linz said, nodding toward a landline sitting on an end table in the living room.

"Did the victim live here alone?" I asked.

Everyone turned toward me with surprised looks, as if they'd forgotten I was there or didn't expect me to speak and participate.

"The house is in his name alone," Linz said. "And from the looks of the place, there doesn't appear to be anyone else living here. There's a spare bedroom that doubles as an office, and a third bedroom that's completely empty."

"What about the bathroom, or bathrooms, if there's more than one?" I asked. "Are there any extra personal-care items that don't appear to belong to the victim?"

Linz looked irritated. "We haven't had time to go

through all that stuff yet," he grumbled. "We've been kind of focused on the dead guy."

Duncan looked back at me. "What are you getting at, Mack? Is there something about this balloon thing that I should know? Where are you going with this?"

I swallowed hard and in a low voice said, "I think we need to take a closer look at those rooms off the hall, because I suspect we may not be alone."

Just then the HVAC shut off, and for a moment the house was utterly silent. No one said anything and nothing moved, except for those darned balloons.

Then Duncan unholstered his gun and gave me a warning look. "Stay behind me. If you get a clue as to which way I should go, let me know."

I nodded, and the two of us headed down the hall. The others—their curiosity apparently piqued by our conversation—turned to watch us. Everyone remained quiet, and at that moment the HVAC system kicked on again. It seemed incredibly loud after the eerie silence from a moment ago.

We reached the first door on the right, and a quick look inside revealed a bathroom. The shower had glass doors, and other than a large cabinet hanging on the wall, there was nowhere for anyone to hide. Even though it was too small to hold a person, Duncan opened the cabinet, which proved to be full of nothing more than towels and personal hygiene items, but they seemed to be female personal hygiene items: bubble bath soap, hair bands, and some floral-scented lotion. Inside the shower were bottles of shampoo, conditioner, and a liquid body soap—all of them floral-scented as well.

"They could be from an occasional visitor, like a girlfriend who stays over," Duncan whispered.

I reached up and opened the medicine cabinet over

the sink. "I don't think it's a girlfriend," I said, puzzled by what I saw. On the bottom shelf in the medicine cabinet was a children's brand of toothpaste and a toothbrush with a Disney character on the handle.

Duncan looked as baffled as I was by this find.

We went back out into the hallway and headed for the first bedroom door across from the bathroom. The balloons appeared more solid as we drew close, letting me know we were on the right track, and as we approached the door they disappeared inside the room. I expected to see the room being used as a bedroom and home office based on what Linz had told us, but it was neither. It was the empty room. There was no furniture, the walls were blank and painted an off-white color, and the single window in the far wall was darkened by closed blinds. Duncan reached around the corner of the door and felt along the wall until he came upon a light switch. He flipped it and light flooded the room. There was a closet along the wall to the right with double folding metal doors.

Duncan looked back at me with a questioning expression.

"The balloons are hovering by the closet doors," I whispered.

Duncan nodded and pushed me back out into the hallway. Then he splayed his hand to let me know I should stay there. The others, their curiosity getting the better of them, had made their way to us, and everyone other than Duncan was standing in the hallway at this point. The place was so quiet—at least for normal ears—you could have heard the proverbial pin drop. Duncan's breathing had sped up and now he had his own bouquet of balloons hovering above and around his head. I held my breath as he grabbed one of the closet door handles and yanked open the right-hand side. It folded open with a loud clang that made me jump, and Duncan aimed his gun into the closet. The extrusion of the folded open door blocked my view of part of the interior, but I could see enough to tell that the closet, like the rest of the room, was empty. Duncan visibly relaxed, and I heard exhalations from the group behind me. I remained tense until I realized all the balloons had disappeared.

Had I misinterpreted them? Clearly, I had rattled the nerves of the others in the house, who were now muttering and mumbling under their breath. If I'd focused hard enough, I probably could have heard what they were saying, but I tuned it out. I had a pretty good idea what they were thinking, and none of it shed me in a favorable light. After a few seconds of this grumbling, the group behind me all turned and headed back out to the main part of the house and the dead man, leaving just me and Duncan there in the empty bedroom.

Feeling stupid and certain the others were now convinced I was a useless lunatic, I entered the room and stood next to Duncan in front of the empty closet. The balloons weren't gone after all. Duncan's were, now that his breathing had slowed to a more normal pace, but the original balloons, their colors all gray and black, were in the closet, bobbing up and down along the back wall. The open closet door had blocked them from my view.

"What the hell?" I muttered, staring at the balloons.

"What?" Duncan asked.

I winced at him. "I thought the balloons had all disappeared. You even had some behind your head right before you opened that closet door. I suspect if I'd turned and looked at the guys behind us, I might have seen some there, too. But yours disappeared once you saw the closet was empty, most likely because your breathing returned to something more normal. I thought the ones I saw hovering in the hallway earlier, and then here in front of the closet door, had disappeared, too. But they're still here, Duncan. They're hovering inside this closet. This empty closet. I don't understand it, but something about this . . . or maybe something with me is wrong."

"How can you tell which balloons were which?" Duncan asked.

"They're different colors and sizes. And there are different numbers of them. The ones I first saw in the hallway that are now in the closet are black and gray. There's no color to them, and they're small. Yours were larger and colorful—blue and green and red."

I stood there, staring at the balloons and the closet's interior and gave my synesthesia full rein. At one point I even closed my eyes to block out the image of the balloons, forgetting that I can see my synesthetic images with my eyes open or closed. Suddenly, I felt as if I'd been pushed backward. The feeling was so real that I flung my arms out to try to maintain my balance or grab on to something. I opened my eyes and quickly regained my equilibrium. I'd felt that odd pushing sensation before.

"Remember the Cooper case?" I said to Duncan. He nodded, eyeing me curiously. "When I stood in front of the dresser of that little boy who was missing, I felt a pushing sensation, as if a hand was actually shoving me back away from the thing. It was because the drawers had recently been opened."

A light bulb went on in my head then, and I spun on my heel and headed for the master bedroom. It was a good-sized room, and I stood at the foot of the bed for a moment, surveying the entire space and letting my synesthesia work. When I looked at the wall that should've been the back side of the closet in the other room, I experienced another strange physical sensation, only this time it felt like I was falling, as if the floor beneath me had suddenly disappeared.

I hurried back to the empty room, a silent but watchful Duncan on my heels. Staring into the closet at the bobbing bouquet of balloons, I said, "I think there's a void, a space of some sort between this closet and the master bedroom."

Duncan said, "There might be a chase, a channel for the mechanicals or ductwork."

I went out into the hallway again and walked over to the thermostat I'd noticed on the wall earlier. I flipped the heat off and then returned to the empty bedroom. The balloons were still bobbing up and down in front of the back wall of the closet. There was a rhythm to them, an almost frantic up and down, up and down, up and down.

"I need you to go out into the hallway and shut the door to this room," I said to Duncan. This was met with some unintelligible grumbling, but he did as I asked. I watched the balloons for a moment, but they stayed the same. Then I walked over and flipped off the light in the room.

With the silence and darkness surrounding me, many of my synesthetic reactions disappeared. I closed my eyes and tried to steady my own breathing the best I could. After a few seconds I heard it, and even with my eyes closed I saw it. I reached over and flipped the light back on, and then opened the door to let Duncan back in.

"I don't know who's behind that closet wall," I said to him, "and I don't know how you can get to them, but someone is in there, someone who is very nervous and afraid. I hear a racing heartbeat and see the rapidly pulsing light that goes with it."

Duncan once again went on alert. Holding his gun in front of him, he studied the inside of the closet. The floor was concrete, the walls and ceiling were drywall, and there was one long metal shelf—completely empty—that spanned the closet from one side to the other. A single right-angle brace was located beneath the shelf near the center of the closet, providing support. Beneath it, I could see a seam in the back wall that went from the brace to the floor.

I reached past Duncan and grabbed the brace, first pushing, then pulling on it. When I pulled, we heard a distinct click, and the right-hand side of the closet wall gave way. It swung outward as Duncan grabbed my arm and pulled me back. He aimed his gun into the empty space. It was dark, but despite the lack of light, I felt a sense of openness about the space. I took out my cell phone and activated my flashlight app, shining it into the area behind the closet.

The light revealed a mattress, a stuffed bear, an empty paper plate, a plastic cup, and two small bare feet.

Chapter 4

"This is the police," Duncan yelled. "Come out with your hands up."

Out in the main part of the house, I heard someone say, "What the hell?" and the others returned, congregating in the hallway outside the door to the room.

We all stood frozen, eyes riveted on the closet, but nothing happened. After a few seconds, Duncan looked over at me, mouthed the word *light*, and did a gimme gesture with his free hand. I handed the phone to him, and he aimed the light into the closet, shining it into the area we couldn't see. When I saw him drop his gun hand, I stepped closer so I could see what he saw.

Inside the space—arms wrapped around her legs, chin resting on her knees, dressed in a flannel nightgown—was a young girl of maybe eight or nine, pale in color, with dark brown hair. She didn't look at us. After a few seconds, she began to rock back and forth slowly.

Duncan turned and looked at me with his eyebrows raised. "What the hell?" he said.

Their curiosity piqued, the others came into the

room to see what we had found. I heard someone mutter, "Well, I'll be damned." Someone else said, "Go figure." And a third voice, which I recognized as Ortega's, simply said, "Sorry about that."

I focused on the girl, searching for any synesthetic feedback I could get from her. The pulsing red light was still there, flashing faster than before. And the balloons hovered over her head, wafting up and down in conjunction with her rapid breathing. Her eyes stared straight ahead. A smell emanated from her, a mixture of soap and sweat that made me feel a shroud of dampness descend over me.

And then I saw an image of a door slamming shut. It was so vivid that for a moment I thought the closet had somehow closed itself. Then an odd, keening moan filled the air. It took me a second to figure out if it was a real sound. It was, and it was heartbreaking.

Duncan holstered his gun and squatted down beside the child. "Hey there," he said in a calm, low voice. "Who are you?"

The girl didn't answer. She continued to rock, staring straight ahead.

"What's your name?" Duncan said. Still, there was no response. Duncan reached out and touched the girl's shoulder.

The child exploded into action, her arms and legs flying in all directions. The keening moan turned into a loud scream.

"Whoa!" Duncan said, falling back onto his butt. Linz and the two officers started to move closer to the child, but Duncan held up a hand to stop them.

Almost as quickly as she had turned into a human version of the Tasmanian devil, the girl once again withdrew into a tiny, rocking ball of unresponsiveness. Duncan looked over at me with a perplexed expression.

"I think she's in shock . . . or maybe autistic?" I said.

"What the hell is she doing locked away in this little cubbyhole?" Duncan asked rhetorically. "And what are we supposed to do with her? Who is she?" He got back to his feet and looked over at the others in the room. "Were any of you aware the victim had a child?"

There was some mumbling, some shuffling of feet, a couple of abashed expressions, and several shaking heads. No one said a word. The two uniformed officers both looked away. Duncan got up from the floor and approached Miguel Ortega. "You," he said, jabbing a finger toward the man's chest, "start talking to people and doing some inquiries. Find out who this kid is and why she's stashed away in a hidden cubbyhole."

Ortega nodded spastically, turned, and pushed his way past the others into the hallway.

I looked at Duncan and said, "I think the fewer people there are in here, the better she's going to do."

Duncan nodded and gave a pointed look to the others. Hank Johnson, no doubt eager to escape Duncan's accusatory looks and tone, spun on his heel and fled the room. Linz and the others backed out slowly, reluctant to depart from this curious scene. As soon as everyone had passed over the threshold, Duncan shut the door to the room. Then he turned back to me and said, "Any ideas on who she is and what we should do with her?"

I stared at the girl for a moment, letting what little synesthetic reaction I had to her come out. There wasn't much. The bland, faded balloons still hovered, and the red pulsing heart light was still there, but otherwise there was nothing. I approached her and knelt down on one knee where Duncan had been before, an awkward move given my crutches and cast. "My name is Mack," I said, once I was settled and had set my crutches aside. "I don't know your name, so for now I'm going to call you Little Girl, okay?"

That door image appeared to me again, fleeting, but this time it remained slightly ajar. I reached out and placed a hand on the girl's, where it wrapped around the leg closest to me. I half-expected her to jerk away from my touch, but she didn't so much as flinch. Her rocking stopped, and the door image came to me again. It was open a smidge wider this time. After a second of indecision, I decided to go for broke. I leaned in and took the other hand as well, unwrapping her arms from around her legs. "Come on out of there, Little Girl," I said, my voice soft. "You're safe with me."

She didn't look at or acknowledge me other than to allow me to take her hands in mine. I gave them a little squeeze and then let them go. "I need my hands to help me get up," I said. Then I grabbed my crutches and struggled back to a standing position. Once I was balanced, I reached down with one hand. To my surprise, she took it, stood, and stepped out of the closet. Despite this cooperation, her blue eyes remained unfocused, staring off to one side, looking at nothing.

I glanced at Duncan, who stood by watching in silence. I released the girl's hand and took a better look inside the closet cubbyhole. When I realized there was an overhead light with a string hanging down from it, I pulled it, and the space was more fully revealed. It was larger than I had thought initially, approximately six feet deep and eight feet wide. The walls were padded with a foam material that would likely soundproof the area. There was a mattress on the floor covered with a worn sheet and a soft, plush blanket. Beside the mattress was a water bottle that was half full, and a bowl that contained some dry Cheerios. Near the other end of the mattress was a stuffed teddy bear that was

missing one eye. Alongside the bear was a shoebox full
of crayons, dozens of them in various states of use:
some broken, some whole, some worn down to tiny
nubs, while others looked almost brand-new. There was
also a loosely stacked pile of plain white paper and
some well-used coloring books. Hanging on the wall at
the back of the cubbyhole were several pieces of paper
with crayoned scribbles on them, none of them bear-
ing any resemblance to an actual figure or object. They
weren't drawings; they were the mindless, colorful
scribbles one might expect from a two-year-old.

The room was very warm, and I took off my coat and
tossed it over by the door—scene contamination be
damned. Then I ditched my crutches again and got
down on my hands and knees. I crawled into the
cubbyhole, grabbed the teddy bear, the box of crayons,
and several blank pieces of paper. When I came back
out, Little Girl was still standing where I'd left her, staring off into space with that blank expression. I placed
the papers and the crayons on the floor outside the
closet, near her feet. Then I reached up and took hold
of one of her arms. As gently as I could, I tugged on it,
and she obediently dropped to the floor, her legs
tucked beneath her. I put the teddy bear against her
chest and wrapped her arm around it so she could
hold it. I half-expected her arm to go limp and for the
bear to drop, but she hung on to it. I saw a shift in her
eyes; her gaze moved to my face, and for a few seconds,
there was some focus there, a fleeting glimpse of the
child locked inside.

I looked over at Duncan. "Would you be willing to
leave me alone with her in here for a little while?"

Duncan looked hesitant. "I don't know, Mack," he
said. "We don't know anything about her. She could
be prone to outbursts of violence for all we know.

And while she's not all that big in size, based on the way she shoved my arm away earlier, she's quite strong."

"You'll be just outside the door," I said. "If I need any help, I can holler. Why don't you go finish processing your scene and let me see what I can do here? Let me know if you find out anything about her, like a name."

Duncan still looked uncertain. "She's a potential material witness," he said. "She might be our 9-1-1 caller." He hesitated and winced. "She could be more than that, Mack," he said, his voice dripping with hidden meaning.

I knew he was suggesting the child might also be the shooter. "I realize that. But I doubt you're going to get much out of her at this point and there are no weapons here. Let me see what I can do." Duncan's frown deepened. "Go on," I said. "I'll be fine."

He finally acquiesced, but I could tell he did so reluctantly. As soon as he was gone and had closed the door behind him, I shifted my attention back to the girl. I grabbed a piece of paper and placed it on the floor in front of me. After sifting through the box of crayons, I chose a red, a blue, a green, and a brown one. Then I drew a simple, childlike picture of some grass with red and blue flowers growing up from it. Given all the floral scents in her toiletries, I assumed she would like flowers.

She ignored me at first, staring off to one side, seemingly unfocused. But as I drew my fifth flower, she suddenly shifted her gaze to my picture. I paused in my efforts long enough to take a piece of paper and place it in front of her. Then I nudged the box of crayons closer. She began to rock again, moving slowly back and forth.

"Can you make a picture?" I said.

She stopped rocking, staring at the blank white page

before her. I went back to my own drawing and started filling in the blue sky. After a minute or two, she set the one-eyed teddy bear aside, reached into the box of crayons, and withdrew a black one. Then she proceeded to draw a series of wild black circles, a maelstrom of darkness. I continued with my own drawing, sneaking peeks at hers every few seconds. After filling most of the page with the wild black scribbles, she traded the black crayon for a red one and made a small red circle in the middle of the page. Then she drew red lines emanating from the circle toward the edges of the page. The red crayon was returned to the box, and she wrapped her arms about her legs and rested her chin on her knees. Then she began to rock again.

I picked up her drawing and studied it. To me, the image seemed unmistakable: a dark cloud of blackness with a bright red drop of blood at its center, sprays of blood spurting out. Ironically, it was not unlike the synesthetic imagery I experienced in response to the sound of a gunshot.

I turned the picture around so it was facing her and said, "Did you see someone get shot?"

Her rocking ceased for a moment, and for a few seconds, her blue eyes focused on mine. They were huge, rimmed with long, dark lashes. Her pupils were dilated, and despite the lack of any real expression, her eyes were wide, making her look frightened, wary, and alert. It didn't last. The brightness faded, and in an instant, she once again withdrew into whatever world existed behind that blank façade.

I set her picture aside, along with my own, and took two new blank pieces of paper from the pile. I put one in front of her and kept the other for myself. This time I began with a brown crayon and drew the crude outlines of a house, adding in rectangles to signify a door and several windows.

There was a light tap on the door, and the girl stopped rocking, frozen like the proverbial deer caught in headlights. The door opened to reveal Duncan, and a second later, the rocking resumed.

Duncan studied the drawings and the girl for a moment before speaking in a low, soft voice. "Ortega had a chat with a neighbor, a man named John Olbermann who has known Sheldon Janssen for about ten years. Olbermann said he has spoken to Janssen a few times over the years. He said Janssen mentioned having a daughter named Felicity who suffered from severe autism, but Olbermann thought the kid's mother was the custodial parent because Janssen often griped about disagreements they had regarding paying for the child's care. Olbermann also said Janssen told him the kid was something of a handful when she reached toddler age because she reacted violently to any number of sounds, sights, or touches. Whenever she got upset she would throw things, break up furniture, and scream relentlessly, and at times she would bang her head against the wall or furnishings until she sustained severe, bleeding wounds."

I looked at the calm, largely sedate child before me and had a hard time imagining this. "I guess that would explain the lack of furnishings in this room, as well as all the padding in the little cubbyhole there," I surmised. "Janssen must've made that cubbyhole specially for her. It wouldn't have been hard for him to do, given his construction knowledge and background."

"I imagine not," Duncan said. "But it's still a mystery how she ended up here. Olbermann claims Janssen told him the kid had died around a year ago. So he was surprised to learn the kid was living here, not only because he thought she was dead, but because Janssen was often gone for ten to twelve hours at a time, and sometimes went out in the middle of the night. Olbermann never saw any evidence of a babysitter or anything like that, but he also admits he didn't know Janssen all that well. He and the other neighbors all say Janssen was a loner who didn't speak to or socialize much with his neighbors."

"Well, clearly Felicity didn't die," I said.

"No, but according to Olbermann, her mother did, three months ago. Or at least that's what Janssen told him. My guess is that's when Janssen decided to bring his daughter here, though if he thought she was dead . . ." He left the question hanging, a question neither of us could answer for now.

"What was he thinking?" I said. "Given his work hours and such, you would have thought he'd have hired some caregivers, or made arrangements of some sort."

"Maybe he tried," Duncan said. "And we can't be one hundred percent sure this child is Felicity."

I pondered this for a few seconds and then shook my head. "Why would Janssen take in some other autistic child?"

Duncan gave me a grave look, one that suggested some ulterior motives I couldn't bear to consider just yet. "We need to get her checked by a doctor," Duncan said, and I nodded. "And we'll do DNA testing to verify her identity."

"She has to be his daughter," I said. "Look at all the prep work he did creating this hiding place for her. What are the odds of finding another child the same age with the same needs?"

"You're probably right," Duncan said.

I took a moment to contemplate the challenges

Janssen must've faced given Felicity's limitations. I couldn't decide if I admired him for trying to provide some sort of home life for the child, or resented him for essentially locking her away here and leaving her alone for hours on end while he worked. Felicity didn't look abused or neglected—she and her clothing were clean, and she appeared to be developing normally—but surely there were programs her father could've provided for her to try to help her.

"It looks like the two of you are having an art class," Duncan said, interrupting my thoughts.

"Yes, we are," I said, eager to move on to a less onerous topic. I picked up the picture Felicity had drawn and showed it to Duncan.

"That's dark and disturbing," he observed.

"It is. But it's also kind of fascinating."

Duncan's eyebrows shot up. "Fascinating?"

"Yes, because it's nearly identical to the visual manifestation I get whenever I hear a gunshot. It makes me wonder if she not only heard the gunshot but saw it as well."

Duncan narrowed his eyes at me. "Are you implying this child has the same form of synesthesia you have?"

I shrugged. "Not necessarily," I hedged, but the truth was, I was wondering if the child had some form of synesthesia along with her autism. It made sense to me in a way, given that she already had a known neurological disorder. "But who knows? Maybe there are aspects of her autism that allow her to experience the world in a way that is similar to my experiences with synesthesia."

"Does that mean you think you might have a mild form of autism?"

I wasn't sure if the question was a serious one, or if he was just ribbing me. "I don't think so," I said with a frown. "But I suppose it's possible we have some common elements. I know that children who suffer from autism are often overwhelmed by sensory input, so perhaps we share some sort of neurological malfunction."

Duncan digested this for a moment. Then he walked over to the cubbyhole, stepped inside, and examined it more closely. "There's a handle here on the inside that I didn't notice before," he said. He fiddled with the latch on it, testing it. "It looks as if the girl could come and go as she pleased. I thought at first this little hideaway was some sort of cage or prison, but it doesn't look that way."

"If her autism is as bad as the neighbor said, it makes sense," I said. "To you or me that might seem like a prison, but to her it's a safe haven. All the extraneous sensual stimuli are absent. It's safe and secure." I paused a moment and smiled. "I totally understand it. When I was a kid, I often imagined having a hidey-hole like this whenever my synesthetic reactions threatened to overwhelm me. In fact, there have been times in my adult life when I wouldn't have minded having a room like this."

I noticed then that the child had stopped rocking. "Is your name Felicity?" I asked her.

She didn't answer—not that I expected her to—but she did reach into the crayon box and grab a black crayon. Instead of drawing on her own blank sheet of paper, she reached over and took my drawing of the house and proceeded to make big black exes over the windows. Then she dropped the crayon back into the box, got up from the floor, and walked back toward her cubbyhole. She stopped in front of the hidden door because Duncan was still inside, blocking her way. She didn't look at him; she just stood there, shifting her weight from one foot to the other, staring off to her left.

Duncan got the message and sidled past her into the main part of the room. Felicity quickly stepped into the hidden room and then, proving Duncan's speculation, grabbed the inside handle and pulled the doorway closed.

"She must feel like that's her safe place," Duncan said. Then he frowned. "Still, the thought of her being locked away in there alone for hours on end . . ." He shuddered.

"What's going to happen to her?"

"We need to have her checked over by a doctor," Duncan said. "And we should try to find a relative of some sort. If we can't find a living relative, we'll have to contact the Department of Children and Families and have them decide what to do with her. Even if we can find a relative, I'm not sure they'll be equipped or willing to take her. My guess is that, given Felicity's condition and limitations, DCF may try to place her in some sort of facility rather than with a family, at least temporarily."

Now it was my turn to frown. "I'd like to be able to spend more time with her," I said. "I feel like I have a connection with her and might be able to find out if she saw or heard anything."

Duncan chewed his lip in thought. "I can give you another hour or so to spend with her here," he said. "We're going to be here processing the scene at least that much longer. After that, we'll have to see how things go."

I nodded. "Any word on Mal?" I asked, switching subjects.

Duncan shook his head, a worried look on his face. "I've got several feelers out, but nothing yet. I'm sure he'll turn up soon with a logical explanation for everything." Duncan's voice always tasted like chocolate to me, and with this latest comment, that taste turned bitter. He was lying, and I felt my heart ache, both literally and figuratively.

The evidence we found in this house suggested strongly that Mal had been here, but maybe he had been here some other time, and there was another explanation for why his fingerprints were on the murder weapon. And perhaps the blood trail leading into the kitchen hadn't been his blood. Maybe it was Felicity's. Except I knew that wasn't the case. She had no injuries on her that would have created such a trail.

The evidence technician had said he'd found three prints on the gun. One was Mal's, and presumably one belonged to the victim. I had to hope the third one belonged to the killer, and that the blood trail belonged to him or her as well. Felicity wasn't wounded, but was she a killer? I couldn't wrap my mind around the possibility of either her or Mal being the killer.

But I knew from the changes in Duncan's voice that he was more open to the ideas, and all I could do was hope he was wrong. I prayed Mal was okay and alive wherever he was. And I also prayed we would find that someone else had killed Sheldon Janssen.

Of course, that meant that there was a cold-blooded killer on the loose. I didn't like any of the options.

Chapter 5

Duncan left the room, shutting the door behind him. I crawled to my crutches, struggled to my feet, and hobbled my way into the closet. I pulled the bracket that opened the secret door and found Felicity curled on her side on the mattress, her legs drawn into a fetal position. I studied her for a minute or so, trying to decide how to proceed. Finally, I lowered myself to the closet floor beside her and simply started talking.

"Felicity, my name is Mack. I have a feeling you have things you want to tell me, and I know you're probably afraid. Some bad things happened here, and that must be very scary for you. It's scary for me. These kinds of things . . . scary things like this, make me see and hear and feel things that aren't there. For instance, the smell of blood makes me hear a certain kind of music. And the feel of the snow falling outside tastes like bread. Today the snow is light and fluffy, so it tastes like white bread. When it's heavy, it tastes like wheat bread. Do you go outside at all?"

I paused, not so much for an answer as to gather my thoughts. But I noticed that despite not having moved, Felicity was now looking at me, engaging me with her eyes.

"It's cold outside," I said. "And cold air tastes kind of sour to me, like unsweetened lemonade, or the juice from a lime. Everything I experience comes from more than one sense. For instance, I can tell from your smell that you use a shampoo that smells like flowers. I know that not just because of the smells, but because smells have distinct sounds and feelings for me. Even the smell of those crayons we used makes me hear a bubbling sound. When I hear music, I see different colors and shapes. Do you like music?"

Again, I paused. She still hadn't moved, but her eyes were still engaged. I began to sing a ditty I remembered from my childhood about the wheels on the bus going 'round and 'round. My father used to sing it to me, and just hearing the lyrics would make me feel the same sensation I experienced whenever I looked at a bus moving along the street: a vibration in my feet. When I was done with the song—or at least what I could remember of it—I again fell silent.

After a moment, Felicity pushed herself up into a sitting position, her eyes locked on mine. Then she began to hum. It took me a moment to recognize the tune: "Row, Row, Row Your Boat." I listened for a moment, and when she finished the basic tune and started humming it again, I joined her, but did so as if we were singing the song in rounds. She looked surprised, and for a moment, I thought she was going to stop humming, but instead she began to sing the words. Her enunciation was surprisingly clear, and I began singing along with her, still doing the round. After we finished two choruses of the song, she stopped and broke into a loud, happy laugh, the sound of which made me taste sweet strawberries and the sight of which made me feel a warm sensation in my tummy.

I looked at her and said, "You can talk."

Her smile faded. She dropped her gaze and stared at the floor.

"We don't have to talk," I told her. "It's okay if you don't want to. Why don't we draw some more?" I got up and crutched back over to the papers and crayons that were still sitting in the middle of the room. Wordlessly, I sat on the floor, laid my crutches beside me, and picked up a sheet of paper. Then I took a tan crayon from the box and began to draw the figure of a man. My artistic talents were quite limited, and what I ended up with looked more like a gingerbread man than anything else, but I figured the context would be sufficient.

Felicity watched me in silence for several minutes before finally emerging from the closet. But rather than sit down and draw with me, she paced back and forth, watching what I was doing, and pulling at her lips every few seconds. I wondered when she'd last had anything to eat and if she might be hungry. I took out my cell phone and sent a text to Duncan, asking him if there was anything out there in the main part of the house that he could bring in here for us to eat. While I was texting, Felicity cocked her head to one side and watched me with intent curiosity. After sending the text, I handed the phone to Felicity to see what she would do with it. I should've thought it through more. As she was staring at the screen, one hand hovering over it as if she wanted to touch it, it buzzed and dinged with Duncan's response.

Felicity let out a screech that sounded like a bird of prey, and she flung the phone away from her. Fortunately, she flung it in the direction of the closet, so the impact was minimal because it hit the mattress, bounced, and caromed off the foam padding on the soundproofed walls.

My gut response was to get up and try to calm her, but I resisted it, thinking that any sudden physical contact would only heighten her discomfort. After that one primal screech, she made no more noise. She started pacing again—a little faster this time—and again pulled at her lip.

"Felicity," I said in a soft, low voice, "I'm sorry the phone scared you. I used it to send a message to Duncan, the man who was in here earlier. I thought maybe he could bring us something to eat." The pacing slowed, so I scooted into the closet on my rump to retrieve my phone. I read Duncan's reply. "He's going to bring us some food in a moment, okay?"

No response, but the pacing seemed to slow a little more. I returned to my drawing, and a minute later, there was a tap on the door. Felicity dashed into the closet and squatted there, looking out at me. The door opened, and Duncan entered the room carrying a plate that had some crackers, some peanut butter, some baby carrots, and a chocolate bar. He set it down on the floor beside me and said, "Anything?"

"Not really," I answered.

He said nothing more, and after giving me a gentle squeeze on my shoulder, he exited the room, closing the door behind him.

"Come and get something to eat," I said to Felicity. I picked up a cracker and popped it in my mouth. Then I picked up the chocolate bar and unwrapped it, breaking it into several pieces that I then set on the plate.

Felicity darted out of the closet toward the plate, grabbed several of the chocolate pieces, and shoved them in her mouth. She did it with such speed and ferocity that it made me laugh.

"Wow," I said, "you must really like chocolate. You can have the other pieces, too."

She didn't hesitate. Her hand darted out and the rest of the chocolate pieces disappeared.

I smiled at her and said, "You know that man who was just in here, Duncan? The sound of his voice tastes like chocolate to me."

She stared at me with a new intensity. After a moment, she grabbed one of the blank pieces of paper and then retrieved a red crayon from the box. She quickly drew what appeared to be some sort of red fruit, either an apple or cherry. Then she picked it up and showed it to me.

"Is that an apple?" I asked.

She shook her head vigorously. "Cherry," she said. She reached toward me with a finger, touching it to my lips.

I gaped at her. After a moment, I picked up a carrot and showed it to her. Then I bit it in half, chewing the portion in my mouth. "The taste of this carrot makes me hear a clapping sound," I told her with the pieces still in my mouth. "And when I chew it, the feel of it on my teeth makes me see boxes, piles of boxes."

Felicity picked up a carrot and bit it the same way I had. She stared at me as she chewed, the muscles in her face working, frowning one second, looking puzzled the next. She chewed slowly, methodically, never taking her eyes off me. When she was done and had swallowed, she popped the other half into her mouth. She positioned it between her teeth and then crunched down hard just one time. Then, with the carrot still in her mouth, she leaned forward and drew a triangular shape on the same page where she had drawn the cherry.

I gaped at the picture for a moment, and then I gaped at her. I felt a trill of excitement, certain I had just met a fellow synesthete. Just to be sure, I picked up a cracker and smelled it. In an instant, I heard something that sounded like ocean waves crashing. I dug in the box of crayons until I found a blue one, and then I drew a caricature of a series of waves. "This is what these crackers smell like to me," I said.

Felicity reached over, took the cracker from my hand, and then held it up to her nose. I watched as she sniffed and then set it back down on the plate. She looked at the box of crayons for a moment, and then she reached in and retrieved a red one. Grabbing a new piece of paper, she started to draw, making a series of shapes that I thought were leaves at first.

"The cracker smells like crumbling leaves?" I asked her.

She shook her head.

"Like fresh leaves? Does it make you hear something, or are you describing the actual taste?"

She shook her head again and huffed out a breath of impatience. After drawing several of the leafy shapes in a bouquet of sorts, she returned the red crayon to the box and took out a black one. Then she drew a series of wavy lines above her red leaf shapes. Then she replaced the black crayon with a brown one and drew a small stack of brown horizontal lines beneath the red leaf shapes. I finally realized what her picture was.

"That's a fire," I said.

Her expression brightened, and she smiled at me.

"Does the cracker smell like a fire?"

Felicity shook her head spastically, and then touched

her ear. Suddenly she reached forward and pinched a section of my hair between her fingers right next to my left ear. It was all I could do not to pull away from her—the movement was so sudden and unexpected, it startled me—but I managed to sit still. She then began rubbing my hairs together between her fingers.

"Ah," I said with a smile. The rubbing of my hair between her fingers sounded very similar to the crackle of a fire. I gathered from all this that when she smelled the crackers she heard that sound. I decided to try another one. After clearing my throat, I sang, "'Row, row, row your boat, gently down the stream.'" When I was done, I picked up a piece of paper, raised my knees, and placed the paper against my thighs so Felicity couldn't see it. Then I removed a series of crayons from the box and drew on the paper, keeping it from her sight the entire time.

She watched patiently as I drew, a bemused smile on her face. When I was done, I turned the paper over and set it on the floor with my drawing facing down.

"When I sing the song, does it make you see something?" I asked her. She nodded. I pushed the box of crayons toward her and gave her a blank piece of paper. "Show me," I said.

I sang the song again, and when I was done, I nodded toward the paper.

Felicity's smile broadened, and her expression turned sly. She picked up the piece of paper, pulled her knees up the same way I had, and placed the paper on her thighs. Then she proceeded to remove a series of crayons from the box and draw on the paper. When she was done, she put her paper face down on the floor.

"Let's turn them over when I say three," I said. "Do you understand?"

Felicity nodded, and reached over to take the edge of her piece of paper. I did the same with mine and said, "Okay, here we go. One, two, three."

We flipped our papers over at the same time. Felicity clapped her hands with glee and there was a huge smile on her face, a fleeting one because it was gone almost as quickly as it appeared. But a sparkle remained in her eye that told me she was enjoying this little game.

I expected her drawing to be nearly identical to mine, which consisted of a series of different shapes in different colors. Music always presents itself to me that way: boxes, circles, triangles, random shapes, squiggly lines . . . any number of shapes and designs in any number of colors. Each song is a unique combination of these.

Felicity's drawing had some similar characteristics in that it was a series of colors I imagined would seem random to most people. But rather than shapes and lines, she had drawn numbers. There were single, double, and triple digit numbers drawn in a sequence, a space in between signifying which groups of numerals went together. Each individual numeral had its own color, and the color wasn't necessarily consistent. For instance, the first number she had drawn was a forty-eight, with the four in green and the eight in red. A few digits later, she had drawn the number eight by itself, but in this case, it was yellow. And in a subsequent number, 452, the numeral four was drawn in purple.

Our colors didn't match up in any way I could detect, but I did notice that Felicity had written down the same amount of numbers as I had shapes in my picture. This led me to believe she saw each individual musical note as a number with colors, whereas I saw them as some sort of shape with color. Our experiences were somewhat similar, but also vastly different. Regardless, I was convinced Felicity had some form of synesthesia.

Chapter 6

My excitement over this bonding moment with Felicity didn't last long. The door to the room opened, and Duncan entered with a woman behind him. Felicity shot up from the floor and went back to her hidey-hole, squatting down and staring off into a corner. Duncan did the introductions.

"Mack, this is Julie Parnell, a social worker with DCF. She's here to take Felicity." Duncan turned toward Julie Parnell and said, "This is Mack Dalton. She's a consultant for the police department."

"Pleasure to meet you," Parnell said in a rote tone. Even as she said the words, her eyes weren't on me; they were on Felicity. "Is that room back there where you found her?" she asked with a look of disbelief.

"It is," Duncan said. "It's actually a hidden room of sorts. As I mentioned to you on the phone, the child seems to have some severe form of autism."

"She may be autistic," I said, "but she understands what's going on around her better than she lets on. She's also a synesthete."

Parnell turned and looked at me with a bemused expression. "She's a what?" she said.

"A synesthete; someone with synesthesia."

Parnell gave me a skeptical look. "I'm not familiar with that term."

"It's a sensory disorder," I explained. "I have it myself. My senses are cross-wired so that I experience each of them in more than one way. For instance, smells come with certain sounds for me, and some sounds come with a taste. When Duncan speaks to me, I taste chocolate. When Felicity spoke to me earlier, I tasted strawberries. You, Ms. Parnell, are an exception. Rather than a taste, I get a visual manifestation with the sound of your voice. When you speak, I see tiny sparkles of light."

I half-expected the woman to look at me like I was crazy and then dismiss me. She did neither. "Are you saying the child was able to speak to you?" she asked.

I nodded. "It wasn't much, a word or two. And she sang a song. We communicated more through our drawings." I pointed toward the various crayon pictures spread around on the floor.

"Interesting," Parnell said, nodding her head slowly and studying the pictures.

"What are you going to do with her?" I asked.

"First, I'm going to have her checked over by our physician to make sure she's okay, and that there are no signs of abuse. Assuming that checks out okay, I'm going to place her temporarily with foster parents, a couple who specialize in taking care of special needs children like this. I've placed other children with them who had similar issues."

"I suspect her synesthesia may play a big role in some of her behaviors," I said. "All of that sensory input can be very overwhelming. It makes one feel like they want to hide and withdraw from the world. That little cubbyhole she hides in is perfect insulation for her condition."

Parnell cocked her head to one side and gave me a tolerant smile. "Do you have some sort of training as a psychologist, or are you a social worker?"

"No," I said with a smile. "I'm just relaying my own personal experience with this disorder because I think it will help you in managing Felicity."

"Thank you for your advice," Parnell said, a bit tight-lipped. "I think I can manage. I've had a lot of experience with this sort of thing. If you don't mind, I'd like some time with Felicity alone."

I frowned at this, suspecting things weren't going to be as easy as Parnell thought. But I didn't want to ruffle any feathers or create a scene, so I got up from the floor and crutched out of the room.

Duncan followed me out, and Parnell shut the bedroom door behind us. I turned around and gave Duncan a pleading look. Before I could say a word, he held up his hand like a cop stopping traffic. "I know, I know, the woman is a bit pushy. But this is what she does for a living, so let's let her do her job, okay?"

I bit back the protest I wanted to make, my shoulders sagging with resignation. Duncan steered me back out to Janssen's dead body, which had been removed from its spot on the floor and was now inside a body bag. As Dr. Spencer zipped the bag closed, we heard a high-pitched screech emanate from the bedroom down the hall. I knew from the sharply tart taste of strawberries that Felicity was the source of that screech. Then I heard Parnell speak Felicity's name in a clipped, sharp tone. I saw the little sparkly lights, except they were duller than before. With the lights came the sound of indistinct soft murmurs, no doubt Parnell's attempts to calm Felicity.

I tried to push down thoughts of Felicity and Parnell and concentrate on the crime scene instead, in case there was something else I could detect. But the screeches continued, and hard as I tried, I couldn't shift my focus away from that bedroom. After a few minutes, a flustered-looking Julie Parnell emerged from the bedroom and walked up to us, her face beet red, her hair out of place, a small scratch on her arm that was red, raised, and angry-looking.

"That child is going to be harder to manage than I thought," she said, taking out her cell phone. "We're going to have to restrain her and I'm going to need some help. If you guys can help me hold her down, I'll call for an ambulance and we can have the EMTs help us restrain her and then take her to the hospital."

"You don't need to restrain her," I said, my tone sharper than I'd intended. "She understands what's going on if you take the time to explain things to her."

Parnell shot me an irritated look. "I've been doing this for a long time, Ms. Dalton, so if you don't mind, just let me do my job, okay?"

"No, it's not okay," I said, not bothering to temper my tone this time. "She's just a little girl, and she's frightened. The more you get in her face, the worse she's going to be."

Parnell shot Duncan a pleading look, her way of begging him to make me shut up and go away. But Duncan had already seen how I had connected with Felicity, and while he may not have had a full understanding of the intricacies of her autism, he understood the complications synesthesia added to the picture, thanks to the time he had spent around me.

"There's no need to cause any undue trauma to the child," he said to Parnell. "Why not let Mack have a try at it to see what happens?"

Clearly, Parnell had expected unquestioning support from Duncan, and when she didn't get it, she gaped at him, her mouth hanging open, a deep frown on her face. She stared at him that way for a moment, and when she finally closed her mouth in preparation for speech, Duncan made a move before she could get a word out.

"Come on, Mack," he said, taking me by the arm and steering me back toward the bedroom. "See if you can convince Felicity to leave with Ms. Parnell."

We made our way back to the bedroom with Parnell hot on our heels. Evidence of the skirmish that had taken place was obvious. The neat stack of paper that had been on the floor was now spread all over the room, and several of the pictures we had drawn were torn. The crayon box had been spilled, scattering its contents about the room, and a couple of crayons were smashed and broken. Felicity had retreated into the closet and the door was closed. I made my way inside and knocked on the wall.

"Felicity, it's me, Mack," I said in a soft voice. "I'm going to open the door, okay?"

There was no response, so after a moment, I pulled on the brace and swung the door open. Felicity was squatting on her haunches atop the mattress, her arms wrapped around her legs, rocking back and forth. I knelt down on the floor beside her, propping my crutches against the wall.

"Felicity, we need to take you to a hospital to get you checked out. The people there need to look at you. They won't do anything to hurt you; they just want to make sure you're okay. Once that's done, you need to go spend the night somewhere other than here. It will be a safe place, and Ms. Parnell will make sure it's a place where you can have quiet if you want." I turned and gave Parnell a pointed look. "Isn't that right, Ms. Parnell?"

Parnell looked irritated, and she answered me with a tight-lipped, "Of course."

I reached over and touched Felicity's shoulder. She stopped rocking, but she remained in her wrapped-up position. "Will you come out of the closet please?" I said.

Felicity stayed still and continued staring straight ahead. I was about to ask her again, when she said, "Mack."

"Ms. Dalton is not trained in this sort of thing," Parnell said officiously.

I rolled my eyes and sighed. "I can't go to the hospital with you," I said to Felicity. "But maybe I can come and visit you later where you're staying." This suggestion was met with Parnell's scoffing *harrumph* from behind me. I ignored her and continued talking to Felicity. "It's very important that you do what Ms. Parnell says, Felicity. I promise you no one will hurt you if you do what she says. If you don't, they may put you someplace where I won't be able to see you again. I don't want that to happen."

Felicity remained motionless, and her gaze remained fixed, but a small tear fell from her lower lid, tracking down her cheek. It broke my heart to look at her.

"Ms. Parnell wants you to ride with her in her car," I said. "You've ridden in a car before, haven't you? When I'm in a car, the sound of the engine makes me see blue clouds. And whenever I'm in a car that goes over a bump, I taste peanut butter. How crazy is that, huh?"

I saw the corner of Felicity's mouth twitch up just a hair. There was a hint of a dimple in her cheek. I'd seen the full dimple when she'd laughed earlier. I leaned into the space, got close to Felicity's ear, and whispered to her. When I was done, she looked me straight in the eye and giggled. It was the sweetest sound I could've heard at that moment, and it filled my mouth with the taste of honey.

I clambered to my feet, balanced on my crutches, and extended a hand to Felicity. After a moment's hesitation, she took it, got up, and came out of the closet. She kept her eyes on the floor and refused to look at Parnell.

"She's going to need some warm clothes," I said.

Felicity let go of my hand and grabbed my shirttail. She gave it a tug and then, still holding my hand, she headed for the bedroom door, pulling me behind her. In the hallway, she turned left toward the master bedroom. There were three dressers in the room, and she pulled me toward a white one on the left. She stopped in front of it, let go of my shirt, and stood there with her arms at her sides, facing the dresser, shifting slowly back and forth from one foot to the other.

I started opening drawers, and removed underwear, pants, shirts, and pajamas. After I put them on the bed, Felicity walked over and selected the items she liked and, presumably, wanted to wear. After searching through a closet, I found a small suitcase and started packing the other items in it.

Felicity stood at the bedside hugging the clothing items she had chosen while I did this, watching me pack and then hand the suitcase to Parnell.

I draped an arm over Felicity's shoulders and said, "Let's go into the bathroom and dress, okay?" I nudged her toward the bathroom that was connected to the master bedroom, but she slipped beneath my arm and went down the hall toward her closet hideaway and the other bathroom. I wasn't sure where she was headed, but let her go and choose. Unfortunately, Dr. Spencer was hauling Sheldon Janssen's body out at that very moment.

Felicity stood rigid in the hallway, watching them carry the body bag out. Even though the body itself wasn't visible, I sensed Felicity knew what was inside. Though the rest of her body remained stock-still, one hand hung at her side, and she kept opening and closing it into a fist. The uniformed cops, Miguel Ortega and Hank Johnson, stared back at her, and for a moment this grim tableau was frozen in time.

As soon as the body was outside and the front door of the house had closed, Felicity turned and headed into the empty bedroom. I followed, and by the time I got in there I saw she had gone into her cubbyhole and closed the door. Parnell and Duncan came in behind me, and the three of us stood there in silence, staring at the back of the closet wall. I'm sure we were all thinking the same thing: would she come back out, or had she gone into hiding again?

"Let's give her some time," I said finally. "I don't think we should push her too hard."

Parnell, looking impatient, said, "Let me know if and when she reemerges. I have some phone calls to make." She spun around and left the room.

"Charming woman," I said to Duncan as soon as she was gone, my tone dripping with sarcasm.

"Take your own advice and give her some time," Duncan said with a wan smile. "You, and this child, are an acquired taste. It can take some getting used to."

"I suppose," I said. "But given what Parnell does for a living, I would have expected her to be more open and understanding."

Duncan didn't agree; nor did he disagree. After another span of silence, he said, "I'll leave you to handle

Felicity. I'm going to go out to see how the guys are doing with processing the scene. And I'm going to see if I can find out anything more about where Mal might be."

I heard—and tasted—the worry in his voice. Where was Mal? Was he okay?

And then I got an idea. I took out my phone and sent a text message to Cora, asking her for a favor. A moment later, she answered me back.

I started pacing, anxious for Felicity to come out of the closet—a term that made me smile as I thought it. I busied myself gathering up the spewed crayons and pieces of paper—a task made difficult by the need to manage my crutches—returning the crayons to the box and putting all the papers into two neat piles, one for the drawings and one for the blank sheets. When I was done with that, I decided Felicity had gone back into hiding and wasn't going to come out. I was going to have to go in and get her.

I headed for the interior of the closet, but just as I reached for the brace to open the door, it opened on its own. Felicity stood there, dressed in the clothing she had chosen. Her discarded clothes lay in a neat, folded pile atop the mattress.

"Good job," I said. "Are you ready to go see the doctor?"

She didn't answer. But she frowned.

"It will be okay," I assured her. "They won't hurt you."

"I want Mack," she said.

"I'll come to see you again, as soon as you're settled in your new house, okay?" I had no idea if this would be possible, but I felt I needed to give the girl some sort of reassurance. Then, to distract her, I said, "Can you help me with something, Felicity?"

No answer, but she looked me straight in the eye,

and I took this as acceptance. I took my phone out of my pocket and opened up the text message Cora had sent me. "Look at this," I said, showing the phone to Felicity. On the screen was a picture of me and Mal that Cora had taken on the first night we had met. Mal and I both looked a bit awkward and shy, understandable given that we were faking a blind date. "Do you know this man, Felicity?"

She stared at the picture for a long time. Finally, she looked up at me, her eyes budding with tears. Slowly, she nodded. Then she clapped her hands over her ears and started chanting. "No, no, no, no, no . . ." She kept repeating the word, the timbre and level of anxiety in her voice rising with each repetition.

Fearful she was building up to a full-blown meltdown, I reached over and placed a hand over hers. "It's okay, Felicity," I said. "You don't have to tell me, or remember anything if you don't want to."

Her chanting stopped. She looked me in the eye, and then said, "Bad man!"

I wondered who she was referring to. Could it be Mal? Did she think Mal was a bad man for some reason? I didn't want to push her, afraid she would start to chant again, so I switched subjects. "Are you ready to go?"

She looked sad, and for a moment, I thought she was going to dart back into the closet and shut the door again. But after a few seconds she nodded, and after dropping her arms to her sides, she headed out of the bedroom.

Chapter 7

Duncan drove us back to the bar after we saw Parnell and Felicity on their way. Parnell, still not convinced the child would cooperate, had called in her cavalry. Two strapping young men had shown up to ride with her and Felicity to the hospital. With a little cajoling from me, Felicity went willingly and quietly. I asked Parnell if it would be possible for me to see Felicity once her medical exam was finished and she was settled in somewhere.

"I think your involvement with this is done at this point," she said, her tone curt. "Thank you for your help so far, but we have it from here."

I was about to say something back to her, something rather rude, but a look from Duncan stopped me. He shook his head ever so slightly, warning me not to go there. Feeling frustrated and angry, I let him steer me toward his car. The first couple of minutes of our ride was spent in silence. Then Duncan posed a question to me.

"What did you say to Felicity to make her laugh when you whispered in her ear?" he asked.

"I told her that the color of Parnell's pants made me smell dog poop."

Duncan shot me a look that was half-amused, half-disbelieving. "Did it really?"

I shook my head and smiled. "No, but I thought it might put Felicity at ease and help strengthen the bond we were already building."

"Nice work," Duncan said.

My smile faded. "Thanks, but I feel like it was all for naught. I would've liked to have spent more time with her rather than turn her over to the clutches of that Parnell woman."

"You never know what might happen," Duncan said prophetically. "On another subject, once we get to the bar, I'm going to check in with Mal's family and get a key to his house. I want to head over there as soon as possible. Do you want to come along?"

"Of course."

Our stop at the bar was intended to be a short one, but it wasn't to be. The first delay came from Cora and the Signoriello brothers, Joe and Frank. The trio was seated at a table near the front entrance, and the remnants of whatever they had ordered to eat for lunch was on the table, as was Cora's laptop, something she never went anywhere without.

"There they are!" Cora said as we walked in. "How did the first official crime investigation go?"

"Sit down and give us all the gory details," Joe said, grabbing a chair and pulling it out from the table.

"I'd love to guys," I said, "but we're only here for a short while. We just stopped by to pick up something. The investigation is still very much ongoing. You guys haven't seen or heard anything from Mal today, have you?"

All three of them shrugged and shook their heads. Then Cora said, "Is Mal involved in your case?"

In a calm, reasoned voice, Duncan avoided a direct answer. "We really need to talk to him as soon as possible."

"I assume you've tried to call him?" Cora said.

"I have," Duncan said. "The calls keep going to voice mail."

"Maybe he forgot to charge his phone," Joe offered.

"Or maybe he forgot his phone," Frank suggested.

"Both are good possibilities," Duncan said, though I knew from the change in the taste of his voice that he didn't believe this for a moment. "If you see him, please ask him to call me right away."

The threesome nodded, but I could tell from their expressions that Duncan's efforts to downplay the situation hadn't fooled them. Joe and Frank's bodies might be slowing down a little—to be expected when you hit your midseventies—but their minds were as bright and sharp as they had been in their heydays. They'd been around the block a time or two, and seen plenty in their combined lifetimes.

Cora hadn't been around nearly as long, but she'd been coming to the bar for the better part of a decade or more. She and I had grown much closer recently, sharing confidences, thoughts, ideas, relationship frustrations, and of course, the database of my synesthetic reactions. Her talents when it came to computer hacking had proven to be a very valuable asset to both me and Duncan, though Duncan kept her participation strictly on the lowdown. Cora didn't always play by the rules.

We moved to the bar so I could check in with my staff to make sure things were running smoothly. My day bartender, Pete, was working behind it and, at the moment, Debra, my head waitress, was back there also, helping him slice oranges.

"How is everything going?" I asked them.

"Swimmingly of course," Debra said, looking smug. "We've been doing this long enough to handle things just fine on our own. And you know that if any problems came up, we would call you. So the more important question is, how did your first day as an official crime consultant go?"

"It's been interesting, and that's all I can say about it for now." Pete shrugged; Debra looked disappointed. "I'm going to be leaving again in a few minutes," I told them. "Keep up the good work."

Duncan and I then headed into the newest section of the bar, an adjoining space I bought a few months ago. We crossed the room toward the raised stage at one end. Off to one side of the stage was a door to a stairwell going down to the basement. Beside it was the door to my new elevator, which was almost completed and ready to use. The elevator was primarily intended to provide an alternative access to the second floor, which could also be reached by stairs on the far side of the room. It would go down to the basement, too, but only if one had a key to override the normal access points.

I opened the door to the basement and hollered down the stairs. "Anyone down here?"

"We are," came back a voice I recognized as that of Connor O'Reilly, Mal's father.

Mal had given me an overly generous Christmas gift by having members of his family, who owned a construction company in Yakima, Washington, come to build my elevator. They weren't doing it for free, but I knew the price Mal was charging me was far below what I would have had to pay anyone else. In exchange, I provided free food and drink while they were working.

For the past two weeks, Mal's brothers, Ryan, who was a carpenter, and Patrick, who was a master electrician, had been staying at Mal's house at night and working on my elevator in the bar during the day. His sister, Colleen, who was a master carpenter, had also come along. Mal's mother, Josephine, and his other sister, Deirdre, who was a master plumber, had stayed home. With so many family members crowding his house, Mal had been spending his nights on a bed I set up for him in the basement of the bar. I had invited him to stay in my apartment upstairs, and he did for a couple of nights. But once the person who had been stalking me was apprehended, he moved himself into a makeshift bedroom he set up in the basement. This was probably wise of him, given that Duncan and I no longer had to hide our relationship, and Duncan had been spending many nights at my place. The situation could've been awkward because of Mal's feelings for me, but he handled it with uncommon grace and kindness. He was a sweet man, and my feelings for him ran deep. But there was something between me and Duncan—chemistry, magnetism, I didn't know what to call it—that wasn't there with Mal. Mal was more like the brother I never had.

Duncan and I descended the stairs into the basement, and the O'Reilly clan gathered around us.

"Any word from Mal?" Connor asked.

Duncan and I both shook our heads. "We were hoping you guys had heard something, Duncan said. "When is the last time any of you saw or heard from him?"

"He slept here last night, or at least that's what we all assumed," Connor explained. "We left around nine last night and headed back to his house. He was down here doing some finishing work on the elevator car's interior."

"He texted me this morning," Colleen, said. "Said he needed to come by the house to shower and grab some clothes and wanted to know if everyone else was done and gone. We were all headed out the door and I texted him back and told him so."

"What time was that?" Duncan asked.

Colleen took out her phone, swiped the screen a few times, and then said, "Seven fifty-eight."

Given that the time of death the ME had provided was around seven-thirty in the morning, this timing seemed ominous.

"Has Mal been coming back to the house regularly?" Duncan asked.

"Not regularly," Patrick said. "He's been in and out a few times over the past couple of weeks to do laundry and pick up some things. Other than that, he's been sleeping here at the bar. He said Mack was letting him use her shower."

Duncan shot me a look. "I didn't know that."

"He uses my father's shower," I clarified. "Anytime you've been here, you've been up and gone long before Mal needed the shower."

"I want to go take a look at his house," Duncan said, turning his attention back to the O'Reillys. "Can I borrow a key to get in?"

Colleen fished in her jeans pocket and pulled out a single key on a ring. "Here you go," she said. "Is Mal okay?"

"I'm sure he is," Duncan said, lying. "He probably either forgot his phone or forgot to charge it." Before anyone could ask any more awkward questions, Duncan pocketed the key and turned to me. "Can you show me where Mal has been sleeping?"

"Sure. I set up a cot for him in the basement beneath the old section."

We left the O'Reillys after assurances that all parties would inform the others if anyone saw or heard from Mal, and headed back to the main area of the bar. Though we could have cut through downstairs, taking a secret tunnel that connected my apartment and the original site of the bar with the basement in the new section, there were some bad memories associated with that tunnel and I tended to avoid it. Instead, we went back up the stairs and threaded our way over to the back hallway of the original bar area, where the entrances to my apartment and that side of the basement were both located. Once we went back down into the basement, I led Duncan over to Mal's temporary sleeping quarters, which had been set up in a corner near several boxes of liquor.

"Not a bad location," Duncan said with a wry smile, eyeing the boxes. "Convenient if one wants a nightcap."

"I told Mal a long time ago that he has free run of the bar, so he doesn't need any of this."

Duncan shot me a look when I said this, and I sensed my statement had disturbed him for some reason. Whatever it was, he shrugged it off in a second and shifted his focus to Mal's sleeping area.

The bed, which was neatly made, was a double-size, inflatable mattress covered with sheets and blankets I had provided from my apartment. There were empty, upended crates on both sides of it, and one of them was serving as a nightstand. A lamp sat on top of it, plugged in with an extension cord that ran across the floor. There was also a phone charger, a half-empty bottle of water, and a coffee mug that had been cleaned. Stashed in the open area beneath these items were the plans for the elevator, along with some trim samples. The other crate was serving as a makeshift dresser. There were socks and underwear, a couple of T-shirts, and an extra pair of jeans folded inside it. On top were several toiletries I assumed Mal carried upstairs whenever he used my shower. The ceiling overhead was open, and hangers looped over an exposed plumbing pipe held two plaid flannel shirts.

"Not a bad setup," Duncan said.

"I guess," I said, frowning.

"What?" Duncan said, watching me.

I shrugged. "I don't know," I said. "I suppose this area is better than nothing, but it bothers me that Mal is using this as a bedroom when I have a perfectly good unused bedroom in my apartment. I tried to convince him to take over my dad's room, but he adamantly refused."

Duncan opened his mouth as if to say something, but apparently thought better of it and clamped it closed again. He surveyed the area for a moment, and then said, "If we assume Mal spent the night here last night, odds are his phone was charged. He clearly rigged things up so he could charge it every night. So why isn't he answering it?"

I knew it was a rhetorical question, so I didn't bother trying to answer. We headed back upstairs, and I checked in with Pete to let him know I was leaving again. I had complete faith in my employees' abilities to run the bar without me, so my check-ins were driven more by guilt than any real concerns. Assured that all was and would continue to be fine, Duncan and I left and headed for Mal's place.

Mal's house was in the same neighborhood as

Duncan's, though it was several blocks away. It was a small, two-story, Craftsman-style home with three bedrooms and two bathrooms. The neighborhood was an older one, and most of the houses, including Mal's, dated back to the 1920s and '30s. A few looked like they were losing their battle against the ravages of time and neglect. Not surprising, given Mal's construction background, his house appeared to be well maintained. There were a few things that needed fixing on the exterior, but there was also evidence that Mal had been working on these items. Several balusters on the front porch railing had been replaced but not yet painted, a chore that would have to wait for warmer weather. There was also evidence of paint that had been scraped away from some of the window trims.

Duncan knocked and rang the bell on the off chance Mal was there, but when no one answered after a minute or so, he unlocked and opened the front door.

"Mal, you here?" Duncan yelled, creating a burst of chocolate flavor in my mouth. There was no answer, and the utter silence was a bit spooky.

Inside, the house looked like it had been a temporary home to several guests. In the living room, clothing had been strewn here and there: draped over the backs of chairs, hung on a closet doorknob, and tossed onto one of the end tables. Someone had breakfasted at the coffee table and left behind their remnants: a coffee mug with a half inch of cold coffee in the bottom, and a plate with some toast crumbs and a few bits of scrambled egg. Out of habit, I grabbed up both items, positioned them with my fingers so I could carry them and crutch at the same time—something I'd become quite adept at over the past few weeks—and carried them to the kitchen.

I expected something out of the fifties or sixties with

lots of heavy wood trim, older appliances, and either tile or Formica countertops. But the kitchen was a pleasant surprise. Clearly Mal, or whoever he'd bought the house from, because he'd only been living in Milwaukee for a year, had redone the kitchen recently. The appliances were new, stainless steel, and state-of-the-art; the countertops were granite—a gorgeous swirling medley of gold, brown, and silver—and the cabinets were a simple Shaker style with a honey-red finish. The floor was hardwood, clearly the original oak boards based on the appearance of some of the pieces, but newly sanded and polished to a shiny gleam. There were can lights in the ceiling, but the Craftsman style of the house was evident in both a ceiling fixture and a pendant light over the sink, both of which had beautiful stained-glass shades. It wasn't a huge room, not large enough to support an island or kitchen table—and given the large, connected dining room, there was no real need for either—but there was a small, round, bar-style table with two stools in the middle of the room, topped with the same granite as the countertops. It provided a small eating space or an additional work space.

Once again, evidence of a hasty breakfast and morning retreat was evident in the dirty dishes in the sink and the dirty skillet on the stove. I added the dishes from the living room to the collection and then rejoined Duncan in the living room, where he was sifting through a small pile of mail on a table by the front door.

"Anything?" I asked.

He shook his head and kept sorting, so I meandered my way upstairs. My senses reacted to a number of things: the smells of soap, aftershave, and hair products; the squeak of the wooden stairs beneath my feet; the feel of a cold draft as I passed by a stained-glass window on the upper landing; the sight of the sun-washed colors from that window playing on the hallway floor. I pushed all the subsequent reactions down, tamping them into submission, and tried to focus on just what I could see. The first two doors I came to were both bedrooms, one on the right and one on the left. The left, southern-facing room was warmly lit by sunlight; the room on the right was darker and shaded. The wall colors seemed to have been chosen with these differences in mind: a warm, creamy shade of yellow for the darker room, and a cool, forest green for the sunnier room. White trim around the windows and four-panel doors, as well as wide, white baseboards and white crown molding, made each room look like a framed painting. The furnishings were older, not valuable antiques per se, but gently used period pieces.

The next two rooms were the master bedroom, located on the left, and the main bathroom on the right. There was no en suite for the master, but the main bathroom was surprisingly large and did double time as a laundry room.

It looked as if the two brothers were sharing the master bedroom. Based on the toiletries I saw on a dresser in one of the earlier bedrooms, Colleen was using the sunnier of the two rooms, which left Connor to use the remaining one. I looked around the master bedroom, unsure which clothing belonged to Patrick and Ryan as opposed to Mal. Given that I knew Mal to be a relatively neat person, I gathered that most of the strewn items belonged to the brothers. I didn't see anything in particular that looked interesting, but when I entered the bathroom across the hall, I immediately smelled Mal, or rather the particular aftershave he liked to use. That scent always triggered a hair-raising sensation for me in the most literal sense. The few times Mal had used my dad's bathroom in my apartment, the freshly applied smell had made the hairs along my arms raise. As the smell dissipated, so did the sensation, and I knew from past experience that my reaction would fade to nonexistence within an hour or two of Mal having used it unless I got up very close to him.

I supposed Mal's brothers might have used his aftershave, but given that they left the house several hours ago, the lingering scent present now suggested that someone—presumably Mal—had been here within the past hour or so. Plus, I recalled seeing a bottle of that aftershave among the toiletries in the basement bedroom Mal had been using. And I couldn't recall ever detecting the same smell on Connor or either of Mal's brothers. That didn't mean they didn't use it today, and I wondered if there was another bottle of it somewhere here in the house.

I was distracted from this question by a disquieting sound: the shrill, high-pitched tones of a trumpet. I looked around and saw that there was a hamper in the bathroom. It seemed that the trumpet screech had emanated from that area, and this was confirmed for me as I moved closer and the sound grew louder. Using my elbow, I bent down and flipped the lid open. Just then, Duncan joined me in the bathroom.

"Anything in here?" he asked.

I nodded, and told him my thoughts about the aftershave. "I suppose one of the other guys could have used Mal's aftershave if there's any of it here," I said. "And if any of them had been here in the past hour, it would explain my reaction. They haven't, so I have to assume the lingering smell is from Mal having been here."

Duncan nodded, a ponderous expression on his face.

"There's something else," I said, pointing to the open hamper and explaining my reaction to it. Without hesitation, Duncan removed a pair of gloves from his coat pocket—he always carried several pairs on him wherever he went—and put them on. He then began sorting through the clothes in the hamper. After removing a couple of shirts and a pair of jeans, he stopped and stared into the hamper. I stepped up so I could see inside as well. There, buried at the bottom of the hamper, was a hand towel and a T-shirt. Both of them were saturated with blood; not a nick-yourself-shaving amount of blood, but rather a serious-wound amount of blood.

Neither of us said anything more for a moment, both of us lost in our own thoughts and our concern for Mal's welfare. Then I delivered more bad news. "The particular note or sound of this blood matches one of the ones I heard, or smelled, in Janssen's house."

"I need to run out to my car and get some evidence bags," Duncan said. "I'm collecting that towel and shirt." With that, he turned on his heel and headed downstairs.

I stayed in the bathroom, standing in the middle of the room with my eyes closed. I let my other senses take over to see if I could pick up on anything else of use. I felt moisture lingering in the air, as if someone had recently used the shower, and even with my eyes closed I saw drops of water like rain.

Nothing else struck me for the moment, so I opened my eyes. The medicine cabinet door had a mirror in it, and as I looked at its surface, I felt the same sensation I'd felt when I looked at the gun in the condo. I suspected this meant there were fingerprints on the mirror, though how useful that would be remained in question, given the number of people in the house who might have touched it.

It held the typical over-the-counter pain medications, a generic, over-the-counter antihistamine, a bottle of cough medicine, a box of various-size Band-Aids, toothpaste, floss, and razors. I stared at these items and gave my synesthesia full rein.

When I was younger, my father enjoyed testing my synesthetic abilities. He would have me step out of the room, and then he would rearrange something in it. He started off with easy items, large things that would be easily noticeable. But as I aced each test, he upped the odds with each subsequent challenge by moving smaller things, or moving them less. Sometimes he would take some small item and hide it somewhere—in his pocket, or in a drawer, or under a piece of furniture—and then ask me what was different.

I excelled at these little games, and to be honest, I also enjoyed them. Not only was it shared time when I could bond with my father, it allowed me a chance to let my synesthesia out of the box of shame I kept it hidden in most of the time. We discovered through trial and error that my ability to perform this trick waned with time. The longer it was after an item had been moved, removed, or hidden, the harder it was for me to tell what had been done. My father and I debated why this was. One theory was that my brain formed a picture of the room that was exact and precise that I could then compare to the altered room. But this didn't explain why my ability waned with time, and we more or less ruled it out when my father tested me by not allowing me in the room beforehand. I could still tell that something had been moved and identify where the object had been, even though I couldn't identify the specific object itself.

Our next theory was that I might be able to sense pressure changes in the air, tiny drafts created by the movements that had taken place. But we eventually ruled this one out with logic, given that my and my father's movements about the room would have created larger drafts than anything else, and that would have confused things. Finally, we surmised that I was able to see or smell stirred particles of dust and could somehow distinguish between them. This explanation seemed too vague and illogical to me, but it was the one my father clung to. To this day, I'm not sure how I do it, and I long ago quit trying to figure it out because there was no real way to know.

Looking at the contents inside the medicine cabinet, I knew the large container of ibuprofen had been moved recently. So had the wound dressing materials. My heart ached, because I knew this meant Mal had been wounded—probably shot—and judging from the amount of blood on the items in the hamper, it was a serious injury. I said a silent prayer that he was okay.

Duncan returned and bagged the bloody items from the hamper, sealing and labeling them. I shared with him my perceptions regarding the items in the medicine cabinet, and after looking at them, he bagged and tagged those as well.

"I don't understand," I said to Duncan. "If Mal is hurt . . . shot . . . why didn't he seek help?"

Duncan's brow furrowed. "My guess is he's hiding out for some reason."

"Or maybe he has sought help," I countered hopefully. "We should check on the area hospitals. If he was injured badly enough, he might have gone to an ER. If he lost consciousness, he might be somewhere we don't know about."

Duncan considered this for a nanosecond and

shook his head. "If he was here tending to his wounds, my gut tells me he's not that serious yet, and he's hiding out for some reason."

This at least gave me some hope. "So where would he go?" I asked.

Duncan narrowed his eyes in thought for a moment. Then his face lit up. "He'd go to the last place anyone would look for him."

Chapter 8

I had no idea what Duncan meant, but I was willing to follow him. After looking around the rest of the house, we left without gathering any other items. Back in the car, I continued to try to figure out what he had in mind, determined not to ask. If I was going to search for Mal, where was the last place I'd expect him to be? His house wasn't safe over the long term. It was too easy, too obvious. The bar was out because that was the first place anyone would look. His family was there. Help was there. I was there, and up until recently everyone thought we were a couple.

I felt a twinge of guilt, and with it a prickling sensation between my shoulder blades that I knew was a synesthetic response to that emotion. Mal had been honest and open about his feelings for me, but I'd made it clear to him that my allegiance lay with Duncan when it came to things romantic. Still, the façade we'd carried on for so long had to have played hard and fast with his emotions. I was surprised he was willing to spend any time at all with me—with us—given how hurt he must have felt.

Then it hit me. The hurt, the humiliation, the bad

memories. On the heels of a painful breakup—though technically he and I hadn't broken up because we were never really together—the last place one would want to be is in the company of the person who broke one's heart.

"You're thinking Mal might have gone to see his old girlfriend, the one he moved out here to be with," I said.

Duncan looked grudgingly impressed.

"I don't recall her name at the moment," I went on, sensing I was on the right track. "But I recall the story, at least Mal's version of it. They met while she was in Washington on business and they hit it off well enough that he came here to Milwaukee to be with her. And shortly after that, they realized it was a mistake."

"Not bad, Mack," Duncan said. "Her name is Sabrina Cortland."

"Right," I said with a snap of my fingers. At hearing the name, other details came back to me. "Mal told me she works for a brewery here in town and was in Yakima shopping for a new hops distributor. She went to a hops farmer who was a friend of Mal's, and that's how they met. Mal happened to be there."

"All true," Duncan said. "Or at least it's consistent with what I know of the story."

"It makes sense," I said. "The ex who broke your heart is the perfect person to go to if you're running or hiding, assuming the parting was on friendly terms." I looked over at Duncan. "And you know where to find her?"

"I do."

It turned out that Sabrina Cortland was more than just a buyer of hops for a brewery; she was the owner of a brewery called Great Lakes Brewhaha. Duncan gave me some background, informing me that unlike the larger and more well-known breweries in Milwaukee, such as Miller, Pabst, and the Milwaukee Brewing Company, Great Lakes Brewhaha was a small microbrewery that over the years had gained in both popularity and sales. They were known for creating some unusual mixes in their brews, and with the modern-day trend toward micro-brewed beers, they had recently enjoyed a surge in growth.

"Sabrina comes from a wealthy family," Duncan explained as he drove, "but the family money isn't in beer. It's in steel. Sabrina used her trust fund to launch a brewery, something her parents weren't keen on, given the huge amount of competition in the area. But Sabrina forged on anyway, and launched the company when she was still in college. Over the next seven years it enjoyed some steady growth and a small amount of income, but in the past five years they've hit a growth streak."

"Good for her," I said, realizing I'd never tried one of the beers from Sabrina's company, though I do stock some microbrews at the bar. The fact that Sabrina came from a rich family made me uncomfortable. My recent experiences and history with wealthy people hadn't been particularly pleasant, and I often found it difficult to relate to them. I wondered if Mal's blue-collar background had been part of the reason he and Sabrina hadn't worked out.

Duncan parked on Wisconsin Avenue near a five-story office building and helped me out of the car because there was a large ice patch beside my door— treacherous for anyone, but even more so for me and my crutches. We entered the building and took an elevator to the fourth floor. GLB Enterprises, the business name Sabrina used, was located in a small office Sabrina shared with two other women, one of whom greeted us as we entered. Though Duncan knew a lot about Sabrina from talking with Mal, he had never met her. Introductions were made with Duncan flashing his badge, and I quickly learned that the other two women were Sabrina's staff members.

Sabrina herself was an attractive woman, not beautiful in a model or actress sense, but more in a fresh-faced, doe-eyed, pretty kind of way. Her smile was warm, welcoming, and felt genuine. There was nothing intimidating about her, and with her blond hair pulled back into a ponytail, relatively little makeup on, and an outfit that consisted of jeans and a sweatshirt, she gave off an aura of relaxed friendliness. I liked her instantly. Despite the warmth emanating from her, I sensed a wariness about her, a distrust of us and our motives for being there.

"What can I do for you, Detective?" she asked, looking at Duncan.

"I'm trying to get in touch with Malachi O'Reilly," Duncan said. "I thought you might be able to help us out with that."

Sabrina let out a little chuckle. "You thought I could help you track down Mal?" She said this with a strong hint of irony. "I'm not exactly on his Facebook friends list."

"It's imperative that I get in touch with him as soon as possible," Duncan said. "I'm worried about him. I think he's in trouble."

The three women in the office exchanged glances. I tried to read them but couldn't. Finally, Sabrina said, "Let's take a walk and talk." She went to a nearby coatrack and grabbed a parka from one of the hooks. After shrugging into it, she headed for the door, and then held it until we fell into step behind her. We followed in silence to the elevator, down to the first floor, and out the main door.

She headed down the sidewalk at a rapid clip, and we continued to follow, saying nothing. I shot Duncan a questioning look at one point, tired of trying to keep up with Sabrina's pace with my crutches. But Duncan said nothing and kept following her, so I did my best to keep up. After making several turns onto side streets, Sabrina stopped near a large parking structure and spun around to face us.

"I assume this has something to do with police business?" she said, looking at Duncan.

Duncan nodded. "He's been undercover for a while, and this morning we discovered that one of the men who worked with him at this undercover job has been murdered. There was evidence at the scene and elsewhere to suggest that Mal might've been shot. And he's disappeared. He isn't answering his phone and he hasn't been in touch with anyone. I think he's gone to ground, and when I tried to think of somewhere he would go that no one would expect him to be, your name came to mind."

"I take it you know my history with Malachi?" Sabrina said.

"Some," Duncan admitted. "In addition to being a fellow cop, Mal's a good friend of mine, and a good friend of Mack's here, as well. He has shared some of his history with us."

"If that's true, you know Mal and I broke up shortly after he moved here. Things didn't end on a friendly note."

"That's not what he told me," I said.

Sabrina turned toward me sharply, with a who-the-hell-asked-you look on her face.

"He said he was hurt by the breakup, but that the two of you remained friends," I went on.

"I'm afraid he misled you," Sabrina said with an apologetic smile. "I haven't seen or spoken to him in nearly a year."

Up until this point, Sabrina's voice had triggered a visual of tiny white puffs, like dandelions gone to seed, floating around in the air. But when she uttered her last line about not seeing or speaking to Mal, all the little puffs turned black and disintegrated.

"You're lying," I said, trying to keep my voice as benign as possible, though there was no getting around the fact that the words themselves were accusatory.

"I beg your pardon," Sabrina said, shooting me another perturbed look.

I glanced over at Duncan. "She was telling the truth up until she said she hadn't seen or spoken to Mal recently," I explained.

Sabrina didn't give Duncan a chance to respond. "Look, I don't know what sort of games you're playing here, but I don't appreciate it," she said irritably. "And I'm done talking to both of you." She shoved past Duncan and headed back the way we had come.

She was a dozen or so steps away by the time I turned myself around and said, "If something happens to him, if he dies, it will be on your head."

From the periphery of my vision, I saw Duncan shoot me a surprised look. Sabrina halted her retreat, glancing around nervously, taking in who was nearby and who might have overheard. Then, with a look of profound irritation, she backtracked to us, practically stomping with each step. She stopped in front of us, arms folded over her chest, one foot tapping irritably, and glared at us, her gaze bouncing back and forth between me and Duncan. Suddenly, her gaze dropped to the sidewalk.

"Fine," she said in a low voice. "I saw him earlier today very briefly. He said he needed to hide out for a while, so I loaned him the keys to my car and the keys to a lakefront home I own up in Whitefish Bay."

Duncan gave her a perturbed but grateful look. "Why didn't you just tell us that in the first place?" he grumbled.

"Look," Sabrina said, "Mal's a good guy. We're from two different worlds, and that caused some problems between us. But that doesn't mean I don't care for him. I don't begrudge him for breaking things off with me, and I want only the best for him. I was more than willing to help him out, especially because he appeared desperate. And he told me not to talk to anyone about seeing him, or to say where he was going."

Her comment about the breakup surprised me. I had it in my head that Mal had been the one who got dumped, but when I searched my memory for why I thought that, I came up empty. I couldn't recall him saying exactly how the relationship between him and Sabrina had ended, so I must've assumed from the hurt way he spoke of it that he had been the one who had been left behind. I realized Mal's feelings for Sabrina must've been strong.

"Was he okay when you saw him?" I asked her.

She pursed her lips before answering. "He looked like he was hurting, but he said he was okay when I asked him."

"What's the address of this lake house?" Duncan asked.

Sabrina gave us the address, and Duncan wrote it down, while I committed it to memory.

"I assure you that we want only the best for him,

too," Duncan told her. "And along those lines, it's imperative that you not tell anyone else that you saw him, spoke to him, or helped him out. In particular, don't tell anyone where he is. I can't stress the importance of this to you enough. It is literally a matter of life and death—Mal's life and death." He paused and looked at our surroundings, surveying the scene. "I've been watching to see if anyone was tailing us when we drove to your workplace," he went on, his voice low. "And I didn't see anyone then, or during this little walk of ours. I don't think there's a reason for you to be on anyone's radar, so I don't think it will be an issue—"

"I was on your radar," Sabrina pointed out, interrupting him.

Duncan gave her a grudging look. "True, but that's because Mal is a close friend of ours and he told us about you," he said. "I'm guessing he didn't tell anyone else or he wouldn't have come to you. Still, be alert and be careful. If anyone finds out you have connections to him, it could put you in danger, as well."

If I expected Sabrina to look frightened by this, I was disappointed. She trivialized Duncan's warning with a little *pfft* and a dismissive wave of her hand. "I'll be fine," she said.

"That's very cavalier of you," Duncan said with a grim attempt at a smile, "but let me assure you, this situation is very serious. I'd advise you to keep your eyes open and your mouth shut."

Sabrina pulled her head back, as if his words had offended her, but after a few seconds she smiled at him and nodded. "Got it," she said tersely.

"Let's go, Mack," Duncan said. He wrapped his hand around my arm and gave it a little tug, nearly making me lose my balance.

I hesitated a moment and smiled at Sabrina. "You're right," I said. "Mal *is* a good guy. Thank you for helping him. I'm sorry things didn't work out between the two of you."

"So am I," Sabrina said with a brittle smile.

And with that, we parted company.

Chapter 9

Just to be safe, Duncan drove a circuitous route about town before heading for Whitefish Bay to make sure we weren't being followed. It had been a very long, intense, and busy day, and I made Duncan stop for some coffee along the way because I felt myself starting to fade. Thanks to the short days of winter, night was closing in as we headed out, and I wasn't sure if the darkness helped us or made things more frightening. On the one hand, our arrival at the lake house was more likely to go unnoticed, but it also made it harder for us to see who might have been lurking in the surrounding trees or yards of the neighboring houses.

I expected Sabrina's lake house to be an extravagant abode typical of other wealthy homes along the lake but was pleasantly surprised to find a modest-size home nestled between two larger ones. This gave Sabrina's house more yard space and, perhaps, more privacy, though all the houses along the waterfront were close enough together that it would be hard to do anything at any of them without being seen if someone was intent on watching. We had to hope that wasn't the case. The house to the left of Sabrina's was dark, but the one on the right had warm light shining out through semisheer drapes on the first-floor windows.

Duncan parked on the main road near the top of a thirty-foot driveway that led down to Sabrina's house. "Stay here in the car," he instructed. "I'm going to go down and scout around the house to try to get a peek inside. I'd like to verify that Mal is here if I can, and if he hears anything, he might shoot first and ask questions later. I don't want you there if that happens."

"I don't want you there either if that happens."

"I'll be okay. Stay put and I'll let you know when the coast is clear."

There was no light we could see emanating from Sabrina's house, nor was there a car parked in the driveway, or along the road like we were. I worried that Mal hadn't made it here, that he was lying somewhere bleeding . . . or dead. I watched, squinting into the darkness, as Duncan quietly made his way down the driveway and around to the left side, taking advantage of the darkened house next door. I cracked my window open and sat, nervously biting at my thumbnail, listening as hard as I could. I switched my gaze from one side of the house to the other, waiting for Duncan or even Mal to appear. Time ticked by—literally, because I could hear the second hand on my watch working its way around the face—and I felt ready to jump out of my skin.

A good five minutes had gone by, and I was about to get out of the car—Duncan's warning be damned—when someone rapped on the driver side door. I jumped and let out a small yelp of surprise as my heart started trying to box its way out of my chest. My involuntary flinch left me with a banged knee, a bashed elbow, and a bruised ego, because I'd failed to hear anyone approach. In the split-second it took me to realize the person knocking at the window was Duncan, my heart rate had doubled and my adrenaline was surging.

"Dammit, Duncan!" I hissed as he opened the driver side door and slid back behind the wheel. "You scared the crap out of me. How the hell did you get all the way back here to the car without me seeing you?"

"I scouted around that dark house next door to make sure no one was lurking or hiding there and then came back up to the street from the far side of it. Then I just walked up behind the car. Sorry if I scared you."

"Is Mal here?" I asked.

Duncan started the engine and then pulled down the driveway, parking in front of Sabrina's house. "He's here," he said. He shifted the car into park, turned the engine off, and opened his door. "Come on, follow me."

I tailed him down the left side of the house toward the back. There was a large two-story deck built onto the back of the house, and I saw that the place was bigger than it appeared from the front. It was built into the hillside and there was a lower, walk-out level here in the back. A sliding patio door provided access to the ground level, and the interior was hidden behind vertical blinds. But I could see light emanating from between the slats, the only indication that anyone might be in the house.

Duncan walked up to the sliding glass door and knocked on it, using the same coded knock he and I had worked out for the back door to my bar when he was sneaking in during the letter-writer debacle. Mal had known about that knock, and I realized how smart it was of Duncan to use it.

"Did you use that knock when you came back here by yourself?" I asked at a half whisper.

"Of course," Duncan said. "Short of shouting through the door, which I didn't want to do because it might attract unwanted attention, not to mention that it might have also gotten me shot, it seemed like an easy way to let Mal know who was out here."

A moment later, the blinds were pushed aside and the sliding glass door was unlocked. All I saw of Mal before we got indoors was his hand and part of his arm on the door handle. Once we were inside, I saw the rest of him, and it made me gasp. His color was pale, and there was an unhealthy sheen to his skin. He moved like an old man as he pushed the door closed and locked it again, clutching at his left side, and shuffling his way to a nearby chair.

"You look terrible," Duncan said, not mincing his words. "Let me take a look at your wounds."

Mal held out a hand to stop him. "I'm fine," he insisted. "Or rather I will be in a day or two." He shifted in his chair, the action eliciting a small groan from him. He was wearing a loose-fitting beige sweatshirt, but I saw a small brown stain near where he was holding himself and knew from my synesthetic reaction to both the sight and smell of it that the stain was dried blood. I tamped down my worries by reassuring myself that at least it was old, dried blood and not fresh, but I was still bothered by the way Mal looked.

"You are going to let us take a look at that wound," I told him in a tone that brooked no objections.

I moved in on him, half-expecting him to push me away. But he didn't. Gingerly, I lifted his sweatshirt to reveal a gauze dressing crusted with old blood. After carefully loosening the tape around the edges, I pulled the dressing away, making Mal suck in his breath through his teeth. Despite my efforts to keep my expression and reaction as neutral as possible, I couldn't help but suck in my own breath at what I saw. The bullet had grazed his left side, creating an angular wound about three inches long and exposing a lot of red, raw, underlying tissue. There was extensive bruising around it, and areas of skin along the edges were blackened.

"Oh my God, Mal," I said. "This looks serious."

"It looks worse than it is," he said. "It's a superficial wound. The bullet grazed me and then tunneled under my skin, exiting back here." With a grimace and a grunt of pain, he twisted and showed me a second dressing.

Quickly, before he could object, I grabbed the second dressing and removed it. Once again Mal hissed with pain.

"Sorry," I muttered.

The exit wound was swollen and discolored, shades of purple, red, and black.

"We found your clothes at your house," I told him. "You lost a lot of blood."

"It did bleed a lot," Mal admitted through gritted teeth. "But it's under control now, and it wasn't enough to be life-threatening. I just need a couple of days to build my strength back up."

"Do you have any first aid stuff here?" I asked.

Mal nodded as he eased his sweatshirt back down and straightened himself in the chair. This minimal effort obviously drained him, and a surge of worry coursed through me. "There's a bag over there on the table with some supplies," he said, nodding toward a dining area that adjoined the main room. "I had Sabrina buy them for me."

I got up and walked over to the table to retrieve the bag. A glance inside revealed a bottle of hydrogen peroxide, several packages of sterile gauze, some medical tape, some antibiotic ointment, and some nonstick pads. I carried the bag back to Mal's seat, while Duncan settled into a chair beside him.

"What the hell happened?" Duncan asked.

"I think I asked too many questions of the wrong person," Mal said. "I got a call from Sheldon Janssen asking me to meet him at his house at seven this morning. I could tell from the tone in his voice that he was upset about something, and my gut told me not to go. I should've listened."

"Were you outed?" Duncan asked. "Did he figure out you're an undercover cop?"

Mal sucked in his breath as I applied a hydrogen-peroxide-soaked bit of gauze to the wound on his side. The peroxide created a field of pink-tinged foam that percolated and bubbled on top of the wound. Mal's color grew even paler, and beads of sweat broke out on his forehead.

"I'm sorry, Mal," I said.

"It's okay," he said, somewhat breathless. "It has to be done."

I wiped away the foam after a moment and then applied a thin film of antibiotic ointment to the area, covering it with a nonstick pad I taped into place. I sat back on my haunches to give him a break before tackling the second wound.

"Have you been taking anything for the pain?" I asked him.

It took him a few seconds before he could answer. "I swallowed a handful of ibuprofen an hour ago. There's a bottle of it in the bathroom next to the sink. But it's too soon to take any more."

"Do you have anything else?" I asked.

He shook his head.

I got up and headed down a hallway in search of the bathroom. I found it and checked the medicine cabinet. Inside was a bottle of acetaminophen, and I grabbed it. I left the bathroom and headed across the hall to a bedroom. It didn't have its own bathroom, but I struck gold when I searched through one of the bedside tables. In a drawer, I found a prescription bottle for Sabrina Cortland that had eight hydrocodone tablets in it. The date on the prescription was from two years ago, but I figured they'd still be good. I went back into the bathroom and got a glass of water, and took all of it out to Mal.

"Here," I said, offering him the prescription bottle. "Take one of these. I'm sure Sabrina won't mind."

Mal shook his head. "I don't want to take anything that will fog my mind," he argued.

"The pain is already doing that," I said. "If you're that worried about it, just take a half one."

Mal debated for a moment.

"I'm going to have to clean that second wound in a minute," I reminded him.

That seemed to convince him. He took the bottle from me, opened it, and shook out one of the pills. He stared at it in his palm for a moment and then popped the entire thing in his mouth. I handed him the water, and he swallowed it down.

"I'll wait about twenty minutes before I tackle that second wound," I told him. "That will give the pill some time to work."

He nodded weakly and then closed his eyes and leaned his head against the back of the chair, letting out a weary sigh.

"I need you to tell me the rest of the story when you can," Duncan said.

Mal didn't acknowledge this. He just sat there, not moving or saying anything for several minutes. Duncan and I exchanged worried looks.

Mal stayed still and silent for so long, I began to wonder if he'd passed out. "Have you eaten anything?" I asked him, afraid he wouldn't respond. To my relief, he shook his head slowly. I went upstairs, where I found a kitchen, and started searching through the cupboards. I found a couple of cans of soup, grabbed some chicken noodle, and then rummaged through the drawers until I found a can opener. A few minutes later, I had it simmering in a pot on the stove. I scrounged up a bowl and spoon, and then I hollered down to Duncan to come up to help me. There was no way I could carry a bowl of hot soup and maneuver with my crutches, especially when I had stairs to negotiate. Duncan bounded up the stairs, and I gestured toward the soup bowl I had just filled. "Can you carry that for me?"

Without a word, he picked up the bowl and headed back down to the basement with me not-so-hot on his heels.

"Eat that," I said to Mal as Duncan offered him the bowl.

Mal looked at the soup, grimaced, and shook his head.

"If you're going to get your strength back you have to eat," I insisted.

"I'm not hungry."

"I didn't ask you if you're hungry," I said in a stern tone. "Eat it."

Mal's eyebrows arched, and he looked over at

Duncan, who shrugged, cocked his head to the side, and arched his own eyebrows in return.

"She sounds pretty serious," Duncan said in a warning tone. "I wouldn't challenge her if I were you. She can be quite persistent."

With one last wary glance at me, Mal took the bowl and started eating. It looked like he was having to force himself, but after eating half the soup, some of his color returned. Duncan and I sat in silence, watching him.

By the time Mal finished the soup, he looked noticeably better than he had when we first arrived.

"Okay," Mal said reluctantly. "I've eaten." He shot me a grudging look. "And I have to admit, I feel a little better."

I tried not to look too smug.

"So tell us what happened," Duncan said. "I gather things went wrong when you were summoned to Sheldon Janssen's house. Give me the details."

Mal leaned back in his seat and closed his eyes for a moment. "Let me give you a little background first," he began. "Janssen is Wade Klein's top foreman, and he's the person I generally report to on the job. Klein is the guy we're after, but Janssen is no angel. And lately, he's been giving me a hard time, asking a lot of questions, watching me closer than usual, and looking at me suspiciously. So when I got called into Klein's office last week, I was anticipating a firing of some sort, or at the very least a thorough grilling."

"I take it that didn't happen," Duncan said as Mal paused to take a slow, deep breath.

"Not even close," Mal said when he was ready to continue. "Klein's office is a mobile trailer, and he takes it with him wherever he goes. He keeps it hooked up to his pickup. It's a brilliant setup really; he can take his office to any job site, and he has every file or piece of paper he might need right there at his disposal. So when he called me into his office, it was into this trailer that was on our job site, though it was some distance away from the area we were currently working on."

"Klein shocked the hell out of me. He wanted to know if I'd be willing to act as one of his foremen. He said he'd had a lot of staff turnover lately—a bunch of his guys apparently got busted for possession and they're in jail now, leaving me as one of the on-site workers with seniority." Mal huffed a laugh at that, which was quickly followed by a grimace and a wince.

"That kind of turnover is pretty typical in the construction industry," Mal went on. "Klein was going to have to hire a bunch of newbies, so I suddenly became a valued employee. While he was explaining the new job to me, he got a text and said it was from Janssen. He read it, cussed, said there'd been an accident on-site and he needed to go check on it. With that, he got up and left." Mal paused again, and his obvious weakness worried me. Simply talking this long was taxing him, but he continued after a few seconds.

"I'm sure Klein assumed I'd leave, too, but I couldn't pass up the opportunity. There I was, all alone in his office. So I got up and started looking through his papers and files. I found three ledger books in a drawer that's normally locked, and a quick flip through the first one made me think it might be a record of bribes Klein paid to certain building inspectors. There were no names mentioned—just initials—but a couple of them matched the names of inspectors I knew had been on the site. The second ledger book had dates, dollar amounts, and weights listed. The weights and money didn't make much sense when I tried to equate them with something construction related, and then I wondered if it might be drugs of some sort. The third book had company names—building supply companies, a catering business, a hardware store, a couple of trucking companies—and columns of dollar amounts and dates. I can't be sure, but I think it might be an accounting of Klein's money-laundering connections and transactions. I was about to start snapping pictures of the pages with my phone when I heard gravel crunching outside the trailer. So I quickly shoved the books into the drawer, closed it, and went back to my seat. I had barely sat down when the door opened and Janssen walked in."

Mal paused and shifted his position, the action making him wince with pain. He leaned forward, elbows on his knees, and massaged his temples with his hands.

"I thought it would be Klein, because the office door stays locked on the inside and Klein gets in with a key. But apparently, Janssen has a key also. Needless to say," Mal went on, "Janssen wasn't pleased to see me there. He looked around the office area, checking it out, and asked me what the hell I was doing in there. I explained about my meeting with Klein and his abrupt departure, and said I'd assumed he'd be back because we hadn't finished our discussion."

"Did he buy it?" Duncan asked.

Mal shrugged, and again the movement made him wince. "He seemed to, but I could tell he was suspicious. And then, a few days after that, he caught me taking some pictures of some questionable structures at the job site. I told him I was simply trying to study and learn new ideas and techniques, but I could tell he was even more suspicious. And that night when I went home—back to the bar, actually—I think I was followed. I can't be sure it was Janssen, but I'm fairly certain someone was tailing me."

He paused, shifting again with a wince. "So, given all that, I was a little concerned when Janssen called yesterday and said he wanted to meet with me at his place first thing this morning. He said it was to go over some upcoming jobs I'd need to supervise in my new role as foreman, and that made sense given what Klein had said. But when I got there, it became clear to me very quickly that Janssen was ticked off at me. He started asking me who I was really working for, and when I answered with Klein's name, it incensed him even more. We argued, and things got heated. I thought sure he'd made me as a cop, but then he accused me of being a construction company's version of a corporate spy, working for the competition and trying to infiltrate Klein's business so I could report back. No matter how much I denied that, he clearly wasn't having it, so I finally told him I was leaving. I almost made it to the door when he pulled a gun on me."

Mal had to take another break, and he leaned back in his chair and closed his eyes for a few seconds. When he continued, he kept his eyes closed, and I knew he was envisioning the scene that had gone down at Janssen's house. "There was a struggle," he said in a surprisingly calm voice. "I was able to wrestle the gun away from Janssen, but not before he fired off a shot." He raised his head and opened his eyes, looking directly at me. "You've seen the results of that," he concluded with a grimace, nodding toward the side where his wound was. "Anyway, when I got the gun away from Janssen it fell to the floor and I kicked it away. It scuttled across the room, and I hit him hard enough to daze him for a moment. I didn't want to kill him because he's a potential material witness, so I focused on getting away from him. I wasn't armed—I'd left my weapon in my car—so he had the upper hand. My best option was to run. Janssen went for the gun, but I was faster than he was and beat foot out of the house before he could get off another shot."

"Why didn't you call for help, or backup?" Duncan asked.

"For one thing, I didn't want to jeopardize the investigation. My ability to infiltrate Klein's company might be over, but they don't know I'm a cop, so someone else could pick up where I left off. Especially because Klein was in the process of hiring a bunch of new people. I also didn't have my cell phone on me. I'd left it in the car, and it was a good thing I did, because Janssen wanted me to hand it over to him so he could see what pictures I had on it. I'd downloaded the ones I'd already taken to my computer and deleted the originals from my phone, so there wouldn't have been anything there for him to see. But I didn't want him to have access to the phone numbers and such I had in it."

"So you have some documented evidence?" Duncan asked.

Mal made an equivocal face. "I have some pictures, but while they're incriminating to some degree, they aren't enough to shut Klein's company down, or prosecute him. We need to get a better look at those ledgers. I wish I'd thought sooner to take pictures of the pages with my phone, but I didn't have much time, and I didn't realize what they were at first. I'm still not one hundred percent sure, which is why we need to get a better look at them." He paused, grimaced, and then went on. "I'm pretty confident neither Janssen nor Klein knows I'm a cop. I'm not sure what Klein knows at all. I don't know if Janssen shared his suspicions with him or not. But after what happened at his house, it's a moot point. I'm done there, but I didn't want to blow the whole case. And I knew Janssen might come after me. So I decided it would be wise to lay low for a bit."

Duncan and I exchanged perplexed looks.

Mal didn't miss it. "What?" he asked, looking from me to Duncan and back at me again, his eyes narrowed.

"What you've told us doesn't quite match up with the evidence we found in Janssen's house," Duncan explained.

"How so?"

"You're saying Janssen was alive when you left, correct?"

Mal was clearly surprised by the question. His eyebrows arched and he leaned back in his chair, staring at Duncan with an expression as perplexed as ours had been moments ago. "Why would you ask me that? Are you telling me Janssen is dead?"

"Not only dead," Duncan said, his tone sobering "He was shot in the back of the head."

Mal looked up at the ceiling and ran a hand through his hair His eyes grew wide. "Well, hell," he said, lowering his head and looking at Duncan. "I swear to you; he was alive when I left."

"Did you see the little girl while you were there?" Duncan asked. "Did you see his daughter?"

Mal looked even more confused. "I didn't even know he had a daughter."

"He not only has a daughter," Duncan explained, "she was there when all this went down."

Mal looked stunned.

"Mal," I said, "did you shoot Sheldon Janssen?"

Mal shook off his astonishment, looked me straight in the eye, and without hesitation, said, "No, I did not. I swear to you; he was alive when I left there."

Mal's voice, like Duncan's, tasted like chocolate to me. Most of the time the flavor was sweet and rich. I knew from past experience that when he told a lie the chocolate taste grew bitter, but with this last statement the flavor had stayed sweet, albeit weakly so. I suspected the faint flavoring was because his voice was also weak.

I looked over at Duncan. "He's telling the truth."

"Good to know," Duncan said, but he looked troubled. "Now all we have to do is convince the rest of the world, even though all the evidence so far points to Mal."

Chapter 10

Once Mal recovered from the shock of our information, Duncan filled him in on the crime scene we'd found at Janssen's house. Mal was clearly surprised by it all and had no idea who might have killed Janssen, or that the man had a child who lived in a closet. Like Duncan, Mal did suggest that perhaps Felicity had been the one who'd fired the fatal shot, but when he saw the scowl on my face he dropped the matter. He and Duncan agreed it was probably best for Mal to lay low from both Klein and his other henchmen, as well as the police for now, until we could get a better grip on exactly what had gone down at the Janssen house.

With that out of the way, the conversation shifted to more practical things. While I went about cleaning and dressing his second wound, he and Duncan discussed the use of Mal's cell phone. Mal had the phone with him, but he had turned it off and had removed the battery shortly after leaving Janssen's house. Duncan agreed it was probably best to leave it off unless it was a dire emergency.

"I'll get you a burner and bring it out here," Duncan offered.

"You have a car, don't you?" I asked, not liking the idea of him staying out here all by himself. I hadn't seen any car parked in the driveway or in the street near the house, so I wondered what Mal had done with it, and if he had a way to leave if he needed to in an emergency.

"According to Sabrina, the people who own the house on this side," he gestured with a nod of his head toward the house that was dark, "are snowbirds who spend all winter in Florida and return at the end of March. So the house is vacant all winter. I parked in their driveway, and I've tried to show as little evidence as possible of anyone staying in this house."

"Well you did a good job," I said. "The place looked totally vacant when we pulled up out front."

When it was time for us to leave, I walked over and gave Mal a careful, gentle hug. "Rest and take care of yourself," I whispered in his ear. "And don't hesitate to call if you need anything."

The one arm he wrapped around my waist to return my hug was tentative. I wasn't sure if it was because he was weak, or if he felt uncomfortable being this close to me physically, given both his feelings for me and the fact that Duncan was there.

I hated leaving Mal in that house alone.

We headed back to the bar, and as soon as we were inside, we made straight for the O'Reillys. It was after seven and they had knocked off work for the day, but they were having dinner and drinks before heading home, home being Mal's house. We knew they were still at the bar because I'd called and asked my evening bartender, Billy, during the drive back, and then instructed him and Teddy Bear, my bouncer and assistant bartender, to keep them there until Duncan and I arrived.

"Any word on Mal?" Connor asked as soon as he saw us. Ryan, Patrick, and Colleen were all focused on us, eager for information.

"We know where he is and he's okay," Duncan told them, and there was a collective sigh from the O'Reilly clan. "But he's in a bit of a situation right now, and that situation might make it dangerous for you guys to be staying at his house."

"No worries," Ryan said, puffing out his chest. "We can handle ourselves."

"I have no doubt you can, under the right circumstances," Duncan said. "However, this is a very serious issue involving some very dangerous people."

"I can board all of you right here at the bar," I told them. "I've got two double beds upstairs, and a pretty comfortable couch. Plus, there's the bed down in the basement that Mal was using. He won't be back for a while, so it's available."

Colleen frowned at me. "You shouldn't have to put yourself out for us, Mack," she said.

"It's not a problem," I assured her. "Besides, I owe you for giving up your time to come here and do this elevator installation for me. Please let me do this as a way of saying thank-you. There are two bathrooms with showers upstairs in my apartment, and you can have free run of the kitchen and bar as often as you want. You're pretty close to done with this elevator job anyway, aren't you?"

Connor nodded. "That's true," he said. "Another two days and I think we'll have it. But if Mal's in trouble, we're not leaving until we know he's okay."

"And a lot of our stuff is back at his house," Patrick said.

"I figured as much," Duncan said. "I've got a couple of guys over there at the house now, making sure it's safe and secure for the moment. I'll provide a police escort so you folks can go over there and get whatever you need. I'm sorry I can't come up with the man-hours to have someone there for you all the time."

"Fair enough," Connor said. He looked at his children with a questioning expression, and they all nodded their agreement. He turned his attention back to Duncan. "When do you want us to go to the house?"

"Actually, now would be a good time, if that works for you."

"We'll make it work," Connor said.

With that, they set aside the various items they were holding and removed their tool belts. Without another word, they followed Duncan back upstairs and out to the main area of the bar. I remained in the basement for a few minutes, checking out my new elevator. I hit the button on the wall and the door slid open. The interior looked slick and shiny new, something I doubted would last long once my staff and/or customers spilled some drinks and a plate or two of food in it. But for now, it was pristine except for a thin layer of construction dust. I knew it was functional because I'd seen one of Mal's brothers ride it up to the second floor yesterday, and then ride it back down to the basement. I stepped inside and thought about taking it for a ride but talked myself out of it. I had no way of knowing how much of its function was completed and I didn't want to risk injuring myself or getting stuck in the darned thing.

The door closed, and I hit the inside button to open it again. It moved almost silently, and I marveled at the construction of both it and the surrounding area. The O'Reillys knew what they were doing.

Eventually, I quit gawking and headed back upstairs and out to the main bar area. All the tables in the old section and most of those in the newer one were occupied, as were all but two of the barstools. Billy was on duty behind the bar along with Teddy Bear.

"How are things, guys?" I asked them.

Teddy Bear, whose physical traits—six-foot-six, big brown eyes, weighing in somewhere around three hundred pounds, and leaning toward the hairy side— helped earn him that nickname, answered first. "It's been a little crazy, but I suppose that's good for business. Debra, Linda, and Missy have all been hustling. Lots of food orders."

"That's good," I said, shifting my attention to Billy. "How are you doing, Billy?" I asked.

He knew I wasn't asking about work. After the fiasco that had occurred in my bar on New Year's Eve, when we'd exposed the culprits behind the letter-writer debacle, Billy had decided to break things off with his long-term girlfriend and fiancée, Whitney. I had to admit I was relieved; the two of them were so different in their outlooks on life, their personalities, their philosophies, and their backgrounds. Whitney came from money and a comfortable life, whereas Billy had had to scramble and work hard for everything. He was close to graduating from law school, and with a combination of hard work, determination, and good tips— he related well to male customers, and his café-au-lait-colored skin, green eyes, and general good looks were irresistible to most women—he had done it all on his own, much to Whitney's chagrin. Basically, Whitney was a snob. She considered Billy's job, and by correlation my bar, to be beneath her and him. These differences came to a head during the New Year's Eve party, and I think Billy finally saw Whitney in a light that opened his eyes to the truth of their future together.

Billy seemed steadfast in his decision, and he had stuck to his guns for the past couple of weeks. But that hadn't made it any easier for him. We had chatted several times about the breakup, and the occasional doubts that haunted him over his decision.

"Whitney called him today," Teddy Bear offered when Billy didn't look like he wanted to talk.

"What did she have to say?" I asked, looking directly at Billy.

"She asked me if I'd come to my senses yet and realized the error of my ways."

"I see," I said, trying to sound objective. "And have you?"

Billy shot me a wary, befuddled look, like he thought I was crazy and had only just then realized it. He let out a long weary sigh. "I'm not going to lie," he said. "I miss her. Sometimes I miss her a lot. We had some good times together. She wasn't always haughty and condescending, though it did seem as if that was her default personality lately. When I could get her away from her rich friends and her parents, she would let her hair down and relax. She was a completely different person when we were alone together."

"Then maybe you should reconsider," I suggested.

Billy shook his head. "It would never work," he said forlornly. "I'd have to kidnap her and take her somewhere where she couldn't be around any of her family and regular friends. And I'd have to hide her out there forever."

"Did you ever suggest a move to her?" I asked. "Maybe a change of venue is just what she needs."

Billy scoffed. "She'd never go for it. She likes her wealth and all the entitlements that come with it."

"I'm sorry, Billy," I said. And though I disliked Whitney immensely, I meant it. I hated to see Billy hurting this way. "You know," I said in a conspiratorial tone, "if you're looking for a way to forget about it all for a while, you should think about asking Alicia out."

Billy's brows drew together in confusion. "Alicia from the Capone Club?" he said.

"One and the same. That girl has it bad for you."

"Really?" Billy seemed genuinely surprised by this revelation.

Teddy Bear was apparently as surprised as I was because he shot Billy a skeptical look. "Come on, dude," he said. "Don't tell me you didn't pick up on it. The girl practically drools every time you're near her. And don't get me started on the goo-goo eyes." Teddy Bear rolled his own eyes in mockery, making me smile.

"I just figured she was flirting, like all the others do," Billy said. "I didn't think it was anything serious."

"Well, it is," I told him. "Do you like her?"

"She's a great conversationalist and whip smart," he said. Then he shrugged and gave us a sly grin. "She's also pretty and has some fantastic booty."

I smiled. It was typical of Billy to list the intellectual qualities ahead of the physical ones.

"She isn't seeing anyone?" Billy asked.

"I don't think so, but you could ask her to be sure," I suggested.

"I might just do that."

Having done my duty as matchmaker for the evening, I headed to my office and took care of some paperwork. Duncan and the O'Reillys returned a little under an hour later, hauling suitcases and bags behind them. Duncan and I took them upstairs, where I gave them the nickel tour, and again raised the topic of the sleeping arrangements.

"It makes sense for me to sleep in the basement," I told them. "My hours are strange, and I don't want to come upstairs and wake all of you at three in the morning after I've closed down the bar. Nor do I want you guys waking me when you typically get up at six. So you guys take over my place, and I'll sleep in the basement in Mal's bed."

The expected objections were voiced, but I held firm, watching Duncan out of the corner of my eye. Part of me hoped he'd offer up his place for me to stay for the two or three days I'd be ousted from my own. I'd already decided I'd turn him down—it would be too much of a hassle driving back and forth with my crazy hours, and I'd get a lot more done if I stayed here. But it would be nice if he at least offered me the chance. It would communicate a certain level of commitment I had yet to see from him.

The O'Reillys continued to protest, even arguing among themselves, something I'd discovered they did a lot. It was always good-natured bantering where no one's feelings were truly hurt despite some robust name-calling. Their behavior gave me a glimpse into another type of life, one with lots of family and siblings, one that took place in an ordinary home, one that had two parents. It was the polar opposite of my upbringing, and for the first time in my life, I felt like I had missed out on something important and crucial. I shook it off almost as quickly as I felt it, because it seemed like I was betraying my father with the thought. He had done the best he could to raise and provide for me, and I'd never felt lacking or wanting when I was growing up. Sure, there were some awkward moments when not having a mother made things difficult. The onset of my menses was one, and my father had eventually solicited help and guidance from some of our female customers who came often enough for me to feel comfortable talking to them about such a delicate topic. And when I got old enough to start dating, I sought advice from my female friends and other women I knew, because my father's take on me dating was that it would happen only over his dead body.

I wasn't alone in these trials and tribulations. There were always other kids who had similar issues: some with dead or divorced parents who had moved away, some with two moms or two dads instead of one of each, and some who had nothing but foster parents.

I hadn't thought much about kids before this. In the back of my mind, I think I always assumed I'd have one or two, but it was never a driving force or an urgent need. Now, for some reason, I could hear and feel my biological clock ticking. And after watching the loving banter that went on within the O'Reilly clan, I suddenly knew I wanted at least two kids, maybe more. Given that I was already thirty-three and about to turn thirty-four, the time for doing that was running out.

These thoughts arose in my mind unexpected, unbidden, and a tiny bit unwelcome. It unsettled me. I looked over at Duncan, who was watching the O'Reillys with a smile, offering no hint that he was aware of my discomfort.

I finally brought the discussion to a close. "Okay you guys!" I yelled. "This is my house, and my bar, and my town. You people have gone out of your way to help me with this elevator project, leaving your homes and traveling halfway across the country. I can't possibly thank you enough for doing that for me, so please let me have this one piece, this tiny bit of gratitude I can show you. The very least I can do for all of you is make sure you are comfortable and safe. So the decision is made. All of you have the apartment, and I'm sleeping in the basement. End of discussion."

With that, I spun on my crutches, went into my bedroom, and gathered some clothing and other items I would need. Duncan followed me into the room and watched me for a moment as I hobbled back and forth between my bed, my closet, and my dresser.

"How much longer do you have to wear that cast?" he asked finally.

"I'm not sure. The doctor said six to eight weeks, depending on how fast I heal. I have an appointment in the morning and it will have been just shy of six weeks, so I'm hoping it will be gone tomorrow."

"I have to go back to the station soon," he said. "I wish I could stay here with you. I'd offer you my place for tonight, but I won't be there, and I'm not sure you'd be comfortable. And frankly, you're safer here."

"Safer? Why do I need to worry about that now?" I hobbled into my bathroom to gather up some toiletries and add them to the collection on the bed. "The letter-writer thing is resolved, and no one has threatened me lately. At least no one I know of."

"I know. But you're working with the police now. It's a matter of public record. And in some circles, that makes you the enemy. Plus, we've already seen how many crazy people there are out there, people like Apostle Mike."

Apostle Mike was a man who had a cult following in the area, a cult of people who often bordered on the edge of sanity and decency. He had targeted me as a "sinner" early on by sending me a letter that called me an abomination, among other things. We thought at one point that he might have been the letter writer, but it wasn't the case. He was a nutjob, however, and I was on his radar. Duncan had a point, one that I had managed to put out of my mind for a while. I didn't welcome its return.

Seeming to sense my discomfort, Duncan said, "I have patrol guys checking on this place regularly throughout the night. Every night. It's part of their normal routine."

That knowledge helped some, but I also found myself wishing Duncan could stay the night. In addition to wanting him here for my personal and emotional reasons, he made me feel safe. Mal had done the same thing for me. I struggled some with this need to have a man at my side to feel secure, but it was a physical security rather than an emotional one, and that meant I didn't have to turn in my feminist card just yet. At least that's what I told myself.

"It does make me feel better," I told Duncan. "Thank you." I hobbled over to my closest one last time and fetched an overnight bag from the shelf. I tossed it onto the bed and then went about loading my treasures into it.

"I'll carry that downstairs for you," Duncan said as I zipped it closed. "You'll have trouble managing the stairs with it and your crutches."

"Thank you."

We went out into the main area of the apartment and bid the O'Reillys good night. I gave them a key to the apartment and assured them they could help themselves to anything they found in it, or downstairs in the bar and bar kitchen. Then Duncan and I made our way to the basement and Mal's makeshift bedroom.

I plopped down onto the bed, exhausted from the emotional drain of the last hour, as well as the physical exertions. Mal's smell wafted up from the bed linens, and when I looked over at his shirts hanging from the overhead pipes, I felt tears well up in my eyes.

"What is it, Mack?" Duncan asked with sweet, smooth chocolate tones. He sat next to me on the mattress and draped an arm over my shoulders, pulling me toward him.

"Is Mal going to be okay?" I asked.

"He'll be fine," Duncan said, but the taste of his voice changed just enough to let me know he wasn't 100 percent convinced of it. "Is that what has you upset? You're worried about Mal?"

"That's part of it," I said. I let my answer hang out there.

After a good half minute, Duncan finally bit. "What's the rest of it?"

I didn't answer right away; I was trying to find a way to couch my words so they wouldn't sound as needy or desperate as I feared I was. "With everything that's happened to me lately, all the deaths, you coming into my life, Mal and his family, the Capone Club . . . it's been a lot of change. Most of it good, mind you, but I feel unsettled. I feel like I've lost control of my life, like it's slipping away from me and there's nothing I can do to stop it. I'm feeling things I've never felt before, wanting things I've never wanted before." I paused and let out a slow breath. "I don't know. Maybe it's a midlife crisis of some sort."

"That's all understandable, given everything you've been through," Duncan said. "You've lost the only family you ever had, you were betrayed by someone in your new, adopted family, and you've nearly lost your own life a couple of times. You're embarking on a new career of sorts, and even making some significant changes with your old one. That's a lot of stress for anyone, Mack."

"Do you want to have kids?" I asked him.

The suddenness and unexpectedness of this segue made him stiffen. But he didn't hesitate to answer. "I do," he said. "I've always wanted to be a father. What about you?"

"I never really wanted to be a father," I said, hoping to lighten the mood. It worked. Duncan chuckled, and I felt him relax, though the arm holding me tightened ever so slightly. "I guess I've always wanted kids," I went on. "Or at least I assumed I'd have them one day. But to be honest, it was always off in the distance, a thing in the future, something to think about but not seriously consider. And now . . ."

"Now you're considering it, thinking about it more seriously," Duncan finished for me.

"Yes."

"And do I figure in to that equation at all?"

"I don't know," I said, pushing myself away from him so I could look him in the eye. "Do you?"

He leaned in closer. "I sure hope so," he said, his voice rich with sweet chocolate. Then he kissed me, and before long we discovered that the makeshift bed was plenty comfortable and accommodating for the two of us.

I slept alone in a strange bed, in a strange place, with noises and smells I didn't typically experience during a night's sleep. But I slept deep and well, dreaming of both Duncan and Mal, and then, oddly, about my mother. I say oddly, because I have no memories of her, only the pictures my dad showed me from time to time. But in my dream, I heard her voice before I saw the face, before I had any reason to expect her to be there. And I knew it right away. I'm sure I heard that voice plenty of times while she carried me in her belly, and perhaps some vestigial memory of it lingered in my brain. Or perhaps I made the whole thing up. I had no way of knowing. What I did know, is that when I woke the next morning I felt closer to my mother than I ever had before in my life. And I believed her when she told me in my dream that everything was going to be okay.

Chapter 11

I arose in my basement bedroom at eight the next morning—much earlier than my usual time, but I had my doctor's appointment to go to at nine. I headed upstairs to the bar bathroom and did a sponge bath, brushed my teeth, and tried to tame my hair. Then I dressed and went out to the bar to put on some coffee so I'd have a cup to take with me. I heard the now familiar sounds of the O'Reillys working on the elevator and went by to say good morning to them before I left. Not only was I impressed with the O'Reillys' commitment to early rising day after day, I couldn't help but envy how chipper and energetic they always were. I've never been much of a morning person, and me before and after my first cup of coffee each day is like the saga of Mr. Hyde and Dr. Jekyll.

The O'Reillys' high spirits buoyed my own as I left for my appointment. An hour and one X-ray later, I returned in a mood more exuberant than theirs. My doctor had determined my bones had healed enough to do away with my cast and crutches. I felt pounds lighter and so much freer without these encumbrances, though the sight of all the hair growth on my newly revealed leg kept making me feel a tickle in my nose that made me want to sneeze. As soon as I was inside, I headed upstairs to my apartment, which was vacant now that the O'Reillys were downstairs working, so I could wash, shave, and apply some lotion to my poor neglected leg.

By the time I returned downstairs to the bar, my day crew was in getting things ready for opening at eleven. Pete, my day bartender, noticed the difference right away.

"Mack, you're back on two legs!" he said with a big smile.

Missy, who was behind the bar with him setting things up, turned and looked at me. "That must feel good," she said.

"Oh, it does," I told them. "Is Jon here?"

Jon was my day cook, and both Missy and Pete nodded.

"Great. I have some work to do in my office, but holler if you need me for anything." As I headed into my office, I relished the simple task of being able to open a door and walk through it without having to prop myself up on a crutch and risk losing my balance. I knew the excitement and delight I felt over this new-found freedom wouldn't last long—soon enough, things would be back to what had been normal for thirtysome years. But for now, I felt like kicking up my heels with joy, though the site of the break remained just tender enough that I wasn't going to try it. It would take a little longer before the muscles in that leg were back to normal.

I had just settled in behind my desk when Duncan called me.

"What's up?" I said, not even bothering with a greeting.

"You sound chipper," he said.

"I am. I got that annoying cast removed this morning."

"Congratulations."

"Thanks. Do you have any news on Mal?"

"He's doing okay," he said. "I went back out to the lake house last night so I could give him a burner phone. But I'm getting some pressure from Chief Holland regarding this Sheldon Janssen shooting, and the fact that Mal's fingerprints were found on the gun. Holland wants to know if you were able to contribute anything to the scene analysis. I told him what you provided for us while we were there, but he feels that's all stuff we would have discovered on our own in time. He's hinting around that he wants you to come up with something better."

"Such as?" I asked, feeling annoyed and wondering if I'd made a deal with the devil when I agreed to this consulting work. "Did you tell Holland I spoke with Mal and asked him if he shot Janssen? And that Mal denied it and was telling the truth?"

"Ah, no, I didn't. I don't want him to know that I know where Mal is just yet. Besides, I'm not sure your little lie-detector trick is what he wants at this point."

"Do you want me to go back to the scene? It's been long enough since it all happened that I'm not sure I'll be much use, but I can try."

"No, I agree with you there's probably little you could come up with there that our evidence techs didn't find. But I'm thinking there's another way, something else that might help."

"What?" I said, feeling—and sounding—a little perturbed.

"I want you to see what else you can get out of Felicity.

She was there when all of this happened, and I have a feeling she knows more than we realize. Plus, I think we're going to need your help in getting her fingerprints."

This was a mixed surprise. Felicity had been on my mind ever since Parnell had taken her away yesterday, and I was eager to see her again. But lurking in the back of my mind was a fear for what the child might have done.

"I'm happy to try to talk to Felicity some more," I said. "In fact, I'd welcome the chance. But I'm not sure that social worker woman is going to go for it. She seemed dead set against me getting any more involved."

"Yeah, let me work on that. I'll let you know."

"Why do you want her fingerprints?" I was a little hesitant in asking this question. I hoped Duncan would tell me it was so they could rule her prints out from any they found in the house. As it turned out, that was the gist of his answer, but it was worse than I'd feared.

"It turned out those three prints on Janssen's gun were from three different people," Duncan said. "You already know that one came back belonging to Mal and another came back as belonging to the victim. But we haven't been able to identify the third print yet."

This gave me pause. "You think Felicity might have shot her father?"

"Well, she was there, and he was shot in the back of the head. Maybe she picked up the gun from the floor and used it. It could have been an accident. Maybe she didn't know what it was, and fired it without meaning to."

This idea was disturbing but also plausible. Poor Felicity. If she did shoot her father, the trauma of that would likely haunt her for the rest of her life. And the kid was damaged enough already.

"Please tell me there is someone else on your list of suspects," I said.

"Well, there are all of Janssen's coworkers. And his boss, of course. We need to bring Klein in for questioning and have you listen in."

"I'm game for that whenever you're ready," I said. "And let me know when you can get me more time with Felicity. I'll be around. Unless you think I should go to visit Mal. Those wounds of his could probably use another cleaning and a dressing change."

This suggestion was met with silence, and I wondered if Duncan was harboring some jealousy regarding my relationship with Mal. "I don't think you need to do that," he said finally. "But I also know you have a mind of your own and will do what you want regardless of what I say. So if you do go there, just be absolutely sure no one is tailing you. And make sure you call Mal to let him know you're coming so he doesn't shoot you." He gave me the number of Mal's burner cell, which I entered into my phone.

We disconnected our call, and I spent another hour or so in my office, finishing up the paperwork I had to do—payroll, financial statements, and ordering. When I was done, I headed back out to the bar and saw that lunch hour was in full swing. It was busy, and everyone was hustling. They seemed to have things well under control, so I decided to pay a visit to the Capone Club room to check in with whoever was present for the day.

Climbing the stairs without the encumbrance of my cast and crutches was a treat, and I realized how ironic it was that the elevator would be done soon, now that I didn't need it so much. But I didn't regret the decision to put it in. My time as a somewhat handicapped person made me realize how necessary it was. It would be a good and valuable addition to the bar, and it would bring me into better compliance with all the rules and laws created by the Americans with Disabilities Act.

When my father's girlfriend, Ginny Rifkin, was murdered a few months back, I was shocked to discover she had left me an inheritance—a quite generous one, in fact. I had used some of the money to buy the building that adjoined mine so I could expand the bar. It allowed me to increase my overall seating area on the main floor, as well as to create a stage and dance floor. My future plans included live music, though I planned to start out with a DJ to see how things went. On the second floor of the new addition, I had added several rooms, including a meeting room I could rent out to groups for a little extra income or use for overflow seating, and a game room that had since been dubbed the Man Cave, though plenty of women used it. I also added a second bar area and a small kitchenette that could be concealed behind a drop-down door when not in use. These would make it easier to wait on people on the second floor when we were busy. I should have thought of putting in the elevator back when I did these renovations, but it hadn't been on my radar then.

The other room I created on the second floor of the new section was one designed specifically for the Capone Club. It was cozy, with cushy chairs, movable tables, a gas fireplace—a feature that had seen a lot of use lately with the bitter Milwaukee winter—and bookshelves. I'd furnished the bookshelves with a few tomes—some *Sherlock Holmes* novels and a couple of other mysteries I found lying about my apartment—and the members of the club quickly expanded the collection with their own additions. Now the shelves sported several types of nonfiction books related to crimes and crime solving: evidentiary processes, fingerprinting, the psychology of killers, blood analysis, and methods of murder that ranged from poisons to weapons.

When I entered the Capone Club room, I saw that the core group was present. Joe and Frank Signoriello were in their usual spot, as close to the fireplace as they could get without combusting. Cora was there, too, her ubiquitous laptop in front of her and her current paramour, Jurgen "Tiny" Gruber, seated beside her. Tiny, whose nickname was the ultimate irony because he stood six-and-a-half feet tall and weighed around three hundred fifty pounds, had brought us one of our first cases: the unsolved murder of his little sister, which had occurred more than a decade earlier.

Carter Fitzpatrick, who was as much of a regular as Cora and the Signoriello brothers these days, had become one of the de facto leaders of the group. Carter had been a part-time waiter and wannabe writer when he first joined the group. The Capone Club had been very kind to him in the pursuit of his writing career, as he had managed to segue several of the cases the group had investigated and solved into book deals with a New York City publisher that produced a line of true crime books. As a result, he had given up his waiter job to focus on his writing full time, and he spent a goodly portion of his day at the bar in the Capone Club room. His girlfriend, Holly Martinson, worked at a nearby bank as a teller. She, along with a friend and coworker named Alicia Maldonado—the girl with the big crush on Billy—joined the group as often as they could and were typically here every weekend, most evenings, and most lunch hours.

I was surprised but delighted to see one of the founding members of the club present because he had been missing from the group for the past two weeks. Tad

Amundsen, a local investor and tax adviser to some of the area's richest residents, had been married to a wealthy woman named Suzanne Collier. It wasn't a happy marriage—Tad's role was primarily that of a trophy husband—but things had changed dramatically when Suzanne was murdered on New Year's Eve in my bar. Suzanne had been the primary perpetrator behind the whole letter-writer scheme. Her death, while sad, had solved a thorny problem for me and the police. Suzanne's wealth and connections, and the general lack of usable evidence we had against her, would've made it difficult, if not impossible, to actually convict her.

I'd spoken with Tad a couple of times since that terrible night. He'd been busy with the funeral arrangements and the investigations into Suzanne's death and the letter-writer thing, but he was getting through it. It didn't help that there was some speculation that Tad knew what Suzanne was up to the whole time, but in my talks with him, I became convinced that was not the case. And apparently, the authorities eventually became convinced as well, because Tad was exonerated.

Tad had been genuinely shocked by the news of his wife's deadly obsession. Over the years I'd known him, I often got the sense he was searching for a way to escape his marriage and not lose the financial comfort that went with it. He got his wish in the end, but Suzanne's death had hit him harder than he expected. It was lucky for him that Suzanne's murderer had been caught because Tad would have been the likely suspect otherwise. I don't know if he ever loved Suzanne, but he did care about her and he was grieving, though the fact that he was about to inherit a very large sum of money would likely help soothe things over for him.

Tad's motives for marrying might not have been the

purest, but I liked the guy and was happy to see him back here with the others. I wasn't sure if he was ready to deal with the sometimes-grim discussions of death that typically took place among the group, but I trusted him to leave if things got too uncomfortable for him.

The bigger issue was that I wasn't sure all the other group members were as confident as I was in Tad's innocence, and I knew things were likely to be awkward for a while. Adding to all this tension was the fact that Suzanne Collier hadn't been working alone, and her partner had turned out to be one of our own, a trusted member of the club.

That betrayal hit the group hard, changing the dynamic. There was an underlying uneasiness I'd felt every time I entered the room since that fateful night, and it was there regardless of which club members were present at any given time. It was something I hoped would fade away over time, but for now, everyone seemed afraid to trust themselves or anyone else.

In addition to the core group of regulars on this particular day, there were a couple of newer members present as well, members who had joined within the last month: Stephen McGregor, a physics teacher at a local high school; Sonja West, the owner of an upscale hair salon named Aphrodite's located a few blocks from my bar; and Clay Sanders, an investigative reporter with the *Milwaukee Journal Sentinel*. There was a time when I had thought of Clay as my nemesis, but he had since proven himself to be a very valuable ally.

There were others who attended the club on a semi-regular basis but were missing at the moment. Karen Tannenbaum, or Dr. T, as we called her, was an ER physician at a nearby hospital whose long and irregular hours sometimes kept her away for days on end. Kevin Baldwin was a local trash collector—though he preferred the title of sanitation engineer—who stopped by whenever he could. And there were a couple of members from the local police department who also dropped in on occasion when their shifts allowed: Tyrese Washington and Nicodemus "Nick" Kavinsky, the cop Miguel Ortega had mentioned.

The Capone Club was a diverse and fluid group of people with varied backgrounds, resources, experiences, and degrees of knowledge. That made for an odd mix at times—people who might never otherwise know or cross paths with one another—but their shared love of mysteries and crime solving brought them together and made it not only work but work well. While the crimes we'd recently solved had been largely credited to me, they had all been group efforts. Recent events had threatened to undermine the group's enthusiasm and cohesiveness, and I felt determined to make sure that didn't happen. I needed to get them back to doing what they loved—crime solving. I wasn't sure how I was going to do that because I didn't know how much, if any, of today's crime scene I could share with them, but as it turned out, the group took care of that problem themselves.

Chapter 12

My entrance to the room was heralded by the usual chorus of routine greetings, but things ramped up quickly.

"Mack, your cast is gone!" said Carter.

This led to a chorus of kudos and congratulations, a couple of backslaps, and a whole lot of smiles. I'd been sporting the cast long enough that some of the newer members didn't know me without it.

"Yes, my cast and crutches are gone," I said in a celebratory tone, hoping to maintain the high spirits in the room for as long as possible. I grabbed a chair from a corner and moved it closer to the others. Such a simple task had been more or less impossible for me over the past five weeks, and my new independence was liberating. "The doctor surprised me today," I said as I sat down. "I thought I was going to be stuck with the cast for another week or two, but he said the bones were healed well enough for it to come off. I have to say, I don't miss it at all. And my staff had better be on the alert because this means I can kick butt again."

Everyone laughed, and more congratulations followed. When they died down, I sensed a palpable awkwardness in the room. Determined to keep spirits high, I decided some liquid spirits were in order. "I think this calls for a celebration," I said. "Free drinks and food for all of you. I'll get Debra up here, and you guys can order what you want. Today, lunch is on the house."

My announcement seemed to do the trick as the group started discussing menu items and drinks, some giving and some asking for recommendations. I got up and went downstairs long enough to find Debra to ask her to come up to get our orders.

"Is the elevator working yet?" she asked after I explained what I wanted.

"It is, but I don't know if it's safe to use," I told her. "I think the dumbwaiter might be, though." In addition to the elevator, Mal had suggested—quite wisely, it turned out—that I also install a dumbwaiter that ran from the downstairs kitchen to the one upstairs. "I can open the upstairs kitchen for you if you want," I told Debra. "And, of course, I can also help you."

"No need," Debra said. "Missy and I can handle it. You go join the group and I'll be right up."

I was about to argue with her refusal of my help, but she spun away from me so fast I didn't have a chance. Instead, I went over to the basement door beneath the stairs and hollered down to the O'Reillys with a request.

"We can do that," Connor said after I told him what I wanted.

Satisfied that I had made everyone a little happier, I went back upstairs to the Capone Club room. Debra showed up right behind me, and over the next five minutes she took down everyone's orders. I placed one for myself and then told her the good news.

"The elevator is functional, and you and Missy are to

be the first people to use it. Connor is waiting for the two of you by the first-floor elevator door, and when you're ready to bring our stuff up, you can christen the elevator and make it officially open for business."

"Sweet," Debra said. She tried to downplay things, but I could tell she was tickled by the idea of being the first person to "christen" the elevator.

I felt good about how things were going and the overall mood of the room until Alicia asked, "Mack, where's Mal?"

I should've anticipated this question. Mal and I had pretended to be a couple to everyone here in the group for several weeks while we investigated the letter-writer case. The two of us were seen together a lot, so much so that we were given the nickname M&M, and we had been dubbed inseparable. Most of the Capone Club group had no idea Mal was a cop. They thought he worked in construction and I met him on a blind date. The only people who knew the truth in the beginning were Cora, Joe, and Frank. Cora's beau, Tiny, had been let in on the fact that my romance with Mal was a fraud, but he didn't know Mal's true occupation. Tyrese was eventually brought into the loop, and Clay, smart reporter that he was, had figured it out on his own.

Once the letter-writer case was resolved, we revealed the relationship as a ruse to everyone, though Mal's true occupation still remained a secret. Even though it was now known that Mal and I weren't really a couple, everyone was so used to seeing us together, they often asked where Mal was whenever I entered the room alone.

"Mal probably won't be around for a while," I told the group. "Between my elevator installation and his regular job, he's working a lot of extra hours. Speaking of extra hours, did I mention I had my first official consultation case yesterday?"

My distracting ruse worked, though it left me in the position of having to hem and haw about the details of the case because I wasn't sure yet how much I could share with the group. In negotiating my contract for this consulting work, I had requested that the Capone Club members be allowed to hear details about cases because they were a large part of my ability to interpret things correctly. Not unexpectedly, that was met with a great deal of resistance. In the end, we reached something of a compromise. I could discuss my specific reactions to specific elements I had been exposed to at a crime scene, but only if Duncan okayed it first. And Duncan, as well as the detective in charge of any particular case, would have the right to declare any specific detail of a crime scene off-limits.

The group grilled me about the case and the scene, and I shared a few generic details with them, as well as some of my synesthetic reactions to certain things. I avoided any mention of who the victim was, Mal's connection to him, and the discovery of Felicity. The group wasn't so easily put off, however, and they continued to probe and prod me for details until my relief arrived in the form of Debra and Missy, who were pushing a cart loaded with food and drinks.

"That elevator is freaking awesome!" Missy said.

"It *is* pretty nice," Debra agreed with a big smile as the two of them started dishing out the goods. Once everything was handed out and the group was focused on eating and drinking, I was desperately trying to think of another topic to discuss that would keep spirits up in the room, but not be about the Janssen case. Fortunately, Carter did it for me.

"Sonja brought us something interesting," he said to

me. "We were talking about it right before you came in. It's not an official murder, at least not yet. I'll let her explain."

I looked over at Sonja, who sucked in her lower lip and gave me an equivocal look before she spoke. "I might be making a mountain of a molehill here," she began, "but I can't shake the feeling that something bad has happened, and no one knows it."

"How so?" I asked.

"I think one of my clients, a woman named Caroline Knutson, might have gotten away with murder," she said in a near whisper. "She's been complaining about her husband, Oliver, for well over a year now, stating how much she hates him and can't stand living with him. Her protestations have gotten more and more vociferous with time. Then yesterday, he suddenly turned up dead."

"It could be coincidental," I said.

"I know, but my gut tells me no," Sonja said, looking less certain than she sounded.

As someone who operated on gut instinct myself much of the time, I didn't feel like I could dismiss Sonja's suspicions outright. But I also knew we'd need more than her gut feeling if we were going to get the police involved.

"We've been playing devil's advocate," Holly said. "Hate is a strong motive, and a common one, but there are far easier ways to escape someone you hate. So we asked Sonja if there was any other motive."

"And there is," Sonja said. "Money. Lots of it. Oliver Knutson is . . . was quite wealthy. Once, when Caroline was complaining about him, I suggested she should simply leave him, divorce him. But she told me that prior to marrying him, she signed an ironclad prenup.

The money she would get if she tried to divorce him would be a pittance."

"And in addition to the money she would inherit as his wife," Alicia said, "there was apparently a rather large life insurance policy as well."

"I can see why you're suspicious," I said, "but if she killed him, I'm sure the police will figure it out."

"Not if she did it in a way that doesn't arouse suspicion," Carter said pointedly. There was a gleam in his eyes, one I recognized all too well. Others in the room had the same look. They were on the trail, and they weren't going to give it up easily.

Resigned, I asked, "When did you say he died?"

"Yesterday morning," Sonja said. "That's what's so odd about it. His wife was in my salon yesterday evening asking for 'the works.' She wanted a complete makeover: a massage, a spray tan, a mani/pedi, a new haircut and color . . . pretty much every service I offer. She was in a very chipper mood. Then I heard on the news this morning that her husband had died yesterday." Sonja paused for dramatic effect, and then in a low voice added, "She never once mentioned it to me while she was in the salon. Doesn't that strike you as strange?"

"Maybe the woman is tactless," I said. "Or maybe she was in shock. None of that means she's a killer, though. What evidence is there?"

Sonja frowned and shrugged. "I don't know, of course." Then her expression lightened. "I thought maybe you could run it by Duncan to see if the police are investigating the case at all. I was going to ask Tyrese or Nick to look in to it, but they aren't here."

I considered this request and shrugged. "I can ask him when I talk to him." I shifted my attention to Clay. Given that Oliver Knutson was probably a mover and shaker in the Milwaukee area, I figured Clay's paper might have some basic information about him prepared for an obituary. "What can you tell us about Oliver Knutson?"

Clay smiled and looked over at Cora, who handed him her laptop. "We were looking in to that very thing when you came in," Clay said, taking the laptop. "Give me a second to log in to my work account at the paper and pull up the preliminary obit for the man."

The room fell silent except for the sound of Clay tapping away on the computer keyboard. I looked over at Tad. He was sitting at the back of the group, looking wary and withdrawn. I wondered if the rest of the group had made him feel welcome.

"Here we go," Clay said, leaning back in his chair and reading from the computer screen. "Oliver Knutson was fifty-seven years old at the time of his death. According to the obituary info, he was a 'self-made man' who struck it rich when he was in his twenties by developing a software program that was bought by Microsoft. That initial boost of wealth grew exponentially thanks to some wise stock investments, and he used the rest of it to start up a novelty and party supply store called Pizzazzeria. The store did quite well for him, and he has since opened a dozen more throughout Wisconsin, Indiana, and Illinois, and he has franchises in six other states. He was predeceased by his son, James, who died in an automobile accident six years ago at the age of seventeen. James was the son of Oliver's first wife, Anne. Knutson has been married to his second wife, Caroline, for four years. No kids for those two." Clay looked up at me. "That's it."

"Not much," I said.

"I could dig up some back articles on him, but I can't

do that search outside of my office," Clay said. "I do know Knutson's first wife, Anne, came from family money. And if I remember correctly, their divorce was a surprisingly benevolent one. If there was any bickering or fighting over money, no one heard about it." Clay paused and shrugged. "I'm not sure that information is helpful, or even relevant. One thing that might be, though, is I know Knutson had some health issues. He was a heavy smoker for a lot of years, and he liked his food. He wasn't a small man."

Sonja nodded. "That was one of the things Caroline complained about a lot." She gave me an embarrassed, apologetic look before continuing. "She called him a beached whale, and she said the thought of having sex with him disgusted her."

"She told you that?" Alicia said, looking aghast. Several people in the room shifted uneasily in their chairs.

Sonja shrugged. "You'd be surprised at some of the stuff our clients share with us. They're often trapped with us for several hours at a time. Plus, in addition to basic hair, manicure, and pedicure services, we offer massages, spray tans, and waxing. Working with, or exposing certain delicate body parts, tends to foster a sense of intimacy. People get to talking and they share things they might not otherwise. Especially the ones who have been coming to us for a long time."

"Don't you think it's odd that the woman came into Sonja's shop for a complete makeover the day her husband died?" Holly asked.

"And in such high spirits," Sonja added. "Almost gleeful."

"It is odd, but it could be nothing more than a bizarre grief reaction," I said, playing devil's advocate. "Or maybe she's being honest about it all. If she's been wanting out of the marriage for a long time, this must seem like a gift." Too late, I realized my words might hit home with Tad. I glanced over and saw him studiously staring at the plate in his lap. He had ordered a burger and, so far, he'd only taken one bite of it. I couldn't see his expression, but I sensed his uneasiness and cursed to myself.

"Presumably the police have already looked in to it," Joe said.

Tiny, a first-generation American whose parents were Norwegian, felt the police had botched the investigation into his sister's death twelve years earlier, and he still held something of a grudge over it. "Da police aren't perfect, ya know," he said. "Dey miss stuff all da time."

Clay, who was still tapping away on Cora's laptop, much to her annoyance, said, "According to the news release, the police don't suspect foul play, but the exact cause of death is still pending an autopsy."

"It can't hurt to ask the cops to look in to it, can it?" Holly asked.

"Ya, but it might not help eeder," Tiny grumbled.

I sighed and shrugged. "I don't see the harm in asking, though it would help if we had something more to go on. I'll run it by Duncan to see what he says."

"Thank you," Sonja said.

At that point, Tad set aside his unfinished burger and fries, got up, and left the room without a word. As soon as he was gone, I looked at the others with a sad expression. "Did anyone reach out to him?" I asked. "Did you guys make him feel welcome?"

The guilty looks and lack of responses gave me my answer.

"Come on, you guys," I pleaded. "Tad is one of the good guys. I promise you, he had no knowledge of what his wife was up to, and he wasn't involved at all."

"We believe that," Carter said. "But it's still awkward. I don't know what to say to the guy."

"None of us do," Holly said.

"How about something like *sorry about what happened and we hope you're doing okay*, or *we're glad to see you back here*, or even just a simple *how are you doing*?" There was more shifting in chairs, and a lot of guilty side glances. My phone rang, and I saw it was Duncan. "I have to take this," I said. "But I hope you guys will reach out to Tad. He's one of us. He's family."

With that, I got up and walked out into the hallway to answer Duncan's call.

"I got you some time with Felicity," he said.

"That's great. How did you get Parnell to cave?"

"Actually, she called me to ask for you. Apparently, Felicity has been a bit of a handful for the foster parents who have her, and they can't seem to get through to her. So Parnell wants you to go by to see what you can do."

"I'm ready any time."

"I'll pick you up in ten."

"Wait," I said. "Before you hang up, there's something else I want to run by you." I told him about Caroline Knutson's odd behavior, and the group's concerns about the nature of Oliver Knutson's death.

Not surprisingly, Duncan sounded skeptical. "It's not much to go on," he said. "And it's not my case. In fact, I don't think the case is being handled by our district. I'll see what I can find out."

"Thank you. I'll meet you out front in ten minutes."

I disconnected the call and went back into the Capone Club room. "I just spoke with Duncan," I told the group. "He said he would look in to the Knutson case. No promises; it's not even his district's case. But at least he's going to check into it."

Judging from the pleased expressions and smiles I saw in response to my news, the group was glad Duncan hadn't simply dismissed their concerns. There was no guarantee he wouldn't eventually do that anyway, but at least for now he was playing along.

I told the group I would check back in with them later, then went downstairs to my office to grab my coat, hat, and gloves. On the way into my office, I saw Tad sitting at the bar looking morose, nursing a drink. By the time I emerged, he was no longer alone. The Signoriello brothers —bless those two dear men—had left the warmth and comfort of the upstairs fireplace and come down to join Tad. So had Carter and Holly. They flanked him at the bar, and I saw Carter give Tad a friendly pat on the shoulder. As I made my way to the door to watch for Duncan's car, I heard the wonderful sound of Tad's laughter.

Maybe everything would turn out all right after all.

Chapter 13

Duncan filled me in as he drove. "The couple who is fostering Felicity focus on caring for kids with special needs. The wife is a nurse and her husband is a psychologist. Neither of them works outside of the house anymore, so it's kind of an ideal setup for these kids. According to Parnell, they've dealt with all manner of kids with a variety of problems. They're the ones who are insisting we bring you by because, apparently, Felicity has been acting out by hitting, kicking, and yelling any time anyone tries to interact with her. When they ignore her, she squats in a corner and doesn't move for hours. They haven't been able to get her to say anything other than one word."

"Which is what?" I asked

Duncan shot me an amused look. "She keeps saying *Mack*, over and over again. The Varners—that's the name of the couple caring for her—thought at first the word represented some item or a food she wanted, like mac and cheese. They finally called Parnell to see if she knew what it meant."

"That had to have been painful for Parnell," I said, unable to suppress a small smile.

"I'll admit, she didn't sound happy when she called me. But in her defense, I do think she has the best interests of the child in mind. So try not to be too smug or antagonistic."

"Parnell is going to be there?" I asked, my smile fading.

"Yes, I'm afraid so."

"Yippee," I said, my voice dripping with sarcasm. On that somber note, the rest of our drive was made in silence.

The Varners lived in a split-level home on the outskirts of the city. I guessed their ages to be somewhere in their late fifties, and judging from the multitude of pictures I saw displayed, they must've fostered and/or had a lot of kids.

The psychologist, whose name was Jerry, had a neatly trimmed mustache and beard that were all gray, while the hair on his head was more of a salt-and-pepper color. He had a receding hairline, pale blue eyes, and a rather large nose. He was tall and stood very erect. Something about him reminded me of pictures I had seen of Sigmund Freud in his later years, and I wondered if the similarities were intentional or coincidental.

His wife's name was Irene, and I figured she must have been a knockout when she was younger, because she was a looker even now. Her skin was creamy and unblemished, her facial features were refined with a small, pert nose, pouty lips, and large, round eyes that were a shade of green one rarely sees. It made me wonder if she was wearing tinted contact lenses. Her strawberry-blond hair was streaked with white, and the fact that she didn't bother to touch up the color made me like her for some reason. She looked patient, capable, and caring, and she greeted us with a warm smile that looked apologetic.

Parnell was indeed present, just as I'd been warned, and her expression was a mix of pouting petulance and annoying irritation. She avoided looking at me as she did the necessary introductions, and then said, "I'll leave it to the four of you to figure out what you want to do from here." Finally, her gaze settled on me. "I don't mean to put a lot of pressure on you, Ms. Dalton, but the Varners have determined that Felicity's behavior warrants a more controlled and professional environment if it continues."

"Do you mean an institution of some sort?" I asked. Parnell nodded.

"It's not a decision we take lightly," Irene said. "But Felicity's behavior borders on dangerous, both for her and for us. If we can't get her under control, we might need to experiment with some medications to try to calm her."

"Of course," Jerry said, "we'd prefer to keep her here and not medicate her, if possible. So we're hoping you can work some magic."

"I'll do my best," I said. "I definitely had a connection with her yesterday, but who's to say if that will continue?" I looked around the house, let out a heavy sigh, and said, "Well, let's get to it. Where is she?"

Irene pointed toward the stairs. "She's in a bedroom in the lower level, the second door on the left. We had to empty the room of all its furnishings because she kept pounding her fists on them, ripping the bed-clothes apart, and banging her head against things. She seemed to like it better when the room was empty, and Ms. Parnell told us that's the way things were set up at her home."

"Sort of," I said, shooting Parnell a questioning look. "Did she tell you about the cubbyhole?"

"She did," Jerry said. "We tried to create a small closet space in her bedroom here, similar to what she had there, but she didn't seem particularly interested in it."

"The space she had there, while hidden away, was actually quite roomy," I told him. "And she had some comfort items in there. Maybe your spot is just too small for her."

Jerry nodded. "You might be right. Come on," he said, heading for the stairs. "I'll take you to her." He turned and made his way down the stairs, stopping in front of one of the doors in the basement level.

As he reached for the knob, I put my hand on his arm and stopped him. "Would it be all right if I went in by myself?" I asked.

Jerry hesitated, made eye contact with Parnell, and gave her a questioning look, apparently conferring with her. Or deferring to her.

"Let her go," Parnell said with a shrug. Then she looked at me, her eyes narrowing. "It's your funeral," she said, demonstrating a complete lack of tact. "If the kid goes off on you and you get hurt, you'll have no one to blame but yourself."

Jerry stepped aside, and I opened the bedroom door.

The room, like the one in Felicity's home, was completely empty. Felicity was settled on her haunches in the far corner, her arms wrapped around her knees, her expression frightened. But her face quickly morphed into something different when she saw me. She stood, her face alight with happiness, and said, "Mack!" She moved toward me, and for a moment, I thought she was going to hug me. I extended my arms in anticipation, but she stopped a foot away and took hold of one of my hands. She lifted it to her face and positioned my palm against her cheek, leaning into my hand.

Judging from the gasps and murmurs I heard behind me, this behavior stunned our onlookers. I don't think any of them were more astonished than I was. I had anticipated a much more fragile, damaged version of Felicity than what I had seen yesterday. I feared the change of scenery and people would have overwhelmed her, and I wasn't sure she would even remember me.

"Hi, Felicity," I said. I studied her face, which looked calm and composed at the moment, though she wasn't making eye contact with me. I saw a bruise and a couple of small scrapes on her forehead and chin, no doubt from banging her head against the wall. "It's good to see you again."

She stared off at one of the side walls of the room but continued to hold my hand against her face. I let her stay that way for a moment, and then said, "Irene, could you round up some markers or crayons, and some blank paper to use them on?"

"Sure."

"Felicity, can we sit down and talk?" I said.

She still didn't look at me, but I caught the slightest shift in the focus of her eyes.

"Your hair smells like coconuts," I said, getting a whiff of whatever shampoo had been used on her. My mind briefly imagined what bathing an uncooperative Felicity had to have been like, and it made me wince. "The smell of coconut sounds like a hammer hitting a nail to me," I said to Felicity. "Isn't that funny?"

She finally lifted her face away from my palm, though she didn't let go of my hand. Her eyes met mine, and I saw a twinkle there that, for a moment, I thought might be some sort of synesthetic reaction. Suddenly, her face lunged toward mine. The movement was so unexpected and so fast that I didn't have time to back away. But I did blink and flinch—an involuntary response. If Felicity noticed, she didn't show it. In the next nanosecond, I realized she was sniffing at my hair, and I willed myself to be still. I hoped my heart would stay in my chest, because the adrenaline surge triggered by her lunge made my heart race and pound like it wanted to bust out of there. After a few seconds, she backed away and smiled at me.

"Hair smells purple," she said.

Behind me, I heard Jerry whisper, "Well, I'll be damned."

Irene returned with a plastic bag full of crayons and a short stack of printer paper. "Will these do?" she asked, handing them to me.

"They're perfect."

Felicity had squatted at my feet, and she reached over and rubbed one side of my left leg. "Gone," she said. "All better?"

I nodded and smiled at her. "Yes, Felicity, it is all better. I broke the bones in my leg and that's why I had that cast on there. But the bones healed up, and today the doctor took off the cast. It's much easier for me to get around now."

Felicity had continued to rub my leg as I spoke. She paused, cocked her head to one side, and said, "Hurt?"

"Not now," I said. "It hurt when I first broke the bone, but only for a little while." I looked over at Irene. "Why don't you sit down on the floor with us to draw?"

"No!" Felicity said. She crab-walked away from me, scuttling toward her corner.

"It's okay, Felicity," I said. "Irene and Jerry are friends of mine. They won't hurt you. They want to help you.

They want to help me help you. They are nice people, although they don't see colors and shapes like we do." I saw Irene shoot me a curious look. Behind me, I heard Parnell mutter, "Oh, for cripes' sake."

Then, much to my surprise, I heard Jerry say, "Mack, do you have synesthesia?"

I turned and gave him a grateful, though slightly disbelieving smile. "I do," I said. "You're familiar with it?"

"Somewhat," Jerry said. "One of my instructors, an older man who was retired from his practice, told us about the disorder, and one particular case he had that was an unusual and severe type of synesthesia. It was a girl, a teenager who had a particularly complex overlap of all her senses. She'd been diagnosed as schizophrenic because she saw and heard things that weren't there, but our professor was able to determine it was just a function of her synesthesia."

I stared at Jerry for a moment. "Was your professor's name Dr. Whitman by any chance?"

Jerry cocked his head to one side and smiled. "Indeed, it was." His face lit up. "Don't tell me . . . are you the patient he talked about?"

"I believe I am," I said. "What's more, I think Felicity here has synesthesia, too. I don't think her case is as messed up as mine, but I'm certain she has some form of it. That's why she said my hair smelled like purple."

Felicity had retreated into her corner, and she squatted there, hugging her legs, listening and watching as we spoke. I looked over at her and smiled.

"Everybody here is your friend, Felicity," I said to her. "Won't you come sit with us and draw some pictures?" I didn't wait for her to answer. I sat down cross-legged on the floor—my newly freed leg protesting with a dull ache that reminded me I wasn't fully healed yet—and opened the bag of crayons. I took a piece of paper and found a flesh-colored crayon that was more orange than anything. Using it, I drew the shape of a face and then added a nose and some ears. Then I swapped the crayon for a blue one and colored in some eyes. Next, I used a black crayon to provide the outline of the eyes, some eyelashes, and a head of short black hair. I finished it off in red, drawing some lips and adding a rosy color to the cheeks.

Irene had joined me, and she began to draw as well. Her picture was of a flower: a bright green stem, several green leaves, and red petals. The woman obviously had some artistic talent; the flower she had drawn was a rose, and there was shadowing, color fades, and linear details that gave it a three-dimensional look.

Duncan, Ms. Parnell, and Jerry stood in the doorway, watching quietly. Felicity stood, sliding up the wall, and took a step toward me and Irene. But then she stopped and eyed the trio in the doorway suspiciously.

"Mind if I join you?" Jerry said. He stepped into the room, sat down on the floor next to his wife, and took a piece of paper and a crayon.

Duncan and Parnell remained standing in the doorway. "I need to make some calls," Duncan said. "Do you mind if I go upstairs?"

"Not at all," Irene said. "Make yourself at home."

Ms. Parnell glanced at her watch and said, "It seems you have things under control now. If it's all right with all of you, I'm going to head out. I have another case I need to follow up on."

I waved her away, glad to be rid of her. I got the sense that Ms. Parnell was suffering from a bad case of job burnout, and her presence here would only complicate things.

Both she and Duncan disappeared upstairs. The rest of us sat on the floor coloring pictures, and after a moment, Felicity walked over and sat down with us, positioning herself close to me. She pulled up her knees and wrapped her arms around them, watching us but not participating.

"Felicity, I'd like to ask you some questions about what happened at your house," I said. I kept drawing and didn't look at her. Irene and Jerry glanced at her, but they, too, kept drawing. "Something bad happened at your house yesterday," I said. "I'm wondering if you saw any of it."

Felicity began to rock back and forth.

"If you did see something," I continued, "you could draw a picture of it."

A minute, perhaps two, ticked by. Felicity continued to watch and rock, and I was about to try coaxing her some more when she suddenly reached forward and grabbed a piece of paper. She set it on the floor in front of her, turned it ninety degrees, stared at it, and then turned it back to its original position. She then repositioned herself so she was lying on her side. After studying the bag of crayons for a moment, she reached in and pulled out a red one. Holding it in her fist like a dagger, she put it to the paper and began scribbling. The crayon slashed across the page over and over and over again, eventually becoming more circular. Felicity quickly filled the middle of the page with a deep, red blotch. Gradually, she increased the pressure on the crayon, and the paper began to tear.

Irene, Jerry, and I had ceased our own efforts, and we watched Felicity with a mixture of worry and curiosity. Once the tear in the paper made it nearly impossible for Felicity to continue scribbling on it, she raised her hand up and stabbed the paper, breaking the crayon in the process. Then she looked up at us, her eyes huge, and yelled a single word at the top of her lungs.

"BANG!"

All three of us jumped. I waited, expecting Felicity to burst into tears or crawl back into her corner, or do some other version of an emotional withdrawal. But instead she sat there staring at me with those big eyes, the most direct eye contact I'd ever had with her.

After taking a few seconds to calm myself, I pointed to the torn, red, scribbled page and said, "Is this blood, Felicity?"

She nodded. I swallowed hard, realizing this meant she had likely seen her father's dead body at the least, and perhaps had seen him get shot. Then the darker thought came to mind, the one I didn't want to consider. Perhaps she was the one who had shot him. Even as the thought went through my mind, I shook my head. I didn't want to accept the idea.

I took out my cell phone and pulled up the picture of Mal that I had shown her before. "Felicity, do you know this man? I showed you this picture yesterday. Do you remember?" I was tense, half-expecting her to scream or scramble backward toward her corner, but she did none of those things. She simply nodded.

"This man was in your house yesterday. Did you see him?"

Clear as a bell, she said, "Yes." She looked away toward the wall, made a fist with one hand, and then punched the palm of her other hand, saying, "Pow!"

I gathered from this that she had seen Mal struggle with her father. She must've come out of her cubbyhole, though in the heat of the moment Mal hadn't seen her.

"Bad man," Felicity said, the same descriptor she'd

used the day before. It made sense, given Mal's recitation of the events that had taken place. But I also knew Mal hadn't shot Sheldon Janssen. And I didn't want to believe Felicity had either.

"Did you see anyone else in your house yesterday?" I asked Felicity next.

She nodded again, and my heart leaped. "Can you tell me who you saw? Or if you don't want to talk, can you draw who you saw?"

There was no response from her for a minute or so. Then she reached over, picked up a black crayon, and drew an arch of black circles on a piece of paper. She paused and studied it a moment, and then traded the black crayon for a pink one and drew an oval shape beneath the black circles. I realized she was drawing a face. Over the next couple of minutes, she added brown eyes, a pink nose, and a red mouth to the face. Then she picked out a blue crayon and drew wavy blue lines running down from both of the eyes. When she was done, she set the blue crayon aside and sat there, her face bent over the picture, her arms hugging her torso.

"This looks like a woman," I said. "Is it a woman?"

Felicity nodded, her head still down, staring at the picture.

I studied the blue lines and asked, "Is she crying?"

Again, Felicity nodded.

"Do you know her name?"

Felicity finally looked up at me. "Little peach," she said in a soft, sad voice.

I pondered her answer, trying to figure out what it meant. Was she referring to some sort of synesthetic reaction to the woman? Or some reference to the woman's name?

"Is that her name?" I asked.

Felicity turned and crawled back to her corner, curling into a sitting fetal position, her knees drawn up and her arms wrapped around her legs. She began to rock.

I looked over at Irene. "Does the term *little peach* make any sense, or mean anything to you?"

Irene shook her head.

Duncan returned then, and he paused in the doorway, studying the scene in the room. "Any progress?" he asked.

"I don't know," I said. "Maybe." I showed him the picture, explained how it had come to be, and then told him what Felicity had said. "I have no idea what she means by *little peach*," I concluded.

Duncan's brow furrowed as he contemplated the term.

"And I don't know if she's going to give us anything more right now," I added. "Perhaps we should take the picture she drew and show it to someone else, to see if it rings any bells?"

I knew Duncan understood right away what I was referring to. We could show the picture to Mal and ask him if he recognized the woman, or had any idea what the little peach reference might mean. Duncan nodded. "Good idea."

I grabbed the picture and got up from the floor. I walked over and handed it to him. "Let me see if I can get her settled down for the night before we leave." Again, he nodded. I switched my attention to Irene. "Do you have a mattress of some sort that we can put on the floor in here?"

She nodded, and gave her husband a questioning look. Jerry disappeared and returned a moment later with a twin-size mattress that had a sheet on it. He carried it into the room and set it on the floor next to where Felicity was sitting.

"I'd like some time alone with her, if you don't mind," I said to the room. "I'll see if I can talk her into being a little more cooperative and a little less upset with things."

No one questioned or objected, and I soon found myself alone in the room with Felicity.

"Okay, Felicity," I said. "It's just you and me now, and we need to have an important talk."

Chapter 14

I spent an hour with Felicity, bringing her some food and making sure she ate it, getting her to the bathroom to wash up and brush her teeth, and giving her the clean water glass Duncan brought us to use, which I then carefully handed back to him. He dropped it into an evidence bag so it could be used to lift Felicity's fingerprints. Felicity and I then returned to the bedroom, and I settled her on the mattress, which Jerry had kindly augmented with a top sheet, two blankets, and a pillow. I talked to Felicity the entire time, sharing my synesthetic reactions to the various things we encountered, and explaining to her that Jerry and Irene were good, friendly people who wouldn't hurt her and wanted to help her. She cooperated fully and showed no signs of revolt. I told her I would be back to see her again, but I wasn't sure when.

"Just be patient and wait for me, okay?" I said, and she nodded, studying her thumbnail like it was the most fascinating thing she'd ever seen. "And do what Irene and Jerry ask you to do." Again, she nodded. "I'm your friend, Felicity, okay? You and I are friends."

She looked me in the eye for the first time during this hour of one-on-one companionship, and her face broke into a tentative smile. On impulse, I leaned over and gave her a kiss on the forehead. As soon as I did it, I realized it might be too aggressive a move for her. She didn't like people touching her. I anticipated a sudden withdrawal, but instead, she shocked me by letting forth with a hearty laugh.

I left her, still smiling, and closed the door to her room. Then I went upstairs to clue the others in on what had transpired. The mood in the house, now that Parnell was gone, was noticeably lighter. Irene and Jerry thanked me profusely and had no objection to my coming back to see Felicity again. In fact, I got the sense they wouldn't mind if I simply moved in with them for a while.

It was dark when we left, and Duncan and I rode in silence for the first five minutes or so. I was content with the quiet—my head creates enough noise all on its own—and was almost disappointed when Duncan finally spoke.

"You've got quite a way with the kid," he said.

I shrugged. "Just lucky, I think."

"I think not."

I looked over at him, smiled, and said, "Thanks."

"While you were working your magic with Felicity, I made some calls regarding the case your Capone Club members were curious about."

"And?"

"And the lead detective on the case said it was closed. The victim was overweight and smoked, and it seemed apparent he died of a heart attack in his sleep. The ME decided not to do an autopsy."

"So we're just going to let it go?" I said with a frown, dreading the passing on of this news to the group.

"No. I persuaded the detective on the case to convince the ME to post the guy."

"You did?" I gave him a grateful smile.

"I did. It wasn't easy."

"Thank you."

"Don't thank me yet," he said in a cautionary tone. "Odds are the ME either won't do the post, or will do it and find exactly what they expect."

"At least if they do the autopsy, I can tell the group there's nothing to the case," I ventured. I realized then that we weren't on our way back to the bar. "Where are we going?"

"To see Mal. I want to show him that picture the kid drew."

"Good," I said. "I want to check in on him anyway, to make sure he's okay."

I saw Duncan shoot me a glance. "You're quite fond of him, aren't you?"

"I am," I admitted. "He's a great guy."

"I'm a little jealous."

"You don't need to be," I assured him. "Though I understand why you are. I do care a lot for Mal, and if you weren't in the picture, I suppose I might try to make something work between the two of us."

"Then I best make sure I stay in the picture," Duncan said, sounding grave. He reached over with one hand and took mine.

He drove one-handed the rest of the way, holding my hand the entire time. His touch and warmth were reassuring and comforting to me, and it was with reluctance that I finally pulled my hand free when we had reached our destination. I started to get out of the car once Duncan had parked and turned off the engine, but he reached over and grabbed my arm, stopping me.

"Hold on a second," he said. He pulled me toward him and leaned into me at the same time. Then he gave me a nice, long, delicious kiss on the mouth.

"Wow. I kind of like this slightly jealous version of you," I said when we finally pulled apart.

"Good," he said with a wink and a smile. "There's plenty more where that came from."

We finally got out of the car and headed around to the back of the house, entering through the same basement sliding door we'd used on our previous trip. Duncan had called Mal to let him know it was us, using the burner phone he'd gotten for him earlier.

I was heartened by the sight of Mal. His color had improved, and he no longer looked haggard and sickly. He wasn't back to his old self yet, but I could tell he was on the mend. I greeted him with a hug—a gentle one, lest I aggravate his wounds—and told him his family was safe but worried about him.

"I thought they might be worried," he said, looking pained. He handed me an envelope. "I wrote them a letter. Would you mind giving it to them?"

"Of course."

He stepped back then, and eyed me from head to toe. "You got your cast off," he said with a smile.

"I did. And I don't miss it a bit."

"I'll bet not. How's the elevator project going?"

"It's almost done. And it's fantastic. Thanks so much for tackling the project for me."

Duncan cleared his throat behind us, and I gave Mal a guilty smile and rolled my eyes before turning away from him.

"Mal, I've got something I need you to look at," Duncan said, taking Felicity's drawing from his pocket.

"The little girl, Sheldon Janssen's daughter, drew this for Mack today. She indicated that she saw someone at the house when Janssen was killed, and when Mack asked her who it was, she drew this. Does it look familiar to you?"

Mal took the picture and studied it. Despite the crudeness of the drawing, the basic descriptors were apparent. He gave it a full minute and then shook his head.

"No worries," Duncan said, taking the picture back. "How are you fixed for food and supplies?"

"I'm good for another few days," he said. "Any other leads in the Janssen case?"

Duncan shook his head. "I talked to Klein and asked him when he last saw Janssen. He said it was on the night before he was killed, and only for a few minutes. Janssen dropped by his house, and when I asked him why Janssen was there, he said it was to discuss some problems with one of the job sites. When I asked him what sort of problems, he gave me some vague answer about personnel issues."

"I'm guessing I was that issue," Mal said. "And I'm certain Janssen shared his concerns regarding me."

"Assuming that's true, you need to stay hidden for now," Duncan said. "Work on that picture. If that woman was there when Janssen was killed, there's a good chance she was the one who killed him."

"When I asked Felicity if she knew the woman's name, she said *little peach*," I told Mal. "Does that trigger anything for you?"

Mal arched his eyebrows. "Actually, yes, it does. Though I'm not sure how it relates. I overheard Janssen talking to one of the other guys on the job site about a kid of his who he said had died. He never mentioned her by name, but he referred to her as his little peach."

This information was disappointing. "So maybe Felicity was referring to her dad being there," I said. "Maybe she didn't understand what I was asking. Except . . ." I hesitated, thinking.

"Except what?" Duncan asked.

"Well, that picture she drew definitely wasn't her father, and it certainly looks like a woman."

Mal scratched his head. "You might want to try talking to a guy named Norman Chandler," he said. "He works for the company, and he and Janssen were good friends. Based on conversations I've heard between the two of them, they go back a long way and socialize together. Maybe he'll know who this woman is."

Duncan nodded. "Okay. I'll see if I can track him down."

We spent an hour with Mal, chatting about the case and other things, including his family and the elevator. He thanked me for taking his family in and ensuring their safety, and said he felt bad they had put me out.

"I'm not out," I said. "I'm sleeping in a very cozy bedroom set up in my basement."

Mal looked surprised at this. "You mean the bed I've been sleeping in?"

I nodded. "I hope that's okay," I said.

"Of course it is," Mal said with a chuckle. "It's your house, your bar. You can sleep anywhere you want to. I just assumed you were staying at Duncan's."

There was a brief tick of awkward silence. "We considered that option," I said. "But Duncan felt the bar was safer, and I didn't want to have to travel back and forth with my hours being the way they are." Eager to change the subject, I said, "I need to take another look at your wounds and change those dressings." I got up and fetched the necessary materials while Mal dutifully removed his shirt.

To ensure we didn't go back to the subject of sleeping arrangements, I asked Mal about his ex, Sabrina. "I like her," I said. "I like her a lot. She seems nice, down-to-earth, and friendly. Not to mention protective. It's a shame the two of you couldn't make it work."

Mal sighed. "Bad timing, I think."

"Maybe you two should give it another try," I suggested. "She seems to care about you a lot. I mean, look what she did for you, letting you stay here in this house."

"She's a good egg," Mal said, nodding in agreement. "But we're very different people. I'm just glad that despite what happened between us, we parted on friendly terms and she isn't the kind to hold a grudge."

"She was fiercely protective of you," Duncan said. "I agree with Mack. There are some feelings there still. It might be worth another shot, once all this is resolved."

We left Mal with that thought to ponder, and promised we would be back in a day or two. "If you need anything before then, anything at all, just call on that burner I gave you," Duncan instructed.

Mal looked morose as we prepared to leave, and I wondered if he was lonely out here in this house by himself. He was used to a large family and lots of people around, so I imagined the isolation of this place, and being cut off from everyone he knew, must be hard for him.

Duncan must have sensed Mal's mood, too, because as we were leaving he gave Mal a light, friendly punch on one arm. "Buck up, my friend," Duncan said. "I'm going to get you out of this mess. I owe you for what you did for me and Mack, and I intend to pay you back."

"You don't owe me anything," Mal said, giving me a hangdog look. "I enjoyed every minute of it."

I gave him a kiss on the cheek, and then whispered in his ear, "I enjoyed it, too."

When Duncan and I were settled back in the car, he asked me what I had said to Mal when we were leaving.

"I just gave him a bit of encouragement," I said vaguely. "He looked so dejected and lonely. It breaks my heart to see him like that."

Our return drive was comfortably quiet, and at one point, Duncan reached over to hold my hand again. When we arrived at the bar, he parked the car, and as he turned off the engine, he turned to me and said, "Is it okay if I spend the night?"

"I was hoping you would. But you're going to have to share the inflatable bed in the basement with me because Mal's family has taken over my apartment."

"That's fine," Duncan said. "As long as I'm with you, it doesn't matter where we sleep."

His words made my heart squeeze, or at least that's how it felt in my chest.

"I know you've got some free time tomorrow because it's Sunday," he went on, "but I'm going to have to get up early and head into the office. I want to try to hunt down this Chandler guy Mal mentioned to see if he can add any insight into Janssen for us, and also to see if he recognizes the woman in the picture."

"I understand," I said. "Resolving this case is as important to me as it is to you. Not only is it my first official case as a consultant with the police department, but there's this whole business with Mal. We need to clear him as soon as we can."

"Agreed."

Once we were inside, we hunted down Mal's family. They had quit work for the day and were seated at a table enjoying food and drink. We joined them, and, in a low, quiet voice, Duncan updated them on Mal's status. Then he gave them the letter Mal had written.

"Are you sure he's okay?" Connor asked.

"He's fine," Duncan answered. "We have a bit of a mess to resolve, but I'm going to get to the bottom of it."

"We're about done with the elevator project," Connor said. "We're going to take tomorrow off and do a little bit of sightseeing here in Milwaukee. Perhaps you could suggest some sights?"

"I'd be happy to," I said.

"We appreciate it," Connor said. "We should be able to tie up the elevator project on Monday, and I've arranged for us to head back to Washington on Tuesday. Do you think Mal will be able to come out of hiding before then?"

Duncan and I exchanged looks. "I honestly don't know," Duncan said. "I'll do my very best to make that happen, but I can't make any promises. If it doesn't happen, we can probably arrange for you to see him before you go."

"That would be nice," Connor said.

After providing them with a list of sightseeing options to choose from, Duncan and I excused ourselves from the group. I went to check in with Billy and the rest of my staff, while Duncan disappeared into my office, no doubt to take care of some business. The remainder of the night up to closing time was uneventful. I let my staff leave early, telling them I would take care of all the closing duties. Now that I was no longer encumbered by my cast and crutches, I felt the need to repay all of them for the extra time and effort they put in to help me when I did have them.

Duncan emerged from my office just before closing, and he assisted me in my efforts. As soon as we had things taken care of, we retired to the basement and settled in Mal's makeshift bedroom. I was exhausted from the day's efforts—both physically and mentally—but Duncan managed to reawaken some energy in me, and trigger a host of wonderful synesthetic reactions in my body.

Chapter 15

Despite the fact that I'm normally able to sleep in on Sunday mornings, it wasn't to be on this particular one. Not only did the unfamiliar sleeping area interfere, Duncan received a phone call a little after eight. I listened to his end of the conversation, but it didn't reveal any details to me. I had no idea who was on the other end of the line. As soon as he disconnected the call, I asked him.

"What was that all about?"

"That was the detective covering the Knutson case. Apparently, the night shift at the medical examiner's office tackled Mr. Knutson's autopsy."

"Do tell," I said, feeling a little trill of excitement.

"First, I need to hit up the bathroom," he said, swinging his feet over the edge of the bed and sitting upright.

"You'll have to go upstairs," I said. "That's one of the downsides to this little bedroom setup. There's no bathroom down here." I, too, swung myself out of bed and threw on a robe. "I'll come with you. I need to go myself, and I want to throw on a pot of coffee."

Some ten minutes later, the two of us had taken care

of our morning ablutions and we were settled in at a table in the bar with two steaming-hot mugs of coffee.

"Want me to fix you something to eat for breakfast?" Duncan offered.

I shook my head. "We can eat later. I want to hear about the Knutson case."

Duncan smiled and shook his head wryly. "Curiosity killed the cat, you know," he teased.

"If you don't hurry up and tell me, I'm going to kill *you*," I countered.

"Okay, okay." Duncan held both of his hands in front of him, warding me off. "According to Detective Bobby Dillon—that's who's handling the case—the medical examiner said there were signs of ischemia, meaning tissue death due to a lack of oxygen, in Knutson's heart. He said that's something commonly seen when someone has a heart attack."

"So it probably was a death from natural causes," I said, unable to hide the disappointment in my voice.

"Not so fast," Duncan said with a crafty smile. "Despite the evidence of a lack of oxygen to the tissues, and the fact that the man was overweight, his arteries were in surprisingly good shape. According to the medical examiner's findings, there was no blockage of any sort that would have caused a heart attack. Typically, a heart attack causes damage to a portion of the heart muscle, the area served by the arteries that are blocked. But in this case, the entire heart showed signs of tissue death, as did other parts of the body. Basically, Oliver Knutson suffered a general lack of oxygen to his entire system."

"You mean like suffocation?"

"That's one way," Duncan said, looking troubled. "But there wasn't any evidence of suffocation. Typically, there are some signs of strangulation, or pressure applied to the face with a pillow . . . something like that. People don't realize it, but those things do leave marks that are identifiable. There weren't any in this case, though."

"That seems odd," I said. Duncan nodded thoughtfully but said nothing. "Were there other health problems Knutson had that might've caused his death?"

"Some minor things," Duncan said. "He was diabetic, but apparently, it wasn't bad enough for him to have to take any medication for it. He controlled it with diet. And speaking of diet, he was on one to try to lose some weight, so the medical examiner thought there might have been some electrolyte imbalances that caused an arrhythmia. But once he got the bloodwork back, there was no evidence to support that theory. Knutson also suffered from sleep apnea related to his weight, and he used one of those CPAP machines at night. The medical examiner thought the machine might have malfunctioned somehow, but it was tested and appeared to be working fine. Plus, there was no evidence of any struggling on Knutson's part. In general, when someone feels like they're not breathing properly and the oxygen level drops, it triggers anxiety and agitation. But Knutson was found in bed on his back, the bedcovers in place, cold, blue, and not breathing. According to his wife, his CPAP machine was turned on and working when she found him that morning, but he didn't have his mask on. By the time the police got there, the wife had turned the machine off."

"I'm not familiar with these CPAP machines," I said.

"Basically, it's a breathing mechanism that provides air under pressure to the person using it. It's meant to help people who have sleep apnea and other respiratory ailments. According to what the ME said, these people often have floppy tissue in their airways. The

CPAP machine's pressure helps prevent that floppy tissue from blocking the airway. The pressure it delivers keeps things open, kind of like an inflated balloon."

The mention of balloons made me briefly flash on Felicity. I wondered how the night had gone with her and the Varners. "So it involves wearing some sort of mask?" I asked, getting back on track. Duncan nodded. "Is it possible the mask somehow suffocated him?"

"No," Duncan said with a shake of his head. "The ME said this particular mask had an anti-asphyxiation valve in it to prevent something like that from happening."

"So even if the power went out while the person was sleeping with the mask on, they'd still be able to breathe?"

"They would. But it's more likely the person would simply wake up, aware of the sudden loss of pressure and air. Of course, that's assuming the person was able to wake up. If he was sedated in some way, he might not have been able to remove the mask, or perhaps he managed to take it off but lacked the wherewithal to put it back on."

"Any evidence of sedation?" I asked.

"Not yet," Duncan said. "The preliminary tests for the presence of any sort of sedating drugs or paralyzing agents were negative. The ME told Dillon there are other, less common drugs he can test for, but that will take a while."

"So Sonja may have been right after all," I said.

"Perhaps so," Duncan said with a sobering nod. "Though Detective Dillon had already decided to take a closer look at the scene, and have another chat with Knutson's wife for some reason. My interest in the case came as something of a surprise, but Bobby is willing to let me work on the investigation, and even let you participate."

"You make it sound like such a burden to have me involved."

Duncan gave me a tolerant smile. "Mack, you have to understand, there are still a few people out there who are skeptical about you and your ability. The fact that Chief Holland and Tony Dixon both agreed to use you as a consultant doesn't mean everyone on the force is convinced it's a good idea. But it does mean they have to let you work with them if the boss says so. And in this case, the boss will say so. It's a high-profile case with a wealthy and well-known victim. It's bound to garner a lot of press. The chief will want to hedge all his bets the best he can, and assure the DA's office has all the necessary information and evidence to properly prosecute."

I let out a weary sigh. "Right," I said tiredly. "I forgot that it's an election year."

"You don't have to play if you don't want to," Duncan said.

"No, I won't back out. I admit I'm not excited about the attention it's likely to draw to me, but in fairness, Holland and Dixon did warn me. I knew what I was getting into when I agreed to work with them."

"Does that mean you're ready to go to work?"

"You mean now?"

"Soon," Duncan said. "Dillon is waiting on a search warrant for the Knutson house and said we can come along. I don't know if his wife will be there or not, but if she is, we can have a chat with her, and you can do your lie-detector thing. Or perhaps Dillon will want to bring her in to the station to talk. Either way, you're welcome to listen in and provide whatever feedback you can."

"Do I have enough time to take a shower?"

"Make it a quick one. I'm expecting to hear from Bobby about the search warrant any minute."

"Will do." I picked up my coffee cup and headed for the stairs to my apartment. I managed all of four steps when I remembered the O'Reilly's were camped out up there and, because they intended to take the day off, they were likely hoping to sleep in.

I turned back to Duncan. "On second thought, I think I'll grab some bar towels and do a spit bath in the ladies' room down here," I told him. "I don't want to disturb Mal's family."

Fifteen minutes later, I looked reasonably presentable. I'd managed to do a quick wash-up at the sink, fix my hair, and get dressed. I even put on a touch of eyeliner and some lipstick. I wanted to make something of a good impression in my new role as a consultant. By the time I emerged from the bathroom, Duncan was ready to roll.

"We're on with the search warrant," he said. "Let's go."

Twenty minutes later, we arrived at the home of Oliver and Caroline Knutson. I expected, given Oliver Knutson's purported wealth, that we might end up in a home in one of the ritzy neighborhoods bordering Lake Michigan. It was a well-to-do neighborhood all right, but not one on the lake.

Duncan parked on the street and waved at someone once we were out of the car. To my surprise, the person who waved back was a woman with blond hair and a tall, slender figure. She had just emerged from a car— an older-model Toyota sedan—and she headed toward us with a curious but friendly smile.

"So, Albright, this is the infamous secret weapon I've heard so much about," she said, giving me a quick once-over. There was a hint of skepticism in her tone, and her voice tasted like buttery cheese with just a hint of sharpness to it.

"Bobby Dillon, meet Mack Dalton," Duncan said.

"Please, call me Roberta," Bobby said, extending a hand.

I smiled and made a face at Duncan. "Duncan neglected to tell me that you were a woman," I said, shaking her hand.

"Well, that's because I'm just one of the guys to all the cops in town. Ever since my coworkers heard one of my brothers call me Bobby, it's been my nickname on the force ever since. I suppose it makes sense given that I have three older brothers, and I'm the only girl in the family. My mom passed away shortly after I was born, so I was raised in a house full of testosterone."

"I'm sorry about your mom," I said. "My mother died right after I was born, too, and I was raised by my father. So we have something in common, although I never had any siblings, and my house had more alcohol than testosterone."

This triggered a bemused and slightly worried look from Roberta.

Duncan explained. "Her father owned the bar Mack now owns, and they lived in an apartment above it. Mack still lives there."

"Ah," Roberta said with a look of understanding. "You grew up in a bar. How fun that must have been."

"It was never boring."

"I'll bet not." Roberta shifted her attention to two marked police cars that were pulling onto the street. "Ah, here comes our backup," she said.

The marked vehicles jockeyed into parking spaces, and then two uniformed cops and two people in plainclothes got out and walked over to join us. The people in plainclothes were each carrying two large tackle-type boxes. Roberta did the introductions.

"Officers Barrow and Vasquez, this is Detective Duncan Albright and his assistant, Mack Dalton." I nodded at the two uniformed men. Barrow was tall and slender, pale skinned with a blond buzz cut, a large hawk nose, and almost no lips. He looked to be somewhere in his early thirties. Vasquez was short—I guessed him at around five-foot-eight or -nine—and tended toward the stocky side, though I suspected some of that width beneath his uniform was due to muscle—he looked like a weight lifter. His dark-complected skin, black hair, and brown eyes were a direct contrast to Barrow. That, combined with the differences in their heights and physiques, made these two guys look like the opposite ends of a spectrum.

Roberta moved on to the two people in plainclothes, one woman and one man. "This is Amelia and Brian," she said. "They are two of our best evidence technicians."

With the introductions done, Roberta gave me one last assessing look before shifting her attention to the stately homes on our side of the street. She reached into her coat pocket, removed a wad of latex gloves, and peeled off a pair, which she handed to me. Then she did the same for Duncan and the two uniformed officers. Amelia and Brian were already wearing some.

Amelia said, "I have booties in my case for us to slip over our shoes before we go inside."

Roberta nodded, and waved a hand toward a large stone mansion. "Shall we?" she said.

I removed my weather gloves, stuffed them in my coat pocket, and then pulled on the latex gloves as we made our way toward the Knutson house.

Knutson lived in one of Milwaukee's elite, older

neighborhoods. On the outside, with its boxy shape and stone façade complete with carved pillars, his house looked cold and unwelcoming. It reminded me of a mausoleum, and I had to suppress a shiver that I wasn't sure came from the winter temperature outside.

After we climbed onto the porch, Amelia set down the case she was carrying and took out several pairs of paper booties, which we all dutifully donned over our boots. When everyone was ready, Roberta used the lion's head knocker to announce our arrival. Just to make sure, she also rang the doorbell.

A woman I assumed was Caroline Knutson opened the massive, wooden front door and greeted us with a puzzled but welcoming smile. "Hello, Detective Dillon," she said, casting a somewhat annoyed glance at Roberta before eyeing me, Duncan, and the rest of our entourage with a curious frown. With the sound of her voice, I saw a faintly undulating yellow line floating in the air.

"Mrs. Knutson," Roberta acknowledged. "May we come in?"

Caroline frowned. "May I ask what this is about?"

I couldn't help but notice that she looked freshly pampered. Her hair was cut in one of those geometric dos and colored a pale blond with darker blond highlights that were beautifully and subtly done. Her fingernails were newly polished, done in a French manicure. Her skin glowed from a spray tan and who knew what sorts of facials or other skin treatments, and I felt certain if I could have seen her toes, they would have been immaculate as well. Sonja did nice work.

"We need to have another look around your house," Roberta said.

Caroline narrowed her eyes at Roberta, chewing on

her lip. "It's not a good time," she said. "What exactly are you looking for?"

Roberta, borrowing from a book I gathered all the cops learned from because I had seen Duncan use the same tactic many times, didn't answer Caroline's question. Instead, she fired back with one of her own. "Did Mr. Knutson take any regular medications?"

"No," Caroline said. "Occasionally, he'd borrow one of my Ambiens to help him sleep. But like I told you before, he didn't like doctors, and despite my nagging, I could never get him to go see one." Her face took on a sad expression and in a mournful tone, she added, "If only he'd listened to me, he might still be alive today. His heart attack might have been prevented."

"Your husband didn't have a heart attack," Roberta said.

Judging from the expression on Caroline's face, she was clearly stunned by this information. "He didn't?" she said, blinking fast several times.

Roberta shook her head, and I thought I saw a glimmer of a smile on her lips.

"How do you know that?" Caroline asked.

"His autopsy showed it."

The two women were staring at each other with an intensity that was both unnerving and fascinating. It was as if they were the only two people in the world at that moment.

"Autopsy?" Caroline said, and her voice was a little shaky. "I thought the coroner said it looked like natural causes and an autopsy wasn't going to be necessary."

"Yes, well, that changed. The medical examiner has full discretion in deciding whether or not to perform an autopsy when there is an unexpected or unexplained death." She paused, giving Caroline a moment to digest this.

"If he didn't die of a heart attack, what did he die from?" Caroline asked.

"That's what we need to find out," Roberta said. "And it's why we want to take a second look around your house." I wondered why Roberta didn't just show Caroline the search warrant straightaway, and wondered if she was toying with the woman—the way a cat teases a mouse—before moving in for the kill.

Caroline gnawed at one of those perfectly manicured nails.

"Mrs. Knutson, it's quite cold out here," Roberta said with a grimace after several seconds of weighty silence. "May we please come in?"

This plea to Caroline's politeness and sensibilities worked. She stepped aside, and our little entourage moved indoors.

"I don't understand why you did an autopsy," Caroline said as she closed the door. "Ollie wasn't a healthy man. The coroner said so when he was here. He said it looked like natural causes."

"Yes, well, some information came up that made the ME decide to take a closer look at things," Roberta explained. "And when he did, some irregularities turned up."

"What sort of irregularities?" Caroline asked, and I noticed the yellow line of her voice began to undulate a little faster.

"I'm not at liberty to say right now," Roberta said. She started to move deeper into the house, but Caroline stopped her.

"Hold on a minute. I don't think it's a good idea to let you guys traipse all over my house again. You had your chance yesterday, when Ollie died."

Apparently, this was Roberta's cue to play her trump card. "It doesn't matter if you think it's a good idea," she said. Though the words were smug, Roberta's voice was not. She sounded genuinely sympathetic. But with her next words, the taste of her voice turned rancid, and I knew there was no sincerity there. "I'm truly sorry to be such a nuisance to you, Mrs. Knutson. But you see, I have this search warrant that says I can look through your house now." She pulled the search warrant paperwork from her jacket pocket and handed it to Caroline. "I'm sorry if our presence is compounding your grief," she said, not sounding sorry at all. "But we are going to look around. Here's our warrant."

Caroline took the paperwork and scanned it, her expression shifting from simple concern to mightily pissed off in record time. She'd been played, and she knew it. "I think I need to call my lawyer," she said.

"You go right ahead," Roberta said. "Show him that paperwork when he arrives. In the meantime, Officer Vasquez here is going to keep you company, to make sure you don't get rid of anything we might want to look at."

Caroline's face flushed a vivid red. She looked like a teapot ready to boil over. "Are you suggesting I have something to hide?" she asked through gritted teeth.

"Do you?" Roberta shot back.

Caroline stuttered and stammered for a second before stomping her foot in a fit of petulance and storming away from us toward the kitchen I could see at the back of the house. Vasquez followed her, and as Caroline started swiping through her cell phone—probably searching for her lawyer's phone number—Roberta waved for us to follow her.

Chapter 16

The inside of the Knutson house was the exact opposite of the outside. In stark contrast to the cold, sharp, colorless stone on the outside, the interior decor consisted of warm colors, plush furnishings, and gleaming, refinished hardwood floors.

The entrance had placed us in a great room that included a living room, a dining area, and the aforementioned kitchen. It was obvious the inside of the house had been remodeled over the years, providing a sharp contrast to the nearly century-old façade on the outside. The kitchen was state-of-the-art, and the open concept design of the main living area was a modern touch that never would have existed when the house was originally built.

Roberta, a woman I decided I never wanted to cross, led us down a narrow hallway off the great room to what was clearly the master suite. Though it lacked the enormity of the modern-day McMansion-size bedrooms—there were limits as to how much one could do with these older homes without building an add-on—it was still a good-sized room with beautiful, glossy-white trim around the floor, doors, and windows.

The same glossy-white framing was evident in the crown molding near the high ceiling. There was a stone fireplace in the room, but it looked like it had been converted over to gas.

Just off the bedroom was a bathroom, again a smaller version than what one might see in a more modern home belonging to someone of Knutson's wealth, but still nice. There was a claw-foot tub, black and white hexagon tiles on the floor, a pedestal sink, and a tiled shower stall in one corner that looked oddly out of place.

The bed was an old-fashioned four-poster with a canopy. There was a distinctly feminine feel to the decor, not only in the bed but in the frilly furnishings, curtains, and accessories. I suspected immediately that these touches were Caroline's doing, but it turned out I was wrong.

"This is where Oliver slept," Roberta told us. "Caroline has her own room at the other end of the house."

I stared at Roberta in disbelief.

"I know, I know," she said with a roll of her eyes. "The room is definitely girlie. It shocked me, too, the first time I saw it. Apparently, Oliver's first wife, Anne, decorated it. Caroline told me she had intentions of redoing the room but never got around to it. Oliver snored so bad that it was keeping her awake at night, so she took over what used to be the servants' quarters at the other end of the house and renovated it as her own sleeping space instead."

"Is Oliver's first wife still in the picture?" I asked.

"She is," Roberta said. "In fact, she was the primary impetus behind our investigation into Oliver's death . . . other than your inquiry," she added, giving Duncan a pointed look. "Anne has been quite insistent about Caroline's motives for marrying Oliver, and was concerned that his death wasn't from natural causes."

"So she lives here in the area?" I asked. Roberta nodded. "Did she have access to the house?"

"Not that I know of. Besides, Anne has no real motive. She's a wealthy woman in her own right." Roberta narrowed her eyes at me. "Why do you ask?"

Duncan was watching me closely. "Have you picked up on something, Mack?"

I shook my head. "Nothing significant yet," I said, though this wasn't entirely true. There was something odd about the ceiling in the bedroom. When I looked at it, or at the crown molding bordering it, I felt a strange sensation, as if my body was lighter suddenly and wanted to take off and fly. But I had no idea if this was anything significant, or even exactly what it was that was triggering the response. "I was just trying to get a picture of who had access to the house," I explained. "Did Oliver and Caroline use any sort of in-house help, like a cook or house cleaner?"

"Good question," Roberta said with a grudging smile of admiration. "And yes, they did. There is a woman who comes every Monday to clean, and a grounds-keeper who takes care of the snow clearing in the winter and the lawn and gardening needs the rest of the year. But he hasn't been here since we had the last snowfall. That was four days ago."

"And Oliver died on a Saturday, so it's safe to assume the house cleaner wasn't here either," I noted, getting a nod from Roberta. "So the only people who were in the house that we know of were Caroline and Oliver?" Another nod. "And what did Caroline say about how she found him?"

A voice came from behind me and, judging from the wavy yellow line I saw, I knew it was Caroline. I turned and saw her standing in the hallway behind us, Vasquez at her side. "My lawyer will be here shortly. I'd like you to stop this search until she gets here."

"That's not going to happen," Roberta said.

Caroline dismissed her and shifted her gaze to me. "I'll tell you the same thing I told Detective Dillon yesterday. I always get up earlier than Ollie, and I make a pot of coffee for the two of us. Then I go and wake him up. When I went in to wake him yesterday, he was cold, blue, and wasn't breathing. I called 9-1-1 right away. When the paramedics got here, they pronounced him dead right away. The police were here at the same time. And then I was escorted out into the kitchen and not allowed to see Ollie again." She gives Roberta a hurt look.

Sensing that Caroline was in a chatty mood—something I'm sure her lawyer would have advised her against—Roberta egged her on.

"I don't have my notes from yesterday with me," Roberta said to Caroline. "Can you go over the details again?"

"I explained it all to you very specifically yesterday, Detective. Clearly you don't believe me and think I had something to do with Ollie's death. The idea is ludicrous, of course, and while he might not have died of a heart attack, the coroner—"

"Medical examiner," Roberta corrected.

"Whatever," Caroline said impatiently, rolling her eyes. "Whoever it was that was here yesterday felt certain Ollie had died of natural causes. You being here today is nothing more than a form of harassment. And I can't believe you let someone cut poor Ollie open." Caroline looked genuinely hurt, but the yellow line of her voice suddenly sagged, making me think she was being less than sincere. Then she pouted, spun on her heel, and retreated, giving Vasquez an irritated look when he fell into step beside her.

Roberta sighed, no doubt disappointed over the missed opportunity to get a lawyerless Caroline to repeat more of her story from yesterday to see if it remained consistent.

While all this was going on, I kept sneaking peeks at the bedroom ceiling and then shifting my gaze to the ceiling out in the great room area. There was something different in the bedroom, but at the moment I wasn't sure what it was. The floating sensation I felt in my body was definitely a synesthetic reaction, but I didn't know what I was reacting to. Was it something I was seeing or smelling? Or was it simply a side effect of some emotion? The way my synesthesia worked, it could've been any of those things.

I ventured deeper into the bedroom and made my way over to the bed. The covers were still rumpled from where Oliver's body had been, but the bottom sheet had been stripped from the bed. I wondered if it had been taken along with the body. I looked over at the nightstand beside the bed and knew that something there had been moved or removed. Currently, there was a book—a paperback mystery, the irony of which didn't escape me—lying open with its pages down to mark the spot where Oliver had stopped reading. Beside it was a pair of reading glasses, and one of those clip-on book lights. The rest of the surface of the nightstand was empty, but I sensed a distinct void in the light covering of dust and knew something else had recently been there.

"Detective Dillon?" I said.

"Please, call me Roberta."

"Okay, Roberta, was there something else on the nightstand here when the police first arrived?"

"There was," she said, giving me a curious look. "How did you know that?"

"It's just something I can do," I said with a shrug. "Can you tell me what it was?"

"It was an empty drinking glass. We took it as evidence in case it turned out that Mr. Knutson had been drugged. According to his wife, he sometimes took a sleeping pill."

"And did you find anything?"

"The ME did test for Ambien, the sleep medication, because we knew he took it. It came back positive, but at the normal level one would expect to find in someone who had taken the proper dose at bedtime."

"And what was beside the bed, in front of the nightstand?" I asked, looking at faint impressions in an area rug beside the bed.

Roberta looked at me, impressed. "I see why you call her your secret weapon," she said to Duncan. Then she turned back to me. "Knutson had a machine and an oxygen tank there because he suffered from sleep apnea and had to use one of those CPAP devices," she explained, verifying the information Duncan had already given me. "I imagine the sleep apnea is why he had such a snoring problem. We confiscated the machine, of course, and had our techs look it over to make sure it was functioning properly. And we also alerted the medical examiner to the fact that the victim used a CPAP machine. We thought perhaps the machine might have somehow malfunctioned, or been blocked so that air couldn't get to the mask Mr. Knutson wore, and that he might have succumbed from breathing in his own exhaled carbon dioxide. The medical examiner said that was unlikely as the lack of oxygen typically would awaken a patient, who would then remove the mask. Besides, this mask had a special valve in it that made accidental asphyxiation impossible."

"What about a power outage?" Duncan asked.

"There is a backup battery and an alarm on the machine—quite a loud one, in fact—that seemed to be in proper working order when our techs tested it." Roberta paused and sighed. So far everything she was telling us jibed with what Duncan had shared with me earlier. "We checked the CPAP machine thoroughly," Roberta went on, "but I don't think it's relevant. Caro line told us Oliver wasn't wearing his CPAP mask when she came in to wake him yesterday morning. According to her, he often took it off during the night because it annoyed him. Sometimes he did it in his sleep without realizing it, and other times he did it intentionally. The medical examiner tested Knutson's blood for oxygen, carbon monoxide, and carbon dioxide levels."

"Carbon monoxide?" I said.

"From the furnace or the fireplace," Roberta explained. "But the air in Mr. Knutson's lungs had a normal level of oxygen, and there was no indication of high levels of carbon dioxide or carbon monoxide. That would seem to indicate a sudden death, which is why we assumed he died of some sort of catastrophic cardiac event. The sudden onset of chest pain and an inability to breathe might have made him tear his mask off just before he died."

"I assume the oxygen tank was full enough?" I asked.

"It was over three quarters full and functioning properly."

I thought a moment. "You'd think if Mr. Knutson had any sort of warning for whatever happened that his agitation prior to death would have been evident," I said. "Yet he was supposedly found in perfect repose, right?"

Roberta nodded. She shot Duncan a look I couldn't quite interpret, though I sensed she was annoyed. Then she just stared at me, waiting.

I walked around the room, letting my synesthesia take over. I looked, smelled, and listened, though I tried not to touch anything for fear of contaminating the scene. Aside from what I had already mentioned to Roberta, I didn't pick up on anything except for the weird feeling I got when I looked toward the ceiling.

After doing the full circuit of the bedroom, I moved into the bathroom. There were plenty of synesthetic reactions here, but nothing that seemed significant. They were reactions I recognized in response to the smells, sights, and sounds, like the dripping faucet in the sink. There was a drinking glass—actually, a paper cup—next to the sink, and Brian bagged and tagged it. Amelia gathered up the soaps, shampoos, and shaving cream, and bagged and tagged those as well. Brian tackled the medicine cabinet, bagging containers of several over-the-counter medications for pain relief and allergies, as well as some generic vitamins.

"I'm afraid I don't have anything else to offer," I said with an apologetic look at Roberta and Duncan, both of whom had watched and followed me around in silence. "Do you want me to look at other parts of the house?"

"Might as well," Roberta said. "Though I'm not sure we'll find anything helpful."

"You never know," Duncan said. "She's pulled some pretty neat surprises out of her hat for me."

I felt the pressure was on to prove myself and my abilities, but given that Caroline had been in the house since Oliver's body was found yesterday morning, I had my doubts as to how helpful I could be. Things were bound to have been moved, added, or deleted from the household between then and now. Depending on how much time had transpired, I might not be able to tell. I'd gotten lucky with the dust on the nightstand and the faint impressions in the area rug, but without those I wouldn't have been able to detect anything missing from the room. Still, I was willing to give it a try. I let Roberta lead the way and followed her, with Duncan bringing up the tail.

We came across Caroline and Officer Vasquez in the kitchen. "My lawyer should be here in a few minutes," Caroline said, looking cross.

"That's fine," Roberta said, sounding as if she couldn't have cared less. "Just show her that paperwork I gave you when she gets here." Roberta shifted her attention to Vasquez. "Would you mind escorting Mrs. Knutson into the living room so we can have a look around the kitchen?"

Vasquez nodded and, without saying a word, he waved a hand toward the living room and gave Caroline a pointed look. Caroline rolled her eyes in annoyance and left the kitchen area in a huff, dropping onto a leather couch in the living room. She folded her arms over her chest and pouted, glaring at us the entire time.

Roberta made her way around the kitchen, opening cupboards and drawers, inspecting the contents of the refrigerator, and even opening and looking inside the oven and microwave. There was a small butler's pantry off the kitchen, and she looked in there as well.

I dutifully followed her around like a devoted puppy dog, once again letting my synesthesia do its thing. But all the reactions I had were expected ones, reactions I recognized and knew well because they were related to common, everyday things.

After finishing our circuit of the kitchen area,

Roberta looked at me with a questioning expression. I simply shook my head, triggering a sigh from her. We moved on into the area at the end of the house opposite Oliver's bedroom. There was a second bedroom here that had clearly been created out of several smaller rooms. Its shape was irregular, with odd little nooks, irregularly aligned moldings, and patched-in areas on the wooden floor. Based on the contents and decor, plus the fact that we knew Caroline's bedroom was at this end of the house, it was easy to guess this was her room. Caroline's tastes were much more in line with my own: basic furniture with simple lines, warmer colors, and a focus on comfort. The room lacked the flowery, frilly, feminine touches that had been present in Oliver's room. It didn't have its own bathroom, but there was a second one in the hallway just outside the bedroom door. We toured both rooms, and the techs once again collected items from the medicine cabinet and shower. Roberta informed me that they had already collected Caroline's Ambien bottle the day before.

There was a second floor to explore, and when we reached the base of the stairs, which were located by the front door, the doorbell rang. Caroline leaped from her seat and hurried over to see who it was. She peered through the peephole and then turned to look at us with a smug expression.

"My lawyer is here," she said. She flung the door open to reveal a dark-haired woman who appeared to be in her fifties. She was carrying a briefcase and dressed like a professional. "Thank goodness you're here, Natalie," Caroline said. "These people are digging and pawing through my house, treating me like some common criminal. You need to stop them."

Natalie graced us with her professional smile as she

set her briefcase on the floor, removed her gloves, and extended a hand. "Natalie Sokoloff," she said as Roberta displayed her gloved hands with an apologetic look. "Right," Sokoloff said, withdrawing her hand. "I'm here on Caroline's behalf as her attorney. May I ask why you're here?"

"We're exercising a search warrant," Roberta explained. "Your client has her copy."

Natalie turned and raised her eyebrows at Caroline. With a scowl, Caroline handed over the paperwork. Natalie unfolded it and scanned the contents. "The warrant appears to be in order," she said eventually. She looked over at Roberta. "Have you seized anything yet?"

"We took some stuff from both bathrooms, some medications and some personal hygiene items. And also a cup we found in Mr. Knutson's bathroom. We collected a full mug of coffee and the contents yesterday that we found on his bedside table. And we took his CPAP machine so we could test it to make sure it was functioning properly. We haven't had a chance to look upstairs yet. We're headed there now."

Natalie nodded sagely, and then walked over and settled in beside Caroline, who had retaken her spot on the couch. "Have you been questioned at all?" Natalie asked Caroline.

Caroline frowned, looking deep in thought, though I didn't think deep thought was something the woman was capable of. "No, not really," she said. "We talked some, about why they're here."

"Did the detective ask you any questions?"

Once again, Caroline frowned, and she took several seconds to answer. I guessed she was replaying a mental reel of our visit. "Detective Dillon did ask me if I wanted to reiterate my story about how I found Ollie yesterday."

"And did you?"

Caroline winced. "All I did was repeat what I told her yesterday."

Natalie rolled her eyes. "Don't repeat anything, don't say another word," she said in a chastising tone. Then she looked over at Roberta and gave her a nod.

Natalie's marching orders to Caroline eliminated any chance I had of talking to the woman anymore to determine if she was lying. Duncan and I exchanged looks communicating our shared disappointment, and I knew he was probably kicking himself for not trying to talk to her right away, when we first arrived.

Natalie and Officer Vasquez stayed with Caroline, while Roberta headed up the stairs. Officer Barrow, Amelia, Brian, Duncan, and I all followed.

We reached a landing that was as big as the living and dining areas in my apartment. Boxes were stacked along the walls, and judging from the packing lists and labels I saw, they were supplies destined for Oliver's party supply stores. There were boxes of Mylar balloons for various occasions, packages of streamers and confetti, disposable dishes and silverware, wrapping paper, ribbons, novelty items, and more.

I studied the boxes, giving my synesthesia full rein, trying to determine if anything had recently been moved, added, or removed. Several times, in several different places, I got a sense of something displaced.

"Something was removed from this spot," I said, pointing to one of the areas. "And it was done fairly recently."

"Like what?" Roberta asked me.

I shrugged and gave her an apologetic look. "I can't tell you what it was. All I can tell is that there was something there that isn't now. I think it was something about the size of those boxes over there." I pointed toward some cartons stacked on the other side of the landing that were approximately two feet square. "Some of these boxes have been moved around recently," I said, pointing to two spots where my synesthesia reacted. "But I don't think they were removed, just moved."

"Well, that doesn't help us much," Roberta said, giving Duncan a pointed look.

"It seems odd that he would keep this stuff here in his house, doesn't it?" I said. "I mean, I would think that if he owned a string of these stores, he would keep most of his supplies in the stores themselves, or in a warehouse somewhere."

Roberta conceded the point with a slight sideways tilt of her head. "I suppose," she said, sounding unsure.

From there, we moved on to explore the rest of the floor. There were three more bedrooms and two more bathrooms on this level, though two of the bedrooms had been converted into home offices. It wasn't hard to tell whose was whose. One of the offices had more of the party supply boxes in it, and the furnishings were the heavy, wooden affairs one might find in an old-fashioned home library. The other office had a drafting table, a glossy black bookcase filled with graph paper, drawing pads, and an assortment of colored pencils and markers. On the drafting table was a sheet of plain white paper with various drawings on it. On one side of the paper was a detailed picture of a table covered in a lavender-colored cloth, and a chair with a white cloth cover and a lavender bow at the back. In another corner was a detailed close-up of what appeared to be a centerpiece: a simple glass vase filled with lilac cuttings and adorned with white ribbons. In the middle of the page was a sketch of a room featuring several of the drawn tables beneath a ceiling of lavender and white balloons and crystal lights. The sight of the balloons made me flash back to the Sheldon Janssen case again, and the synesthetic balloons that led me to Felicity.

"It looks as if Caroline was the special occasion planner for the company," I said. I looked over at Roberta. "Does she inherit the business with her husband's death?"

"She does," Roberta said, giving me a smile. She shot a glance at Duncan. "Looks like you've trained her well. She's already thinking motives."

Duncan smiled but said nothing,

"It doesn't take much of a genius to figure out money as a motive," I said.

Roberta looked over at the evidence techs, Amelia and Brian, and said, "Let's confiscate all the computers from up here. And any tablets you may find. It might be enlightening to see what sort of things Caroline searched for on the internet."

While the techs bagged and tagged the various computers, Duncan, Roberta, and I moved on to finish examining the second floor. We didn't find anything that seemed significant to anyone, and we regrouped back in the landing area amid all the boxes.

"Anything to add?" Roberta asked me.

"Sorry, no."

"Are you planning on inviting Caroline down to your station for a chat?" Duncan asked.

Roberta nodded. "Not sure we'll get much out of her with the attorney there, but I'd like to give it a try."

"Then you should let Mack listen in and observe," Duncan said. "She has a very helpful ability when it comes to listening to people. She can tell when they're lying."

Roberta arched her eyebrows at me. "Really?" She sounded cynical.

"It's true, at least with most people," I told her. "My synesthesia makes people's voices either taste or look a certain way," I explained. I was about to continue, but the confused and skeptical expression on Roberta's face made me pause.

"I haven't explained your condition to Bobby," Duncan said.

"Condition?" Roberta repeated, sounding wary. She gave Duncan an exasperated look. "Are you telling me your secret weapon is some kind of mind reader?"

"No, not at all," I said. "I have a neurological condition called synesthesia. It's a cross-wiring of my senses that makes me experience the world around me differently from you, or most other people."

Roberta cast a tired look at Duncan. "I thought she was some kind of Sherlock Holmes savant or something."

"Not exactly," Duncan said. "It's a little difficult to explain. It might be better if she just showed you how it works."

"Oookaaay," Roberta said, her voice now rife with doubt. She folded her arms over her chest and cocked one hip to the side, a stance that told me all I needed to know about her take on things.

Duncan looked over at me. "Do your thing," he said.

I sighed. This constant testing of my abilities was getting old, but I knew it was a necessary evil until I could establish myself with this and other groups of investigators.

"I'd like you to say three things to me," I said to Roberta. "Make them statements about yourself, or your life, things no one would know from any sort of routine search on the internet or any other resource. Have two of the statements be true and one of them a lie. I'll tell you which one is the lie."

"A one-in-three chance of guessing correctly doesn't sound all that convincing," Roberta said.

"Fine," I said tiredly. "How many statements would you like to make?"

"How about five?"

"Five it is."

Roberta narrowed her eyes at me, and thought for a moment. "Okay," she said finally. "Statement one: the first boy I ever kissed was named Bradley. Statement two: I have a heart-shaped birthmark on my left hip. Statement three: the first pet my brothers and I ever had was a cat named Tiger. Statement four: I was born in a taxi. Statement five: my kindergarten teacher's name was Miss Terwilliger." She arched her brows at me again and gave me a challenging look as she waited for me to respond.

Officer Barrow, Amelia, and Brian stared at me, their attention riveted.

"Well, your statements are a little tricky," I began, and I watched Roberta take on an I-knew-it expression. "At least one of them was," I amended. "Your third statement, the one about the cat . . . that's the one that isn't true, although I suspect you had a pet named Tiger, either it wasn't your first pet or it wasn't a cat.

Roberta's expression rapidly morphed from smug satisfaction to one of surprise. Amelia and Brian stared at her expectantly. "Our first pet *was* named Tiger," Roberta said. "But you're right; it wasn't a cat. It was a fish."

Amelia muttered, "Wow," under her breath, and Brian gaped at me.

"Okay," Roberta said, finally letting her arms loose to hang at her sides. "You've convinced me. So, shall we head on down to the station?"

"Lead the way," Duncan said.

As we all fell into step behind Roberta, Duncan and I brought up the rear.

"Way to go, Mack," Duncan whispered in my ear, his voice tasting of sweet milk chocolate.

I couldn't help but smile.

Chapter 17

The police station where Roberta worked was on the far north side of town. It bore similarities to Duncan's, but the interview rooms were quite different. At Duncan's station there were rooms surrounding a central observation area where one could both watch and listen to what was going on. At Roberta's station, each room—much smaller rooms than the others I'd seen—had a camera and audio feed that could be observed from a computer located virtually anywhere in the station.

Caroline and her attorney, Natalie Sokoloff, were directed to one of the tiny interview rooms, which contained a small, square table and four chairs. They were left alone until the feed from the room could be set up. Roberta directed Duncan and me to what appeared to be a break room and sat us at a table with a laptop. A technician accompanied us, and once he had the visual set up, Roberta left us and went into the interview room. She looked up at the camera and gave our technician, a man named Gregory, a thumbs-up signal; with a couple of taps on the keys, we also had audio.

"I don't know if my synesthesia will work like this," I told Duncan, soliciting a curious, sidelong glance from Gregory. "It may be too distant, too mechanical."

He nodded, looking thoughtful. "Let's give it a try and see what happens," he said. "If it doesn't work, perhaps Bobby can arrange for something a little more up close and personal."

I settled into a chair, and Gregory turned the laptop toward us. "The entire interview will be automatically recorded," he told us. "Please don't touch the laptop, particularly the keyboard."

"Got it," I said.

Roberta began by stating the date, time, the relevant case, and the person being interviewed, with a mention that the attorney of record with Caroline was Natalie Sokoloff. After that, she read Caroline her rights and asked her if she understood them.

"We do," Natalie said. "I'd like it noted for the record that I have advised my client not to partake in this interview, but she has decided to do so anyway, against my objections."

"So noted," Roberta said.

Natalie turned to Caroline and said, "I want to give you one more chance to rethink this."

"I have nothing to hide," Caroline said. She sounded convincing, but I couldn't tell if she was telling the truth or not because the wavy, yellow line did not appear.

"I'm not getting anything," I told Duncan.

"Very well," Natalie said, looking both annoyed and resigned.

Duncan scowled.

"I appreciate your concern," Caroline said to Natalie, "but the sooner we can get this silly business resolved, the better."

"Wait," I said to Duncan, feeling a trill of excitement. "I can see it now. For whatever reason, it wasn't there at first, but now it is."

Gregory studied me, eyes narrowed, the back of his hand rubbing over his bearded chin. I wondered what he was thinking.

"Okay, then," Roberta said. "Let's begin with yesterday morning, when you found your husband. Tell me again everything that happened."

I realized I could taste Roberta's voice and relaxed, determined to focus. It was working.

"I woke up around six, my usual time," Caroline said. "Ollie and I had a routine in the mornings. He typically didn't wake up until around six-thirty or so, and because I woke first, I'd go out and put on a pot of coffee for the two of us. Then I'd take a cup in to him. If he wasn't awake already, I'd wake him."

"And you were sleeping in a separate bedroom?" Roberta asked.

Caroline nodded.

"Did you see Oliver during the night at all?" Roberta asked.

Caroline hesitated before answering. "I checked on him once, around two, when I got up to go to the bathroom."

Roberta's eyebrows arched. "You didn't mention that earlier. Did you typically do that? Check on him in the middle of the night?"

"No," Caroline answered. "But I did that night because he'd been complaining of feeling off before we went to bed. And he'd taken one of my Ambiens. I was worried about him."

The wavy yellow line disappeared with this statement. I frowned at the computer, confused as to why this had happened. I started to say something to Duncan about it when Caroline continued and the wavy yellow line reappeared.

"He was sleeping soundly when I checked on him. I went back to bed."

"Okay, let's go back to the morning. You made the coffee. Then what happened?"

"I fixed a cup for Ollie. Two sugars and some milk . . . that's how he liked it."

"And you took it to his bedroom?"

"I did."

"Did you have a cup for yourself as well?"

"Yes, I did."

"And what happened when you entered the bedroom?"

"I saw that Ollie's CPAP mask was off. It was hanging from the machine next to the bed."

"Did that concern you?"

"A little, yes," she said. The yellow line disappeared again. "But it wasn't unusual. Ollie sometimes took it off during the night, because he said it made it hard for him to get comfortable when he wanted to change positions and sleep on his side. His sleep apnea isn't bad if he's on his side, only when he's on his back. If he woke up at some point after taking off the mask and turned onto his back, he'd typically put the mask on again." The line reappeared.

"And you know this because you saw him do it?"

"A few times, back when I used to try to sleep in the same bed with him." Caroline made a sad face, looking as if she was about to cry, though there were no tears. "I should've been harder on him about his diet, and exercise, and visits to the doctor. The doctor made it clear his weight contributed to the sleep apnea, and I promised I would help him eat healthier. I tried for a while, but he would only pick at the stuff I prepared, and then he would sneak out and buy himself some fast food. I know he did it because I found the wrappers and bags stashed under the seat of his car." She paused, burying her face in her hands for a moment. When she raised her head again, her eyes were red-rimmed but still dry. "I should've been more insistent," she said in a sobbing voice that sounded fake. "I should've been harder on him."

Roberta was unimpressed by this show. She rolled her eyes and then asked, "What position was Oliver in when you entered the bedroom?"

Caroline looked taken aback for a moment, as if in shock that her emotional outburst hadn't been believed. She cleared her throat and shifted in her chair. "He was on his back," she said.

"What position were the blankets on the bed?"

"They were up to about midchest level," Caroline said with a pout.

"Tell me everything you did," Roberta urged.

Caroline looked away for a few seconds, appearing to be deep in thought. "I walked over to the bed, saying it was time to wake up. I set his cup of coffee on the bedside stand and turned off the CPAP machine. Then I realized the room was unusually quiet. I looked closer at Ollie then, and noticed his color was off."

"Off how?"

"He looked . . . dusky. His lips were blue. And then I saw how still he was. Nothing was moving. His chest wasn't rising."

"What did you do next?" Roberta asked.

"I . . . um . . . I called out to him."

"His name?"

"Yes."

"How many times did you say his name?"

"What?" Caroline said. She frowned, sounding a little rattled.

"How many times did you call out his name?" Roberta repeated. "Once? Twice? Several times?"

"I . . . I don't know . . . several, I think." The wavy line started to sag and droop.

"Three times? Four?" Roberta pushed.

"I don't know for sure," Caroline said, sounding whiny. "I wasn't focused on counting."

Natalie closed her eyes, pursed her lips, and shook her head.

"Okay, what happened next?" Roberta asked.

"When he still hadn't moved, or answered me, or opened his eyes at all, I reached down and touched him on his shoulder."

"Which hand did you use?"

Caroline thought a moment. "My left hand."

"Where was your cup of coffee at this time?"

"What?"

"You said you set his cup on the nightstand," Roberta said, leaning closer to Caroline and pinning her with those piercing eyes. "But you also said you had two cups of coffee when you entered the room. Where was yours?"

Caroline blinked several times really fast and squirmed in her seat. "Still in my hand, I think."

"You think? You're not sure?"

"Detective," Natalie said in a testy tone.

Caroline used the interruption to gather herself. She looked over at her attorney, then back at Roberta. "Yes, I had it in my hand. In my right hand."

Roberta sat back in her seat. "What happened when you touched him?"

"Nothing," Caroline said. She made another unconvincing sad face. "He felt . . . hard . . . cold. I pushed on his shoulder several times, but nothing happened."

"Your husband was wearing pajamas when we arrived," Roberta said. "So I assume you touched the fabric when you touched his shoulder?"

"Yes."

"And this hard coldness you felt, you felt that through the material?"

Caroline hesitated, her eyes narrowing. I got the sense she was parsing both the question and her answer before committing. "Yes," she said finally.

"Okay," Roberta said, her voice rife with skepticism. "What did you do next?"

"I pulled the covers down a little to get a better look at him. I . . . I thought that maybe he was breathing, but it was so shallow I couldn't see or hear it. But there was nothing. No movement. I bent over and put my ear on his chest to see if I could hear his heart, but . . ."

"You bent over?" Roberta interrupted. "Were you still holding your coffee at this point?"

Caroline sucked in her lower lip, and her eyes started darting from side to side. "I must have set it down," she said. The wavy line was undulating like crazy. Caroline was nervous.

"Set it down where?"

"On the nightstand, next to his cup."

"Did you unbutton Oliver's pajama top when you put your ear on his chest?"

Caroline shook her head.

"Did you consider trying to do CPR or any other resuscitative measures?"

"I don't know how to do CPR," Caroline said. The wavy yellow line disappeared again.

"Oh, come now," Roberta said in a disbelieving and chastising tone. "You may not have had any official training in CPR, but surely you've seen people push on the chest of someone who appears dead on TV, or in a movie."

"I suppose," Caroline said, sucking in her lip again. She'd been wringing her hands and now she shoved them down between her legs. "It just didn't occur to me. Besides, he was so . . . so . . . cold. His skin felt hard. He looked . . ." Her voice trailed off as she thought. Then she shrugged. "He looked very dead," she said bluntly, and the yellow line reappeared.

Roberta stared at her for a long moment until Caroline shifted uncomfortably and looked away, glancing over at Natalie, whose expression had remained irritated throughout the entire interview.

"All right; what happened next?" Roberta said eventually.

Caroline looked back at Roberta, appearing more composed. "I went out to the kitchen to get my cell phone and call 9-1-1."

Roberta's eyes narrowed again. "And what did the 9-1-1 operator say to you?"

Caroline looked surprised by this question. "She said she was sending some help."

"I listened to your 9-1-1 call," Roberta said. "The operator asked you if you had tried to perform CPR. Do you recall that?"

"Oh . . . yes," Caroline said, raking a hand through that perfectly highlighted hair. "I told her that I didn't know how to do it. She said she could talk me through it, but I told her that Oliver was cold and blue, and that his skin felt hard."

"You stayed on the phone until help arrived," Roberta said.

"Yes."

"Where were you during that time?"

"I went and stood by the front door to watch for the ambulance. But two police officers showed up first. The 9-1-1 operator hung up once the police arrived. I let them in and directed them to Oliver's bedroom."

"Did you go with them?"

"I followed them, but I didn't go back into the bedroom. I watched them from the door. They took one look at Oliver and shook their heads. They knew he was beyond help." She said this last bit with a hint of self-righteousness, as if their actions justified her own.

"You never went back into the bedroom once the police arrived, is that correct?"

"It is."

"The photos of the scene the police took showed one cup of coffee on the nightstand. Where was yours?"

Caroline's eyes darted around. "Um, I took it with me when I went out to the kitchen to call 9-1-1."

"You found your husband dead in bed, set your coffee on the nightstand so you could listen to his chest, and when you went to call for help, you thought to pick up your coffee and take it with you?"

Caroline didn't answer. Natalie rolled her eyes and leaned forward. "Caroline, that's enough. I'm begging of you, stop this interview now."

Caroline looked back and forth between the two women, that lower lip once again sucked in. She looked unsure, a bit panicked, and that yellow line was undulating like crazy. "Okay," she said finally. "I don't want to talk about this anymore."

"Thank goodness," Natalie said with obvious relief. She shot out of her seat and went to the door. "Let's go."

Caroline did as she was told, looking contrite. Natalie held the door to the room open and glared at her client as she passed by. Just before leaving, she shot Roberta an irritated look and then stormed out.

"Wow," I said, leaning back in my seat. "Roberta is one tough cookie."

"That she is," Duncan said. "Did you pick up on anything during all that?"

Gregory reached over and slid the laptop away from us and started tapping away at the keyboard. But he kept glancing at me with a curious look in his eyes.

"I don't know," I said. "Maybe. There were some odd moments."

The door to the room opened and Roberta walked in, looking annoyed. "Well?" she said, not bothering with any preliminary pleasantries.

"Mack was just about to share her impressions with me," Duncan said.

Roberta settled into a chair across from me and leaned forward, elbows on the table, her eyes pinning me in place.

"When I hear Caroline's voice I see a wavy yellow line," I began. Gregory had stopped typing and he leaned back, arms folded over his chest, watching me. "At first, I thought the computer feed wasn't going to work because the line wasn't there when you first started. Though I realize now that I was able to taste your voice just fine. Anyway, after the first thing Caroline said, the line suddenly appeared. Whenever you had her nervous, the line undulated very fast. But there were a couple of times when it disappeared completely. I suspect those occurrences were when she was lying."

Roberta took a moment to digest this. "You say this line wasn't there when Caroline first spoke?"

I shook my head.

She looked over at Gregory. "What was it she said at the very beginning?"

Gregory leaned forward and poised his fingers over the keyboard, but I provided the answer before he could strike a single key.

"It was when she said she had nothing to hide."

Roberta looked at me, impressed.

"I have excellent memory recall, most likely due to my synesthesia," I explained with a shrug and a half smile.

"Interesting," Roberta said. "What did Caroline say the other times this line disappeared?"

I thought back. "It disappeared when she said she didn't know how to do CPR. And when you asked her if it concerned her that Oliver wasn't wearing his mask, and she said yes. It also disappeared when she said Oliver had complained of feeling off the night before, and she was worried about him."

"Interesting," Roberta said again. She thought a moment and then looked over at Duncan. "What's your take on all this?"

He gave an equivocal shrug. "Based on what Mack has just said, it sounds like Caroline has something to hide. We just need to figure out what it is."

Roberta's face furrowed in thought for a moment, and I caught her staring at me, pondering. "If Oliver Knutson didn't die of natural causes, and there's no evidence of any obvious physical injuries, what's our cause of death?"

"Poison?" Gregory suggested.

Roberta nodded slowly, still deep in thought. "If that's the case, the most likely source would be the coffee Caroline said she brought to Oliver. But according to her, he didn't drink any of it. She said he was cold and dead when she brought it into the room. And the cup we collected *was* full."

"If he drank any of it, it should be present in his stomach contents," Duncan said. "I suggest you get the ME to analyze those contents carefully, and search for other, less common poisons."

Roberta's expression brightened some. "Good point. I'll give him a call now." She took out her phone and prepared to dial but hesitated, looking over at me. "It can take a while to get results from a test like that, and I feel like we've lost a lot of valuable time already. Tell me something, Ms. Dalton. Does your synesthesia help you identify odors and smells?"

"It does."

"So . . . would you be able to identify the presence of something other than coffee in those stomach contents if you had a chance to . . . smell it?"

The mere suggestion made my stomach roil.

Duncan frowned at Roberta. "That's going a bit above and beyond," he said, making a face.

I thought about what Roberta was suggesting. I knew my synesthesia would react in a predictable manner to the smell of coffee, but how would the acids of the stomach affect that? And how would I know if any additional reactions to the smell were due to a foreign substance, or the stomach acid?

"I can't be sure it would work," I told her. "I'd have to experiment a little with a baseline."

"What sort of baseline?" Roberta asked.

I explained to her how my synesthesia worked, and how I might be able to identify the presence of coffee based on the reaction I had to the smell of the contents of the stomach. "But the addition of stomach acids complicates things a little. I own a bar, so I've been exposed to vomit in the past," I said with a grimace. "But each exposure had its own unique synesthetic reaction, presumably based on the contents of the stomach at the time. I might be able to identify a unique and different synesthetic reaction to Oliver's stomach contents, but who's to say if it would be related to the presence of a foreign substance in the stomach?" I gave Roberta an apologetic look and shrugged.

"Correct me if I'm wrong," I went on, "but based on what I've learned working with Duncan, it's the testing for the various foreign substances, like poisons, that will take time. The ME should be able to identify the presence of coffee in the stomach fairly quickly, right?"

"Yes," Roberta said.

"So, if you found coffee in his stomach, it would disprove part of Caroline's story. According to her, Oliver was already dead when she brought the coffee in to him. So the presence of coffee by itself would be meaningful, right?"

"Yes," Roberta said again.

"So test for the coffee, and if it's present, I'll do what I can to try to determine if there's anything else present."

"Seems reasonable," Roberta said.

"I have a couple of other questions, if you don't mind," I said. Roberta shrugged. "What do you have as the time of death for Oliver?"

"According to the ME, he'd been dead about four hours when we found him."

"And do you know whether or not the coffee was still warm when the police arrived? Or perhaps it was still warm when you arrived?"

Roberta cocked her head to the side and grinned at me. "As a matter of fact, I do remember," she said. "The mug was still warm when I touched it, and Oliver definitely wasn't. So it's unlikely the coffee had anything to do with it, at least the particular coffee that was in the mug we collected."

"I think that gets me off the hook," I said with a smile.

"Not entirely," Roberta said with a sly look. "I might still ask you to sniff at some stomach contents. It just depends on what we find. I'll let you know."

On that rather dour note, Duncan and I left the station and headed back to my bar.

Chapter 18

"I think it's fair to say you won Bobby over," Duncan said during our ride back.

"I'm not sure that's a good thing. Sniffing vomit isn't what I had in mind when I agreed to this consulting arrangement." He chuckled. "Do you think Caroline had something to do with Oliver's death?" I asked him.

He thought a moment before answering me. "My gut says yes. It seems clear to me that there was little romance left in their relationship, and all that money has to be a powerful motive. What do you think?"

"I think she's definitely hiding something. I should've had Roberta ask Caroline outright if she killed her husband. If she said no and I determined she was lying, it wouldn't be admissible in court, but at least it would have given us a guideline for whether to keep digging. Although, if that guilt trip of hers about nagging Oliver more about his health was genuine, she might feel like she did kill him in a way, even if she didn't commit murder. And that could make her answer to the question ring false."

Duncan's phone rang, putting an end to our speculations for the moment. I listened to his end of the conversation, which consisted of little more than a few grunts of acknowledgment and a couple of single-word responses. I tried to hear what was being said on the other end, but there was too much ambient noise in the car, and Duncan had the phone up tight to his ear. Fortunately, I didn't have to wait long.

"We may have a new lead in the Sheldon Janssen case," he said once he disconnected the call. "A more thorough canvass of the neighbors found someone who saw a woman knocking on Janssen's door the day before he was killed."

"The one in the picture maybe?" I posed hopefully. "A girlfriend perhaps?"

"Maybe," Duncan said, though the look on his face suggested otherwise. "Except according to the neighbor, Janssen wasn't home at the time. You'd think if it was a girlfriend, she would know that, what with cell phones and texting and all."

"Was this neighbor able to provide any sort of description?"

"Yeah, but I don't know how useful it will be. The neighbor is a man, and he didn't notice the same sorts of attributes a woman might." Duncan shot me a sidelong look—eyebrows raised—that told me what sort of attributes the man had focused on. "He said the woman looked to be in her thirties, maybe early forties, with curly, shoulder-length brown hair. She was too far away for him to be able to tell what color her eyes were, but he said she was a larger woman and that her chest appeared impressively big beneath a plain, tan wool coat."

"Well, other than the description of her chest, it's a rather ordinary description that could fit hundreds of women in the city," I said. "But who knows? His observation about the chest might prove helpful."

We arrived at the bar, and Duncan found a parking

spot half a block away. Once we were inside, we went straight to my office. Duncan said he needed to make some phone calls, and I told him he could use the office to do so. I shrugged out of my coat and headed out to the main part of the bar to give Duncan some privacy.

I don't open my bar until five on Sundays, so we had the place to ourselves. For the past couple of weeks, the O'Reillys had been my Sunday company, but they had taken the day off and gone sightseeing, so even they weren't around. I did some prep work for the opening later by stocking beer, cutting up fruit for garnishes, replacing a near empty soda canister in the basement, and washing up some glasses. My stomach growled, and I hoped Duncan would finish up with his calls soon so I could fix the two of us something to eat for lunch. It was after one, and I hadn't eaten breakfast. I decided if he took much longer, I was going to eat without him.

Fortunately, he came out a few minutes later. He looked excited and eager to share news with me, but before he could get a single word out, I told him, "Food is the priority at the moment. I have to eat now or I'm going to pass out from hunger. Do you want something?"

He smiled and said, "Surprise me."

I was too hungry to play games, so I took him at his word and disappeared into the kitchen, deciding then and there that he was getting the same thing I was going to eat: a cheeseburger and fries. I'd already turned on the fryers in anticipation, so it only took me ten minutes to fix us up two plates. If it wasn't for Duncan's preference for well-done meat, I could have had it ready in seven. After fixing up both plates with lettuce, tomato, some ketchup for Duncan and some herbed mayo for me, I carried them out to the main area, where I found Duncan seated at one of the tables close to the bar. He had a soft drink in front of him already, so after setting down our plates, I fixed myself a cup of coffee and joined him.

"Okay," I said, picking up my burger. "You can talk now." I sank in my teeth and bit off a huge chunk of cheeseburger, savoring the flavors and all the synesthetic responses that came with them.

Duncan watched me chew for a moment, an amused expression on his face, before he spoke. "I tracked down this Norman Chandler fellow Mal mentioned, the one who's good friends with Janssen. I called him, and he's going to come down to the station to talk with me at three this afternoon."

"The station?" I said, speaking rudely with a mouth half full of burger that I struggled to swallow. "Why there?"

"I want whatever he has to say to be on the record. If he's that close to our victim, he has the potential for being a suspect."

"You want me to go with you?" I mumbled, holding a hand in front of my mouth because I had just stuffed a couple of fries in there.

"Of course. And because you're an official consultant now, I think I'm going to have you sit in the interview room with me rather than observe from outside."

I made no comment to this, though I conceded the idea to him with a nod and a shrug.

"I'm going to have a chat with Klein, too," Duncan went on, nibbling at his fries.

"Are you going to ask him about Mal?"

Duncan shook his head without hesitation, but he didn't answer right away because he'd just taken a big bite of his burger. "No, I don't want Klein to think we know anything about Mal. He won't be surprised by me wanting to talk to him, given that Janssen was his right-hand man and someone killed him. But if there is a connection in Klein's mind between Janssen's death and Mal, I want him to tell me, not the other way around. If there is even a remote chance Mal's true identity hasn't been discovered, I don't want to blow the case. Mal may not be able to go back there, but that doesn't mean they can't put another undercover cop in there in his place."

"Do you know yet when you're going to talk to Klein?" I asked him.

"I called him but got his voice mail. I left a message, explaining who I was and that I needed to speak with him regarding Janssen, and to call me back as soon as possible. Hopefully, he'll call back today, but if not, I'm sure we'll hook up tomorrow sometime. I want to go to him rather than have him come in to the station. I want to see him in his element, in this mobile office he has. Maybe we can get a glimpse at these books Mal was describing."

"And am I going along for that one, too?"

"Of course," Duncan said, winking at me.

"Any chance I can go see Felicity again sometime soon?"

Duncan frowned, and I thought he was going to tell me no, but it turned out to be different news. "I don't see why not," he said. "But there's something you should know. That third fingerprint we found on the gun was definitely hers."

I frowned at this. "So she touched it, or maybe she picked it up when she found her father. It doesn't mean she shot him."

"True," Duncan admitted. "I found out a few other things, too. I had some of my guys dig into the life of

Janssen's wife, Hope, to see what they could find. They found a death certificate from three months ago that says she died from a drug overdose, so that part is verified. But there wasn't a lot else. Hope lived very much off the grid. She and Sheldon split when Felicity was three, though they never actually divorced. Sheldon paid her child support for the next five years. When the kid was four, she was placed in an institution by her mother."

"Wait," I said around a french fry. "Why did Sheldon pay Hope child support all those years if Felicity was placed in an institution?"

"Hope didn't tell Sheldon that. She let him think Felicity was living with her all that time, and she kept the child support money for herself."

"That's cold," I said. "Didn't she have to pay for Felicity's care?"

"Ah, there's the rub," Duncan said, in a tone that let me know something juicy was about to follow. "Hope took Felicity to an out-of-state residential mental health facility in Illinois and said she was scoping the place out for a possible admission there. Then Hope disappeared, leaving Felicity behind. She used a false name for both Felicity and herself, so no one knew who Felicity really was. Hope told them the kid's name was Jean, which happens to be Felicity's middle name, so the place called her Jean Doe. They couldn't just toss her out at that point, and efforts to find Hope were unsuccessful, so the kid became a ward of the court and stayed there, her care being provided at the taxpayers' expense."

"So how did Sheldon find her?"

"We found some payments in Sheldon's files from a year ago that were for a private investigator. A couple of my guys talked to that PI this morning and learned Sheldon had hired him to see if he could find out how

Felicity had died, and where her grave was, so he could visit it. According to the PI, Sheldon had just been told by Hope that Felicity had died, and Sheldon, knowing Hope had a history of drug abuse, was suspicious about the circumstances. Coincidentally, just before Hope told him Felicity had died, Sheldon had written a letter to her that he sent with one of his child support payments, saying that he wanted to see Felicity, and maybe even talk about setting up some sort of shared custody."

"Why? I wonder."

Duncan shrugged. "Maybe his conscience was getting to him. Maybe it was some kind of midlife-crisis thing. Or maybe he was trying to mitigate his child support payments. Who knows?

"Anyway, Hope didn't want to lose out on the child support payments, but clearly, she couldn't have Sheldon asking too many questions or trying to visit his daughter, because then he'd discover the truth. So she accepted she was going to have to give up on the child support money and came up with the death story, thinking that would make Sheldon go away."

"So how did Sheldon find his daughter?"

"The PI tailed Hope, saw she was homeless, which explained why Sheldon was mailing his payments to one of those mailbox stores, and that she was heavily into the drug scene. He found her high as a kite one night, pretended to be high himself, and started questioning her. She admitted the whole story to him. She told him that Felicity was still alive, and what facility she was in. Once the PI took the information back to Sheldon, he found Felicity and went about establishing his paternity through DNA testing. Then he simply checked her out of the place. I'm guessing he built that hidey-hole before he took her out of the facility so it would be ready when he brought her home. And apparently, he didn't tell anyone about her."

"Odd," I said, wiping my mouth with a napkin. "I wonder why he felt the need to have her living with him when he didn't have anyone to care for her while he was gone, and didn't try to get her into any programs."

Duncan shrugged. "It *is* a bit puzzling."

A terrible thought came to me then. "When the doctor examined her, was there any evidence of sexual assault?" I asked.

"No, thank goodness," Duncan said. "That was one of the first things I thought of, that Janssen was abusing the child in some way. But there was no evidence of that, or any other abuse for that matter. The kid appears well nourished, she doesn't have any unexplained or unusual marks, injuries, or bruises, and while it's impossible to tell if she's suffered any sort of emotional or mental abuse, given her condition, she doesn't strike me as someone who's been severely traumatized in any way. And since there are DNA records proving Sheldon is her father, we know Felicity is who we think she is. Just to be sure, we emailed a picture of her to the facility, and they confirmed it's her. Granted, Sheldon's means of caring for her were less than ideal, but it doesn't appear to have caused the kid any harm."

I had to agree with his assessment of the situation. At first blush, the whole hidey-hole business had seemed like some form of abuse, or captivity at the very least, but in the end, it had turned out to be a comforting factor for Felicity.

Duncan finished off his burger and pushed his empty plate away. "We need to get going," he said, glancing at his watch. "Our Mr. Chandler will be at the station in twenty."

I popped my last fry into my mouth and gathered

up our plates, carrying them into the kitchen. Then I went to my office to get my coat.

The sky outside was leaden and heavy, threatening a winter storm. I hunched down inside my coat and hoped Duncan's car heater would warm up fast. It reached a comfortable level about the same time we reached the station, and it was all I could do to coax myself out of the car and into the frigid world outside. That cold seemed so ominous.

Chapter 19

I'd been to Duncan's station before to observe suspect interviews, but on the other occasions I'd stayed inside an observation room that let me see and listen in to the interrogation without the room's occupants being the wiser. This time, things would be more nerve-racking because I would be in the room with the suspect, though I reassured myself some by remembering Chandler wasn't a suspect at this point. He was what Duncan and the other cops often referred to as a *person of interest*.

"Want a cup of coffee or some water to take into the room with you?" Duncan asked me as I shucked my coat and handed it to him so he could hang it on a hook in the station break room.

"I've heard about the coffee you have here and I think I'll pass," I said sardonically.

"Wise choice. Water? It's bottled, so we haven't had a chance to ruin it."

"Sure. Thanks."

Duncan bought two bottles of water from a vending machine, handed me one of them, and then led the way to the interview room. "You can have a seat here," he said, pointing to a chair in one corner of the room. There was a table with three other chairs positioned around it, and I knew from my past observations that Mr. Chandler would be directed to the one at the end farthest from the door. That would put him opposite me, with a healthy distance between us and the door nearest to me, which helped my rattled nerves a bit.

"I need to go set up some things to make sure this is recorded," he told me. "Make yourself comfortable and I'll be right back."

I settled into the chair, which was clearly not designed for comfort—I wondered if this was intentional—and sat with my water bottle between my legs and my hands primly folded in my lap. The walls in the room were bare, and the table and chairs were plain wood, scarred in places, and cheap in design. From a synesthetic point of view, it was a calming place. There was no sound other than that of my breathing, little visual stimulation, and no overwhelming smells for me to pick up. Then I remembered Duncan was very likely watching me at this very moment from the observation room. I looked at the mirrored window and gave a tentative smile. Not knowing who was back there watching me didn't do much to further settle my jangling nerves.

Fortunately, I didn't have to wait long. Minutes after he left, Duncan returned. I felt relief at his presence until I realized Norman Chandler was right behind him, or at least some man I assumed was Norman Chandler. My brain barely had time to register the incongruence of Duncan letting a potential suspect walk behind him when I saw there was a third person: Chief Holland.

The presence of the chief unsettled me even more. I shot Duncan a look, but he ignored me.

The chief gave me a cursory nod and a smile. "Ms. Dalton," he said. He then summarily dismissed me, shifting his attention to Norman Chandler, so I did the same.

Chandler's face was leathery and weathered, befitting someone who had spent a lot of time working outdoors in all seasons. His build was lean and sinewy; his hands looked like thick slabs of meat and his fingers bore the many scars of his work. His eyes were a pale blue—almost watery—and his nose bore a roadmap of superficial and burst blood vessels that I had seen hundreds of times in people who worshipped alcohol a little too much and a little too often. As he walked past me, I caught a whiff of him and was surprised not to smell any alcohol. But there was a lingering scent of old sweat that emanated from his blue jeans and his wool winter jacket, which looked like it had seen better years. Stains blotted the front of it, there was a button missing from both the top and the bottom, and the material looked threadbare. His feet were clad in work boots that were creased and discolored, and the soles appeared to be unevenly worn. On his head was a knit cap, dirty-blond hair escaping from the sides and back.

Duncan directed Chandler to the seat at the far end of the table, and he walked over and plopped down like someone who was exhausted and could barely stand. Duncan took the seat closest to him, while the chief took the remaining chair at the opposite end of the table, close to me.

Before starting any questioning, Duncan pulled a small notebook from his shirt pocket, opened it, and flipped to a page. He then stated the date, the time, the people present, and the fact that we were talking with Mr. Chandler regarding the Sheldon Janssen homicide case. When he was done with that, he shifted his gaze to Chandler and informed him that our talk was being recorded. He did not recite the Miranda to him. Chandler said nothing, did nothing in response to all this.

"Mr. Chandler, thank you again for coming down here to talk with us," Duncan went on. "As I explained to you on the phone, one of your coworkers and someone I've been told was a personal friend of yours, Sheldon Janssen, was found murdered on Friday. We're trying to establish some background and history on the man in hopes of getting a better idea about why someone would want to kill him."

Chandler eyed Duncan with casual indifference. If he was nervous, it didn't show. "Damned shame, what happened to him," he mumbled. His voice was gravelly, and it tasted like bland barbecue sauce. "Hope you catch the bastard what did it."

Duncan made some brief introductions, introducing the chief with the caveat that he was Duncan's boss and there to observe him in action, and introducing me as Ms. Dalton and stating I was his assistant. Chandler barely spared the chief or me a glance.

"I would like to ask you some questions about Mr. Janssen," Duncan went on once the introductions were done, "starting with how long you've known him."

Chandler narrowed his eyes and glanced at the ceiling for a moment. "About six years, maybe seven." He sniffed, swiped at his nose with the back of his hand, and shrugged. "Met him when I started on with Klein."

"Did the two of you work together often?" Duncan asked.

"Pretty much every day the place had work," Chandler said. He undid the remaining buttons on his coat but didn't take it off.

"And did the two of you become friends right away?"

"I s'pose," Chandler said, sticking out his lower lip.

His remaining teeth—many of them were missing—were stained brown, and I suspected he was a user of chew. This supposition was supported by the round shape worn into the pocket of his shirt, which was the same size and shape as a can of chewing tobacco, a threadbare ring of white on the otherwise blue shirt.

"Did the two of you do things together outside of work?" Duncan asked.

"Sometimes. Wasn't always just us, though. The whole crew would go out after work for drinks from time to time."

"Did you and Mr. Janssen go out for drinks without the rest of the crew?"

Chandler narrowed his eyes at Duncan. "You suggestin' sump'in?" he said in a suspicious tone. "We wasn't secret lovers or nothing like that. I ain't no pervert."

Duncan smiled and shook his head. "No, sir," he said. "I'm just trying to get a feel for how well you knew Mr. Janssen."

"We was friends. That's all."

"Okay. Did Mr. Janssen talk to you about his private life at all?"

"Yeah, some."

"What about his family? Did he talk about them at all?"

Chandler shifted in his chair. I didn't need my synesthesia to tell me he was starting to feel a bit anxious. "He wasn't close with his family," he said, looking away. "Said they all lived back in New York and they didn't talk much."

"How about his wife, his ex-wife?" Duncan asked.

Chandler looked at Duncan briefly, then away again.

"Did he ever talk about her?" Duncan pushed.

"Mighta mentioned her once or twice," Chandler said. He looked back at Duncan, his steely reserve back in place. "But she's dead, so I'm pretty sure she didn't kill Sheldon."

"Did his wife have any family in the area?"

"How the hell would I know that?" Chandler said, punctuating the question with a little *harrumph*.

"I thought perhaps Sheldon might have mentioned them," Duncan said, and I noticed he had switched from the more formal "Mr. Janssen" to the use of his first name.

Chandler frowned and reached up to scratch his head, and when he was done, the knit cap was tilted sideways. "Now that you mention it, he did say sump'in one time about a sista who lived in Waukesha. Name was something weird, one of those hippie-dippie names parents liked to use back in the sixties, ya know? Freedom or Happy or some crap like that."

Duncan scribbled something in his notebook. I wondered if he did it out of habit, because all this was being recorded, or if he did it to create a pause of uncomfortable silence to see if Chandler offered up anything more. If it was the latter, it worked.

Chandler let out a long, deep sigh and leaned forward, elbows on knees. "I know you know about the kid 'cause she ain't there no more."

This surprised me, and judging from the look on Duncan's face, it surprised him, too. "What kid?" Duncan asked after a few seconds of stunned silence.

"Sheldon's daughter," Chandler said with huge impatience, as if Duncan had asked the dumbest question possible. "I know she ain't there 'cause I checked to make sure she's okay. And she was gone."

"What do you mean, you checked?" Duncan asked, frowning.

"I went by Sheldon's place last night and let myself in. He gave me a key a long time ago. Said if anything ever happened to him, I was s'posed to take care of his girl."

"You went into Sheldon's house last night?" Duncan asked, his irritation obvious both in his tone and his rapidly reddening face. He didn't give Chandler time to answer. "Didn't you see those big yellow tapes on the door that said not to enter? His house is a crime scene. Do you have any idea what you've done?"

Duncan's high ire startled Chandler. The man was leaning as far back into his chair as he could go, and if he could have melted into it, I think he would have. He stared at Duncan with wide eyes, one arm folded over his chest, the fist on that arm propping the elbow of his other arm, the hand of which was clamped over his mouth, as if he was trying to keep any more damaging information from escaping. I was sure the chief's presence during this revelation didn't help Duncan's mood any.

Duncan paused, sputtering for a few seconds. Then he closed his eyes and took a few more seconds to gather himself.

"Let's all take a breath, shall we?" Chief Holland said in a calm voice. "Mr. Chandler, what time last night did you go to Mr. Janssen's house?"

Chandler eyed the chief warily, and appeared to be debating whether it was safe for him to answer. Apparently, he decided it was. "Round about nine or so, I think." He hesitated, his eyes darting from the chief to Duncan and back to the chief. "I didn't damage your tape or nothin'," he said. "I used my key, unlocked the door, and stepped between the strips."

I covered my mouth with my hand because I couldn't help but smile at Chandler's naïveté. He thought it was the integrity of the tape that had Duncan upset.

"And what did you do once you were inside the house?" the chief asked.

"I called out for the girl, and then checked to see if she was in her special place."

"You knew about the hiding place?" Duncan asked, resuming control.

Chandler snorted back a laugh. "Of course I knew about it. I helped Sheldon build it."

Duncan, and the chief for that matter, seemed momentarily stymied. Finally, Duncan asked, "When was the last time you saw Sheldon?"

Chandler squinted at the ceiling. "Day before he was killed," he said. "At work."

"Did Sheldon indicate to you that he was worried about anything? Or afraid of anything?"

Chandler chuckled. "He was afraid of the boss. We all of us are. Klein can be a mean bastard."

"Did he say he was afraid of Klein the last time you saw him?"

"Yup, sure did. Said he knew Klein was gonna be real ticked off because of some on-the-job shenanigans." Chandler pronounced the word like it was gender specific: she-nanigans.

"What sort of shenanigans?" Duncan asked. He leaned a little closer, and I knew he was wondering if this might have something to do with Mal.

"Don't know for sure," Chandler said with a shrug. He explored the inside of one cheek with his tongue. "Said something about a spy, but that didn't make no sense to me," he concluded.

"Did Sheldon say who he thought the spy was?" Duncan asked.

"Nah, he kept that kind of stuff private. I know he

did other things for Klein. Side jobs, ya know? But he never talked about it."

"Do you have any ideas about who the spy might be?" Duncan asked.

Chandler squinted at the ceiling again, appearing deep in thought. After a moment, he looked at Duncan and said, "There's this one guy, kind of new to us. He asks a lot of questions and takes a lot of pictures with his phone. And he and Klein always seem to be butting heads, ya know? And he didn't show up for work on Friday."

"What is this person's name?" Duncan asked.

Chandler shook his head and chuckled. "It's Malachi O'Reilly. That's rich, ain't it? He's got one of those Israeli first names, but his last name is as Irish as they come."

"Mr. Chandler, you can't go back inside Sheldon's house. In fact, I'm going to ask you to turn over the key you have."

Chandler shrugged at this, fished in one of his pants pockets, and pulled out a key ring. He found the key in question, removed it from the ring, and handed it to Duncan. "The kid . . . she's okay?" he said.

"She is," Duncan said.

"What's going to happen to her?"

"We don't know yet," Duncan said. "She's with a family right now who is well equipped to take care of her and her special needs. She's safe."

Chandler nodded, his brow furrowed. He seemed genuinely concerned about Felicity, and despite his somewhat uncouth appearance, demeanor, and speech, I felt a twinge of affection for him and his devotion to the child.

"You mentioned Sheldon did some side jobs for

Mr. Klein," Duncan went on, changing the subject. "What sort of jobs were they?"

"I don't know for sure," Chandler said, wiping his nose on his sleeve. "He paid a lot of visits to people, and he always seemed to have packages to deliver."

"What kinds of packages?"

Chandler shrugged. "Boxes, bags . . . who knows what was in 'em. I know there was money in one of the boxes he had one time because I saw it. But that was the only one I saw."

Duncan digested this for a few seconds, and I took advantage of the moment. "Mr. Chandler, does the term *little peach* mean anything to you?"

"I guess. Shelly sometimes referred to the kid as his little peach. He said his wife, or ex-wife rather, started using it, and it stuck."

"Did you kill Sheldon Janssen?" I asked.

Everyone in the room appeared surprised by my question, or perhaps the sudden segue. All three men looked at me, their expressions equally bemused.

"Hell no," Chandler said after a slight hesitation.

The taste of his voice remained unchanged, and because he was cooperating, I decided to go a step further. "Is there anyone you know of who would have wanted Sheldon Janssen dead?"

Chandler gave the question some serious thought. "Well," he said finally, letting out a weighty sigh, "Mr. Klein is a scary dude. I don't know what kind of stuff he and Shelly did together, but I got the sense from Shelly that it wasn't strictly legal at times." He paused, winced, and eyed Duncan and the chief to see if they had reacted to this revelation. When they didn't, he continued. "I s'pose Shelly might a gone and got himself into a sitch-ee-a-shun"—Chandler enunciated the syllables with great care and emphasis—"that got him in trouble with the wrong kind of people, ya know? Or maybe he just got on the wrong side of Klein."

Duncan looked over at me, eyebrows raised in question. I shook my head, and Duncan turned back to Chandler and said, "Okay, sir, you are free to go. Thanks for talking to us."

Chandler looked a little surprised, but after a moment's hesitation where he seemed to be waiting for someone to say *just kidding* or something like that, he got out of his seat and headed for the door. As he opened the door, he looked over at me and said, "You should prolly look purdy close at that O'Reilly guy, too. There's sump'in shifty about that man."

And with that, he left.

Chapter 20

The three of us sat there in silence after Chandler left the interview room. A good minute passed before anyone moved or said anything. It was Chief Holland who finally broke the silence.

"Ms. Dalton, I assume you asked Mr. Chandler if he killed this Janssen fellow so you could see if he was lying?"

I nodded.

"And?"

"And he didn't kill the guy. What's more, he believes either Klein or this O'Reilly guy might have done it." I saw Duncan give me a sharp look. "Of course, Mr. Chandler's beliefs aren't facts, so the only thing I can tell you for sure is that he didn't do it and he genuinely cares about Janssen's daughter."

The chief switched his attention to Duncan. "Who is this O'Reilly character? Is that the person whose fingerprints were found on the gun?"

Duncan nodded. "It is, but I'm certain he didn't do it."

Chief Holland gave him a quizzical look. "How so?"

Duncan hesitated just long enough to give away the

fact that he was hiding something. "Because I found him, and asked him with Mack here as my lie detector," he said, apparently deciding to come clean. He paused, and we both waited to see if Holland would accept this as proof of innocence.

"You're sure?" Holland asked me, and I nodded. "Then I'm okay with that. How does he figure into this? And why were his prints on the gun?"

"He's a cop," Duncan said. "He's been working undercover at one of Klein's sites. And he admits to struggling with Janssen when a gun was pulled on him, explaining how his prints ended up on it."

"I see," Holland said, looking worried. "Do you think he's on the take or something? Because we've suspected Klein of money laundering, possibly even drug smuggling, for a while now."

Duncan shook his head. "O'Reilly is a personal friend of mine, and of Mack's, too."

Holland gave Duncan a look of disapproval. "So your level of objectivity with regard to him is basically none?" he said, his voice rife with skepticism.

"You're going to have to trust me on this one, Chief," Duncan said.

"And me," I threw out for good measure. "Mal O'Reilly did not kill Sheldon Janssen."

Holland looked less than convinced. "So where is he? Why isn't he assisting with the investigation?"

"He is," Duncan said. "But he's doing it on the sly. He's been trying to get a handle on just what Klein's other activities are. I doubt he's going to be able to continue that assignment, particularly if he's persona non grata with Klein at this point. But while he may not be in Klein's favor, I don't know if his cover is blown. And until we can figure that out, we're trying to keep a low profile with that part of the investigation, in case his superiors want to try to put another undercover person in there. O'Reilly did come across some books Klein had in his office that might be valuable as evidence."

Holland didn't look pleased with this explanation, but he didn't question it any further. Instead, he pushed back his chair, stood, and narrowed his eyes on me for a second. Then, without another word, he left the room.

"We really need to talk to this Klein fellow," I said. Duncan shot me an amused look. "What?" I said, feeling annoyed at being the apparent butt of a joke I didn't get.

"You sound like one of us. Like a cop."

"Well, in this consulting role, I sort of am one of you, aren't I?"

"I suppose you are."

"But I'm also the owner of a bar, and I should really get back to it." I glanced at my watch. "I imagine any other inquiries will have to wait until tomorrow?"

Duncan's phone rang before he could answer me. "It's the Syracuse cops who did the Janssen family notification," he said. Then he tapped the screen of the phone, put it to his ear, and said, "This is Detective Albright."

Once again, I tried to listen in. But I was unable to hear the other end of the conversation and Duncan's only comments were a couple of *uh-huh*s, a *thank you*, and then an intriguing, *really?* After listening for a full minute or more, he finally said, "That's interesting." Another pause and then, "I don't know, but I hope to find out." He ended the call with another thanks to whoever was on the other end and closed with, "I will."

I was literally on the edge of my seat, waiting for him to explain.

"Well, that's interesting," he said. "Sheldon Janssen's family said they haven't heard from him in years."

I shrugged. "He was estranged, perhaps?"

"It would seem so. His family said they had no idea he was ever married, or that he had a child."

"That's odd. Felicity is what, eight or nine? Even if he hadn't spoken to his family in two or three years, you would have thought he'd have mentioned a child somewhere along the line."

"Apparently not."

"Any idea how Janssen ended up out in Milwaukee?"

"He attended the U of W here. Moved out here when he was a young man, and apparently never went back or had any further contact with his family."

"Interesting," I repeated, thinking. "What about Hope? I know she's dead, but Chandler said something about a sister. Have you found any family for her out this way?"

"We're working on it," Duncan said.

Having exhausted our contemporaneous analysis of the case for the moment, Duncan drove us back to the bar. It had started snowing, big, fat, fluffy flakes that drifted lazily from the sky. When we arrived at the bar, Duncan asked if he could use my office and my computer for a while. "If I can check on a few things from here, I can stay and spend the night," he said with a salacious wink.

I was more than happy to accommodate his request and, after asking him if he wanted something to drink, and offering to have one of my waitresses bring it to him in the office, I left him to his work while I made my rounds of the bar.

The place was busy for a Sunday evening, but as usual, my staff had things well under control. After checking in with Billy and Teddy Bear behind the bar, and asking Missy if she and Linda were managing okay, I poked my head into the kitchen to make sure things were going well there, too, and to order some coffee for me and Duncan. With that done, I headed upstairs to the Capone Club room.

The gas fireplace was turned on its highest setting, and the room both looked and felt warm and inviting. Through the window at the far end of the room I could see the snow falling, heavier now, though the flakes were still fat and fluffy. This room was by far my favorite part of my new section remodel, so much so that I had been considering turning my dad's office in the apartment upstairs into a similar type of room.

Nearly all the chairs were filled, and as I scanned the faces, I saw most of the usual suspects were present: Joe, Frank, and Cora, of course, along with Carter, Holly, Tad, Alicia, Sonja, and Stephen. Greg Nash, our resident real estate agent, was also there. He had just returned from a two-week trip to the Caribbean, and he looked refreshed and tanned. He had decided to take a vacation back when I formulated my New Year's Eve plan to out the letter writer and her cohort. Greg had had a scary experience around that time regarding the showing of a high-end home where no one showed up and he sensed something wasn't right. It was later that same day I made the revelation to the Capone Club members about the letter writer, something I had kept secret up until then. When Greg learned the details of the deadly history I'd been keeping from him and the others, he'd decided departure was the better part of valor, at least until the letter-writer thing was resolved. I wasn't sure he'd come back to the Capone Club at all after that, so I was happy to see he had returned to the fold.

Everyone looked happy and relaxed, and I was

greeted with the usual chorus of hellos as I settled into one of the few empty seats. "What are you guys talking about?" I asked.

"Sonja brought up the situation with her client whose husband died yesterday," Holly said. "We were discussing how peculiar the woman's behavior was at the salon, and that segued into unusual grief reactions, and how unreliable such things can be when you're trying to determine guilt."

"Well, I have an interesting update," I said with a knowing smile.

"Do tell," Cora said.

"Okay, but this information doesn't leave this room, agreed?" Everyone nodded. "The first leak that comes from here will end my ability to share any information with you guys about the cases I'm working with the police department."

"We all understand that," Carter said. "I think everyone here agreed to the background checks and signed the nondisclosure agreements the police department gave us."

"Good," I said. "So . . . it seems Sonja's instincts may have been spot-on. We don't know for sure if the woman killed her husband, but there are definite questions surrounding his death, and it wasn't as straightforward as it initially seemed."

"Are you saying he didn't die of a heart attack?" Sonja asked.

"He did not," I said.

This information elicited a self-satisfied smile from Sonja. "I knew it," she said. "Did you do your lie-detector thing and ask her if she killed him?"

"I didn't get a chance," I said. "She lawyered up pretty fast, and while she agreed to answer some questions, the lawyer convinced her to stop before too long."

"Did you get any kind of synesthetic reaction to the scene or anything else?" Cora asked.

"Not really," I said, recalling the weird sensation I'd felt when I looked at the ceiling of the bedroom where Knutson had died. "Nothing that made any sense to me anyway." I then explained to them how I'd felt light-headed, or rather light-bodied, in the bedroom. Cora searched her database of my reactions and informed me what I already knew. "That's not one we have on file," she said.

"So what's the working theory regarding the husband's death?" Carter asked, shifting the subject.

"It's a bit of a puzzle," I admitted. "There were no signs of a struggle, no evidence of any physical harm, but also relatively clean arteries in his heart, according to the medical examiner. Given that the man was overweight and smoked, the assumption of a heart attack made sense. Now we're looking more toward the possibility of him being sedated, poisoned, and/or suffocated. He used one of those breathing machines—"

"A CPAP machine?" Greg asked.

I nodded. "According to his wife, he wasn't wearing it when she found him yesterday morning, so there's a possibility he simply suffocated in his sleep from his sleep apnea. But it doesn't usually happen without signs of some sort of struggle. The lack of oxygen to the brain tends to trigger enough panic to awaken someone. And assuming we can believe what his wife said, Oliver Knutson was found lying peacefully on his back with the covers in place."

"Interesting," Carter said.

I looked over at Clay. "Have you come up with anything new on Oliver Knutson or his wife?"

"Nothing official, but I did dig up some gossip. Rumor has it Knutson and his first wife, Anne, were separated for a year and then had an amicable divorce four years ago, which was somewhat surprising, given all the money at stake. Word is Oliver didn't ask for any money from Anne; he simply wanted to keep his business for himself, and they split the marital assets down the middle."

"When did wife number two come into the picture?" I asked.

"I'm not sure," Clay said.

"I can answer that one," Sonja offered. "Assuming what Caroline has told me at the salon over the years is true, Oliver hired her five years ago to help with the event planning end of the business. Caroline was already doing something similar on her own, but she was struggling to make ends meet because of competition—ironically, from Oliver himself—and because she was a one-woman show who often overestimated her own abilities. Oliver had seen her work and liked what she did. Caroline said he told her she had a good eye for color and structure and a good head for details. Oliver really liked some of her designs and plans, and that was not his forte. So he hit on the idea of bringing her into his company, thereby eliminating some of his competition and helping Caroline. Of course, I'm sure the fact that he was separated from his wife at the time, and Caroline was an attractive single woman who was fifteen years younger than him and flirtatious, had something to do with it. Anyway, one thing led to another, and as soon as Oliver's divorce was final, he and Caroline got married."

"So is she an employee of the company or a partner?" I asked.

"Good question," Carter said.

"And one I can answer," Tad said.

One of the perks of being a trophy husband to one

of the richest women in Milwaukee was that Tad's small accounting business had grown into one of the elite money management firms in the city. All of Suzanne's wealthy friends and compatriots had come to Tad, and he had done well for them. I'd asked him a few days ago if his clientele seemed stable now that Suzanne was no longer in the picture. After all, she was the one who had brought most of his customers to him. But Tad had assured me the business was still going strong, and his successful management of the portfolios that had been entrusted to him ensured he would continue as before.

"As luck would have it, I provided money management services to Oliver Knutson," Tad told the group. "I can tell you that his estate is worth millions, and his wife is a partner in the business. However, the agreement made when she became a partner limits her access to a lot of Oliver's money, money he made before they married." Tad paused a moment and then added, "I'm not privy to any prenuptial agreements. Caroline became a partner before the marriage, and her funds were limited to whatever portion of the business she brought in with her end of things. And, as I understand it, she was primarily in charge of the event planning. The monies from the party supply stores were held by Oliver in separate funds that Caroline didn't have access to."

"I'll have to check with Duncan to see if he can find out what kind of prenup might exist," I said. "I'm sure the detective in charge of the case must have access to that sort of information."

I spent another half hour or so with the group, discussing various aspects of the case, including some potential poisons Caroline might have used. That led to me sharing my discussion with Roberta about smelling the stomach contents of Oliver Knutson.

"That's a pukey job," Cora joked.

"And one I'd rather avoid," I added. "I'm hoping the stomach contents will be negative for any coffee, so it won't be necessary."

On that note, I excused myself from the group and headed back downstairs to my office to see what Duncan was up to. He was on his phone when I entered, seated behind my desk, tapping away on my laptop. I settled on the couch and waited for him to finish, not even bothering to try to hear the other end of the conversation this time.

"That was Mal," he said once he had disconnected the call.

I frowned, wishing I had known that before he hung up. I would have liked to have said hi to him. "Is he doing okay?"

"He is. He says he feels stronger, and his wound is healing. I asked him about this woman who was seen at Sheldon Janssen's place, but he says he doesn't know of anyone fitting that description in Janssen's life. But he did say he didn't think it was a girlfriend, because the only woman Sheldon Janssen ever dated or talked about was a heavyset woman with blond hair. Apparently, he had something of a casual relationship with this woman. No commitments, just the occasional hook up."

"That doesn't mean he wasn't seeing someone else on the side," I pointed out.

"True."

"Have you heard anything back from Roberta on the stomach contents of Oliver Knutson, or the details of the prenup?" I asked him.

"As a matter of fact, I have," he said. "I spoke to her

right before I talked to Mal. The prenup specified that in the event of a divorce, Caroline was only entitled to the funds she brought into the company during the time she worked there. And Bobby found a will."

I could tell from the look on Duncan's face that the will was going to be an interesting piece of this puzzle. "And?" I prompted.

"Oliver Knutson was in the process of changing his will when he died. Bobby—"

"She prefers Roberta," I said.

"Sorry. Habit. Anyway, she found some emails between him and his lawyer specifying the changes he wanted. They had been deleted recently, but the tech guys were able to resurrect them. I would assume the lawyer had copies as well, so deleting them wasn't a smart move. The original will left all Knutson's money and the stores he owned to his offspring, should there be any. There weren't, and in that case, all the money was to go to Caroline. The new will states that all his money and the stores should go to a children's charity and a church."

"Did he sign the new will?" I asked.

Duncan shook his head, giving me what I can only describe as a gotcha smile.

"So Caroline definitely had motive, assuming she knew about the changes he was going to make."

Duncan nodded, and his smile faded.

"Why so glum?" I asked.

"There's no evidence that points to her, at least none that's worth anything," Duncan said. "All we have is supposition. We weren't able to find Caroline's fingerprints on Knutson's computer, and there's no evidence they've found on her computer to indicate she had access to his email account. And we still don't know what killed him."

"What about the stomach contents?"

Duncan frowned, shaking his head. "There was no coffee in his stomach. In fact, there was nothing in his stomach at all except some bile. The ME said he can analyze the liver tissue and look for traces of some poisons there, but according to Bobby, er, Roberta, he didn't sound hopeful."

I made a face that matched Duncan's frown. "So what's next?"

He shrugged. "Roberta thought it might be helpful to chat with some of Knutson's employees, to see if they know anything. She said you and I are welcome to come along."

"When?"

"First thing in the morning."

"Okay, then. After that, do you think I might be able to see Felicity?"

Duncan cocked his head to one side and smiled at me. "That little girl really got to you, didn't she?"

"If by *got to me* you mean I'm interested in seeing that she's properly cared for, then yes."

"You told me you want to have kids of your own," Duncan said, his brown eyes darkened to nearly black. His breathing sped up a notch. "Want to go practice making some?"

"You're putting the cart before the horse here, aren't you?" I teased, my heart starting to pound.

"It's just practice," he countered.

I debated all of a nanosecond. "Let me go see if my staff will close up for me."

"I already talked to Billy, and he said he'd be happy to."

I arched my eyebrows at him. "That's rather presumptuous of you, isn't it?"

He got up from his seat and came around the desk

to me, pulling me up and into his arms. His breath was warm on my face, and he held me so close I could feel his heart pounding in his chest. "I've never met anyone like you, Mack," he said, just above a whisper. "And I can't imagine my life without you in it. I admit I'm a little gun-shy after my experience with my last relationship, but if you can give me a little time, I think you and I have a long future together. That is, if you'll have me."

It was the first time he'd spoken of any sort of commitment, and it literally made my heart skip a beat. "There's a problem," I said, and he stepped back from me, looking both hurt and confused. It probably didn't help that I then laughed at him. "Not a problem with you and the future, silly," I clarified. "A problem with the here and now." His look of confusion deepened. "My apartment has been taken over by the O'Reillys, remember? And our basement bedroom isn't exactly private during the bar's open hours. Anyone could come down there."

His relief was obvious in the smile on his face, the relaxing of his shoulders, and the retaking of the space he had opened between us moments before. "So let's go to my place," he said.

And that's what we did.

Chapter 21

I awoke the next morning alone, temporarily confused as to where I was. Understandable, given that I'd slept in a different bed every night for the past three nights. After a few seconds, I remembered, and then the smell of fresh coffee reached me. I smiled, and let myself luxuriate in the other smells around me before getting out of bed.

It was early for me, only a little past eight, but I felt well rested and relaxed. There was a bathrobe draped over the bottom of the bed and I shrugged into it, smelling Duncan's scent as I wrapped it around me. I shuffled out to the kitchen, where I found Duncan standing before the stove, whipping up some bacon and eggs.

"I hope you don't mind a cholesterol laden breakfast," he said over his shoulder. "Coffee is in the pot over there."

I walked over to where he indicated, found a clean, empty mug in front of the pot, and poured myself a cup. I was resigned to drinking it black, figuring Duncan wouldn't have any of the heavy cream I liked, but I was wrong.

"There's cream in the fridge," he said.

Half an hour later, I was fully awake, fully sated, and ready to tackle the day. "What's on our agenda?" I asked him.

"Do you need to go by the bar this morning?"

I shook my head. "Debra and Pete can handle things. So I'm yours for the time being."

"I like the sound of that," Duncan said with a wink. He drained his coffee cup, got up, and carried it and both of our plates to the sink. "I already showered, so it's all yours," he said. "We'll head out whenever you're ready. Our first visit is going to be with Mr. Klein."

Forty-five minutes later, we arrived at the construction site where Klein's mobile office was located, which was not, Duncan informed me, the place where Mal had been working. We discussed our approach to the man along the way, but it was a brief conversation because the site—one of several Klein was currently managing—wasn't far from Duncan's house. This particular site was a commercial building being put up in an industrial park. The site was half a block long and still in the early stages of construction: three stories high with girders, some flooring, and sheets of plastic covering parts of the interior. Duncan had to park near one end of the building, and we walked along the front of it to get to Klein's mobile office, which had been parked in a small gated lot at the other end of the building. The lot, and much of the street in front of the building, was filled with other vehicles.

Duncan had called ahead, and Klein greeted us at the door and invited us inside. I'm not sure what I expected the mobile office to look like, but I was surprised by how well organized it was. It reminded me of some of those tiny houses I'd seen on the HGTV channel, small monuments to multiuse functions, smart planning, and clever use of space. The trailer itself wasn't very large, yet when we went inside, I didn't feel like the quarters were tight. It was easy to recognize the items Mal had described: the desk, the chairs, and the filing cabinet. I wondered which of the drawers contained the books Mal had mentioned.

Klein himself was a small man—slender but fit-looking, and about five-foot-seven—and that may have contributed to the perception of space inside his office. In direct contrast to his small stature, his personality was large. He greeted us with a big smile, a booming voice, and a vigorous handshake. His hair, which was mostly white, though the original red could be seen in spots, was fashioned in a military-style crew cut. Freckles, some of which had merged into larger, sun-damaged areas of skin, dotted his face.

Klein invited us to have a seat, and Duncan and I settled into two metal folding chairs that he had removed from a cabinet and placed beside his desk. The desk was positioned near the middle of the space, against one of the side walls. There was a louvered window—the only one in the trailer—above it that kept Klein from having to stare at a wall. It also, depending on how the louvers were angled, provided him with a view of anyone who was approaching the entrance.

It was chilly inside the office, so we kept our coats on. Based on the insulated undershirt I saw peeking out of the neck of Klein's flannel shirt, which was covered by a quilted vest, I guessed it stayed chilly most of the time. The walls were thin, and most likely Klein and others were frequently going in and out the door, which would make it hard to maintain any heat inside.

"How can I help you, Detective?" Klein said once we were all seated. I noticed his desk chair was a metal folding one like ours. "I assume you're here to talk about Sheldon?"

"That is correct," Duncan said. "I'm hoping you can provide us with some details about Mr. Janssen's life, both here at work and during his off time. The better I can get to know him, the easier it will be to figure out what happened."

"It's a damn shame what happened to him," Klein said, shaking his head woefully. "I'm going to miss him a great deal. Not only was he my most trusted employee, he was a good friend."

Duncan removed a small notebook from his pocket and flipped it open. He then removed a pen from the same pocket, pulling the cap off with his teeth. As he removed the cap with his free hand, he looked at Klein and made a face, like he had just tasted something that was a bit rancid. "Before I get too deep into my questions, there are some awkward but necessary basics I need to cover with you, Mr. Klein. To start, can you tell me where you were last Friday morning between the hours of seven and nine?"

I thought Klein might adopt an offended posture and attitude with the question, but I was wrong. "I understand," he said. "Fortunately, I do have an alibi for that period of time. I was right here, on this job site, sitting at my desk. Fridays are my payroll days, and I spend every Friday morning calculating hours and writing checks."

"You do your own payroll?" Duncan said.

"I handle most of my own money matters," Klein said. "I have a degree in finance and I'm a CPA. I find that the fewer hands there are in the pot, the better."

"Can anyone verify you were here in your trailer during those hours?" Duncan asked.

Klein narrowed his eyes and stared at the ceiling, his

hands tented beneath his chin, his fingertips tapping lightly at a cleft there. After a few seconds, he said, "I believe one of my employees, a man named Roger Mulligan, came into the trailer at one point." He paused, and dropped his head to look at Duncan. "He wanted to know if he could borrow some money against his next check."

"What time was that?" Duncan asked.

"I'm not sure," Klein said with a frown. "But I was here in my trailer from about six-thirty in the morning until well after ten. So it would've been somewhere during that time. The men usually show up on site around six forty-five. I do recall I had several checks written by the time Roger came in, and I hadn't yet written his. I do the payroll alphabetically, and it takes me about three hours total, so you can estimate the time based on that." He smiled and gave Duncan an apologetic shrug. "I'm sorry, but that's the best I can do."

"That's fine," Duncan said. He looked over at me with a questioning expression. I nodded and gave him a thumbs-up. Klein's voice tasted like corn bread, and that taste hadn't altered at all yet.

Klein didn't miss this exchange between me and Duncan, and while he gave us a curious smile, he made no mention of it.

Duncan turned his attention back to Klein. "I'm curious, did you give Mr. Mulligan the advance?"

Klein shook his head. "I don't like to complicate the payroll process. But I also like to help out my employees, particularly the good, reliable ones, as much as I can. So I loaned him the money he needed and we wrote out an IOU agreement. If he pays me back from his next paycheck, there will be no interest. After that . . ." He shrugged, the conclusion needing no explanation. Given our suspicions about Klein being a money launderer, I couldn't help but wonder if *loan shark* should be added to his résumé.

"How long had you known Mr. Janssen?" Duncan asked.

"We went to college together," Klein said. "So I guess it's been about twenty years."

"So, did you know his wife?" Duncan asked.

"Oh, yeah," Klein said with an ironic chuckle. "She was a real piece of work, that one."

"How so?"

"Let's just say she had a bit of a problem saying no," Klein said. "She couldn't say no to men, she couldn't say no to booze, and she couldn't say no to drugs." He sighed. "It all caught up to her in the end. I heard she died of an overdose."

"It would seem so," Duncan said, garnering an odd look from Klein. "So I take it you know about his daughter also?"

"Yeah, a sad case, though I suspect her death was all for the best given her . . . um . . . problems."

There was a moment of silence, and it was all I could do not to look at Duncan. But I didn't want to interrupt his flow and I wasn't sure where he was going with this.

"Then, I guess you and Mr. Janssen weren't that close," Duncan said after the pause. "Because his daughter is not only alive, she was living with him."

Klein seemed surprised at the news, more than I would have expected. "Really?" he said after another pregnant pause.

"Yes, really. We're hoping to find some next of kin who might want to take the girl in," Duncan went on. "It appears Mr. Janssen wasn't very close with his family. They didn't know he'd ever had a daughter. Do you know if Janssen's wife had any other family in the area?"

Klein, still looking disturbed by Duncan's revelation, simply stared at him.

"Mr. Klein?"

Klein's expression turned angry for the briefest of moments. It was there and gone so fast, I began to wonder if I'd really seen it. Was he simply upset that someone he thought was a close friend had kept something this significant from him? Or was it something else?

"Um, I heard Hope mention something about a sister once," Klein said finally. "But I never met her, and I don't even know her name. I'm not sure they were that close."

Duncan moved on. "How long did Mr. Janssen work for you?"

"I hired him on about a year after college. Sheldon never finished, and he started taking odd jobs here and there. He did a lot of construction work, so it seemed like a good fit."

"So you hired him on as a regular worker?"

"At first, yes. But I promoted him pretty quickly after that. He might not have finished college, but Sheldon was a smart guy. And he's a good supervisor. He knows . . ." He paused and winced, and then corrected himself. "He knew how to get the most out of people."

"Did Mr. Janssen oversee all your work sites and employees?"

"He did."

"Were you aware of anyone he was having trouble with recently?"

Klein sighed and folded his hands in his lap, taking another look at the ceiling. "There was someone: a worker on one of my other sites downtown. Sheldon mentioned that he thought one of the guys on that job might be a spy of some sort. Said he caught him taking pictures at the site with his phone, and that he was asking a lot of questions of the other guys."

"Did he tell you who this worker was?" Duncan asked, and I held my breath waiting for the answer.

"No," Klein said, pursing his lips and sighing again. I let out one myself. "He didn't. He said he wanted to get more evidence first, that he didn't want to color my attitude toward the guy because he was reliable, a hard worker, and quite talented. Sheldon said he really knew his stuff."

"Do you have any idea who this worker was? Even a guess might be helpful."

Klein shook his head. "Sorry, but I have no clue. To be honest, I let Sheldon handle most of the hiring and firing stuff. He knew the workers, and I left all that personnel crap to him. It's not my favorite thing to do."

"Okay, then," Duncan said. "That's all I have." He looked over at me. "Do you have anything?"

We had discussed our strategy in the car on the way over, and Duncan had given me a few questions he wanted me to ask.

"Mr. Klein, I've heard some rumors that your business practices might not be on the up-and-up. Can you clarify that for me?"

I expected the man to be angry, or confused, or defensive. But all he did was laugh. "Let me guess," he said when he was done chuckling. "You heard these rumors"—he made air quotes with his fingers when he said the word *rumors*—"from one of my competitors."

"Does it matter where I heard it from?"

He smiled at me, and there was something slippery and dangerous in that smile. "No, I suppose it doesn't, because it isn't true. It's just wishful thinking on the part of some of my competitors who aren't as good in business as I am."

"I've heard you have certain officials on your bankroll," I said. My heart was pounding in my chest. Provoking this man was like poking a stick at a mad tiger. "I've heard you've been known to bribe building inspectors from time to time, encouraging them to look the other way when your work is, shall we say, shoddy?"

That made the smile disappear. "I think we're done chatting," he said in a cold, dark tone. He stood, hands on his hips. "You can leave now."

We did so, exiting the trailer and hearing the door slam shut behind us. When we were a safe distance away, Duncan said to me, "Well? What was your take?"

"Oh, he's up to no good," I said. "His voice definitely changed when I asked him about the rumors. When he denied them, his voice went from a sweet corn bread taste to something more like sauerkraut. But the good news is, he was telling the truth when he said he didn't know who the suspect worker was. So I think Mal is in the clear."

As we passed a section of the structure draped in plastic, a bitter gust of wind blew down the alleyway, making a large wall flap of that plastic slap in the wind. It furled upward exposing the inside. I saw Klein's crew, or at least some of them, standing on the other side of that plastic, and it made me stop dead in my tracks.

One of the men working on Klein's crew was Tiny Gruber, Cora's current boyfriend and a member of the Capone Club.

Chapter 22

"Duncan, look," I said in a low voice, nudging his arm and pointing to the exposed interior of the structure. "That's Tiny."

Duncan looked where I'd indicated just in time to see the men inside before the plastic sheeting flapped back down, obscuring our view. "Interesting," he said. "I knew Tiny worked in construction, but I didn't know he worked for Klein."

"Cora told me he freelances a lot, working for different contractors, sometimes doing some small, odd jobs himself."

"I wonder if Mal has ever seen him at his site," Duncan mused. We walked the rest of the way to the car in silence, but once we were on our way, Duncan said, "We should have a chat with Tiny. We might be able to use him to gain access to Klein's books."

"What are you thinking?" I asked.

Before he could answer me, his cell phone rang. "This is Detective Albright."

He listened, once again frustrating my efforts to garner who he was talking to and what it was about.

When he looked over at me and smiled, I knew it would be good news.

"Thanks," he said after listening for a minute or so. "Send the info to my cell phone." He disconnected the call, set the phone on the seat between us, and said, "I should be getting an address texted to me in a moment. It's DMV info with an address for a woman I hope is Hope Janssen's sister. She lives in Waukesha. We don't have a phone number, though, so we may have to pay her a surprise visit."

"That's great news. How on earth did you find her?"

"I had some guys research Hope Janssen's history. They found her maiden name on her marriage certificate to Sheldon. Fortunately, it wasn't a very common name, and the sister either never married, or if she did she kept her maiden name, or got divorced and took it back. Then I had them pull up all the women with that same last name and look for a hippie-dippie first name." He looked over at me and winked. "The end result is one Peace Vanderzandt."

"Well, the name Peace certainly fits. I hope she'll be willing to take Felicity. That poor child needs some stability in her life."

Duncan's phone dinged and he said, "Go ahead and look if you want."

I picked up the phone, opened the text message, and studied the info. Along with the address and some info on Peace Vanderzandt's height, weight, eye and hair color, was a picture. She was thirty-three years old with shoulder-length brown hair. According to the other data, her eyes were blue, her height was five-five, and she weighed 185 pounds. My mind adjusted that last number for the typical ten pounds we women tend to fudge on these things and put her at closer to 200 pounds.

"Duncan, she fits the description of the woman who was seen by the neighbor at Janssen's house."

"DMV listed her bust measurement?" he asked with a healthy dose of skepticism and amusement.

"No, but the other parameters fit: brown shoulder-length hair, and based on her weight, she's going to be a little on the hefty side."

"Let's hope she's a buxom woman," he said. "Because those parameters would fit half the women in Milwaukee."

"Should we go there now?"

Duncan considered the question and then shook his head. "I want to hit up the party stores Oliver Knutson owned and chat with some of his employees. Once we've done that, we can pay a visit to Peace Vanderzandt."

"How many stores are we going to?"

"There are five here in the Milwaukee area, and another ten in other parts of the state. Bobby didn't see much benefit in visiting the out-of-state stores because they likely didn't see Knutson all that often. So we're splitting the local ones. She's doing three and we have two to visit."

I considered correcting him on Roberta's name again, but decided it was a lost cause.

We reached the first of our assigned stores a few minutes later. It was located in a strip mall, one of the anchoring stores at the end and the largest store in the group. A large sign over the entrance identified the place as simply "Pizzazzeria," but a smaller banner beneath it read, "Party and Special Event Planning and Catering."

Inside, I felt like I was a kid again. The shelves nearest the door were stocked with all kinds of children's party favors: hats, noisemakers, colorful gift bags, disposable plates, confetti, crepe paper, banners for everything from bar mitzvahs to birthdays, glow sticks, glitter, and an assortment of small toys. A colorful assortment of balloons, both vinyl and Mylar, floated at the end of each row of shelving. There were two checkout lanes—one on either side of the door—and both were manned. A portly, rosy-cheeked woman with gray-streaked hair at the register to our right greeted us with a big smile and a cheerful voice laced with energetic enthusiasm.

"Welcome to Knutson's, your full-service party-planning place! How can I help you fine folks today?"

Duncan hesitated a second or two, and I suspected he was trying to figure out a polite way of ignoring the woman. I gathered he quickly determined, as did I, that she wasn't the type of person one could easily dismiss, however, and with a sigh, he pulled his badge and approached her.

"I'm Detective Albright with the Milwaukee Police Department," he said. "I'm here in regard to Mr. Knutson's death and would like to talk with the employees if I may."

The woman, who was wearing a name badge that identified her as Midge, cocked her head to one side, her smile faltering ever so slightly. "I thought the detective in charge of Mr. Knutson's death was a woman," she said, a hint of challenge in her tone.

"You are correct," Duncan said. "Detective Roberta Dillon is the primary on the case. I'm assisting her."

"I see," Midge said. She shifted her gaze—one that I doubted missed much—to me. "And are you a detective also?" she asked.

"No, ma'am," I said. "My name is Mackenzie Dalton and I'm a consultant with the police department."

"A consultant," Midge said, her eyes growing wide. "How impressive." Her tone was mildly mocking, but I shrugged it off, figuring if she was making fun of me now, one could only imagine her reaction if and when she learned just what it was I did in my role as a consultant. "It was my understanding Mr. Knutson died of natural causes," she said, shifting her attention back to Duncan.

"We haven't yet been able to determine a precise cause of death," Duncan said.

With this, the woman's smile faded away, the antithesis of the Cheshire cat. "So, did that woman detective finally decide to listen to me?" she said in a condescending tone.

"What did you tell her?" Duncan asked.

The front door opened and a woman with three kids entered the store. Midge's smile reappeared, and her tone turned chipper again, albeit less loudly so. "Why don't we go back to one of the planning rooms where we can chat privately?" she said. "Follow me."

She promptly turned and left her station, marching toward the back of the store. Not once did she look back to see if we were following her; clearly, she assumed we would obey her command. She was right.

We made our way between shelves toward the back of the store, where the displays gave way to an open area. In the farthest left back corner there was a balloon station, a desk with a wall behind it that featured pinups of the many options available. A young woman stood behind the counter chatting with a male customer as she inflated a balloon from a large helium tank. Something near the ceiling caught my eye, and I stopped and stared for a moment, curious.

My hesitation didn't go unnoticed. I heard a loud *ahem* and tore my attention away from the ceiling. Midge was standing in the doorway of the middle of three glass-walled rooms that ran down the right side of the rear area, each one furnished with a table and four chairs. Each room had pictures on the wall that displayed a variety of party venues, and there were several large notebooks on the tables, presumably filled with more pictures and samples of items for customers to peruse. The first room was occupied by a woman wearing a faux fur coat and hat. A designer handbag sat on the floor beside her chair. Across the table from her was a young man in a suit and tie who was pointing to an anniversary-themed display in an open notebook he was holding up for her.

"Mack?" Duncan said. "What is it?"

"Nothing."

He accepted my answer for the time being, though I could tell from the look on his face that he was going to grill me later. He headed for the open door next to Midge, and I followed. Duncan ignored the seats, opting to stand behind the farthest one. I took a stance behind the closer one, and we waited as Midge closed the door and walked around the table to the other side. Apparently taking her cue from us, she, too, remained standing.

"Now then," she said, her smile once again fading. "Let's talk turkey. I'm guessing you're here because you finally figured out that Oliver's wife is a gold digger. I tried to tell that lady detective something might be fishy about Oliver's death."

"What made you think that?" Duncan asked.

"Well, isn't it obvious? She's so much younger than him, and she targeted him the minute he hired her. Hell, she probably targeted him before that, for all I know. And she's always talking about money—how much Oliver has, how little she has, griping about how unfair Oliver was with the division of assets—and griping about Oliver himself . . . his weight, his snoring, him smoking those cigars of his. She couldn't wait for him to kick the bucket, and I'm guessing she decided not to wait any longer."

"Did she ever say anything to you about wanting to hurt Mr. Knutson?"

"She never said anything to me directly. She knew I wasn't a fan. But I overheard plenty. She liked talking to the younger employees, like Andy and Cheyenne over there." She jutted her chin toward the windows, toward the girl handling the balloons. "She complained about Oliver to Cheyenne all the time."

Midge went on with her diatribe, but I tuned her out. I'd turned to look at Cheyenne, and once again I was distracted by the ceiling above her. My mind started churning, thinking back to things I'd heard, things I'd read. And then it clicked.

I whirled back to face Duncan, grabbing his jacket sleeve. Midge was still going on about Caroline and her kibitzing, but I interrupted her. "Duncan, I think we can go now," I said.

Duncan looked at me, his eyes narrowed. Midge let out a harrumph of annoyance at my interruption.

"You two aren't going to listen to me either, are you?" Midge said indignantly. "You think I'm just some old lady who doesn't know what she's talking about. Well, let me tell you something. I know a whole lot more than you think. You need to . . ."

As Midge rambled on, I gestured with a nod of my head toward the room's exit, still maintaining eye contact with Duncan. He didn't hesitate any longer. "Thank you for talking to us," he said, interrupting Midge. She opened and closed her mouth several times, like the proverbial fish out of water, glaring at us in disbelief and with a fair dose of contempt.

"Well, I never . . ." she huffed, placing her hands on her ample hips.

Duncan slid past me and opened the door to the room, holding it for me. I slipped past him, escaping Midge's wrath. We could hear her muttering as we walked back toward the front of the store.

Once we were back in Duncan's car, he turned to me and said, "Okay, give."

"I think Caroline murdered Oliver, and I think I know how she did it. There are some things I need to check. I need to chat with the medical examiner. And if my suspicions are right, we need to figure out a way to pin it on her."

I shared my theory with Duncan, and he listened intently. I watched his expression morph from curious and mildly skeptical to excited. It was a look I knew well, one that said he was on the hunt and closing in, about to make his kill.

When I was finished, he took out his phone and made a call. Minutes later, we were on our way to the ME's office.

The medical examiner's office was in the basement of a downtown public office building. I thought we might run into Dr. Al Spencer again, but the pathologist in charge of the Knutson case was someone different, a Dr. Gaines. He met us in his office—a relief for me because I was afraid we'd end up in an autopsy suite with a bunch of cadavers in various states of postmortem ugliness, and I wasn't sure I was ready to handle something like that.

The smell of formaldehyde was strong throughout the place, and it triggered a crunching sound, like someone walking in the forest after the autumn leaves have fallen. It also gave me a peculiar headache, a low, throbbing pain in my right temple.

Dr. Gaines's office was filled with large textbooks stuffed into a bookcase, sitting on file cabinets, spread out over his desk, and stacked on a chair. Mixed in with the books was an assortment of papers and reports. A quick glance at those closest to me revealed scientific articles related to various aspects of postmortem analysis. This display of educational material left only one empty seat other than the chair behind the doctor's desk, so both Duncan and I stood on one side of the desk while Dr. Gaines settled in on his side.

"Sorry," he said, waving a hand around the room. "I'm not the neatest person, as you can see, and I don't normally have more than one person at a time visit my office. We can go to a conference or family room if you'd prefer, but because you said you had some theoretical questions regarding Oliver Knutson's death, I figured it would be more helpful to me to have my resources close at hand."

"This is fine," Duncan said, and I nodded my consensus. "As I said on the phone, I . . . or rather Mack here, came up with an idea about Mr. Knutson's death, and we wanted to run it by you. But first we have to explain some things to you. For that, I'm going to let Mack take the lead."

I went about providing Dr. Gaines with a brief explanation of my synesthesia, a subject he fortunately knew something about. After providing several examples of how it manifested itself for me—including my formaldehyde reaction—I explained to him the odd reaction I'd had to Mr. Knutson's bedroom ceiling when I looked at it.

"I had the same reaction earlier today when we were

visiting one of Mr. Knutson's stores," I went on. "And I think I know why." I then explained my theory to him, relieved to see he didn't look skeptical. In fact, he looked intrigued. When I was done, I fell silent, and Duncan and I both stood there staring at him expectantly, waiting for his reaction.

"It's brilliant," Dr. Gaines said after a few moments of silence. He whirled around and started digging through a pile of papers he had on top of a filing cabinet that stood behind his desk. Amazingly, he found what he was looking for in a matter of seconds. Despite the disorganized look of his office, I suspected the man knew exactly where everything in it was located.

"Take a look at this," he said, handing several sheets of paper that were stapled together to Duncan. "It's a printout of an online article I found that was written by the Final Exit Network. Do you know what that is?"

Duncan and I both nodded. "It's a group that supports the right to die, or assisted suicide," I said. "I saw a late-night TV program about it sometime in the past and remembered it when I was in the store. That's what gave me the idea."

"You are correct," Dr. Gaines said, giving me a broad smile. But his delight quickly faded, his smile dropping into a frown. "Your idea is a good one, but unfortunately, I'm not sure it's a valid one." He then explained why.

I was crestfallen. But the doctor took on a thoughtful expression and said, "Although . . ." Duncan and I waited while he again fell silent. Finally, he said, "It's possible your theory is correct, but I suspect our Mrs. Knutson may have been too clever for us." He shared his thoughts on the matter, and when he was done, he sank down into his chair, shaking his head. "Let me think on it for a while, but I don't think there's a way for me to prove it. I'll run it by some of my colleagues as well, to see if they have any ideas, but I'm thinking it's a lost cause. It's a pretty foolproof method of dispatch, if I do say so myself." He sounded as if he bore some grudging admiration for Caroline Knutson.

A dismal silence fell over the room as the three of us contemplated our inability to prove what I strongly suspected was the truth, and the idea that Caroline Knutson might just get away with murder.

Then Duncan said, "Well, we may not be able to prove it, but I'm betting Caroline Knutson doesn't know that."

"What are you thinking?" I asked him.

Duncan shared his thoughts.

"It's a long shot," Dr. Gaines said, and I had to agree with him. "But it's worth a try. After all, what have you got to lose?"

Chapter 23

After leaving the ME's office, we headed back to the bar to get something to eat and regroup. Duncan got a call from the taciturn Ms. Parnell, informing him that he had permission to bring me by again to see Felicity.

"Are you okay with waiting until this evening to do that?" Duncan asked. "I'd like to go pay a visit to Hope's sister next."

"Sure," I said. The truth was, I really wanted to see Felicity again. The kid had wormed her way into my heart, and I felt a near-maternal urge to see her. But I also recognized the importance of solving the case, both for Mal's peace of mind and Felicity's.

After making fast work of our lunch and checking to see that things were under control at the bar, we set out for Waukesha, which was twenty miles outside of suburban Milwaukee to the west. It took us a little over half an hour to arrive at our destination, a cute little Cape Cod–style home that sat at the base of a drumlin outside of town. It was a bucolic setting, a small, semirural development that hadn't been completely stripped of its natural beauty.

There was a car parked in the driveway of Peace Vanderzandt's home—a good sign for us. Duncan rang the doorbell, and seconds later, a woman answered the door. I felt a surge of excitement when I saw she fit the description of the woman the neighbor had seen visiting Sheldon's house: shoulder-length brown hair and very buxom. Her eyes and her basic stature matched that of the vital statistics Duncan had come up with for Peace. Except something about her was wrong.

"Are you Peace Vanderzandt?" Duncan asked.

"I am," the woman said, and her voice made me see the little flashing lights one might see on a warm night during the height of firefly season.

"Are you the sister of Hope Janssen?"

"What has she done now?" the woman said, and the flashing lights faded to specks of glitter.

There was an awkward silence of a few seconds while Duncan parsed this question and its meaning. "Ms. Vanderzandt, I'm sorry to inform you that your sister, Hope, is deceased."

Peace sighed. "Well, I can't say I'm very surprised," she said. "She's had a substance abuse problem since she was a teenager. She wasn't exactly a model of healthy living."

"May we come in for a moment to chat?" Duncan asked.

"About what?"

"There are some things we need to clarify about your sister."

Peace sighed again, this time rolling her eyes. "There isn't much to clarify. She was a loser and a junkie."

"There is the matter of her daughter," Duncan said.

Peace blinked several times really fast. "Daughter? Hope had a daughter?"

Duncan looked behind him, scanning the neighboring homes. "Can we please come in?"

Peace clearly didn't want to invite us inside. She hesitated, chewing on the inside of her cheek. "I suppose. But I have an appointment in an hour, so it's going to have to be a short visit."

We stepped inside the house, which was decorated in a European contemporary style: lots of gray tones, furniture with sleek, minimalist lines, and a dearth of accessories. We settled onto a low-backed, gray leather couch adorned with two bright red throw pillows—one of the only sources of color in the room—while Peace sat on the edge of a white chair with short wooden legs and a throw in the same bright red color.

"Your sister died three months ago," Duncan began. "She and her husband, Sheldon Janssen, had a daughter named Felicity, who is nine years old."

Peace opened her mouth as if to say something, but she bit it back. She was sitting ramrod straight, wringing her hands in her lap, clearly nervous. "Yes?" was all she finally said.

"Felicity was living with her father, but unfortunately, her father has now also passed on, leaving the child an orphan." Peace showed no visible reaction to this news. "Child Protective Services has made temporary arrangements for the child," Duncan went on, "but we were hoping to find a family member who might be interested in assuming the child's care."

Peace's color paled. Something about this conversation had her upset, but I wasn't sure what it was. Was it the information about Sheldon? Or was she acting when she showed surprise at the presence of a niece, a niece she might know well enough to know she didn't want to be saddled with her care?

"I'm hardly in a position to take on a child," Peace said, flashing an apologetic smile. "I'm single, and at the moment, I'm also unemployed."

"I see," Duncan said. "Are your parents still alive?"

Peace shook her head. "Our dad died when we were kids, and my mom passed away from cancer fifteen years ago."

"I'm sorry," I said, knowing how it felt to be parentless. "No other siblings?"

Peace shook her head. "You said temporary arrangements had been made for Felicity?"

Duncan nodded. "She's been placed with a foster family for now."

"Would I be able to see her?"

Duncan shrugged. "I suppose. But you should understand that your niece has some . . . um . . . unique circumstances. She's a special-needs child."

Peace nodded, seeming neither curious nor bothered by this information. "As I said, I'm not a candidate for motherhood at this point in my life, particularly single motherhood. But I would like a chance to meet my sister's daughter."

"I take it you and Hope weren't very close?" Duncan said.

Peace sighed. "My sister and I hadn't spoken in years. We parted ways a long time ago. She started hanging out with a bad crowd, and when she was using, which was all the time it seemed, she wasn't a nice person to be around."

"So you never met her husband?"

"I didn't even know she was married." The fireflies returned, and I frowned, unsure what to make of this visual manifestation.

Duncan feigned a look of confusion and said, "One of Mr. Janssen's neighbors said he saw a woman fitting your description knocking on Janssen's door a few days before he was killed."

Peace let out a nervous titter and swiped her hands down her thighs. "Well, it wasn't me," she said, and the fireflies glowed brighter. "What sort of description did this neighbor provide?"

"He said it was a woman, about your height, with shoulder-length brown hair and, um, a well-endowed chest."

Peace laughed. "Well, surely there are hundreds of other women who fit that description," she said. "I assure you, it wasn't me."

Duncan fell silent for a moment, and Peace fidgeted in her seat. Finally, Duncan said, "Well, I'm sorry to have bothered you." With that he stood, and I did the same.

Peace also got up, and she hurried over to the door to show us out. "I really would like a chance to meet my niece," she said as she opened the door. "Can you arrange that for me?"

"I don't see why not," Duncan said. "I'll be in touch. Is there a phone number I can use to reach you?"

Peace hesitated for two blinks, and then said, "Sure."

Duncan took the notebook and pen he carried from his jacket pocket, opened the notebook, clicked the pen, and then looked at Peace expectantly. She rattled off a phone number, which he dutifully wrote down. Then he closed the notebook, returned it and the pen to his jacket pocket, and said, "I'll be in touch."

When we were back inside his car, Duncan said, "Something is off with her. Did you pick up on anything?"

I explained to him about the fireflies.

"That makes sense. I'm certain she's lying to us. Did you notice she didn't question who Hope *Janssen* was, even though she claimed she didn't know her sister was married? And she didn't so much as flinch when I mentioned that Sheldon had been killed; not just that he died, but that he was killed."

"What reason would she have to lie about that stuff?"

"I don't know for sure. Maybe she's the one who killed Sheldon. Whatever it is, I'm not letting her anywhere near Felicity until we figure it out."

"There was something else about her that seemed odd to me," I said as Duncan did a U-turn in the street. "I'm not sure what it was. Something about her appearance."

Duncan said nothing, giving me time to puzzle it out. He took out his phone and placed a call, and instructed whoever was on the other end to dig up anything they could find on Peace Vanderzandt. When he was done, he ended the call and looked over at me. "Anything?"

I shook my head in frustration. "Give me some more time. Maybe it will come to me. In the meantime, can we go see Felicity now? Maybe I can show her the picture of Peace and see if she reacts to it."

Duncan took out his phone and handed it to me. "The Varners are in my contact list. Go ahead and make the call."

Ms. Parnell was at the Varner house when we arrived. Because the woman and I seemed to rub each other the wrong way, Duncan spoke to her to update her on our finding of Peace Vanderzandt, and her reaction to the news about her sister and niece.

"I was able to get a copy of Felicity's birth certificate," Parnell said. "And based on my research, the sister is correct. There are no surviving family members on the mother's side other than Hope's sister, and while there are plenty of family members on Mr. Janssen's side, no one our office has contacted has any interest in taking the girl in or supporting her. As such, we have started proceedings to have her made a ward of the court."

"Does that mean she'll be placed in an institution again?" Irene Varner asked.

"Most likely," Parnell said. "It's probably for the best. It's not likely anyone is going to want to adopt her, given her condition and issues. An institution is probably the best place for her."

I wasn't sure I agreed with her, but I didn't have any other options to offer. If I was in a different position in my own life, I might consider trying to adopt her myself, but the demands of my bar, my single status, and my new job as a consultant with the police department wouldn't mix well with the demands Felicity's care would place on me. I felt sorry for the child.

Duncan explained to Ms. Parnell and the Varners what we wanted to do with Felicity on this visit, and when no one objected, we made our way down to the basement bedroom where she was staying.

"How has she been since the last time we were here?" I asked Irene as we descended the stairs.

"A little calmer," she said. "She still doesn't engage with us much at all, but she hasn't acted out or had one of her screaming spells like she did her first night here. She draws a lot."

When we reached the bedroom door, I knocked and then opened it. Felicity was in the room, curled up in the corner, her knees drawn up, her arms wrapped around them. She was staring across the room, but her eyes had a vacant look to them that made me think she wasn't seeing what was in front of her. Not that there was much in front of her. Other than some papers, markers, and crayons, and the mattress on the floor, the room was essentially empty.

I walked over to her and sat beside her while the others stood in the doorway, observing. "Hello, Felicity," I said.

Her head turned to look at me, and her eyes focused. "Mack," she said, deadpan.

"That's the most response we've gotten from her since your last visit," I heard Irene whisper.

"Yes," I responded, giving Felicity a smile. "How are you?"

She didn't answer me. Instead, she turned back to look across the room, once again taking on that vacant stare.

I reached for some papers and markers that were nearby and started drawing. I sketched a picture of a pizza slice with circles on it in brown to indicate pepperoni, and then drew an arrow alongside it. At the other end of the arrow I drew a car. When I was done, I pushed it toward Felicity. "When I smell pizza with pepperoni on it—which is my favorite pizza, by the way—I hear the sound of a well-tuned car engine. But if the pizza also has mushrooms on it, which I don't like, the engine skips and coughs."

I saw Felicity's eyes shift down toward my drawing, but she said nothing and maintained her position. Grabbing another piece of paper, I drew a series of red splotches, hoping they looked like blood. Just to make sure of the connection, I drew a finger and made a red slash across it just above the red splotches. Then I drew an arrow, and beside the point of the arrow, I drew a trumpet.

"Blood has a smell to it," I said. "And when I smell it, I hear trumpet music."

From the doorway, I heard Parnell mumble under her breath, "This is a waste of time."

"That woman has gotten more of a response from her than anyone else has," Irene said, a hint of irritation in her voice. "So maybe you can let her be?"

I could only imagine the expression on Parnell's face, because my eyes were fixed on Felicity. I took back my pictures and put a blank piece of paper in front of her, and then reached for the box of crayons, moving them closer. Then I took another sheet for myself and tried to draw an image of my father. My artistic talents were crude at best, and the end product looked little like him, but at least it looked like a man.

"My daddy died like yours did," I said to Felicity. "I really miss him. He used to hug me a lot, and I loved his hugs. Sometimes, like now, I like to pretend he's still alive. That's why I drew this picture of him, so I can pretend for a little while. And you know what else I'm going to draw?" I traded in my current crayon for an aqua-colored one. Then I sketched out wavy blue lines with it alongside the drawing of what was supposed to be my father.

"See these lines?" I said to Felicity. She was looking at my drawings, and her gaze seemed focused. "Whenever my dad would hug me, I would see bluish-green waves of color like this. Isn't that funny?"

Felicity let her arms fall at her side, and she shifted her position, tucking her legs beneath her so that she was on her knees.

"Did your dad ever hug you?" I said.

Felicity nodded.

"What did it feel like when your dad hugged you?"

Felicity reached down and grabbed the hem of her nightgown, a long, flannel, granny type of thing. She rubbed it between her fingers.

"Did it feel like that?" I said, and she nodded slowly.

From the doorway, Irene said, "We discovered she only likes to wear soft cotton material. We tried to give her some nylon panties, but she tossed them aside. She won't wear anything polyester either. And she prefers loose-fitting stuff. I think she'd live in that nightgown if we let her."

I wondered if this preference for certain materials was related to her autism, or if it was due to a synesthetic response. For me, anything leather gave me a nasty taste in my mouth, so I never wore it. And if I was ever near anything made of real fur, I heard a constant, repetitive, and irritating sound of rushing air, almost like an animal panting.

I decided now was as good a time as any to spring Peace's picture on Felicity. She was engaged with me to some degree, and I hoped that because she seemed trusting and comfortable with me, it would temper any reaction she might have to it.

"Let me have your phone with the picture," I said to Duncan.

It took him a minute to get out his phone and bring up the picture. He walked into the room slowly, handed it to me, and then returned to the doorway.

"Do you know who this is?" I said to Felicity. I put the phone in front of her, and her eyes drifted toward the screen.

What happened next came as a total surprise. Felicity reached out and slapped my hand, knocking the phone out of it. Then she pushed herself into the corner, as if she was trying to melt into the wall. A bloodcurdling scream followed.

"Oh, for heaven's sake!" I heard Parnell say.

I hesitated, wanting to say something to Felicity to calm her, but her shrieks were so loud I doubted she'd hear me. Then, on instinct, I scooted over closer to her and slowly wrapped one arm around her shoulder. The shrieks continued, but she didn't try to push my arm away or shrug it off, so I went ahead and snaked my other arm over her other shoulder. Slowly, I pulled her into me, wrapping her inside my arms. And then I began to hum the tune to "Row, Row, Row Your Boat."

Felicity's shrieks stopped. Though I half-expected her to try to wriggle away from me, or shrug me off, she did neither. She let me hold her.

"Wow," I heard Irene say. "That's amazing. She won't let us touch her at all."

After several seconds of hugging, I heard Felicity start to hum along with me.

I continued to hold her for another minute or so, and then I slowly released her. I stopped humming, and so did she. I put my face in front of hers and said, "Do you know the woman in that picture I showed you?"

She nodded slowly. "Little peach," she said. And then she formed one hand into the shape of a gun and said, "Bang, bang!" so loud it made me jump.

Chapter 24

Duncan drove us back to the bar after I said good-bye to Felicity and the Varners. And yes, to Ms. Parnell, too. During our drive, I said, "It seems pretty clear to me that Felicity thinks Peace killed her father."

"I don't think she's going to make a very good witness," Duncan said. "We need something more."

"What if Peace takes off now that she knows we're interested in her?"

"I don't think she will. At least not yet," Duncan said. "She seemed genuinely interested in seeing Felicity, and until we let her do that, I think she'll stick around. But I'll put a watch on her in the meantime, just to be sure."

"You're not seriously thinking about letting her see Felicity, are you?"

Duncan didn't answer right away.

"You can't do that to Felicity," I protested. "You saw how she reacted to just the picture of her. Can you imagine how traumatic it will be if she meets the woman face-to-face?"

"Well, that might be the evidence we need. We could tape the encounter, and it might be usable in court."

"You can't do that to her," I said again. "And if you record her reaction to Peace, you'd have to do the same thing with the other suspects. What if you brought Mal to see her and she did the same thing with him?"

"Maybe we should bring them together then," Duncan said. "See what kind of reaction she has to Mal."

The frustration I felt over this conversation was angering me, so I decided to switch topics. "When do you want to try to get a peek at Klein's books?"

"Let's see if Tiny is at the bar, and if he is, we'll have a chat with him to see if he's willing to help us. I can't force him to, so I'm hoping he'll want to play along."

"I think he will. His sister's murder all those years ago shaped his opinions and his outlook on this kind of stuff. He's all about seeing justice served."

We arrived at the bar, and after checking in with my staff, we made our way over to a table where the O'Reilly clan was congregated, enjoying a meal and some beers.

"Hey, Mack," Connor said, proffering his beer to us as we approached. "Your elevator is officially done."

"That's fantastic," I said. "I can't thank you guys enough for giving up your time and your lives to come here and do this for me."

"We'll do just about anything for free food and beer," Patrick said.

"Hear, hear," Ryan said, holding up his beer.

A chorus of "Hear, hear," combined with the sound of clinking bottles, followed as all four of them toasted this sentiment.

"How's Mal doing?" Colleen asked after they had all taken swigs of beer.

"Better," Duncan said. "He'll be fine. But our suspicions were confirmed regarding his boss. I don't think he knows Mal is a cop, but he might think Mal is a spy of some sort, and that puts him, and you guys, in danger. We're not sure if he knows who Sheldon suspected or not. He says he doesn't have a clue, but I'm not sure we can believe him. Hopefully, we'll have some resolution soon."

"We have plans to return home tomorrow," Connor said. "Any chance we can see Mal before we go?"

Duncan gave this request a few seconds of thought. "Okay, let me see what I can do."

"At least you'll get your apartment back after tonight," Colleen said to me. "Thanks so much for putting us up."

"I'm the one who needs to say thanks," I told her. "You've done me a huge favor. Consider yourselves family from here on out. Anytime you're in Milwaukee, come on by. The food and drinks will always be on me."

"I see some trips to Milwaukee in our future," Ryan said, and he and Patrick high-fived each other.

"It's a great city," Connor said. "Thanks for the sightseeing suggestions."

"Yeah, the brewery trips were a definite highlight," Patrick said with a devilish grin.

"Well, enjoy your last evening here," I told them. "Order anything you want to eat or drink. What time is your flight tomorrow?"

"We need to be at the airport by noon," Connor said.

"Then I'll make sure you have a hearty breakfast to see you off."

After one more round of vociferous thank-yous going both ways, Duncan and I left them. Duncan once again wanted to use my office to make some calls and do some work. I gave him my key and then headed upstairs to the Capone Club room. Tiny wasn't there, so I pulled Cora aside out in the hallway and asked her if she was expecting him to show up this evening.

"I am," she said. "He said he'd come by after work. Why?"

I told her what we had in mind. I wasn't sure what her reaction would be, but if she had any hesitation about Tiny putting his job and, potentially, his life on the line, she didn't show it. What's more, she was quite excited about her role in the plan.

"I'm sure he'll want to do it," she said. "And I have to admit, it'd be nice to get out and do something a little more exciting than tapping computer keys."

"Great," I said. "Thanks, Cora. Duncan and I will both really appreciate it."

We returned to the room and the curious stares of the others.

"What's up, Mack?" Carter said. "You haven't been around much. Busy day?"

Because there were no newcomers, just the usual crowd, I once again reminded them that what I was going to tell them needed to stay with the group. Then I filled them in on the Janssen case, though I kept the part involving Tiny and any information about Mal out of it.

"What about Oliver Knutson?" Sonja asked when I was done.

"I have some good news to report on that account," I told them with a big smile. Then I shared my theory of the case with them, and the discussion we had with the ME.

"You're brilliant, as usual!" Joe said when I was done. "Now all we have to do is figure out a way to prove it."

"Yes, therein lies our dilemma," I said. "Duncan has an idea on how we might be able to do it. Time will tell."

"Can you share the details?" Carter asked.

"Not yet. But I'll let you guys know as soon as I can."

I could tell they were frustrated by this answer, but they accepted it, knowing my new relationship with the police department put some dampers on the information I was willing to share and when.

The group was discussing the brilliance of Caroline's method of murder when Tiny showed up. Before he could have a chance to settle in with the group, Cora and I steered him back out of the room, saying we had a new menu item we wanted him to try. I doubted the others bought that excuse, but once again, they had little choice other than to accept it.

Cora and I escorted Tiny down to my office. Duncan was on my laptop computer when we went in, and he stopped what he was doing to get up and greet Tiny.

"Haven't seen ya in a while," Tiny said, shaking Duncan's hand.

"It has been some time," Duncan said. "Listen, Tiny, I wonder if I could run something by you. There's a case I'm working on, and I could really use your help with it."

"You want *me* to help?" he said, looking skeptical.

Duncan nodded. "It's about your job, your current one." Tiny looked confused. "You're working for Wade Klein, right?"

"Ya, dats right."

"We have reason to think Klein is involved in some illegal activities," Duncan said. "We had an undercover cop working there for a time, but he's no longer able to do that."

Tiny's look of confusion turned into one of enlightenment. "Oh, ya, da guys on dat job were saying dere was a guy who disappeared, and dat maybe he was a spy or somet'in like dat."

Duncan nodded. "That was probably our guy," he said. "It was Mal."

Tiny looked appropriately surprised.

"While he's no longer able to work there," Duncan went on, "he was able to get a look at some books Klein keeps in his office. We think those books might be the evidence we need to finally arrest Klein."

"What do ya t'ink Klein is doin'?" Tiny asked.

"Money laundering," Duncan said. "And perhaps some bribery. There has been talk of him doing shoddy work on some of his jobs and paying inspectors to look the other way." I noticed he left out any mention of suspected drug trafficking. "There's a good chance these books are records of some of his illegal transactions."

"Some of da guys on dat job did say some t'ings about shortcuts dey didn't like," Tiny said, looking troubled.

"Have you worked for Klein before?" I asked.

Tiny shook his head. "Naw. I have a guy I work for most of da time, but he's out right now because of some surgery he had to have. So I got somet'ing temporary." He sighed. "So what da ya want me ta do?"

Duncan described Klein's mobile office to him.

"Ya, I've seen it," Tiny said.

"Klein keeps the doorknob to that office locked so no one can get in without knocking. As far as we know, he and Mr. Janssen are the only ones with keys. So every time he leaves the office, the door locks behind him."

"You want me to try to steal his keys?" Tiny said, looking alarmed.

"No," Duncan said. "I don't want you to steal anything. We found a ring of keys in Mr. Janssen's house, but there are dozens of keys on it and we don't know which one is to the trailer. So we need you to do something else." Duncan outlined the plan for him. When he was done, he said, "So what do you think, Tiny? Are you up for it?"

Tiny looked over at Cora. "What da ya t'ink?" he said.

"I'm totally up for it," Cora said.

"Okay, den," Tiny said with a big smile. "Count me in."

We spent the next half hour discussing the specifics of the plan and arranging to meet the next morning. When that was done, Tiny and Cora went back upstairs, and Duncan and I headed out again. Our next stop was Mal's lakeside hideaway, with a stop along the way for some burgers and fries I told Duncan I could easily have made at the bar.

I was delighted to see Mal looked much better. His color had improved, his step had some spring to it, and his attitude was upbeat. I hugged him—carefully, so as not to irritate his wound—and offered to change his dressing for him. He readily agreed.

"It's hard for me to get to the part around back," he said. "So I'd appreciate your eyes and hands for it."

I gathered the necessary supplies while Mal removed his shirt and settled onto a stool by a bar at one end of the room. He and Duncan dug into the food, and started chatting about the Janssen case. It didn't take me long to realize Duncan had been in regular contact with Mal, keeping him updated.

When it came time to disclose the plan we had cooked up for getting a better look at Klein's books, Mal was eager to get on board.

"This place is starting to get to me," he said. "I'd love to get back out there and actually do something."

We stayed and chatted a while longer, discussing

the morning plans. I ate my burger and some fries in silence, finding them a poor example of the fare compared to my own. When the talk finally ebbed, I finally interjected my own thoughts.

"Mal, your family is leaving tomorrow. They really want to see you before they go. Why don't you come back with us tonight and stay at the bar? It's plenty safe, and your family is staying in my apartment, so you'll be able to spend some time with them. You can have your basement bed back if you want. I can stay at Duncan's."

Mal considered the offer and looked at Duncan. "What do you think?" he asked.

Duncan shrugged. "I was going to suggest the same thing myself. I just hadn't gotten around to it yet. You could show up around closing time so no one sees you."

Mal considered the offer for a few seconds and then said, "I'd really like to see them, too. And it will be easier to coordinate things in the morning that way. Let's do it."

With that resolved, we helped Mal clean up the remnants of our meal and then said our good-byes. It felt good knowing it would be a short-lived one this time.

On the ride back to the bar, Duncan was silent, and that worried me. "I hope it's okay I invited myself to spend another night at your place," I said, wondering if that was what had him so introspective.

"Of course," he said.

"You seem awfully quiet. Is something wrong?"

"I'm just worried about Mal participating in this thing in the morning. He looks better, but I know he isn't one hundred percent yet, and I don't want to push him too hard."

"He'll be okay. Tiny is going to be doing most of the heavy lifting anyway. Mal's role will be a simple one."

"Simple but necessary," Duncan said. "I'd do it myself, but it's his case, and for the sake of the solidity of future search warrants and any potential prosecution, it's better if he does it. But if something goes wrong, Mal could end up getting hurt more."

"What do you think might go wrong?"

"If our little distraction plan doesn't work, the whole thing will be for naught. And even if it does work, Mal might not have enough time."

"If that happens—and I think it's a big *if*—we'll think of something else," I said, and Duncan frowned at me. "What?"

"*We'll* think of something else?" he echoed. "You sound like you think you're coming along."

"Of course I am."

"No, you're not."

"Oh yes I am."

"This is serious stuff, Mack," he said.

"I know that. I'm not treating it like some frivolous outing. And I'm part of the team now, remember?"

"Not for this."

I stared at him, one eyebrow arched. "I can take care of myself," I insisted.

"It's not that," Duncan said. Then he sighed. "I just don't like the idea of putting you in danger." He paused, his lips pinched into a thin line. "I don't know what I'd do if anything happened to you."

His voice choked up on this last statement, and I felt my heart nearly burst. I didn't think I could be any happier at that moment. But then Duncan proved me wrong.

"You know I love you, Mack, right?"

"You do?"

"I do."

I smiled at him. "Well, I happen to think you're a pretty swell guy, too."

He shot me a horrified look, and I burst out laughing. "Relax, you ninny," I said when I had my laughter under control. "I've been in love with you for months. I thought it was obvious."

"Well, I wasn't sure, what with all this stuff with Mal, and that business with my ex."

His ex, Courtney Metcalfe, was a wealthy socialite and the daughter of a Chicago tycoon, who had left Duncan standing at the altar. His history with her was one of the reasons I hadn't felt comfortable around wealthy people. Well, that, and the fact that another wealthy woman had been behind the letter-writer campaign. I'd recently discovered Courtney was not only living in Milwaukee—a fact Duncan hadn't shared with me—but that she was making overtures to win him back.

"Look," Duncan went on, "I know I haven't been around as much as you would like. And I've seen the way you act and look around Mal. You really care for him."

"I do care for Mal," I said. "And I'll admit I wouldn't mind seeing more of you. But my feelings for Mal are more brotherly in nature. And I suspect I'll be spending a lot more time with you in this new role I have. I'm basically your sidekick now."

His face relaxed, and I saw a hint of a smile on it. "I like the sound of that," he said. "In fact, I think maybe we should consider making you a permanent sidekick. Would you consider marrying me?"

I was flabbergasted. "M-m-marry you?" I stammered.

"Too soon?" he said, wincing.

"Maybe a little," I said. How had things gone from hoping for the commitment of an invite to spend the night at his place to a marriage proposal already? Zero to sixty with lightning speed. "We've only known each other for a few months, Duncan. And when you get right down to it, we don't really *know* each other at all."

"I know plenty about you," he insisted.

"Okay, then I don't know all that much about you. I mean I only just discovered this whole business with your ex a few weeks ago. And then there's the matter of living situations. I can't give up my bar and my apartment and you have a house."

"The house is technically my parents'," he said. "They own it. I just live in it rent free in exchange for maintaining it and doing some fix-ups. I'd be fine with us living at your place."

I recalled him telling me this information about his house back when we first met. So I scratched that objection off my list. "I need a little time to think about it, Duncan," I said. "Would that be okay?"

"Of course." He tried to sound dismissive, but I could hear, and taste, the hurt in his voice. I felt bad I was the cause of his pain. Why was I feeling so hesitant? I did love him; that much I knew. And I'd been bemoaning the lack of apparent commitment on his part for the past several weeks. Well, I had my wish. This was the ultimate commitment. So what was holding me back?

I decided it was time to have a serious, heart-to-heart talk with myself. And maybe with Cora and the Signoriello brothers, too. And maybe, just maybe, I needed to have a chat with my father, as well. Yeah, talking with a ghost. That should clear things up just fine.

Chapter 25

When we got back to the bar, we made the final arrangements for our morning rendezvous with Klein and the building site. Our plan required the assistance of Clay as well as the others, so we read him in on the plan and asked for his help. No surprise, he was eager to participate, particularly when we promised him an exclusive on the story.

I took some time to grab a change of clothes and put some clean sheets on Mal's basement bed, and then worked at getting things ready for closing. I sent my staff home right at two, and Duncan helped me whip through the closing duties. The O'Reillys were majorly excited when we informed them of the plan to have Mal spend the night at the bar, and he showed up right on time, just after closing, parking some distance from the bar and coming in through the back-alley entrance so he wouldn't be seen.

It was fun to watch the O'Reillys come together again. The obvious affection and warmth they shared made me long for a big family for the first time ever. I'd been content all my life with just Dad and me, and some of our regular bar patrons often made it seem like we had a larger extended family. But after watching the interactions between the O'Reilly clan, I felt like I might have missed out on something all those years.

Duncan and I left for the night a little after two-thirty, and I told the O'Reillys they had free run of the bar. Predictably, Patrick and Ryan whooped over this, while their sister shook her head in mock disdain.

Duncan kept giving me these sad, little hangdog looks throughout the night, and it only made my remorse worse. Things felt a tad awkward at his place, but we were so exhausted, we both fell asleep with ease.

The following day dawned gray and cloudy, and I could smell snow in the air. Duncan was up before me—already showered, shaved, and dressed for the day by the time I woke up at eight. We were supposed to meet up with the others at the bar at nine, so I hurried through my morning ablutions, which left little time for Duncan and me to talk. This was probably just as well, because I didn't yet know what to say to him.

Our ride to the bar was a silent one, but it didn't feel uncomfortable. Duncan rested one hand on mine throughout the drive, and that reassured me that his tension was due more to the upcoming operation than anything between the two of us.

The O'Reillys were all up and sharing breakfast in the bar when we arrived.

"Good morning, Mack!" Connor greeted me.

"Good morning!"

"Can we fix you something to eat as a way of saying thanks for turning your home and your bar over to us?" Colleen said.

"Thanks, but Duncan and I already ate, and besides, I promised you guys a breakfast today." I realized as soon as I said this that Duncan might have liked to take Colleen up on her offer. All we'd had to eat was a couple of toaster tarts.

"Thanks," Connor said, "but we've already helped ourselves. Hope that's okay."

"Of course," I assured him, and then I went behind the bar to get a cup of coffee. Duncan followed me, and Mal got up from the O'Reilly table and walked over to us.

"Thanks for this," he said, gesturing toward his family. The change in the way he looked only served to prove to me how important the love and company of his family was to him. There was color in his cheeks where there hadn't been any before, and a spark in his eye I hadn't seen in a while.

"I'm the one who needs to thank you," I said. "I still can't believe your family came here and installed my elevator for me. And you did the bulk of the planning and design work. It's worth every penny and then some. In fact, I intend to give you and your family a little bonus."

"That's not necessary," Mal said. "You gave them free food, drink, and lately, housing, so I think we're good."

I let the argument go because I knew Mal wouldn't change his mind, but I intended to provide the bonus nonetheless.

After one last round of good-byes, the O'Reillys climbed into their rental vehicle and headed for the airport. I missed them a surprising amount as soon as they left and could only imagine how Mal felt.

Cora and Clay both arrived at the bar a short while later, and the five of us sat down and once again went over the plan, synchronizing our watches and reviewing the timing. Tiny, whose role was crucial, was already at work, anticipating our arrival. Once we were sure everything was planned down to the last detail, we headed out in Duncan's car.

Duncan parked some distance away from the site and the mobile office trailer. Then we split up, Clay heading for the work site, Cora, Duncan, Mal, and me quietly heading for the back of the mobile office. From there, we positioned ourselves among the parked cars and trucks in the lot, crouching down so we wouldn't be seen. Mal, Duncan, and I went alongside the pickup truck with a topper on the bed that was parked closest to the trailer. Cora crouched beside a car next to us.

A few minutes past the prescribed hour, we saw Tiny hurrying toward the trailer. He mounted the two stairs outside and knocked on the door. When Klein answered, Tiny stepped into the doorway and started talking. We were close enough to hear what he said.

"Mr. Klein, you best come to da site right away. Dere is some reporter dere who says he's here to investigate a story he's working on about how our work is dangerous and not up to da code. He says dere is a camera crew arriving any minute."

I heard Klein mutter some expletives, and a moment later, he came out of the trailer, letting the door bang closed behind him. We watched them cross over to the work site, and as soon as they were out of the way, Mal stepped out from our hiding place and headed for the trailer door, camera in hand. I held my breath as he mounted the steps and pulled on the handle, knowing that if Tiny had failed at his part of the job, the whole thing would end right there. Tiny's job had been to place a cork, which I had provided and Duncan had measured and cut, into the slot where the door latch normally went, preventing the door from latching.

Duncan had applied some double-sided tape to one end of the cork so it would, hopefully, stick in place.

There were a dozen things that could go wrong, including the cork not sticking and falling, Tiny fumbling it, or Klein checking the door before leaving to make sure it was locked. We had rehearsed the moves Tiny should make dozens of times last night, practicing on the door to my basement. He made the moves over and over again until he not only became adept at placing the cork but at positioning himself so Klein would have to slide past him, and then being in a spot where he could prevent the door from bouncing back open again, something that would have made it apparent it hadn't locked.

The door opened, Mal disappeared inside, and I was able to breathe again.

Off in the distance, we heard the muted voices of the others: Klein, Clay, and some of the workers. I couldn't make out what they were saying, but the voices were raised and the tones sounded heated.

Minutes ticked by as the rest of us stayed in our hiding spots and waited. I imagined in my mind what Mal was doing inside: opening the drawer where the books were kept, taking them out, opening them, and photographing the pages. There were so many possible complications, and I kept running through them in my head. Was the drawer locked? This possibility had been discussed, and Mal was carrying a device that would, hopefully, unlock it. How many pages were there? How long would it take? Would Clay and Tiny be able to keep Klein occupied and away long enough?

I glanced at my watch and saw that just over eight minutes had passed. Why was Mal taking so long? I knew Duncan was as worried as I was because I could hear his heart pounding inside his chest. We exchanged a nervous look but said nothing.

Then our worst fear came true. We heard voices approaching, and raised up enough to peek through the side windows of the truck. A red-faced Klein was storming toward his office, Clay and Tiny running behind him, yelling questions at him. "Crap," Duncan muttered. He looked over at Cora, who was watching through the windows of the car she was hiding behind, and pointed toward the men.

Cora needed no further prompting. She popped up and quickly strode toward the group of men, yelling, "There you are, you cheating bastard. I've been looking all over for you." She strode up to Klein in a few quick steps and poked a finger in his chest, stopping him. "I need you to tell me right now if he"—she pointed at Tiny with her free hand—"was really working here yesterday, or if he's been seeing that slut on the side again." She then grabbed Klein's arm and spun him around. "Look at him," she yelled. "That's the face of a cheater! And you're covering for him, aren't you? You men, you're all alike. Sticking up for one another so you can stick it wherever you want. Well, I'm here to tell you right now, that's going to stop."

Cora went on with her tirade, yelling inches away from Klein's face. Klein stood there looking dumbfounded, alternately staring at the crazy woman who was all up in his business and the two men who had stopped several feet away. Duncan darted out of our hiding place, ran up to the door of the office, and rapped three times quickly. Two seconds later, the door opened and Mal stepped out. He clambered down the stairs, and Duncan led him back to the truck that was our shield.

"That was close!" I whispered once we were all crouched down again. "Did you get what you need?"

Mal nodded, then his face took on a horror-stricken expression. "Oh hell," he muttered. "I forgot to grab the cork."

Duncan let out a perturbed sigh and ran a hand through his hair. I squeezed my eyes closed, my heart pounding in my chest. I raised up again to peek at Klein and Cora, and saw Klein shake his head and turn away from Cora, once again heading for his office. This was bad, and I thought fast, trying to decide what to do.

Cora came after Klein and grabbed his sleeve, halting him for the moment. But I knew it wouldn't last for long. She continued her ranting diatribe, having succeeded in turning Klein enough to give me a chance. I took it.

I stood and scrambled out of the hiding place, shaking off Duncan's grab on my arm. I heard him hiss my name, but ignored him and scooted around behind the trailer. I took a second or two to gather my wits and then proceeded to walk back around to the front of the trailer. As I had feared, Klein had once again shaken Cora off, and he was continuing toward his office. I walked over to the base of the stairs and stood there, staring at him. When he saw me, he hesitated for just a second, rolled his eyes, and then continued coming for me.

"Good day, Mr. Klein," I said. "I need to speak with you again regarding the matter we discussed the other day." I looked past him toward the still-shrieking Cora. "Unless you're otherwise occupied, that is," I added with a wide-eyed look.

"I've got nothing more to say to you," he grumbled. He tried to step past me and climb the stairs, but I sidestepped up them, positioning myself by the door.

"I think you want to hear me out," I said, putting my hand up on the door just above the lock and leaning against it. "I happen to think you're innocent, and I have a way to help you. But you're going to have to hear me out."

Klein rolled his eyes again, removed his keys from his pocket, and reached past me to insert one in the lock. He drove it home and turned it, giving me an annoyed look. "I suggest you move out of my way," he said.

I leaned back just enough to allow him to grab the door and open it. Then I feigned losing my balance, acting as if I was about to fall backward off the side of the steps. To stop myself, I grabbed the door's threshold, right where the strike plate was located. To his credit, Klein made a grab for me.

"Thanks," I said, breathing a fake sigh of relief. "Shall we?" I swung my free arm toward the inside of his office.

"Ms. Duncan, I don't—"

"It's Dalton. Mack Dalton. The detective's name was Duncan, Duncan Albright."

"Whatever," Klein said irritably. He looked back at Cora, who was now striding rapidly toward us, still ranting. Klein stepped into his trailer, and as he did so, I maneuvered my fingers around the edge of the cork Tiny had stuck in the depression, pulled it out, and palmed it, lowering my hand to my side. Klein turned and glared at me. "I've had about all I can take today," he said, his face a thundercloud of anger.

I started to say something more, but Klein pulled the door shut, nearly knocking me off the steps for real this time.

I looked toward Cora and gave her a quick thumbs-up. She spun around and went after Tiny and Clay, both of whom began a hasty retreat toward the work area. A quick glance told me that Mal and Duncan were still hunched down beside the truck. I walked a few steps away from the trailer and then turned back to look at it. I saw Klein's face appear in the window, but when he saw me looking at him, he quickly retreated. Feigning frustration, I turned and stomped off toward the main street.

Duncan and Mal met me seconds later, and we continued our way back to where Duncan had parked the car. Cora, Clay, and Tiny met us there a few minutes after that.

"Holy crap!" Cora said, a huge smile on her face. "That was fun!"

"I didn't t'ink so," Tiny said with a frown.

"Did it work?" Clay asked. "Please tell me you got what you need."

Mal smiled at them. "I did. Thanks to all of you."

"And you swear you won't let anyone else have this when you're ready to bust Klein?" Clay said, looking from Mal to Duncan and back again. "I get an exclusive, right?"

"It will be all yours," Duncan told him.

"I need to go get my car," Tiny said. "I'm done working for dis guy."

Cora looked at me. "Can you do without me for a little while? I'd like to go with Tiny."

Judging from the excited, flushed look on Cora's face, I had a good idea what they'd be doing for the next hour or two. "That's fine," I said.

"Where's your car?" Cora said, grabbing Tiny's hand and pulling him away. I started to think they might not make it out of the parking lot before Cora ravaged the poor guy. The two of them headed off, and the rest of us climbed into Duncan's car.

No one said a word as Duncan started up the engine and pulled out. As soon as we left the industrial park, I said, "I think this calls for a celebration. The drinks and lunch are on me."

"It's too soon to celebrate," Duncan said. "We need to look at what Mal got, analyze it, and see if it's what he thinks it is. Then we have to convince a judge to give us a search warrant."

"Oh, come on," I pleaded. "You have to eat."

"I am kind of hungry," Mal said.

The corners of Duncan's mouth twitched up into what was almost a smile. "Okay. I know when I'm outnumbered."

I clapped my hands together and said, "Good."

Duncan shot me a look. "You seem quite jazzed by all this," he observed. "You do realize how dangerous that stunt you pulled back there was, don't you?"

I did. And my pounding heart, which still hadn't fully settled back into a normal rhythm, was proof of it. But a part of me also agreed with Cora. The stunt had been nerve-racking and tense. But it had also been a slice of exhilarating fun.

Chapter 26

I ordered up food and drinks for all of us when we got back to the bar, and because the bar had just opened, I took everyone upstairs to my apartment to eat so we could have some privacy. The O'Reilly clan had been the perfect houseguests. The apartment was spick-and-span clean, the beds had been stripped and the linens were in the dryer, and all the dishes were clean and put away. Except for the naked beds, it was hard to tell anyone had even been there.

We gathered around the dining room table and, while we ate, rehashed the entire affair, recalling how we had experienced both amusement and panic during various aspects of it. Several times I caught Duncan staring at me with expressions that ranged from wistful to annoyed, and I wasn't sure if it was because of what I had done during our escapade or my ambivalence about his proposal the night before. I decided it was probably both.

When Duncan wasn't watching me, he and Mal were going over the photos Mal had taken with his digital camera. They seemed excited at the mention of several names and dates they found among the photographed pages, and I had a feeling Wade Klein's days as a contractor were coming to an end. This was good news, but it still hadn't brought us any closer to figuring out who had killed Sheldon Janssen. At one point I excused myself from the group to use the bathroom. When I was done, I took a moment to check my reflection in the mirror. This crime-solving stuff suited me. My complexion was rosy, my eyes were bright, and my face looked smooth and relaxed. Maybe it wasn't the work, I thought. Maybe it was Duncan's proposal.

As I studied my face in the mirror, I felt a familiar sensation. My mirror image always made my face crawl, for lack of a better word. It felt as if my skin was trying to rearrange itself. It wasn't an uncomfortable feeling, just peculiar. And I'd experienced it thousands of times in my life. But this time, an alarm went off in my brain. Something about the experience felt different . . . more important. I'd felt this sensation recently, but in a different context. I closed my eyes and tried to figure out what my mind was trying to tell me. And then I remembered. I'd had the same sensation when I was looking at Peace Vanderzandt.

My eyes flew open and I turned away, my thoughts racing. Things started clicking—literally, because I could hear a faint clicking type of noise in my head—and my heart started to race. I bolted out of the bathroom and joined the others.

They were laughing at something, no doubt some retelling of the adventure we had just shared, and I stood at the head of the table and waited for them to settle down. Slowly, they all turned to look at me.

"What is it, Mack?" Duncan said. He put down the french fry he'd been about to pop in his mouth and stared at me.

"You need to call Ms. Parnell," I said.

"Okay," Duncan said slowly. "Want to tell me why?"

"She said she had a copy of Felicity's birth certificate. I want to check the birthdate on it."

Duncan narrowed his eyes at me; the others just stared. "Want to tell me why?" Duncan asked.

"Not yet. I need to check on something."

Duncan arched his eyebrows, took out his phone, and punched in the number. Everyone's attention had shifted to him. The room was utterly silent. Ms. Parnell must have answered because Duncan said hello, said who he was, and then asked her if she could please tell him what Felicity's birthdate was on her birth certificate.

"No," I said. "Not Felicity's. Hope's."

Duncan's brow furrowed, and he amended his request. Then he looked at me and said, "She's pulling the birth certificate from her file." While he waited, Duncan propped the phone against his shoulder and removed his notebook and pen from the pocket of his jacket, which was draped over the chair back behind him. Seconds later, he started writing. I walked over and peered over his shoulder at the date: September 16, 1985. When he was done writing it down, he thanked Ms. Parnell and gave me a questioning look. I shook my head, and he said good-bye and disconnected the call. Then he looked at me again. "Well?" he said.

"Check the driver's license info you have on your phone on Peace Vanderzandt," I said. "What's her birthday?"

Duncan started tapping at the screen on his phone. A moment later, he said, "September 16, 1985." He looked back at me, his eyes wide.

I smiled at him. "That's it!" I said, snapping my fingers.

"Hope and Peace weren't just sisters; they were twins. But not identical twins, mirror twins." I saw looks of skepticism on some of the faces staring at me. "Think about it," I said. "No one's face is exactly symmetrical. There are subtle differences in the shape of the eyes, the height of the eyes, the lay of the mouth, the overall structure, even where one's hair parts. Peace and Hope are twins, but their facial shapes and structures are the opposite of each other, like a mirror image." I still saw some doubt, so I continued my explanation. "I get a weird sensation when I look at my own mirror image, and just now in the bathroom, I remembered that I got the same sensation when we met Peace and I looked at her. It was right after studying the picture of Peace that Duncan had on his phone."

Several seconds of silence ensued as the group contemplated what I was saying and the ramifications of it all. It was Clay who finally broke the silence. "So, what are you saying, Mack?"

"I'm saying Peace Vanderzandt isn't really Peace Vanderzandt. It's Hope! She has taken on her sister's identity."

"So what happened to Peace?" Mal asked.

"My guess is that she's the one who died, not Hope. I'll bet that's why Peace, or rather Hope, visited Sheldon. She was looking for Felicity. She found out Sheldon had pulled her from the facility, and she wanted to know where she was. And I'm betting that's why Felicity said little peach killed her father." I looked at Mal. "You said Sheldon once referred to Felicity as his little peach, right?" Mal nodded. "And Norman Chandler told us that Sheldon picked up that nickname from Hope. Maybe it was a take on her sister's name; you know, Little Peace as opposed to Little Peach? Anyway, I'm betting it was Hope who killed Sheldon."

"But why?" Clay said.

"I'm not sure on that count," I admitted. "Perhaps she was angry with him for taking Felicity. Maybe she wanted her back, or wanted to know where she was, and Sheldon wouldn't tell her. Or maybe she wanted to take Felicity without Sheldon being able to come after her."

"Then why didn't she?" Duncan asked. "If she was there in his house, and Felicity saw her, why didn't Hope just take her daughter?"

Another piece of the puzzle fell into place for me. "Because she didn't see Felicity. Felicity saw her, but Hope probably ran from that house in a hurry after shooting Sheldon. Felicity saw Mal, remember? Yet he didn't see her. I'm betting Hope didn't either. Felicity probably heard the raised voices and came out of her hiding place. When a shot was fired, it probably frightened her, and she hid somewhere else. She might have been afraid at first, but eventually, she thought about coming out of her hiding place to see what was going on. But then the door opened again, so she stayed hidden and saw her mother come in."

"It makes some sense," Mal said.

"Of course it does," I said. "Think about it. When we told Peace, who I now believe was Hope, about trying to find someone to take care of Felicity, she looked shocked. And then, after saying she had no interest at all in taking in the girl, she kept insisting she wanted to meet her. Why? I think it's because she thought Felicity was dead."

"I'm with Clay," Mal said, looking puzzled. "Why would Hope kill Sheldon? He was her main chance at finding Felicity."

I shrugged. "Revenge? Anger? Maybe he flipped Hope's trick back on her and told her that Felicity was dead, and that set her off. Maybe there was a struggle similar to what you experienced." I paused and shrugged. "Only Hope herself can answer that question."

"Then we best have another chat with her," Duncan said. "I'm glad I put some guys on a watch over her." He started tapping at his phone again, and made arrangements for the local cops to bring in the woman they thought was Peace Vanderzandt. When he was done, he looked over at me with a smile. "Ready for another interview?" he said.

"Wouldn't miss it."

"Do I get an exclusive on this one, too?" Clay asked.

"It's all yours," Duncan told him. "Let's get to it."

Three hours later, Duncan and I walked into an interview room in Duncan's police station. Seated inside was a very irate Peace Vanderzandt, who I now felt certain was really Hope Vanderzandt Janssen.

"I don't appreciate being left to sit here for an hour without knowing what's going on," she snapped as soon as we walked in. Just before entering the room, I had once again examined the photo of Peace. Now, as I looked at the woman before me, I had that crawly sensation in my face and scalp.

"I'm sorry you had to wait," Duncan said.

"Where is Felicity?" she demanded. "I thought I was being brought here to see her."

"Yes, well, that's not exactly true," Duncan said.

Peace/Hope looked from Duncan to me and back at Duncan again. "What's going on here?"

"Ms. Vanderzandt, there are some questions about the death of your brother-in-law that we need to clear up first. And before we do that, I need to inform you of your rights. It's a standard thing whenever we talk to someone here." Duncan read her the Miranda warning. "Do you wish to have an attorney present?" he asked her.

"What for? I haven't done anything. Only guilty people need attorneys, right?"

I knew she was lying when she said she hadn't done anything, and I gave Duncan a look and a slight nod.

"Ms. Vanderzandt, I understand your sister and you were identical twins; is that correct?"

"Yeah," she said with a shrug. "So?"

"So before we can let you see Felicity, we need to verify your identity."

"Seriously?" she said, gaping at him. "What do you want, a driver's license? A passport? I have both in my purse."

The fact that she had a passport with her was concerning. It wasn't the sort of thing one carried around every day.

"No, that won't suffice," Duncan said. "Those are photo IDs, and given that you and your sister are identical twins, it isn't enough."

She frowned at him. "What, then? Fingerprints? DNA?"

"Well," Duncan said, leaning back in his seat and lacing his fingers together, "identical twins have identical DNA, so that won't help. Fingerprints might, because identical twins don't have matching fingerprints, and we do have your sister's on file from her autopsy. Unfortunately, we have nothing to compare them to. Neither of you was ever fingerprinted before."

The woman fumed and started tapping one foot in irritation.

"However, there are some differences between the

two of you that we can use." Duncan unlaced his fingers and leaned forward, picking up and opening a manila folder he'd brought into the room with him.

Peace/Hope stopped tapping her foot and leaned forward. "Such as?" she said, her voice sounding wary.

"Such as scars. We were able to find an accident report on file, a motor vehicle accident involving Peace Vanderzandt. Do you recall that accident?" Duncan asked.

For the first time, the crusty façade showed a crack. She stared at Duncan, saying nothing.

"No?" Duncan said. "Well, let me refresh your memory. You were involved in a two-car accident four years ago in which you were hit broadside by an elderly motorist who ran a stop light and hit your car. The impact caved in the driver's side door of your car. You sustained several injuries, including a bruise to your left arm and leg, and a rather severe cut on your left arm from the broken glass in the door window. According to the accident report and the ER visit record that followed, that injury required ten stitches."

Duncan closed the file and tossed it back on the table. "So the identification is relatively simple," he said, lacing his fingers again. He focused his gaze on her left arm, currently obscured by the long-sleeved sweater she was wearing. "Show us the scar on your left arm."

A good ten seconds ticked by as Peace/Hope squirmed in her chair, her face contorting into various expressions that ranged from fear, to anger, to resignation, and then back to anger again.

"This is insulting and ridiculous," she said, shoving her left arm through the straps of her purse, pushing out of her chair, and grabbing her coat where it hung on the back of it. "I don't have to put up with this kind of treatment from the likes of you." She spun around and headed for the door, pulling it open.

On the other side of the door stood two uniformed police officers who blocked her way. Peace/Hope stood there and stared at them for several beats. Then her shoulders sagged, and she spun back toward us. "That accident report is wrong," she said, but there was no conviction in her voice. I think even she knew this argument was a feeble one that wouldn't help her out of her jam.

Duncan said, "Show me your left arm."

"I don't have to do that," she insisted, thrusting her chin at him in defiance.

"Okay," Duncan said. "But you aren't going to leave here yet. We're going to hold you. We can get a search warrant to inspect your arm, and even if you try to claim the accident and ER reports are false, we can check your fingerprints to verify who you are."

Peace/Hope looked confused. "But you said you don't have any fingerprints to compare to."

"Yes, well that wasn't exactly true. You see, your sister worked as a dealer for the Potawatomi Casino for a few months several years ago, and to work there, you have to be fingerprinted. We're waiting for the records to show up, and when they do, we should be able to prove who you really are."

All the woman's angry bravado evaporated. She walked back over to the chair and sank into it, collapsing like a deflated balloon.

"You're Hope Janssen, aren't you?" Duncan said. His tone wasn't accusatory. Quite the opposite, in fact; it was soothing and conciliatory, tasting like smooth milk chocolate.

Hope nodded, her head hung in misery. Duncan

waited, and after a moment, she lifted her head and looked at him. "Where did Sheldon put Felicity?"

"She lived with him," Duncan said.

Hope looked confused. "But when I found him, I staked out his place for several weeks, and I never saw her come or go from there. And when I went into his house that day, there was no sign of her."

"He built a special little hidden cubbyhole for her," Duncan told her. "She was there the whole time. She saw what you did to her father."

Hope squeezed her eyes closed and gritted her teeth. "That bastard," she muttered. "He deserved it. When I asked him what he had done with her, he said she was dead, that she'd choked on some food, and by the time he got her to the hospital, it was too late."

"He lied," Duncan said.

Hope shook her head and let out a humorless laugh. "Where is she now?"

"She's safe," Duncan said. "She's with a foster family that is more than capable of caring for her."

"Yeah, good luck with that," Hope scoffed. "That child is a demon."

I wanted to shake the woman. "She is not a demon," I said. "And if you feel that way about her, why on earth did you want her back?"

"I didn't want her back," Hope snapped. "At least not for any length of time. But I needed some money. I lost my home, I lost my car, I wasn't able to get a job—"

"Because of the drugs?" I said.

Hope didn't answer. She just glared at me. After a moment of eye-to-eye standoff, she said, "I realized if I was dead, my sister could claim Felicity and apply for assistance to care for her. That money would have come in real handy."

"It was your sister who died?" Duncan said.

Hope stared at him for the longest time without answering.

"Did you kill her?" he prompted.

"No!" Hope snapped. "She overdosed."

"She's lying," I said.

Hope shot me a dirty look. Her defiance was once again at the forefront, but it didn't last long. After a few seconds of glaring at me, her body sagged. She looked down at her lap. "I went to my sister for help last year," she said. "I was living on the streets; I had nowhere to go. She took me in, and after a while, I was able to convince her to try some cocaine. From there, I talked her into some crystal meth, and then heroin. Pretty soon, she was as hooked as I was. But we were burning through her money pretty fast, and then she lost her job." She paused, sighing heavily. "I knew I was going to have to do something else soon."

She fidgeted with her fingers for a moment. "When she died, I realized I could assume her identity. That's when I got the idea about Felicity. I knew Sheldon had discovered my lie about her, and removed her from the facility where I'd placed her."

More silence, and then Hope looked up at Duncan with tears in her eyes, tears I felt sure were for herself rather than anyone else. "I just thought Felicity would be happier with her momma, and we could get some money, and stay in my sister's house. I was going to get clean, get off the drugs, and try to get a job."

"She's lying again," I said.

Hope's face contorted into a mask of fury. "Screw you!" she said.

"Get her out of here," Duncan said to the uniformed officers.

One of the officers approached Hope and took hold of her arm. "Come with me, please," he said.

I half-expected Hope to put up a fight, but she went with the men without resisting.

I had no sympathy for the woman. Though I knew we'd likely never be able to prove it unless she confessed, I felt certain Hope had intentionally overdosed her sister. She had killed her sister, killed her ex-husband, and I felt certain that in time she would have killed Felicity, if she'd ever been able to get custody of her. Felicity was nothing more than a paycheck to her.

Fortunately, Felicity was safe now. But she was also all alone in the world, and that saddened me.

Chapter 27

The following morning, I awoke to a mishmash of emotions. I was sleeping alone in my bed for the first time in a while, and though it felt good to be back in my own space, I missed waking up to Duncan's smiling face.

I consoled myself with the knowledge that I'd be seeing him soon enough and got out of bed to get ready for the day ahead. As I was setting the coffeepot in my kitchen to brew, my cell phone rang, and I saw it was Mal.

"Hey, Mal," I answered. "I'm just getting the coffee going. Want to come up and have a cup with me?"

"I'd love to. Be there in a sec. Can you meet me at your apartment door?"

I went down to let him in. Mal had a set of keys to the bar, and while both he and Duncan had planned a long late night of follow-ups on the Janssen case, Mal informed me that he was going to continue to stay in my basement for now, until the business with Wade Klein was settled. When I let him in, he looked haggard and worn, and I suspected he hadn't slept at all, but rather had just now returned to the bar from an all-nighter.

I whipped up some scrambled eggs with cheese and some bacon for the two of us, and we settled in at the kitchen table. "How did things go last night?" I asked him.

"Good," he said. "Hope Janssen confessed to shooting Sheldon in exchange for a plea deal. She was staking out Sheldon's place, and she said she saw me go in that morning, heard the gunshot, and saw me come running out shortly afterward. After I was gone, she went over and tried the door and found it unlocked, so she went inside, unsure what had happened. She thought perhaps I had shot Sheldon, and she admitted she was disappointed to find out otherwise. Apparently, she and Sheldon had quite the confrontation. She demanded to know where Felicity was and stormed through the house looking for her. When Sheldon told her that story about Felicity choking and dying, she snapped, grabbed the gun, which Sheldon had left on the dining room table, and shot him. Then she ran. She was waiting on some false IDs to be made so she could disappear when you and Duncan came to visit. Needless to say, she was shocked when she realized Felicity was still alive. Any smart person would have stuck with the original plan and disappeared, but Hope's greed and her need for drugs overruled."

"So you're in the clear?" I asked.

Mal nodded and smiled.

"What about the evidence you got from Klein's books?"

"It looks promising. I'm hoping to get a search warrant soon."

"I'm so happy for you, Mal. But I'm sorry you had to go through all you did."

"Hey," he said with a shrug and a smile, "I came out

on the right side of things in the end, and that's all that matters."

"Speaking of being on the right side of things," I said, "I think a certain young lady who let you stay in her lake house is still harboring some serious feelings for you. Maybe you two should give it another try. You still have feelings for her, don't you?"

Mal smiled again. "Sabrina is a great gal, no doubt about it. But it just didn't work for us. I think we're from two different worlds or something." He paused and sighed. "I don't know what went wrong. It just felt awkward."

"Maybe that's because you guys put too much pressure on yourselves. I mean, you gave up your life and job back in Washington to come out here and be with her. That's a lot of pressure."

Mal nodded slowly, finishing up his last piece of bacon. "It was good to see her again," he said.

"Give her a call," I urged. "I'm betting she's willing to take another stab at it."

"Maybe I will." He grabbed his napkin, wiped his mouth, and pushed back his chair. "In the meantime, I've got more work to do. What's on your agenda for today?"

"I'm waiting to hear from Duncan regarding the Knutson case. If all goes as planned, we're hoping we can bust Caroline today."

Mal chuckled.

"What?" I said.

"Now you're even using cop slang," he said. "I think we've fully converted you."

He got up, gave me a kiss on the head, and then left. I finished my own meal, washed the dishes, and then headed for the shower. It felt good to be back in my own shower again, and I took a little longer than usual.

Once I was dressed and ready for the day, I headed downstairs. It was only nine-thirty, so my day staff hadn't come in yet. I called Cora to see if she was up and about, and invited her to come over early so I could talk to her.

"What about?" she asked.

"I'll tell you when you get here," I said.

"Ooh, a secret," she cooed. "I'll be there in two shakes."

True to her word, she was knocking on the front door seven minutes later. Her office, a portion of which also served as her home, was only blocks away.

"Okay," she said, settling into a chair and placing her laptop on the table. "What's up? Spill the beans." She opened her laptop and booted it up, as if she thought I was going to ask her to do some research for me.

"Duncan proposed to me," I said.

Cora froze, her eyes wide. "No kidding?" she said.

"No kidding."

"Did you give him an answer?"

I shook my head. "I told him I needed some time to think about it."

"Why?" Cora said, making a disbelieving face at me. "You love him, don't you?"

"I do, but come on, Cora. We haven't known each other all that long, and we haven't talked about a lot of things, and we have no idea if we'll be at all compatible over the long term."

Cora waved away my objections. "Nobody knows if they're compatible over the long term when they decide to get married. Even if you're greatly compatible, there will always be compromises to make, and disagreements to have. What matters is your commitment to each other. Are you ready to be committed to him? To making it work?"

"I am," I said. "I'm not as sure about him, though."

"So have a long engagement and live together. See what happens. Don't let the opportunity slip away unless you have some serious doubts."

I said nothing.

"Do you have serious doubts?" she asked me after a while.

Did I? I had doubts, but then, those came with every relationship. When I didn't answer right away, Cora tried a different tack.

"Tell me the things you're sure of," she said.

"I'm sure I love him," I said. "I'm sure I have feelings for him that are stronger than any feelings I've ever had for anyone else." I thought a moment. "I'm sure we are very compatible in the bedroom," I added with a wiggle of my brows.

"That's important."

"I'm also sure I don't want to lose him," I concluded.

"Sounds to me like you've made up your mind."

"But how do I know if he feels the same way about me?"

"Oh, he does."

"Why do you say that?"

"Because I've seen the way he looks at you when you don't know he's looking. And I've heard the way his voice changes when he's talking to or about you, unlike the way it sounds with anyone else. I may not have your synesthesia, but some things are obvious even to we simple mortals."

My phone rang then, and when I saw it was Duncan calling, I had a momentary panic, thinking he somehow knew we were discussing him. "Good morning, Duncan," I said, letting Cora know who was calling.

"Good morning, sunshine. Are you ready to go after Mrs. Knutson with me?"

"I'm ready any time. Do you want me to meet you somewhere, or are you going to pick me up?"

"I'll pick you up in twenty," he said. "I've got to grab something on the way. I'll text you when I'm out front."

I disconnected the call and filled Cora in on our plans. The front door of the bar opened then, and Debra came in to start her shift for the day.

"You're here early," she said to Cora.

"I was called in for a consultation," Cora said with a wink.

"More of that crime stuff?" Debra said in a tired voice. Many of my employees were intrigued by what the Capone Club and I did, and they participated whenever they could. Debra was an exception.

"Nope," Cora said. "Duncan proposed to her and she's not sure what to do."

Debra stopped with her coat half off, gaping at me. "He proposed?"

I nodded, giving Cora a dirty look for letting my secret out of the bag.

"That's fantastic!" Debra said, slipping her coat the rest of the way off and tossing it onto a barstool. "And about time, I might say."

"It hasn't been very long at all," I protested. "That's part of the problem. We've only known each other for a few months."

Debra waved away my objection the same way Cora had. "Time is irrelevant. Sometimes you just know, you know? And with the two of you, it was obvious from day one."

"Really?" My voice was rife with skepticism.

"Yes, really," Debra said. "Ask anyone here." She

headed behind the bar and started her morning prep work. The front door opened again and Pete came in with my cook, Jon, on his tail.

"Morning, guys," Debra hollered from behind the bar. "Guess who finally popped the question?"

Both men turned and looked at me expectantly.

"Hey," I said, "How do you know she isn't talking about Cora and Tiny?"

Jon rolled his eyes at me.

Pete said, "It's about time. You two have been dancing around this thing for far too long."

I looked over at Cora, who gave me back a smug look that said *told you so.*

I shook my head and smiled. "Okay, I give."

"Does that mean you're going to tell him yes?" Cora asked.

"I haven't made my mind up yet," I told her. "But you guys have given me some things to think about."

With that, I got up and helped Pete and Debra with their morning prep until Duncan texted me that he was out front. I thanked them all for their candor and advice, grabbed my coat and gloves, and headed out.

As soon as I was settled in the car, Duncan leaned over and kissed me. "Missed you last night," he said with a sigh.

"I missed you, too," I told him, and it was true. "So what's our plan?"

Duncan filled me in as we drove to Roberta's police station. They'd already made arrangements with Caroline to come down to the station with her attorney, Natalie Sokoloff, in tow.

"Was the ME able to come up with anything?" I asked.

Duncan shook his head. "No, but he did give us

some information we can use. We'll just have to hope Caroline is easily rattled."

We arrived at the station, and Duncan went around to the trunk of his car and took out a small metal tank. He carried it inside and set it on the table in the interview room we were going to use. Roberta found us in there and greeted us both with a cheery, "Good morning."

We removed our coats, which Roberta took somewhere to hang, and when she returned we spent a few minutes going over the plan once again. Five minutes later, a uniformed officer poked his head in the room and said, "Your suspect is here."

"Send them on back," Roberta said. "And make sure the camera is rolling before they enter the room."

"Got it," the officer said.

A few minutes later, Caroline Knutson entered the room with Natalie Sokoloff at her side. As soon as she stepped into the room and saw the tank on the table, Caroline froze. But it was a brief hesitation, there and gone in a second.

"Come on in and take a seat," Roberta said. Extra chairs had been placed in the room prior to our arrival, and Roberta waved a hand toward the two chairs on the far side of the table, right in front of the tank. "Can I take your coats?" Roberta offered.

"No need," Sokoloff said. "I doubt we'll be here very long."

"Suit yourself," Roberta said with a shrug and a smile. She sat across from Caroline, and Duncan sat down beside her. I settled into a chair that was positioned in the corner behind them, giving me full view of Caroline.

Roberta informed them that the interview was being

recorded, stated the date, the time, the case involved, and all the people present. She then recited the Miranda warning to Caroline. Once that was done, she said, "Okay, here's the thing. We've had a hard time dismissing your husband's death, Mrs. Knutson, because the ME wasn't able to find any direct cause. And it seems you have a fair amount of motive for wanting your husband out of the way."

Caroline opened her mouth, presumably to object to this statement, but Sokoloff silenced her with a hand on her arm.

"We researched your computer," Roberta went on, "thinking we might find some internet searches about poisons, or ways to kill someone."

Caroline bristled, but she pursed her lips and remained silent.

"We didn't find anything," Roberta said, and Caroline's mouth relaxed. "We searched your husband's computer, too, thinking you might have used his, but we didn't find anything there either."

Sokoloff tilted her head and gave Roberta an impatient look.

"But we did find something on your computer that made us curious," Roberta went on. "It was an email from the library, informing you that a book you requested was in. You had deleted the email, of course, but those kinds of things often aren't really gone, so we were able to resurrect it."

"And what was the book referenced in the email?" Sokoloff asked, sounding bored.

"It was a design book of some sort," Roberta said dismissively. "The book itself wasn't important. What was important was the fact that Mrs. Knutson used the library. So I went to her branch and had a chat with some of the workers there, and got a look at some of the other books she's checked out in the past."

Caroline looked off to the side, her expression worried for a moment, but after a few seconds, she appeared to relax.

"We didn't find anything interesting there either," Roberta said.

"Is there a point to this?" Sokoloff asked.

"There is," Roberta said. "Your client's history of checked-out books didn't offer anything of interest, but one of the librarians did. She knows you, Mrs. Knutson, and she recalled a day when you came into the library and spent a lot of time on one of the computers. You then pulled a book from the shelves that you sat down and read. She noticed the title of the book and it concerned her; that's why she remembered it. You might recall that one of the library staff members approached you one day and asked if you were okay."

Judging from the worried look on Caroline's face, she did, indeed, recall the event.

"The reason she was concerned was because of the book you were reading, a book titled *Final Exit*."

Caroline shifted nervously in her seat. Sokoloff didn't look bored anymore.

"It's a book about assisted suicide," Roberta went on. "But then, you know that, don't you?"

Caroline said nothing.

"So then we got curious and took a look at the book ourselves. And lo and behold, the recommended way of committing suicide in the book is with the use of helium."

Caroline's eyes darted toward the tank on the table and then back to Roberta.

"Yes, helium," Roberta said. "Just like that tank in front of you. Your husband's stores are full of them because people use them to inflate balloons, some specialty toys, and whatnot. Anyone can rent or buy them if they want."

Caroline licked her lips.

"So we had a chat with the ME and asked him if it was possible that helium might have been used to kill your husband. And he said it was. He also said your husband was the perfect victim for using something like that because of his CPAP machine. It would be very easy to swap out his oxygen tank for one filled with helium. And the reason it's such a popular method for committing suicide is that it causes a loss of consciousness within seconds, and death within minutes. And because of the nature of the helium gas, the victim wouldn't experience any symptoms of asphyxia."

"That's ridiculous," Caroline snapped. Sokoloff grabbed her arm again and gave it a squeeze.

"Not ridiculous at all," Roberta said. "It's something you have readily available not only in your husband's stores but in your house. You have the tanks delivered there, don't you?"

Caroline glared at Roberta but said nothing.

"You don't need to answer that question," Roberta said. "We have copies of the invoices from the company that delivers them. And you know what the most recent one showed? You had three of those tanks delivered to your house the day before Oliver died. And yet, when we searched your house, they weren't there."

"That proves nothing," Caroline said. "Oliver took them to his stores."

Sokoloff gave Caroline's arm another squeeze. Caroline pouted and clamped her mouth closed.

"Actually, he didn't," Roberta said. "We talked to the employees at his stores, and none of them remembered seeing Oliver drop off any tanks that day. But someone at the store closest to your house mentioned that some empty tanks had shown up at the store the day after Oliver died, and they had no idea how they'd gotten there."

Now Sokoloff looked as nervous as Caroline did.

"So we asked them if they still had those empty tanks," Roberta went on. "They did, and we picked them up, so we could dust them for prints."

Caroline narrowed her eyes at this.

Sokoloff said, "If you found my client's prints on any of the tanks at the stores, it means nothing. She deals with those tanks all the time, and takes the deliveries at her house. I'm sure she touches them all the time as a routine part of her duties."

"Yes, I suppose she does," Roberta said.

"And I'm sure there are a lot of other prints on them as well," Sokoloff added.

"This is true," Roberta said with a sigh. "However, we were able to get an internet history from the computer Mrs. Knutson used that day in the library, and imagine our surprise when we saw that there was a lot of research on suicide, the effects of helium, and forensic findings when helium is used to commit suicide." Roberta paused and smiled, a feral, scary smile. "I must admit," she went on, "it was a brilliant way to commit murder because it often leaves no trace in the victim. However, there can be remnants of it trapped in the victim's lungs, and if the ME pokes a needle and syringe into the lung before opening it up, he can sometimes catch a sample of it. So that's what the ME did, and again, imagine our surprise when we found traces of helium in his lungs. You killed your husband, Mrs. Knutson."

"You did *not* find any helium in his lungs," Caroline insisted angrily.

"Oh, but we did. Combine that with the history of your library research and your fingerprints on that tank there," she nodded toward the tank on the table, "and you're going to go away for a very long time. Assuming they don't go for the death penalty."

Caroline's face suffused with red as Roberta spoke. When Roberta was done, she said, "You're lying."

Caroline was right, if my synesthesia was any indication. What Roberta had said wasn't all true. I knew the ME hadn't found any helium in Oliver's lungs, but I wasn't sure how much of the rest of it was true.

Roberta kept on with her attack. "You made sure your husband took an Ambien just to be safe, to make sure he wouldn't awaken and take off his mask for some reason. And we also found traces of an adhesive on his face. Did you apply something to the edges of his mask to make sure there was an airtight seal?"

"No!" Caroline snapped.

"I think we're done here," Sokoloff said. She stood and said, "Come on, Caroline."

"She's not going anywhere," Roberta said. "We're placing her under arrest."

"Arrest?" Caroline sputtered. "But you're lying. I didn't use any kind of adhesive on Oliver's mask."

Sokoloff realized what her client just said, but I don't think Caroline did. And Roberta wasn't about to let Caroline off the hook yet. As Sokoloff told her client to shut up, Roberta continued with her scenario.

"Yep, I'm betting they'll go for the death penalty. You've seen your last of the outside world today, Mrs. Knutson. You are under arrest for—"

"But they're lying," Caroline insisted to Sokoloff, her voice rising to near hysteria.

"—the murder of your husband—"

"We'll figure it out later," Sokoloff said.

"—Oliver Knutson."

"But I *know* they're lying," Caroline insisted, her voice just below shrieking level. "I know because I flushed that line with oxygen afterward and kept the CPAP machine running so there wouldn't be any helium in his lungs."

The room fell deathly silent. The hot flush in Caroline's face drained away, leaving her looking pale, wan, and frightened. Sokoloff muttered an expletive under her breath.

Caroline turned and stared at Roberta as dawning settled in. "You bitch," she hissed. "You lying bitch! You tricked me!"

Roberta got up and walked over to the door. She opened it to reveal two uniformed officers. "Take her away," she said.

As the officers walked over and proceeded to cuff Caroline, she went berserk. "No!" she yelled. "You can't do this."

"Caroline," Sokoloff said in what I presume she meant to be a calming tone.

"But they're lying, Natalie. There's no way they found helium in Oliver's lungs."

As the officers tugged on Caroline's arms, pulling her toward the door, a look of fear and resignation came over the woman's face. "Natalie, do something," she pleaded.

The officers removed Caroline, and I heard her start to sob as they steered her down the hall. I almost felt sorry for her.

"Would you consider a plea deal?" Sokoloff said to

Roberta, clearly giving up on any hope of exonerating her client.

"Talk to the DA," Roberta said.

Sokoloff sighed, and left the room.

"Wow," I said once she was gone. "That was amazing. How much of the evidence you discussed do you really have?"

"Enough," Roberta said. "There was no adhesive. No need for it. The mask fit tight enough as it was. And the ME had already dissected Oliver's lungs, so there was no way to pull off a helium sample from them. If what Caroline said is true, there likely wasn't any anyway. But we do have the statement from the librarian, and to access the internet on the library computers, you have to type in a number from your library card, so we know it was Caroline who was doing the searches for the assisted suicide info and the helium. And we do have her fingerprints on a tank, though not this particular one." Roberta paused and shrugged. "Sokoloff is right about the fingerprints. They won't be of much use. But Caroline's little denial of a confession will certainly help."

"If you hadn't gotten her to say what she did, would you still be able to prosecute her?" I asked.

Roberta made an equivocal face. "It wouldn't be as strong, and her chances of getting off would have been a lot greater."

"Good work, Mack," Duncan said, rubbing my back. "You were the one who figured all this out."

"I'm officially a fan," Roberta said. "I suspect those empty spaces you detected among the supplies upstairs in the Knutson house were the spots where the tanks had been before Caroline took them back to the store. Oh, and we do have one other piece of evidence I never got around to mentioning."

"Which was . . . ?" I asked.

"The business across the street from the party store where the empty tanks turned up has security cameras outside. We looked at their footage and saw Caroline arrive at the store at four in the morning the day after Oliver died. She let herself in with a key, and then transported three boxes—boxes that were large enough to contain one of these helium tanks—into the store. Unfortunately, the footage doesn't show what was in those boxes, but when you put it all together, it will be enough for a conviction."

"I hope so," I said. "She's a coldhearted woman."

Roberta nodded sagely. "Tell me," she said, "what was it that put you on to the helium?"

"I had a strange synesthetic reaction in the Knutson house when we were there. Every time I looked up at the ceiling in Oliver's bedroom, I got a strange feeling, like I was weightless and being lifted off the floor. I didn't think much of it at the time because I didn't know what had triggered it. But then, when we visited one of Oliver's stores, there was a girl in the back, inflating balloons from a helium tank. And when I looked at the ceiling above her, I got the same response."

"Helium is a light gas," Roberta said. "There was probably some residual escaped helium near the ceiling in the bedroom, and also in the store."

"Makes sense," I said. "Anyway, things started clicking for me. I recalled a documentary I'd seen on TV late one night about assisted suicide. And I read some things about it online. It all came together."

"Well, I'm glad it did," Roberta said. "And welcome to the team."

She walked over and extended her hand. I shook it, and said, "Thanks."

When Roberta was gone, I looked over at Duncan, who was beaming at me. He walked over and kissed me. "So, how does it feel to be a crime-solving savant?" he asked when he was done.

"It feels fantastic," I said. "Let's go catch someone else."

"Patience," Duncan said with a chuckle. "There will be plenty more to come, sadly. For now, what do you say we head back to your bar and have a celebratory drink?"

"Sounds good," I said. "And as usual, the drinks are on me."

Chapter 28

When we arrived back at the bar, the lunch crowd was in full swing and the place was busy.

"Will you let me go behind the bar and fix you up a special something?" Duncan asked me.

I gave him a wary look. "Are you sure you learned enough from your undercover days as a bartender?"

"I have a confession to make," he said with a wink. "I've been studying. I figured if we do end up together, I should be able to chip in and help out behind the bar from time to time." He kissed me on the forehead.

"Okay," I said. "Surprise me." We walked over to the bar, and I told Pete to let Duncan do his thing. "I'm going to go upstairs to check in with the Capone Club," I said, and left Duncan to whip up his magic potions. As I walked through the bar toward the stairs, I realized one of the things that had been bothering me about Duncan's proposal. I had feared it was an impromptu, spur-of-the-moment thing he might later come to regret. But his statement a moment before, about how he'd been studying mixology with thoughts of the two of us being together and him needing to help out from time to time, made me realize he'd been thinking about us for some time now.

I reached the stairs and was about to climb them when I remembered the elevator. I detoured and headed for it. The door was closed, and when I hit the Up button, it slid open, revealing a shiny new interior. I stepped inside, hit the button for the second floor, and the door closed. In a smooth, almost silent glide, the elevator took me up. The sensation it gave me was similar to the one I had felt as a kid when I got a new toy I'd been wanting. How could I ever thank Mal enough?

The Capone Club room was surprisingly full. The group had split off into smaller gaggles, and they were all busy talking. In addition to Cora—and the Signoriello brothers, who were practically fixtures here, fixtures who had marked out the chairs closest to the fireplace as their permanent seats—Carter was there, along with Holly and Alicia, who were apparently enjoying a lunch break from their jobs at the bank. Tad was there, too, as was Dr. T, Tiny, Greg, Sonja, and Clay. Even Kevin Baldwin, our local "sanitation engineer," who hadn't been present much of late, was there. Also present were two other people I hadn't seen for a while: Nick Kavinsky and Tyrese Washington, two of the local cops who participated in the group.

When I walked in, everyone looked up, the room fell silent, and the minigroups separated.

"Hey, Mack," Cora said.

"Hello, everyone," I said.

There were some murmured hellos, and I saw several people exchange glances. Something was up.

"This is a big group for a weekday lunchtime hour," I said, settling into one of the empty chairs.

"Word spreads fast when there's something big to discuss," Tyrese said.

"Really? What are you discussing?"

"Is it true?" Holly asked in an excited voice. "Duncan proposed?"

I sighed, gave Cora an exasperated look, and then said, "Yes, he did."

Holly clapped her hands, and I heard several people congratulate me. Tyrese muttered, "It's about time."

"I haven't said yes," I told the group once the cacophony died down.

"Why the hell not?" Alicia said. "Duncan is a catch, and it's obvious the two of you care for each other."

A chorus of agreeing *yeah* comments followed.

"I wanted . . . I need some time to think things through."

There were some moans, and some shaking of heads, but before anyone else could say anything, Duncan came into the room.

"Hello, everyone," he said, handing me a drink.

Everyone returned his greeting.

"I came up in the elevator," he said.

"So did I."

"It's really nice. Mal and his family did a good job."

"Yes, they did."

"It's a smart addition," Clay said.

The rest of the room was oddly quiet, all of them staring intently at me and Duncan. I took a nervous sip of my drink, which was delicious, cool on the way down and triggering a comfortable warmth in my belly when it hit.

"Wow," I said, raising my glass to Duncan. "This is good."

"Thanks. I'm calling it Duncan's Dynamite."

"Listen," I said, "I need to talk to the brothers about

something. Would you mind if I stepped out for a few minutes? You can fill the group in on whatever you feel is appropriate about the Knutson case. I'm sure they'll be eager to hear about it because they're the ones who brought it to us."

"Of course."

I did a finger come-on at the Signoriello brothers, and when I saw them nod, I got up and headed out into the foyer outside the room. It took the brothers a minute or two to join me. Even with the warmth from that fireplace, those old bones of theirs didn't move all that fast.

"I need to talk to you two," I said.

"Figured as much," Joe said.

"Let's go into the banquet room so we can have some privacy."

I led the way to the room I used for group meetings and such. Most of the time it was closed off, but word was out that the space was available, and the number of rentals was increasing every week.

Once we were all seated, Frank said, "I'm guessing this is about Duncan."

I nodded.

"You're wondering what you should do?" Joe said.

I nodded again.

"And you want us to tell you," Frank said.

I just looked at them.

"You know we can't do that," Joe said, giving me an apologetic look. "Only you can make this decision."

"But we're happy to hear your thoughts on the matter," Frank added.

I smiled at them. I adored these two men, the closest thing I had to a parent these days. "I feel like it's too soon."

"Too soon based on what?" Joe asked. "Do you mean

you're not sure about your feelings for Duncan? Or that you don't know him well enough?"

"That's part of it," I admitted. "Although I do love him. That much I'm sure of."

"And does he want to get married right away?" Frank asked.

"No. At least I don't think so."

"So take your time," Frank said. "Maybe you two could live together for a while. That's what all you youngsters do these days, right?"

"Or is that an issue?" Joe jumped in. "Does he want you to get rid of the bar? Or move out of it?"

"No, not at all. In fact, he said he envisioned the two of us living here together." I looked down at the drink Duncan had made me. "He's even been studying mixology so he can help out behind the bar."

"Okay," Frank said slowly, thoughtfully. "Does he make you happy?"

"He does," I said with a smile.

"And this thing with Mal, is that an issue?" Joe asked.

I shook my head. "I love Mal like a brother. My feelings for Duncan are different."

"So then, what are you afraid of?" Frank asked.

I shook my head and sighed. "I don't know. I think I'm afraid of making a mistake."

"You know what I think?" Joe said. "I think you're afraid of being happy. I think you think you don't deserve happiness because of all that's happened. Your father's death, Ginny's death, Lewis and Gary . . . all of it makes you feel like you're responsible somehow, and you should do penance by staying miserable for the rest of your life."

Frank nodded his agreement.

Were they right? Was I sabotaging my own happiness?

"Look at it this way," Frank said. "If you accept his

proposal, you can have a nice long engagement to make sure you're doing the right thing. If it turns out you're not, break it off."

Now it was Joe's turn to nod his agreement.

"Maybe you're right," I said. "I think I need a little more time to think about it."

Joe pushed himself up from his chair, walked over, and kissed me on the cheek. "You know we won't let you do anything stupid, right?"

That made me laugh.

"We got your back, Mack," Frank said, also rising, albeit slowly, from his chair. He walked over and kissed my other cheek. "You deserve to be happy, Mack. Let it happen." With that, the two of them left the room.

I sat a moment, thinking, and then I left the room and headed downstairs, across the bar, and up to my apartment. I made my way into my father's study and stood there, looking at his desk, his chair, his bookcase. During the letter-writer scare, I had come in here one other time, hoping to find an answer. At the time, I had been to a church, thinking that one of the letter writer's clues was hidden there. It hadn't been, and after my search had proven fruitless, I had come into the study and taken my father's Bible from the shelf, an action spurred by words the minister at the church had said to me. With the Bible in hand, I'd asked my father for help and guidance, appealing to his spirit, or ghost, or whatever might be out there. And then I opened the Bible to a random page, closed my eyes, and let my finger point to a bit of scripture.

What I'd found there had given me the answer I needed. It showed me where my interpretation of the clues had been wrong, and it turned me in the right direction. Unfortunately, the time I'd lost searching in the wrong place, and the car accident that happened as I was trying desperately to make it to the right place in time, had combined to cost Gary Gunderson his life.

Hoping for another helpful revelation, I once again held the Bible to my chest, looked up at the ceiling, and said, "Okay, Dad. You helped me once. Can you do it again? I could really use your advice."

I waited a moment, almost expecting to hear his voice emanate from the ceiling. It didn't, and so I opened the book to a random page, closed my eyes, and let my finger drop.

When I opened my eyes and looked, my finger was on a passage in the Book of John that read: "Peace is what I leave with you; it is my own peace that I give you. I do not give it as the world does. Do not be worried and upset; do not be afraid."

I smiled, and then I cried. I spent another ten minutes there, having a private talk with my father. When I was done, I left and headed back up to the Capone Club room.

Duncan was still there with the others. He looked at me with concern. "You were gone a long time," he said. "Is everything okay?"

"Everything is more than okay," I said, smiling at him. Then I looked at the others in the room. "Thanks to all of you for being such good friends and advisers to me," I told them. "All of you have become such big parts of my life. You're my family."

There were some murmured responses, half of which didn't register, and I was surprised to see Cora looked a bit teary-eyed. I turned to Duncan. "You are the biggest part of my life," I told him. "And with you, I can see a future, a different kind of family. I'm not sure it will be easy, and I suspect there will be more than a few bumps in the road ahead, but I'm willing to negotiate those bumps with you. So . . ." I took a deep breath and held it. My throat tightened, and I felt the sting of tears in my own eyes.

Duncan took my hand and smiled at me. "Mackenzie Dalton, are you saying you'll marry me?"

I blew out my breath, and in the utter silence of the room it sounded shockingly loud. "Yes, Duncan. Yes, I am."

Our kiss was backdropped by a cacophony of whoops, hollers, and clapping.

Chapter 29

Six months later . . .

I stood in the Capone Club room with my adopted family: Cora, Mal, Joe, and Frank.

"You look beautiful, Mack," Cora said, and for only the second time in all the years I'd known her, I saw tears in her eyes.

"I couldn't agree more," Joe said. His brother and Mal both nodded their agreement.

"Thank you," I said. I sighed, smoothed the front of the simple white dress I was wearing, and looked around at the otherwise empty room. "So much has happened here in this room, in this place," I said. "And all of you have been through it all with me."

"It's been our pleasure," Joe said with a warm smile.

"It's been a hell of a ride," Frank said, his eyes wide. "You've given us old codgers a new lease on life, Mack."

"And there will be more to come," Cora said. "Do you realize what you've created here, Mack? Do you realize what you, what all of us have accomplished?"

I did, and I said so, uttering the words "I do" for the

first time that day. "I think the greatest, or at least the most important aspect of it all for me has been the validation I've received, the love and affection I feel, and the happiness I have now. And I have all of you to thank for it." I turned and looked at Mal, who had so far remained silent. "This is a day of celebration for me, but also for you. I heard Wade Klein was convicted on all counts."

He nodded, smiling at me. "No small thanks to you."

I felt myself blush. "You were the one who put your life on the line," I said. "And you almost lost it." A wave of affection came over me, and on impulse, I lunged forward and hugged him. He hugged me back, and for a few seconds, we stayed that way. When we finally parted, I swiped at the tears in my eyes and looked him up and down. "May I say you are looking very handsome in that suit?"

"Thanks," he said with a smile, his voice cracking ever so slightly.

"Is Sabrina here?"

He grinned at me. "She is."

"Things are going well in that regard?"

"They are," he said, looking and sounding a bit self-conscious.

"I'm glad. I knew the two of you would find a way to make it work. I'm so happy for you."

"I suspect the next wedding we'll be holding here is going to be theirs," Cora said with a sly wink.

"Or yours and Tiny's," Joe said with a wink of his own.

Cora shook her head and held up a hand. "No, no. I'm not the marrying kind. But for now, Tiny and I are enjoying what we have."

"I should go downstairs to make sure everything is ready," Mal said. He walked over, kissed me on the cheek, and added, "Congrats to you and Duncan. I couldn't be happier for the both of you."

I was heartened to taste sincerity in his voice.

As soon as Mal left, I looked at the three remaining people and said, "I guess the time is nigh."

"Any regrets?" Cora asked.

I shook my head. "None."

It was true. For the past six months, Duncan and I had been sharing my living quarters, and I'd been amazed at how easily we had fallen into a routine that felt both comfortable and destined. Any reservations I'd had in the beginning had quickly faded away. True to his word, Duncan had stepped up when it came to the running of the bar, slipping behind the bar whenever he could, assisting with opening and closing duties, and even helping out in the kitchen a time or two, though it became obvious early on that his abilities when it came to cooking were limited.

We had managed to balance the joint police work we did with the management of the bar without too many issues, though there were some nights when we didn't get much sleep. Duncan admitted he enjoyed his role as a mixologist, and even said he could see the two of us running the place well into our old age and long after he retired from the police force.

It was ironic, and perhaps sad, that it was my father's death that had led me along the path I'd taken to get to today, to my current life and happiness. While I mourned the fact that he, and my mother, couldn't be here in body to share this important event with me, I felt they were there with me in spirit.

Strains of music rose up the stairs to us as the DJ I had hired for the event played the promenading music that would soon segue into the wedding march.

"That's our cue," Cora said. She ran a hand over the front of the dress she was wearing, and picked up the two bouquets of flowers sitting on a nearby table. She handed one to me, and then fiddled with her own, trying to come up with the right way to hold it.

"I should have forgone the flowers and just let you walk down the aisle holding your laptop," I teased her.

"I do feel a bit naked without it," she said, garnering a tolerant shake of the head from Joe. "Are we ready?"

"Let's do it."

Cora left the room, crossed the foyer, and paused a moment at the top of the stairs. Then she began her descent.

I looked at Joe and Frank, stuck both of my arms out to my sides as I clutched my flowers, and said, "Ready when you are."

They each hooked an arm through one of mine, Joe on my right, Frank on my left. We exited the room, crossed the foyer, and then stopped at the top of the stairs. I looked down at all the people gathered below and smiled. Not far beyond the base of the stairs stood Duncan, looking utterly calm and impossibly handsome in his suit, with Mal at his side. As he gazed up at me, the love I saw in his eyes reassured me. Cora reached them and took her place off to one side. Standing right at the base of the stairs was the justice of the peace.

I took a moment to scan the crowd seated behind them, mentally doing an inventory of everyone who was there. My eyes settled briefly on Billy, who had just graduated from law school and was studying for his bar exam. I was both proud and happy for him, even though I was also saddened by the knowledge that he would soon no longer be one of my regular bartenders.

I was even happier to see that Alicia was seated beside him, and the two of them were holding hands.

All my staff members were there; I had closed the bar for the occasion and hired temporary bartenders and waitstaff to work the reception. Everyone from the Capone Club was present, too, people who had at one time been strangers but now felt like extended family to me. And peppered throughout the crowd were several members of the police force, including Roberta Dillon, Tyrese and Nick, Chief Holland, and even Jimmy Patterson, Duncan's one-time partner and someone I'd suspected—wrongly, as it turned out—of being one of the people behind the letter-writer case.

Then I spied a trio of people sitting at the very back of the crowd who made me smile. Irene and Jerry Varner were there, and sitting between them was Felicity, a huge smile on her face as she looked up at me.

The Varners, who to my delight had decided to adopt Felicity, had made great strides with the child. I had invited them to come, of course, but despite the progress Felicity had made, I'd had my doubts about whether she would be able to tolerate the venue. I'd been making regular visits to them so I could spend time with Felicity, but the demands of running the bar, making my wedding arrangements, and a run of crimes that had required my presence as a consultant had kept me away for the past few weeks. So I was delighted to see all three of them in attendance.

The DJ switched the music to the wedding march— a prompt that we needed to get moving—and with one last look at Joe and Frank, we began our descent. I was halfway down when I heard Felicity yell "Mack!" at the top of her voice, and then start to clap her hands.

Everyone laughed, and the last of my nervousness faded away.

I was on top of the world as I took my place beside Duncan, and turned to face the JP. I was more than ready to do my last call as a single woman.

Recipes

Duncan's Dynamite

½ oz. vodka
2½ oz. cold cranberry juice
2½ oz. cold orange juice
Splash of hot sauce

Mix all ingredients in a highball glass and top off with a splash of hot sauce.

Cold Mother

½ cup cold milk
2½ tbsp. half-and-half
1 tsp. vanilla flavoring
4 tsp. confectioner's sugar
2½ oz. bourbon
Ground nutmeg (for garnish)

Fill a cocktail shaker with ice, and add milk, half-and-half, vanilla, sugar, and bourbon. Shake for 30 seconds and then strain into a martini glass. Sprinkle ground nutmeg on top.

Twisted Sister

½ oz. 151 rum
½ oz. white rum
½ oz. sour apple schnapps
1 oz. pineapple juice
½ tsp. lemon juice
Splash of grenadine
Cherry (for garnish)

Fill a highball glass with ice, add the rums, schnapps, pineapple juice, and lemon juice and mix. Stir in a splash of grenadine. Garnish with a cherry.

Deep Dark Secret

1½ oz. dark rum
½ oz. light rum
½ oz. coffee liqueur
½ oz. cream or milk

Fill a cocktail shaker with ice, add all the ingredients, and shake. Strain into a chilled glass.

Wedding Cake

1½ oz. amaretto
½ oz. white crème de cacao
2 oz. cold milk
2 oz. pineapple juice

Fill a cocktail shaker with ice, add all the ingredients, and shake. Strain into a chilled glass.

If you've enjoyed Allyson K. Abbott's books,
please watch for her work,
as she writes under the name
Annelise Ryan!

Dead In The Water
(A Mattie Winston Mystery)

is available at your favorite bookseller and e-retailer!

Death is the ultimate equalizer. It knows no boundaries and visits everyone eventually: the rich, the poor, the young, the old, the beautiful, and the ugly. Sometimes it arrives with relentless predictability; at other times it comes with stealth and surprise. Its arrival may be peaceful, quiet, and well ordered, or it may be agonizing, brash, and messy. The only reliable predictor is that someday it will come. I think knowing this is what gives us humans drive and motivation. It forces us to make the most—or at least the best—of the time we have, because we don't really know when our clocks might stop ticking.

Determining where, when, and how death arrived for someone is the basis of my job. My name is Mattie Winston and I work part-time for the medical examiner's office as a medico-legal death investigator. That's a big fancy term for someone who assists with autopsies and the investigative part of death. Sometimes the investigative part is a slam dunk, like the drunken driver who dies wrapping his car around a tree, or the terminal cancer patient who passes on peacefully in her home. Other times the investigative part can be an annoying, vague, and troubling puzzle of circumstances that may require days, weeks, months, or even years to figure out. When a death is the result of a homicide, it's the job of my office to assist the police in figuring out who, what, when, where, why, and how. The combined efforts of our scientific procedures and law enforcement's investigative work will often provide the necessary answers. But not always. Sometimes we end up with an unsolved case. And sometimes—as is the case with the homicide I'm focused on today—it's a combination of our hard work and a bit of dumb luck. Unfortunately for me, the dumb luck in this case was mine and it might provide enough of a legal loophole for the killer to get off.

Also unfortunate for me is today I have to testify for the first time in the three years I've been doing this job. Since investigation is a key part of what I do, I often get involved in the finding and seizing of evidence and I've been subpoenaed before to testify. I've been coached on the process over the past two years by my boss, Izthak Rybarceski (Izzy to those of us who know and love him), the medical examiner here in Sorenson, Wisconsin. But up until now, I've never had to testify because the cases settled before going to trial, or the evidence I was involved with collecting was either determined irrelevant or simply accepted by both parties.

The investigative process in this current case took a different path than most, however, and the discovery of some key evidence is being contested by the defendant. I'm not going to be able to escape the courtroom this time, and the prosecuting attorney on the case, a thirtysomething man named Roger Beckwith, tried to ease my nervousness by walking me through the planned questions, reminding me to answer only what is asked, and cautioning me not to let my nerves rattle me to the point that I start babbling. Roger Beckwith, though, is only half of the equation. There's the defense attorney for me to reckon with as well.

I'm sitting outside the courtroom, watching the occasional person walk by and waiting for my summons. There are no other people sitting out here with me, and I've been waiting for over half an hour. The murmur of whatever is going on behind the closed courtroom doors is indistinct yet intimidating. At least three times I've caught myself chewing on my lower lip, and twice I've had to force my left leg to stop bouncing up and down with nervous tension. It's a little after nine in the morning and I've just finished my third cup of coffee, but I still feel logy, thanks to a sleepless night marked by nervous anxiety and a kid who didn't want to sleep. I thought the coffee might get and keep me alert, but now I'm worried I'll have to pee really bad just about the time I'm delivering my key testimony, and I'll either have to ask to be excused or wet my pants. The bathroom isn't too far away, but I'm afraid if I go, they'll call me to testify and think I've flown the coop. I make a mental note to buy and wear a pair of Depends if I have to do this again. I've never wet myself before, but I figure testifying in a criminal court case might be enough to scare the piss out of me.

I'm about to get up from my seat and pace, figuring it will at least work off some of my nervous energy, when the courtroom door opens and the court officer says, "Ms. Winston, they're ready for you."

It's not my first time inside a courtroom, but it is my first time doing anything other than observing. At least I'm here as a witness, not as a defendant or claimant, so I don't have to worry about my future, but it's nerve-racking walking down the aisle and feeling the stares of everyone on me. I'm afraid of stumbling before I get to the witness-box, or doing something stupid and embarrassing when I do get there, like stuttering, or stammering, or laughing at an inappropriate moment . . . something I do a lot. My nerves tend to express themselves through laughter, and I'm not talking about some tittering, sniggering, cover-your-mouth-and-hide-it kind of giggle. I'm talking about all-out, belly-shaking guffaws. This quirk has kept me from attending a lot of funerals. People don't take kindly to having this ceremonious ritual marked by the sound of a sitcom laugh track. Oddly enough, the only nerve-racking events that make me cry are weddings. Though perhaps it's not so odd in my case, given my marital history.

As I approach the witness stand, I glance at the defendant, a thirty-three-year-old man named Tomas "Please just call me 'Tommy'" Wyzinski, who is on trial for killing his girlfriend. He is dressed much better today than any other time I've seen him, but his skin is the pasty color of someone who hasn't seen the sun in a while, and his longish hair is slicked back from his face with so much product it looks like the plastic hair on a Ken doll. He doesn't look at me, which is just as well. His eyes creep me out.

I shift my focus to the woman standing in front of the witness stand. I know she's there to swear me in, but suddenly I can't remember for the life of me if I'm supposed to stop before I get into the witness-box or climb straight into it. Then I see her offer the Bible on one extended hand and I stop in front of the witness-box.

"Please place your left hand on the Bible and raise your right hand," the woman instructs. For a moment, my brain is so frozen with nervous tension I can't remember which hand is which. I make a couple of tentative jabs, take a deep breath to center myself, and then do as she instructed.

"Do you solemnly swear that the testimony you shall give in this matter shall be the truth, the whole truth and nothing but the truth, so help you God?"

"I do." Two of the scariest words in the English language. As the woman turns away, I climb the step into the witness-box and take a seat. Roger Beckwith gets up and walks to a lectern centered between his table and the defense's.

"Good morning, Ms. Winston," he says with a warm smile. I return the greeting after making a funny movement with my lips because they're sticking to my dry teeth. "Can you please state for the court your occupation and where you work?"

"Sure. I'm a medico-legal death investigator working out of the medical examiner's office in Sorenson, Wisconsin. I work under the auspices of Dr. Izthak Rybarceski and in conjunction with the Sorenson police when necessary."

"How long have you had this position?"

"For three years."

"And what exactly is it you do in the course of your job?"

"I assist Dr. Rybarceski with autopsies and I investigate the means, locations, situations, and circumstances surrounding any suspicious deaths."

Beckwith makes a somber face that he aims at the jury. "Sounds like difficult, complicated work. It must be hard dealing with death and dying all the time like that, day in and day out."

My nerves relax a little. So far, everything is going the way Beckwith said it would, right down to his comment about my job, which is to provide me with an opening to pontificate on how much I love my work and how dedicated I am to it. I'm supposed to do this in a way that makes me seem friendly and approachable, yet professional. Beckwith's exact words to me were "try to come across to the jury as professional and dedicated, but not macabre or weird." So I practiced in front of my mirror all week, stating how much I enjoyed my work, how satisfying it was, and how those of us in the medical examiner's office have to step in and be the voices of the dead . . . all of it done with various vocal tones and facial expressions that made me seem maniacal and scary one minute and Valiumed to the gills the next. After three days of practice, I felt I had achieved the perfect mix of professionalism and normalcy so that my fascination and daily work with the dead didn't sound like I was someone who kept their mummified mother in a closet somewhere.

I prepare to deliver my well-rehearsed lines, but before I can, the defense attorney—a petite, blond woman named Joan Mackey, who bears a striking resemblance to the murder victim in this case—interrupts.

"Objection," she says in a rote tone of voice as if she's bored. "There is no question there. And the defense is willing to stipulate to Ms. Winston's current job title and experience."

The judge says, "Sustained," sounding as bored as Joan Mackey, an unusually tame response for him.

I'm a little perturbed—after all my practice, I'm going to be bummed if I can't recite my job-loving mantra—but one look at Judge Wesley Kupper makes me swallow my own objection.

Judge Kupper would be an intimidating man even without his position of authority and his wood-cracking hammer. He's six-and-a-half feet tall, weighs in the neighborhood of three-fifty, has no neck, and speaks in a deep, rumbling voice that sounds like thunder. When he walks into the courtroom with his massive black robe billowing out around him, it's hard not to compare him to Darth Vader. His blue eyes are pale and icy—when he looks at you, it's as if he can see right through you—and his head is as bald—and as big—as a bowling ball. Whenever he shifts his position, his large leather chair groans beneath his weight like a house about to be ripped off its moorings.

"Is there a question in there somewhere, Mr. Beckwith?" Judge Kupper asks in a tired tone. "If not, please move on."

"Very well," Beckwith says. He gives the jury members a tolerant smile and then looks back at me. "Ms. Winston, what did you do before taking your current job?"

"Objection!" says Mackey with much more enthusiasm than before. "Relevance?"

"It's very relevant to the issue in question," Beckwith says. "Ms. Winston's background and prior employment directly impacted her actions on the day in question."

Mackey shakes her head and rolls her eyes.

"Overruled," Judge Kupper says.

"Thank you, Your Honor," Beckwith says, and then he shifts his attention back to me. "Ms. Winston, please tell the court what job you held prior to your position in the medical examiner's office."

"I was . . . technically I still am an RN, a registered nurse. I was employed at the hospital in Sorenson for thirteen years—six in the emergency department and seven in the surgical department."

"Thank you," Beckwith says, scanning the jury members' faces. Per his pretrial counseling, pointing out that I'm a nurse—one of the most trusted occupations out there—not only helps to make me seem less "creepy," it also gives my testimony more veracity. In this particular case, it will play another, more significant role as well, one Beckwith is about to get to. "Let's move on to August fourteenth of last year, the day in question, the day you and Detective Bob Richmond arrived at the home of the defendant, Tommy Wyzinski. Can you tell me why the two of you went to his house?"

"It started when Detective Richmond and I were called to the scene of a suspicious death that—"

"Objection!" Mackey hollers. "The characterization of the death as suspicious is inflammatory."

Judge Kupper narrows his eyes at Mackey and in a tight-lipped voice says, "Overruled."

Beckwith nods and looks back at me. "Just to satisfy everyone's curiosity here, can you state why this death was determined to be suspicious?"

"Sure. To begin with, the body was wrapped in plastic sheeting and it was found in some woods about a hundred feet from County Road A. We, Detective Richmond and I, felt pretty confident the victim didn't get there under her own power or wrap herself up prior to dying, because the body had no head, hands, or feet."

I'm surprised none of the jury or audience members gasp at this revelation, but there is a lot of uncomfortable stirring and shifting going on.

"Oh, my," Beckwith says with an overwrought grimace he makes sure the jury members can see. Then, with a pointed look at the defense table, he adds, "I think we can all agree that qualifies as suspicious."

There is a snort from the jury box, whether out of humor or derision I can't tell. I look over at them and try to determine who the culprit might have been, but everyone is straight-faced and somber looking.

"Please continue, Ms. Winston."

"In examining the remains and other evidence at

the scene, we readily determined the victim was a woman. While surveying the scene and the surrounding area, we found a piece of paper in a parking lot that was approximately one hundred feet away from the wooded area where the body was found. It was a prescription for insulin."

"And was there a name on that prescription?" Beckwith asks.

"There was. It was written out to a Tomas Wyzinski."

"Was there an address on this prescription?"

I shake my head. "No, just the name. But fortunately the name is unusual enough that it was easy to do a computer search and find out where Mr. Wyzinski lived."

"And that's how you ended up in Pardeeville, at the defendant's home?"

"Yes."

"What time of day was it when you arrived at Mr. Wyzinski's house?"

"It was a little after ten in the morning."

"Why did you go to the defendant's house?"

"Given the proximity of the prescription to the scene where the body was found, Mr. Wyzinski was considered a potential witness. The police wanted to find out when he was there and determine if he had seen anything that might be relevant."

"So was Mr. Wyzinski a suspect at this time?"

"He was considered a person of interest," I say, using the term the police use until something more can be determined.

"And can you tell me what happened when you arrived at the defendant's house?"

I nod, sorting my thoughts out to make sure I say everything I need to say. "We . ... Detective Richmond and I walked up to the front door and Detective Richmond knocked. We waited, but there was no answer.

After a minute or so, Detective Richmond knocked again. And again there was no answer."

"Did you leave at this point?"

"We did not. There was a car parked in front of the house and Detective Richmond determined it belonged to Mr. Wyzinski. Since the address was out in the country and the closest house was two miles down the road, we figured Wyzinski was probably around, maybe somewhere else on the property. So we headed for the back of the house."

"What did you see at the back of the house?"

"There was another entrance, a back door, and there was also an old barn about fifty feet behind the house."

"What did you and Detective Richmond do next?"

"We climbed the steps to the back door and knocked on it."

"Did anyone answer?"

"No, but this door had glass in the upper half and Detective Richmond looked inside."

"What did he see?"

"Objection!"

Beckwith raises his hand in a conciliatory gesture before Mackey can voice the reason behind her objection and re-words the question. "Did you also look through the window in the back door?"

"I did."

"What did you see?"

"A man prostrate . . ." I hear Beckwith's voice in my head reminding me to keep my terms simple and aimed at the layperson, and amend my answer. "There was a man lying face down on the kitchen floor."

"And what did you do next?"

"I reached down and tried the knob to see if the door was unlocked."

"Was it?"

I nod.

"Please state your answer for the record," Beckwith prompts.

"Sorry. Yes, it was unlocked."

"What happened next?"

"I opened the door, went inside, and knelt down next to the man on the floor. I felt along his neck for a pulse."

"Did you find one?"

I nod, then quickly say, "Yes, I did. But it was very faint, thready, and irregular. I shook him then, and he mumbled, but it wasn't anything intelligible."

"What was Detective Richmond doing at this point?"

"He was calling for an ambulance and checking to see if anyone else was in the house."

"Were there other things you noticed about the man on the floor?"

"Yes, his skin was very cool to the touch, and he was diaph—" I catch myself and do a quick mental conversion. "He was very sweaty."

"Is the man you saw on the kitchen floor that day here in the courtroom today?"

"Yes, it was the defendant." I point. "Mr. Tomas Wyzinski."

"Objection!" Mackey says, shooting out of her seat, her tone one of impatient disbelief. "The witness had no way of knowing at the time if the man on the floor was my client or someone else."

"Actually, I did have a way," I say before anyone else can respond. "Detective Richmond showed me a DMV picture of Mr. Wyzinski prior to our arrival. The man on the floor fit that picture. Though to be honest, knowing who he was wouldn't have changed what I did in any way."

"Your Honor . . ." Mackey says in a strained tone. "Overruled," Judge Kupper thunders.

Mackey drops back into her seat with a pout, and after watching her do this, Beckwith turns to me with a little smile. "Ms. Winston, would you please share with the court some of the thoughts going through your mind when you found this man on the floor and how those thoughts led to what happened next?"

"Of course," I say. "The prescription we found at the body dump site was for insulin and the man on the floor was displaying classic signs of insulin shock— decreased alertness, sweating, and cold, clammy skin. When I rolled him onto his back, his shirt hiked up, and I could see tiny pinpoint bruises on his abdomen. I knew from my years of nursing that those were injection marks. The abdomen is the preferred site for insulin shots in most diabetics. Given all of that, it was a pretty safe assumption the man on the floor was the same one whose name was on that prescription, particularly since he was the owner of record for the house we were in."

Mackey looks apoplectic, like she wants to object, but she doesn't. I don't know if it's because I'm talking as fast as I can to get it all out, or because what I'm saying isn't objectionable—at least from a legal standpoint. Maybe it's both.

Beckwith nods solemnly and then says, "Just to clarify things, did you at any point verify the identity of the man on the floor in any other way?"

"We did. Detective Richmond removed a wallet from the man's pants pocket and the ID inside belonged to Tomas Wyzinski. But as I said before, his identity wasn't an issue at the time and wouldn't have changed what I did next."

Mackey is frowning now, her forehead heavily creased, her mouth turned down at the corners.

Beckwith has the barest hint of a smile on his face as he asks his next question. "What did you do next?"

"Well, the treatment for insulin shock is sugar in some form. If a diabetic is completely unconscious and unresponsive, some form of injectable sugar is preferred to ensure they don't choke. But if they have some level of alertness and appear to be able to swallow, then some juice, like orange juice, preferably with a spoonful of sugar thrown in, is a good option. Hard candies can work, too, but they are slower acting and more likely to be a choking hazard. Mr. Wyzinski wasn't alert enough to walk, or talk sensibly, but he was mumbling and he wasn't drooling, meaning he was able to swallow his own secretions. So I got up and went to the refrigerator in search of some juice to give to him."

"And what did you find in the refrigerator?" Beckwith asks, and I swear the corners of his mouth are twitching in an effort not to smile.

This time my answer garners plenty of gasps, both from the jury and the others in the courtroom. "I found a woman's head."

Catering and Capers with
Isis Crawford!

A Catered Murder	978-1-57566-725-6	$5.99US/$7.99CAN
A Catered Wedding	978-0-7582-0686-2	$6.50US/$8.99CAN
A Catered Christmas	978-0-7582-0688-6	$6.99US/$9.99CAN
A Catered Valentine's Day	978-0-7582-0690-9	$6.99US/$9.99CAN
A Catered Halloween	978-0-7582-2193-3	$6.99US/$8.49CAN
A Catered Birthday Party	978-0-7582-2195-7	$6.99US/$8.99CAN
A Catered Thanksgiving	978-0-7582-4739-1	$7.99US/$8.99CAN
A Catered St. Patrick's Day	978-0-7582-4741-4	$7.99US/$8.99CAN
A Catered Christmas Cookie Exchange	978-0-7582-7490-8	$7.99US/$8.99CAN

Available Wherever Books Are Sold!

All available as e-books, too!

Visit our website at **www.kensingtonbooks.com**

Follow P.I. Savannah Reid
with
G.A. McKevett

Just Desserts	978-0-7582-0061-7	$5.99US/$7.99CAN
Bitter Sweets	978-1-57566-693-8	$5.99US/$7.99CAN
Killer Calories	978-1-57566-521-4	$5.99US/$7.99CAN
Cooked Goose	978-0-7582-0205-5	$6.50US/$8.99CAN
Sugar and Spite	978-1-57566-637-2	$5.99US/$7.99CAN
Sour Grapes	978-1-57566-726-3	$6.50US/$8.99CAN
Peaches and Screams	978-1-57566-727-0	$6.50US/$8.99CAN
Death by Chocolate	978-1-57566-728-7	$6.50US/$8.99CAN
Cereal Killer	978-0-7582-0459-2	$6.50US/$8.99CAN
Murder à la Mode	978-0-7582-0461-5	$6.99US/$9.99CAN
Corpse Suzette	978-0-7582-0463-9	$6.99US/$9.99CAN
Fat Free and Fatal	978-0-7582-1551-2	$6.99US/$8.49CAN
Poisoned Tarts	978-0-7582-1553-6	$6.99US/$8.49CAN
A Body to Die For	978-0-7582-1555-0	$6.99US/$8.99CAN
Wicked Craving	978-0-7582-3809-2	$6.99US/$8.99CAN
A Decadent Way to Die	978-0-7582-3811-5	$7.99US/$8.99CAN
Buried in Buttercream	978-0-7582-3813-9	$7.99US/$8.99CAN
Killer Honeymoon	978-0-7582-7652-0	$7.99US/$8.99CAN
Killer Physique	978-0-7582-7655-1	$7.99US/$8.99CAN

Available Wherever Books Are Sold!

All available as e-books, too!

Visit our website at **www.kensingtonbooks.com**